PRAISE FOR ALIAS O. HENRY

"*Alias O. Henry* finds Ben Yagoda on the prowl, tracking William Sydney Porter through the grime and glitter of turn-of-the-century New York. Here's Porter—not yet O. Henry—hustling poolrooms, conning marks, scribbling tales in rented rooms, and ducking the law while chasing the muse. Yagoda, part literary sleuth, part historian with a novelist's instinct, cracks open the city and the man. The result is pure O. Henry: unexpected, full of heart, and impossible to resist."
—Laurie Gwen Shapiro, author of *The Aviator and the Showman: Amelia Earhart, George Putnam, and the Marriage That Made an American Icon*

"*Alias O. Henry* is a delight—a buoyant fictional conjecture about the writer's hidden life, full of surprise cameos, playful allusions, and other literary and historical Easter eggs. Best of all is Yagoda's rich portrayal of Ragtime-era New York City, an imaginative evocation as vivid and distinctive as O. Henry's own."
—Gary Krist, author of *Trespassers at the Golden Gate: A True Account of Love, Murder, and Madness in Gilded-Age San Francisco*

"Ben Yagoda's imaginative portrait of William Sydney Porter is a jaunty ride through the bustling streets of New York at the dawn of the modern age—when newspaper men, gumshoes and shopgirls rubbed shoulders with the likes of Thomas Edison,

Will Rogers and Bat Masterson. Weaving the facts of Porter's life together with the themes of his stories and the history of the city, Yagoda has created a novel with a vintage vibe and twisty plot worthy of the name O. Henry."
—Wes Davis, author of *American Journey* and *The Ariadne Objective*

"Ben Yagoda, the accomplished biographer, literary historian and linguist, has written his first work of fiction, and the result—*Alias O. Henry*—is a triumph. Blending a fecund imagination with a scholar's mastery of time and place, he has fashioned a beguiling portrait of America's most famous short-story writer (born in 1862 as William Sidney Porter) and the hectic metropolis on the Hudson that inspired 'The Gift of the Magi' and 'The Last Leaf.' With empathy and insight, Yagoda reminds us that New York, New York was the irresistible destination for hustlers and dreamers—including the secretive former pharmacist from North Carolina who became O. Henry—long before Sinatra sang about it."
—David Friedman, author of *Wilde in America: Oscar Wilde and the Invention of Modern Celebrity*

"Ben Yagoda brings the writer O. Henry fully to life with the affection and specificity that animate O. Henry's own stories. It's all here: early-century perfumes and stenches, music and cacophony, confidences and betrayals. That Yagoda—one of our great chroniclers of language — should find his way so masterfully to this story is no surprise. He delivers us into a Gotham cityscape at a time when new languages erupted in the deadline work of newspaper reporters, sports scribes, cartoonists and movie makers, years before their rugged glories congealed into mass media. Yet he also locates a certain promise for our media-drenched time: all is not lost if there is but a solitary writer using all six senses—the sixth being compassion— o return pen to paper."
—Michael Tisserand, author of *Krazy: George Herriman, a Life in Black and White*

"In this masterful and inspired exercise that can only be called researched-based time travel, author Ben Yagoda breathes new life into the rich spirit of O. Henry. Drawing on a library's worth of vintage material, Yagoda treats us to an accurate, vivid portrait of a quintessentially American character in his own time and place."
—Ken Finkel, professor emeritus, Temple University

"*Alias O. Henry* transports you into the world of the peripatetic—and sometimes prevaricating—William Sydney Porter. Ben Yagoda weaves two origin stories, Porter's and the inspirations for his works written as O. Henry. Yagoda takes you back to Porter's muse, that is, New York City, at the beginning of the 20th century from its gritty underbelly to the colorful characters that populate its noisy streets. This is a novel that entertains and delights."
—Delia Cabe, author of *Storied Bars of New York: Where Literary Luminaries Go to Drink*

Also by Ben Yagoda

Will Rogers: A Biography

About Town: The New Yorker and the World It Made

The Sound on the Page: Style and Voice in Writing

When You Catch an Adjective, Kill It: The Parts of Speech, for Better and/or Worse

Memoir: A History

How to Not Write Bad: The Most Common Writing Problems and the Best Ways to Avoid Them

The B Side: The Death of Tin Pan Alley and the Rebirth of the Great American Song

Gobsmacked! The British Invasion of American English

Edited by Ben Yagoda

The Art of Fact: A Historical Anthology of Literary Journalism (with Kevin Kerrane)

O. Henry: 101 Stories

ALIAS O. HENRY

ALIAS O. HENRY

A Novel

Ben Yagoda

PAUL DRY BOOKS
Philadelphia 2025

First Paul Dry Books Edition, 2025

Paul Dry Books, Inc.
Philadelphia, Pennsylvania
www.pauldrybooks.com

Printed in the United States of America

Photo credits:
Part I: *Close-up photograph of the Flatiron Building*, 1902,
Robert L. Bracklow. Public domain.

Part II: Still from *What Happened on Twenty-third Street*, New York City, 1901,
Edwin S. Porter. Wikimedia commons.

Part III: Detroit Publishing Co., Copyright Claimant, and Publisher Detroit
Publishing Co. *A Characteristic sidewalk newstand sic*, New York City.
New York State New York United States, ca. 1903.
Photograph. https://www.loc.gov/item/2016803067/.

Chapter VI: *Two Sons of the West* © Eric Hanson.

Design by Gopa & Ted2, Inc.

Library of Congress Control Number: 2025937996

ISBN: 978-1-58988-206-5

To the memory of Louis Yagoda, New York native

1909-1990

NOTE: One dollar in 1903 was the equivalent of roughly $36 in 2025.

DECEMBER 24, 1904

ONE DOLLAR and eighty-seven cents. That was all. And sixty cents of it was in pennies. Anna had saved those pennies one and two at a time by bulldozing the grocer and the vegetable man and the butcher until her cheeks burned with the silent accusations of close-dealing she felt them hurling her way. She counted the coins three times. One dollar and eighty-seven cents. And tomorrow was Christmas.

There had been a bit more in the purse yesterday, but that was before she had bought ingredients for the Christmas Eve supper she had already begun preparing: oyster soup, celery, roast chicken (a holiday goose, so dear, would have to wait a year), mashed turnips, baked squash. The dessert, in recognition of her Canadian heritage, was already completed: a nutmeg-flavored egg tart. And there would be one bottle of Burgundy, shared among the three of them—herself, her husband, and their guest.

Now, there was clearly nothing to do but fling her coins to the ground, flop down on the largest piece of furniture in the furnished flat—the small couch—and cry.

As her tears subsided, and then started to dry, she forced herself to consider the only piece of good news she could think of. Which was that she had only one person to buy a Christmas present for. She had made their guest's gift herself, and she had to admit she was pleased with her handiwork. That left her husband, Bob. And she could *not* buy the present she wanted for him for $1.87.

It wasn't as though Bob didn't have a decent salary, nor was he tight-fisted with it. But circumstances had conspired against their finances. Bob's job as assistant Sunday editor at *The World* paid him thirty dollars a week (ten dollars less than it had been before the crash of '02). Her type-writing brought in, at the most, five dollars more—which was exactly the amount they owed each week to the bank, for the loan they had taken to pay off what should in all rights have been that scoundrel Magnuson's obligation.

Thirty dollars was enough to put food on their table, a roof over their heads, and clothes on their backs (when a threadbare garment absolutely had to be replaced), but didn't leave anything over. And their savings . . . well, there weren't any savings. Anna hadn't exactly brought an immense dowery to their marriage, two months before. In point of fact, beyond a few changes of clothing, some art supplies, and a handful of keepsakes, she hadn't brought anything. Bob's nest egg, meanwhile, had been significantly depleted by the wedding: not the modest celebration but what it had cost to allow it to take place at all. What was left went to the move to this modest apartment following the wedding.

Things would have been easier if Anna had a proper job. But the unspoken understanding between the couple ruled that out. Bob, loving and solicitous in every other way, turned rigid on this one topic.

The understanding wasn't completely unspoken, because every couple of weeks, she would bring the matter up. They could use the money, she'd gently offer. Carefully phrasing the issue so as not to hurt his male pride, she'd sketch out a brief that it was hard to make ends meet on his salary and her small earnings, much less put anything aside. And, she'd add, she could use something to occupy herself. Keeping house in a two-room flat was hardly a full-time job. When she was done with the shopping, the cooking, the cleaning, and any type-writing assignments, she'd read the magazines Bob brought home from the office, or—at any other time of year than this—put together a few extra pennies and go to a nickelodeon to take in the latest offering. But even then, there were hours left to fill. One day, she knew, she would once again pick up her paintbrush. But she wasn't quite ready to take that step.

In the meantime, she'd conclude, what would be so terrible about going back to work at Siegel-Cooper? She was sure she could get back her old job in the toy department. Bob's answer was always the same. "We've settled this," he'd say with a sigh, looking out the window and not at her. "Your working days are over." He acted as though the matter was propriety and pride, the idea that in the class they belonged (or aspired) to, for a wife to be working meant the husband had failed. But they both knew—and this really was unspoken—there was more to it than that: that in a warped sort of way, he was punishing her for the choices she had made over the last terrible year.

On the one hand she was grateful to him for the life they were starting to build together. On the other, she felt like shouting, "What about my pride?" What she wanted to say was, "What happened, happened. I can't change the past, but at least have enough faith in me to let me be part of our future." What she wanted to say was, "You make yourself out as sensible and considerate, but sometimes you're so stubborn I want to scream." Someday, maybe, she would say those things. But not just yet.

Anna rose from the couch, stood by one of the windows on the rear wall, and looked out at a gray cat walking a gray fence in a gray backyard. There was a looking glass between that window and the one next to it. A looking glass in a twelve-dollar-a-week flat is very narrow, but a thin and agile person may, by moving about the room in a particular rapid sequence, obtain a fairly accurate conception of her looks. Anna had mastered the art. She stepped from the window and stood before the glass. Her eyes seemed to be assessing what they beheld, with an evenhanded calculation.

She picked up the coins from the carpet. There was no use counting them again. It was already past noon, and if she was to go, now was the time. On went her old brown jacket; on went her old brown hat, her abundant hair precariously arranged beneath it. With a whirl of skirts, she fluttered out the door and into the street.

. . . And into the remnants of yesterday's snowstorm, which had left seven inches on the city—a total of two million cubic yards (she'd read the figure in the *World* over breakfast that morning). Up in Central Park and along Riverside Drive, the snow looked very beautiful, no doubt. By a stroke of fortune, it had fallen on a Friday night: the children, the skaters, and the coasters, those who had horses and sleighs, were enjoying it, and the Saturday-morning workers who had offices up in the sky-scrapers were probably inspired by the white tableau far beneath them. But down in 18th Street, where Anna had to contend with it, it wasn't inspiring at all. Already, the snow was mingling with the dust and being churned dirty by hoofs and wheels. The White Wings—the streets-department workers dressed in their white duck uniforms and matching peculiar pith helmets, an unintended seasonal camouflage—were out in full force, heaping the snow into huge mounds for carts and carriages and trucks to ultimately haul to the docks and so into the rivers.

But that would take weeks. In the meantime, with the day's mild temperature, there was slush to contend with. As Anna reached Fourth Avenue, she saw people wading through pools of it, muttering in grouchy, indistinct voices. Anna didn't feel especially grumpy but couldn't allow her shoes to get wet; she had only one other pair. So she stepped carefully, every now and then having to leap through the air to hurdle an especially expansive puddle.

It was tempting, and would have been a lot dryer—and faster—to take the Manhattan Main Line to her destination. But the fare was five cents. Even though more money would soon be hers, she didn't know exactly how much, and she needed to hold on to every penny. So she turned right at the corner and joined a crowd walking downtown on Fourth. Slowly, her mood lightened. It was agreeable to be out and about the day before Christmas; the shoppers and the shop windows alike were lively and animated.

At 14th Street, next door to Luchow's, she came to Huber's Dime Museum. It was doing a brisk business. The outside talker, in shirtsleeves and a top hat, bellowed out his routine in staccato rhythm: "*Hear* J. M. Moore's Minstrels, *see* Madame Jucca lifting a horse with her teeth, *and* the seven-foot six-inch giantess Leah May, *and* Del Kanon breaking handcuffs. Wohena the Indian Princess will dazzle you, Derkia the Magician will amaze you. And *you will be astonished* by the lifelike picture of the crucifixion on Abbot Parker's back, the world's twentieth-century wonder." Once, she had been a rube in the city, and thus subject to come-ons of that sort. But that was a lifetime ago, and she walked by without so much as a second glance.

At 9th Street, she could have turned left and then followed Second or First Avenue downtown, but something kept her on her path, and onto the Bowery. Over the years, the street had steadily been shedding its reputation as a den of iniquity. Still, even in the last week of 1904, the name had a slightly naughty overtone. It hovered above what Anna heard and saw as she walked: the din of the elevated trains passing overhead, their engines belching smoke and sending down showers of sparks and cinders that hissed on the snow and slush; the raised voices and piano playing escaping through the swinging doors of the many saloons that remained; the spectacle of drunkards swaying and teetering and muttering loudly to themselves.

There were plenty of sober people on the street as well. They were drawn to it, as to a magnet—tradespeople, clerks, mechanics, truckmen, longshoremen, sailors, janitors, politicians, peddlers, pawnbrokers, old-clothes men, shopgirls, sewing-women, piece workers, concert-hall singers, chorus girls. And as the grand river of the Bowery flowed to its terminus at Chatham Square, nationalities of all varieties fed into it via their respective tributaries: the Italians from Elizabeth Street, the Jews from points east, the Chinese from Pell and Doyers streets, the Germans from beyond Houston Street, the Hungarians from Second Avenue.

Anna picked up snatches of conversation, in what seemed like dozens of tongues. She couldn't understand a bit of it, but she could apprehend the *feeling* behind the words. The people spoke explosively, with much use of their hands, and accord or dissent expressed with animated head movements. The pantomime was helpful for, besides the roaring elevated trains, there were four lines of street cars on the Bowery, plus innumerable vans, trucks, beer wagons, delivery wagons, and pushcarts rattling over the pavements. The crowd pressed closely to hear what the patent-medicine fakir was saying, the policeman bent over with his hand on a tourist's shoulder to get his question, the "puller-in" dragged his prey into the store and shut the door to hear his own voice.

Despite herself, Anna opened her purse and reminded herself of how little was in it. If she had had more, she surely would have spent some, for on the day before Christmas, commerce hummed at even a higher pitch than usual. Old-clothes men with pushcarts in the gutter sold boots, stockings, shirts, hats; peddlers trailed along the curb, hung deep with shoestrings and suspenders, or carrying trays of collar buttons and neckties; the cheap stores had women's garments, toilet articles, knick-knacks, and tawdry ornaments inside, all "marked down." And the pawn shops, a half-dozen to a block, had windows packed with enticing items, attached to every one of them a sad story momentarily arrested. Anna paused at one of them, just below Third Street, and looked in the window. Her heart quickened. And then calmed. The item she had been tracking for many weeks was still there, as was the price tag next to it. "$10.00," it read.

Just before Houston Street, she passed the site of the most notorious saloon of them all, McGurk's, a.k.a. "Suicide Hall." She shivered, and not from the cold. The cops had finally closed the place two years before, and now it was a flophouse with a grand name—the Liberty Hotel. As she walked past, Anna could make out the words on the large sign in the lobby. They read: "When did you write to Mother?" The line would make for a nice detail in one of Bill's stories, she thought to herself. She would have to tell him about it over their Christmas dinner.

At Broome Street, where Miner's Theatre stood on the corner, she turned to the east; immediately, the ambient noise changed from engines and trains and raised adult voices to the shouts and shrieks of children. What seemed like a thousand of them were pouring into the street from alleyways and the six-story tenements that lined both sides of Broome. The snow had been cleared to form a narrow path in the middle of the road, in which carriages could pass. Everywhere else was snow and slush, which the kids jumped in, around, and through with delight.

The tenements, scaffolded with fire escapes, had lofty names etched into their faux-elegant facades. They were interrupted only by a small shop here and there, a synagogue with Hebrew letters on the front, a bath house. Anna noticed the doorways of the tenements, the door frames grimy and scratched, from all the hands that had grasped them and all the things that had been forced through them. Here and there was a vacant lot between the buildings, each one crisscrossed with clotheslines hung with laundry like flags.

After three blocks she reached Allen Street and looked up to notice the afternoon sun brightening the houses on the eastern side. Glancing to the north and south, she wasn't surprised that even on the day before Christmas, women were sitting on the stoops or in chairs, calling their wares like pushcart vendors, winking and jeering, making lascivious gestures at any male over the age of ten who happened to pass by. Anna pulled her hat down as far as she could and kept her gaze on the sidewalk.

She could still hear the shouts a block past Allen, just beyond the corner of Orchard Street, when she reached her destination. In the first-floor window, just next to the stoop, was a small hand-lettered sign: "Mme Sofronie. Hair Goods of All Kinds. Bought and Sold." She opened the door and walked in.

PART I

CHAPTER I

SEPTEMBER 23, 1903

Only a handful of people, all men, stood on the platform of the Harrisburg, Pennsylvania, railroad station. One of them was a tall fellow in a light overcoat and a boater. He stood reading *The Daily Patriot*, lifting his gaze every few minutes to scan the platform. Presently he put down the paper and approached another gentleman, in spectacles and a plaid suit.

"Looks like the rain'll hold off," he said, gesturing to the heavens.

Plaid Suit indicated his assent with what might be termed a muffled grunt.

"Where are you off to?"

"Philadelphia.

"Ah, the same. What's your name?" he asked, extending his hand. "Mine's Jim Valentine."

"Thomas Miller," was the promising reply. Promising, because the length of Miller's answers was increasing, if only by one word at a time. The man in the boater hat had contended with less promising material.

He looked at his watch. "Well, Mr. Miller," he said. "The train doesn't pull out for an hour. What do you say we walk up town and look the city over a little?"

They left the station and began to stroll toward Walnut Street. In not less than 200 seconds, Miller had volunteered that he was from Erie, that he was the proprietor of the biggest fabric store in town, and that he traveled to Philadelphia twice a year to replenish his stock.

Just as the man who had introduced himself as Valentine appeared to be offering a reciprocal portion of information, he was interrupted by the approach of a heavy-set gent, who, judging by the furrow in his brow and the perspiration on his shirt, was agitated.

"I beg your pardon," he said—his Southern accent making the last word sound like "pawhdon." "Could you tell me the location of the Market Bank building?"

Valentine turned to face him. "No, we can't."

The stranger looked him in the eye and snorted. "You wouldn't tell me if you could."

"What's that?"

"I said you wouldn't help me if you could, you damned cheap Yankees.

"What do you mean, cheap?" Valentine demanded. "We've got just as much money as you do. And how can we possibly tell you where the Market Bank is when we're both strangers here! Isn't that right?" He turned to Miller.

"Indeed it is," he said.

"I beg your pardon," said the Southerner. "I thought you gentlemen lived here in Harrisburg. Down in North Carolina, where I come from, folks aren't so abrupt. I apologize for misconstruing your intentions."

"That's all right, friend," Valentine said. "I spoke sharply as well. Say, we don't want you to think we're cheap. We just didn't realize you were a stranger here, too. I'd like to buy a round of drinks at that saloon." He gestured to an open door at the end of the block, underneath a sign that said "O'Reilly's."

"No, you don't," the man from North Carolina replied. "The drinks are on me."

The three men made their way into the bar. It was nearly empty and—after the bright sunlight—it took their eyes a full minute to adjust. They all ordered whisky and sodas, and the Southerner took from his pocket a thick roll of bills. He peeled a ten-dollar note from the top, paid the barman, and collected his change.

The three men toasted each other's health, and, once they had knocked back the drinks, introduced themselves. The Southerner said his name was Bob Cannon.

Valentine declared that the next round was on him, but Cannon demurred. "That's not the way we do things where I come from," he said. "I offended you gentleman, and no one is buying this afternoon but yours truly."

The two men remonstrated, but Cannon would have none of it. Finally, Valentine said: "Then I'll tell you what we'll do. For the first round, I'll accept your hospitality, but for the next, we'll play the match game. Odd man pays."

"That seems sporting," Cannon said. "Now, if you gentlemen will excuse me for a minute, I have to see a man about a dog."

As soon as he left, Valentine spoke softly and rapidly to Miller. "Say, did you lamp that roll? This fellow's got dough. Now, you and I might as well get a little of it. When he comes back, we'll start matching. You always hold your coin head's up, and leave the rest to me. We can trim him for fair. Afterward, I'll meet you in that alley we passed on the way here, and we'll divide up."

"Do you think it's all right?" asked Miller.

"Sure, there's nothing to it."

Valentine didn't really have to look, but if he had, he would have observed a familiar transition in the Erie man's eyes: uncertain skepticism effectively banished by the prospect of easy money.

Cannon returned, and the matching commenced. Each man took out a coin and smacked it on the back of his hand. The Southerner called heads. Valentine was the odd man and paid for the drinks.

When their glasses were about empty, Valentine said, "Mr. Cannon, it was a great pleasure, but I'm afraid Mr. Miller and I have a train to catch. But you are all clearly sporting men, and before we leave, I have a proposition for you both. One more match game, this time for all the money we have on us." Cannon looked at one, then the other. "You're on," he finally said. He tossed his money roll on the table. After a few seconds' hesitation, Miller took off his hat and from the band removed four fifty-dollar bills. Valentine put his wallet on the table.

Each man smacked his coin on his wrist. Valentine revealed his tails, Miller his heads. Cannon slowly lifted his hand. The penny showed heads. Valentine was the victor.

He picked up Miller's fifties and Cannon's bankroll. Miller left the bar, shaking his head and saying, "Confound my luck!" Cannon was silent for a minute. He watched Valentine pocket his roll. Then he said, "Three minutes," and walked out of the bar.

One hundred eighty seconds later, Valentine and Miller were in the alley. The former had just emptied his pockets and put all the money on the ground, when the Southerner himself turned the corner and saw them.

"My God!" he said. "I might have known this was a trick. You two are dividing up the money, aren't you?"

"No, no, no," said Valentine. "Calm yourself. We were just talking."

"Then what the hell is my money doing on the ground?" Cannon pulled a revolver out from his pocket and pointed it at Valentine. "Hand it over to me. Real slow."

The other two men lifted their hands. Valentine said, "Now, take it easy, friend. I can explain everything. But in the meantime, I'll do just what you say."

He slowly knelt and grasped the big bankroll. As he drew it in, he suddenly brought his hand to his left foot. In an instant, he had dropped the roll, pulled out a pistol from under his stocking, and fired it at the Southerner, who fell to the ground. Blood started to spurt from his mouth.

Miller stared at the spectacle, his mouth open, his eyes wide, and his hands still in the air. Valentine quickly turned to him. "Get out of here—quick," he said. "We can't be seen together. That train is leaving soon and if we're both on it, the cops will never finger us for this. But we can't be seen together. I'll meet up with you on the train."

Miller took one more look at the large man on the ground, then turned on his heels and walked toward the station as fast as a fabric purveyor can be expected to walk.

Five minutes later, the 2:35 to Philadelphia was pulling into the Harrisburg station. Miller was on the platform but there was no sign of his confederate. No sign of the police, either. As soon as the train stopped, he clambered aboard. He would need to press for a somewhat lower price than he had intended from his Philadelphia supplier.

At that very moment, two men walked into O'Reilly's Bar, one wearing a boater hat, the other dabbing at his face with a handkerchief and holding in his other hand a small rubber bladder, streaked with a red liquid.

The first man—"Valentine"—looked at the other—"Cannon"—and grinned. "Well, Bill," he said, "the two of us have earned our touch. It took all I could do not to break up when that mark pulled the fifties out of his hatband."

He took from one pocket four fifty-dollar bills, and from the other a roll that consisted of two ten-dollar bills wrapped around a fat wad of newspaper clippings. He presented one of the tens to the bartender and the other to his confederate, along with two of the fifties.

"That puts you a little ahead, Bill, but you can use it to pay for the drinks the next time through," the man in the boater hat said. "And you can put that half a C on top of your boodle. It'll make the mark's eyes go wide as a prairie."

"I didn't think we'd have to use the cackle-bladder," he went on. "But time was getting short. And that blood looked convincing, I must say."

"Colonel," said the heavy-set man, "I'm afraid Mr. . . . Miller, was it? . . . was the last mark for me for the time being. I have an appointment in New York City tomorrow afternoon, and I'm on the next train heading east. If my meeting goes well, it'll lead to some straight work. But these proceeds will put me in good stead as a newcomer in Gotham. It was a pleasure doing business with you."

William Sydney Porter stood up from his stool, shook the other fellow's hand, and walked out of the bar.

Some twenty-six hours later, he stood in front of the outer gate of the offices of *Ainslee's Magazine*, in Duane Street in lower Manhattan. He rang the bell, and presented the office boy a card bearing his name.

The boy gave it to Gilman Hall, the editor, who shouted across the office to his assistant, Richard Duffy, "Our Pittsburgh correspondent has arrived!" He told the boy first to get hold of the magazine's owner, George Smith, and then to bring the visitor up.

Porter walked through the door a minute later, with a springy, noiseless step. He wore a dark suit of clothes and a brightly colored four-in-hand tie and carried a black derby, high-crowned. The two editors and the proprietor stood as one.

"So you exist in flesh and blood," Hall exclaimed, extending his hand.

Porter took it, shook with the other two men, then made a light bow. "Perhaps a bit too much flesh," he said. "But I am glad to be here, very grateful for the funds you advanced to make it possible."

"Don't mention it," Smith said. "I was born and brought up amid Pittsburgh's dark Satanic mills and was only too happy to assist in your escape."

Duffy and Hall gathered some chairs around the latter's desk, and the four men sat down. "To tell you the truth . . ." Hall started, then hesitated. "I confess I don't know what to call you, Mr. Porter. William? Sydney? Or are you now going by Olivier Henry?"

Porter chuckled. "No, never Olivier. As you may remember, when you were preparing your annual prospectus last year, you told me an initial wouldn't do—'O. Henry' wouldn't stick fast in the minds of readers. I had a bit of fun picking out a name starting with 'O' that had the maximum advertising effectiveness. But all that is for editorial pages—outside of them, just plain Bill will turn the trick."

"All right then, Bill," Hall said. "I was about to say we didn't know what to expect when we finally met you. Your first stories were posted to us from New Orleans, then you apparently moved to Pittsburgh, for reasons I can't fathom. The first few tales were Westerns. Then there were a couple set in Central America, as if you were setting out to rival Crane and Harding Davis. And now that I meet you, I hear that your accent is markedly Southern."

"Well, I have had my fair share of peregrinations, that's true," Porter said. The others seemed to expect him to go on. But he just sat there, looking from one to another with a tight smile.

Smith glanced at the clock. "Bill, the work day is just about done. Why don't you tell us a bit about yourself. I have to say, since we've been publishing you, your life has been an endless source of fascination to Duffy and Hall."

Porter looked a little uncomfortable, like a little boy expected to waltz at a dance recital. "The fascination is quite mild, from where I sit, but I'll gladly tell you my life story, such as it is. I was born in 1867, which would make me . . . ?" he made some marks on a scrap of paper. "Thirty-five, almost thirty-six. Let's put it at thirty-five.

"My home town is Greensboro, North Carolina—as you discerned, I am a son of the South. As for my ancestors, some of them were governors of the state. I went to Texas when I was quite a youngster. Delicacy of health and not of purse was the cause of the trip. I spent two and half years on a ranch. I was studying the cattle business, with the idea of taking it up. Then the pastures dried up because it quit raining, and then I quit the business."

The editors exchanged a glance. Each had an idea what the other was thinking: Bill Porter talked as if he had plenty of practice drawing out tales in front of the hot stove of a Carolina general store.

"Not long after that," he was saying, "I got a job on the *Houston Post.* I had a daily column and eventually a moniker—'The Post Man.' After about a year, I left to start a ten-page weekly story paper. It was called *The Rolling Stone.* It rolled for about a year and then showed unmistakable signs of getting mossy. Moss and I never were friends, and so I said good-bye to *The Rolling Stone.*"

"And after that?" Hall asked. He and the other two found themselves on the edge of their chairs.

"Then a friend of mine who had a little money—wonderful thing that, isn't it, a friend with a little money?—suggested that I join him in a trip to Central America, where he was going with the intention of getting into the fruit business. Well, it takes a long time and costs a lot of money to learn how the little banana grows. We didn't have quite enough of either commodity, and so never did learn the whole secret of bananas' development."

"So that explains your tropical tales," Duffy said.

"You can hear a lot of them in a banana republic, knocking around among the consuls and the refugees," Porter said.

It appeared that he was expected to continue, and he did. "The banana plantation faded into nothing; I drifted back to Texas. In Austin I got a job in a drug store. That was a rotten two weeks. They made me draw soda water, and I gave up."

Hall: "And after the two weeks at the soda fountain, then what?"

"Let me see. After the soda water, I think there came the highball stage. I went to New Orleans and took up literary work in earnest. And that's where I started to correspond with you gentlemen.

"As for the move to Pittsburgh"—he preempted their next question—"let's just say there is a disgruntled lady in Louisiana."

"And how did you acquire your nom de plume?" Duffy wanted to know.

Porter's ready answer suggested he might have been expecting the question. "I always had a fondness for an old tune the cowboys used to favor in my Texas days. They called it 'Root Hog or

Die.' Towards the end there's a bit. . . " He cleared his throat and then, to the surprise of everyone, sang in a strong, clear tenor:

> Along came my love about twelve o'clock
> Saying Henry, O' Henry, what sentence have you got?

"It seemed a bit of poetic justice to sign 'O. Henry' to *my* sentences."

"And why a pen name at all?" Duffy asked.

"Gentlemen, that is enough autobiography for the time being." Porter stood up. In recounting the chronicle of his life, he had uttered seven more or less truthful statements and told seven lies. It would be difficult if not impossible to enumerate everything he'd left out, from the six years he had deducted from his age, to the existence of his deceased wife and his daughter, to the cackle-bladder grift in Harrisburg, to the pair of grand omissions. But he considered what he had revealed to be a fair trade for the travel expenses he had been advanced and the editorial platform he had been afforded. And now he wanted a drink.

Porter, Duffy, and Hall repaired to a nearby saloon, where the editors quickly discovered that the writer's hotel and their residences were all uptown. So, after each man had consumed two Manhattan cocktails, they proposed a stroll toward that compass point, starting on West Broadway towards Washington Square. Hall and Duffy told him they'd spare him the Bowery and its dens of iniquity. Porter refrained from telling them he'd spent much of the previous evening there, being separated from some of his money at a tavern and winning it back, and then some, by hustling all comers at a shooting gallery. (Among the less consequential omissions from his autobiographical narrative was the proficiency he'd acquired with firearms during lazy days on Olson's ranch, shooting not at bad men or Indians but at tin cans in the middle distance.)

As the three men set off on their walk, Porter was struck, maybe even more forcefully than when he'd arrived the day before—by the spectacle of the city. Especially the people. He had never experienced in his forty-one (not thirty-five) years of wide wanderings anything like the mass of humanity on New York streets on a September afternoon. Not even close. The crowds fascinated him. That man with a limp, the young woman in a shirtwaist, doing the Kangaroo Walk, the one-armed beggar, the fresh-faced cop . . . for all of them, a story seemed to be written on their faces, not yet legible but tantalizing nonetheless. And the crowd itself was a balm. Individually, each face was piquant and unique. But taken together they lost their individual qualities and became a broad smooth expanse, like the ocean seen from the beach in Honduras. He had the pleasant fantasy of leaping into it and becoming faceless himself. And he allowed himself to consider that the wild notion he was pursuing, of planting himself in the biggest city in America in the middle of his life's journey and establishing himself as, of all things, an author, might not be so wild after all.

. . . Duffy was talking, he realized—asking him about the writers he liked. Porter turned to him and said, "I did more reading between my thirteenth and nineteenth years than in all the years since. And my taste was much better then. I used to read nothing but classics. Burton's *Anatomy of Melancholy* and Lane's *Arabian Nights* were my favorites. Dickens and Mark Twain, of course. And I spent many an afternoon with the Rubaiyat of Omar Khayyam."

"Not Maupassant?" Hall asked. "I sense a . . . congeniality between his work and yours."

"French, I presume? I don't know the man. Write down his name and I'll seek him out the next time I'm exploring in a bookshop."

Hall did so. "I commend 'The Necklace' to your attention."

There was one thing Porter found disconcerting in the street scene. Hall noticed it. "You keep looking up, Bill. I can imagine that you'd find New York sky-scrapers rather remarkable."

"It's not that," Porter said. "It's that elevated railway." He gestured at the Sixth Avenue line, screeching to a halt overhead. "How can people dare to ride on such trains, and not be afraid to fall into the street?"

"It's a matter of faith, I suppose," the editor said. "I noticed you had a story in *Munsey's* a few months back. The next piece you send to them will go to their new offices on the eighteenth floor of the Flatiron Building. Frank Munsey had a platform built at the very point of the building, so he can sit at his desk and see a river at port and starboard, and Central Park dead ahead. A fine view, to be sure, but how do you imagine he feels when he sits there and can feel the building swaying in the wind? Or Whitehead, when he goes up in one of his flying machines. Faith, I tell you."

"Colonel," Porter said, "I reserve my faith for providence. And perhaps the sun coming up in the morning. At all events, I'll keep my feet close to the ground."

At Washington Square, they turned up University Place, and three girls approached them from the opposite direction. They were a year or two older than Margaret, but his fancy persuaded him they were the same age, and even suggested that the one in the middle had a certain facial resemblance. As he looked at them, his buoyant mood started to take on water and slowly sink. For the first time since leaving Pittsburgh, he permitted himself to think about what he had left behind. The girls were arm in arm and chattering away, seemingly elated at being released from school for the day. Porter watched them, straining to hear some scraps of conversation. But with the giggles and interruptions, that wasn't possible. As they passed his group, he longed to turn around and just look at them a little bit longer. That wasn't possible, either. He hoped Duffy and Hall wouldn't notice his reaction because if they did, he'd have to make up a story, and for the first time that day he didn't feel up to the task. Fortunately, the editors were in the middle of a brief but heated dispute over whether the New York Giants' new manager, McGraw, and their grand pitchers, McGinnity and young Mathewson, would turn the club's fortunes around.

By this time, the group had entered Union Square, and the baseball argument was interrupted by some kind of commotion at the opposite end, to the north. As they walked toward it, they saw a crowd of people, who turned out to be surrounding a man on the ground wearing a Rough Riders hat. He appeared to be experiencing an epileptic attack. As his writhing intensified, he grabbed for a nearby stick and put it between his teeth. As Porter, Duffy, and Hall moved closer, they could see that one of the man's front teeth was missing.

A resident of one of the stately houses bordering the square had apparently heard the shouts of the man and the spectators; he walked down his steps, helped the poor victim—who had calmed himself considerably—to his feet, and began walking with him back to the house, presumably to offer care and assistance. But at that moment, a young mustachioed police officer arrived on the scene on a bicycle—a cop on a bicycle was something new to Porter—and within half a minute, the policeman had taken possession of the epileptic, placed his right arm around the man's shoulders, and begun to guide him along 17th Street to the east.

The editors and the writer stood there a minute as the crowd dispersed. "Well, Bill," Hall finally said. "I suggested you come to New York because it's the center of the publishing industry. But I think you'll find, when you're through with the tropics and the plains, that the city will provide excellent and abundant material for your stories. I, for one, don't know what to make of the scene we just witnessed. But perhaps something will strike your fancy and you can spin a tale from it."

They turned up Broadway and had the rare—for New York—experience of walking along a line that traversed the grid diagonally. There were no further commotions, just the spectacle of a good portion of humanity on their way home for their dinners, which they had good expectations of enjoying if they could successfully dodge the streetcars, the automobiles, and the horse-drawn carriages.

And the late-day shoppers, who were out in significant number.

Porter had never seen anything like the stores in and out of which they streamed: offering leather goods, haberdashery, jewels, paintings, furs, and much more. The establishments were modest in size, until the block between 18th and 19th streets. On the east side was the massive W. & J. Sloane rug and furniture emporium—six stories of brick, stone, cast iron, and terra cotta, decorated with renderings of birds, monsters, angels, and other fantastic figures. The west side of the block consisted of just two large cast-iron buildings, one shared by Aitken Son & Co. for ladies' clothing and Vandine's for Oriental imports. The other, six stories high, contained Arnold, Constable—the city's oldest department store, Hall explained, with a measure of civic pride, extending all the way through to Fifth Avenue. He gestured one block to the north, to the turreted and even grander Lord & Taylor. "We are standing at roughly the heart of Ladies' Mile," he said. "You can procure virtually any item you desire here, whether you are lady or gentleman. The only sticking point might be the price. Even in the automobile age, it's still the home of the carriage trade."

Just a few blocks to the north were 23rd Street and the Flatiron itself, already looming into view. As they approached 22nd Street, Porter noted little groups of men standing in knots at the corners. "What are those fellows watching?" he asked.

"They're art students and connoisseurs," Duffy said, "though some of them, I think, must be dry-goods men, waiting to learn the newest styles in hosiery."

Hall chuckled. "One thing Burnham apparently didn't account for in his design of the building was the wind. Whichever direction it comes from, it rams into the building, and creates a sort of natural wind tunnel. Just last week that shop window"—he gestured across Broadway—"was smashed by the wind, and the owner is suing Fuller for damages. But the real casualties are women's skirts. That lot over there are mashers, nothing less, just hanging about for a glimpse of ankle or something higher."

After crossing 22nd, standing at the foot of the building, Porter understood what Hall was talking about. A wicked gust reared up and all three men simultaneously shot up their hands, to keep their hats from blowing away. And sure enough, ladies' skirts shot up, too.

The trio walked another block up Fifth Avenue to get a better view of the building. It seemed as though everyone was rubbering up at it, including a man in a boater hat, who was setting up some elaborate photographic equipment. The only person who appeared oblivious was one of Waring's White Wings, whose complete attention was on his street-cleaning duties.

"I would say it qualifies as a Ninth Wonder of the World," Porter said. "And to be sure: the next time I submit a story to Munsey, it will be by post, not hand."

They shook hands and parted ways, the editors walking to the east through Madison Square, Porter to the south, down Fifth Avenue towards 23rd Street, where he had spotted a Western Union office. October was still a week away, but he thought he'd be early this month, maybe as a way of celebrating new beginnings. Plus, he had a fifty-dollar bill in his wallet. He walked into the office, extracted the fifty, and gave it and the familiar address to the man behind the desk.

CHAPTER II

PORTER RETURNED to his small and rather mean third-floor room in a West 30th Street hostelry that catered to traveling salesmen. His trunk lay on the floor in the middle of it, still full, or nearly so. In the first minute of his arrival, naturally, he'd taken out Margaret's picture, and placed it on the small oak table that looked out on a narrow air shaft and which, for a few days at least, would be serving as his place of business. He fingered the silver frame and thought about the girls he'd seen on the street an hour or so earlier. Was his daughter giggling and whispering secrets? Most likely not. He knew her well enough to know that she favored him, in being solitary and prone to secrets and melancholy. Not that he knew her so very well. Since the spring of 1898—when she was eight and half years old—Porter had spent not much more than a few months in her company.

At this point in his life, breaking ties was an old story. It started when he left Greensboro, never to return. Long before then, his mother had left *him*, succumbing to consumption when he was just three. His father drifted away in spirit after that, his attention and energies devoted, on the one hand, to drink; on the other, to the fervently hoped for, never achieved, invention of a perpetual-motion water wheel. In Will's boyhood and youth, Dr. Algernon Porter had largely abandoned his medical practice and spent most of his time in the barn with his machines and his bottle; most of *that* time, he was fast asleep.

Will had been educated and effectively raised by his aunt, the doctor's sister, known to one and all as "Miss Lina." At eighteen, he had left her, all the home folks, and his job as a pharmacist to go to Texas, largely to forestall the dreaded consumption. That part of the narrative he had told Duffy and Hall was true. As was, in the main, the account of his activities in the West. But what it left out was key. For one thing, his marriage to an Austin girl named Athol Estes and the birth of their daughter. For another, the fact that, for three years, he was a teller and bookkeeper at the First National Bank of Austin. In the third year, the owners of the bank concluded that Porter had embezzled a sum of money that, while not exorbitant, was also not trivial, and dismissed him.

By that time, he had started his humor magazine, *The Rolling Stone*. Before it finally stopped rolling, Porter's sketches and articles had caught the attention of the editor of the *Houston Post*, who hired him as a reporter. (Porter didn't even know why he had transposed the sequence when talking to Hall and Duffy, probably just the habit of prevarication.) Facts and William Sydney Porter—by this time, he had replaced the "i" in his middle name with a "y"—never got along very well. After a few disastrous assignments to cover burglaries and fires (the number and names of casualties either found their way into the last paragraph or were left out altogether), he was given his column and "Post Man" designation. He contributed the sorts of humorous sketches and anecdotes that had filled *Rolling Stone*'s pages, but also short narratives that showed a knack for well-turned phrases and ingenious denouements, and they began to gain him a following.

But by then an over-assiduous federal bank inspector had developed an interest in the workings of the First National Bank of Austin. The fellow, terrier-like, would simply not let go, and eventually Porter was indicted and arrested on charges of embezzlement. After his father-in-law posted bail, he fled, first to New Orleans and then to Honduras, with which the United States had no extradition treaty. His wife and daughter stayed in Austin with Athol's parents.

Porter had become the embodiment of the title of his erstwhile magazine—always rolling away from mossy encumbrances, legal, financial, and emotional. He had met and married Athol while she was still in her last year of high school; almost immediately the difference between them in age, interest, temperament . . . everything . . . began to feel vexingly large, and he had found himself drifting away from her. Margaret's birth gave the family unit a center, for a time, but the centripetal urge to wander eventually prevailed. The wandering, in many forms, had started long before he decamped to Honduras. He had heard from a friend, who had heard it from someone else, that the statute of limitations for embezzlement was seven years. There was vague talk that he would return to America after that time had elapsed, but it was vague, and it was only talk. Porter didn't like to dwell on this point but in his heart of hearts, he recognized that, had he found a reliable source of income—maybe something in the export trade, maybe a post at the Embassy, which was hardly assiduous in checking references—he would likely have stayed in the tropics forever.

However, after six months, perhaps the only thing that could have drawn him back to Austin happened. He received word that Athol's consumption (a malady which seemed to pursue him at every phase of his life) had worsened. Almost to his own amazement, he did the right thing: for once in his life, he returned to the scene, surrendered to the authorities, and re-took his place in the family home. But only for a couple of months. Before the trial began, the disease claimed Athol. Another blessing in disguise, perhaps, for she was spared the shame of the court proceedings (at which, to his family's and friends' astonishment, he said barely a word in his defense), of the guilty verdict, and of his sentence to five years at the Ohio Penitentiary. Days after the verdict, he was put on a train, handcuffed to a federal marshal, on his way to Columbus. No one was at the station to see him off because he let no one know of his departure. He told Margaret he was leaving on a long business trip and walked out the door. The marshal had the decency to wait for him around the corner for the walk to the station.

Porter had had a vague notion that prison might be in the nature of a stay at a hotel from which one could not check out. That notion was erased by his first meal. As the door of the dining-room opened, he was greeted with the surging odor of slumgullion made from meat well past its prime. There was the clatter of tin, the shuffle of uneasy feet, the waving of upraised hands signaling the guards for bread. No sound of the human voice, but that God-forsaken, weighty, brutal dumbness imposed upon convicts in the penitentiary. At each place there was a tin of the stew. Not a few maggots floated in the gravy. A hunk of bread and a saucer of molasses and flies filled out the menu.

Shoved into the cell for the night, he felt forgotten by all the world. The cell was in reality a stone vault, four by eight feet. It had no sanitary equipment or window, the only ventilation coming from the barred door that opened on the closed corridor. There were two straw ticks on wooden shelves. These were the bunks. Another man shared the hole with him. No words were exchanged. Two days later, on Saturday night, the men were locked up until Monday morning. Two men sleeping, breathing, tramping about, turned that closet into a hell. It was no longer air that filled the place, but a reeking stench.

After six weeks, he had a stroke of good fortune. He was able to get word to the authorities of his training as a pharmacist, and they in turn assigned him to the position of night druggist. He was given an apartment without charm but with ventilation and a door, not bars. He also now had the privilege of taking his meals not with the general population but in a smaller mess hall, shared with trusties and larcenists on the grand scale who had crossed the warden's palm with silver.

Not long after that, he met and befriended an Oklahoma train robber named Al Jennings, who paved the way for him to join a secret society known ironically as the Recluse Club, which met once a week for Sunday dinner. The club was the brainchild of a burglar, long sprung by the time Porter and Jennings got there. Once this fellow had the plan, the other charter members worked like beavers on it. They got some of the expert burglars and counterfeiters—all fine mechanics—to cut a cupboard in the loft above the construction office, where one of them worked. Over this they fitted a secret panel. These same mechanics made a gas stove, and connected it with the prison mains. It stood on a shelf, which swung out and back into the wall; when it was swung in, another fake panel hid it from view. Piece by piece, the boys picked up from the kitchen, pantries, and dining rooms a complete set of dishes, knives, forks, spoons, and pots. Every Sunday at the regular meeting the president appointed a dinner committee. It was their duty to collect what supplies were needed for the next Sunday. The committee prowled through the prison all the week, using every trick and device to obtain what they needed.

It was unanimously agreed that Bill Porter was the best forager of all. From his position and talents, he could get more provisions in a day than the rest of the Recluses combined. He had made slits in the lining of his coat, and there he carried his plunder. He would walk through the gate, looking neither to right nor left, his coat bulging with a Mother Hubbard effect. As he passed the patrol guard, he would cast one quiet glance, and the guard would look in the opposite direction. Had the gate closed on him suddenly, his coat would have resembled the wreck of a grocery wagon. Once he even brought in six bottles of wine.

Porter and a defaulting French cashier named Jean acted as chefs. They knew nothing of cookery when they began, but Jean was, after all, a Frenchman, and Porter, from his youthful pharmaceutical training, had a sense for how ingredients interacted. Perhaps surprisingly, he tended to cook by instinct, and Jean by weight and measure. Porter would measure out a pinch of this or that, and Jean would say, "Let's weigh it." Porter would reply by dumping it in, saying: "It's in the soup now." Jean liked things high-seasoned, French fashion, about which he and Porter frequently quarreled. "There's no taste to it," Jean would say. "All right," Porter would answer, "wait until our guests object." No one ever did.

But neither the club nor Porter's new position shielded him

from the prison's realities. He saw the broken bodies brought up from the basement when men were all but done to death in vicious floggings. And it wasn't a rare occurrence that some bitter wretch, driven desperate and insane, would attempt suicide in his cell. Porter had been forced to accompany the prison doctor and help him revive the convict. More often than not, their efforts were unsuccessful.

Still, he had two commodities he had never fully appreciated on the outside: solitude and time. He was on duty from five p.m. to five a.m., but usually after ten or so there was little to be done. The rest of the day was his. His sense of shame was such that, at least at first, he didn't care to consort with anyone—prisoner or prison employee; the mere act of conversing was a reminder of his circumstances. Instead, he spent most of his waking time with pencil and paper. While awaiting trial in Austin, in a fit of industry whose origins were still a mystery to him, he had written a handful of proper short stories and submitted them to New York magazines. All were rejected, but the words of encouragement in the return letters—however few and however mild—made him resolve to keep at it. Deep down, he sensed that this represented his last, best chance at . . . what would you call it? Redemption, perhaps.

He didn't have sufficient faith in his powers of invention to embark on a full-length book, but the short-story form suited him. He'd start with some versions of his fellow inmates, or a cowboy he'd run into in Texas, some member of the Austin crowd he had run with, or some dissipated character from Honduras. Then a complication, and a secondary character or two would occur to him, and perhaps a pithy ironic line. Then he was off. If he built up momentum, he could finish a story in the course of a night. His favorite part of the process was the ending. He would arrive at the last couple of pages with a feeling of anticipation, almost excitement. The resolution was a secret, usually even to him, and secrets had always been his stock in trade. In life he tended to horde them like a miser, as if the accumulation were a form of wealth. But in stories, once he glimpsed the denouement, he would delicately nurture it; when it was revealed, he took a proud parent's pleasure.

But by the time he joined the Recluse Club he was willing to have intercourse with his fellow prisoners, such as the man who had called himself "Jim Valentine" at the Harrisburg train station. The fellow's real name was Dick Price and he was a safe-cracker and confidence man originally from Missouri, with two years to go in his sentence when Porter arrived. For the fledgling writer, Price's tales of bank robbery and grifting—including the smack and the cackle-bladder—were prime source material. (And, as it turned out, a way he could make a few extra simoleons after his release. Trying his luck with various marks he encountered on Pittsburgh's streets and in its taverns, he discovered, a bit to his surprise, that he was a born conman. Despite—or maybe because of—his secretive nature, he had the gift of gab when confabulating. Noting that his Southern accent seemed to grease the wheels, he played it up while grifting. And he didn't have any qualms about separating pigeons from their boodle. "If they weren't greedy they wouldn't have gotten into a mess in the first place": within weeks, he'd heard some version of this byword enough times from his fellow inmates to have fully absorbed it.)

In his prison apartment, he would write for about two hours starting at midnight, make a round of the hospital, then return to his desk and work till his shift was done. All told, he completed nearly twenty stories. He had posted all of them to a bartender he'd met in New Orleans, with instructions on which magazines to send them to; it went without saying that a postmark from the OP would not do. He had rejections (thirteen for one piece alone, "The Emancipation of Billy," it was called), but he also had acceptances—a half dozen, by the end of his term. As for his fees, he'd set up the New Orleans barkeep with permission to forge his signature on the checks, an introduction to a local rounder who'd cash them (withholding a fifteen percent commission), and strict instructions on what to do with the proceeds.

Prison breaks some men. Others (a smaller group), it rehabilitates. Porter was one of an even smaller number whose determination it stiffens to the point of steely rigidity. Confinement, a regular schedule, the elimination of virtually all distractions, and the discovery of a calling, such as it was, transformed him from a rolling stone to a man on a single-minded quest. He had never truly applied himself to anything before. Now, work seemed to at least temporarily relieve the feeling of shame that otherwise cruelly oppressed him. Idle, he would have waking dreams in which he saw a succession of faces gazing at him with stern disappointment. Miss Lina, Athol, even his mother, of whom he had only painfully fleeting memories—drying him after a bath, holding him by the hand as they walked about the house, drawing him in for an embrace. He had no memory of her face, so in his imagination she appeared just as she did in the daguerreotype wedding portrait that had rested on his father's bureau and was one of the few possessions he had taken with him when he left North Carolina for Texas. He was ashamed that he didn't know where it was at the moment. Probably in the trunk he'd hastily packed that now lay in the basement of his in-laws' home.

Margaret's dear face appeared to him as well. He always carried with him, folded in the front pocket of his prison pants, the first letter he'd gotten from her. He knew it by heart:

> Dear Papa,
>
> I would like to know why don't you come home?
>
> P.S. Why don't you come home and read Uncle Remus?

(What he didn't know was that Margaret kept all his letters in a cardboard folder on a table next to her bed. The one on top was the reply he sent in July, a couple of months after his arrival in the OP:

> You dont know how glad I was to get your nice little letter today. I am so sorry

> I couldn't come to tell you goodbye when I left Austin.
> You know I would have done
> so if I could have.
>
> Well, I think it's a shame some men folks have to go away from home to work
> and stay away so long—dont you? But I tell you what's fact when I come home next
> time I'm going to stay there. You bet your boots I'm getting tired of staying away
> so long.
>
> So you be just as happy as you can, and it wont be long 'till we'll be reading
> Uncle Remus again of nights.)

If he served out his full term, he would be forty-two on his release. That would give him, generously, twenty more years on the planet. Sitting in his quiet room, surrounded on all sides by sleeping souls, he resolved that he would devote those years to one goal and one goal only. He would gain acceptance, and renown, through what now seemed the only avenue available to him. The written word.

In the event, his behavior was judged good enough that he was set free in July 1903, a year and a half early. He went to Pittsburgh because Margaret was living there with his in-laws, who had purchased and were operating a small hotel. He and his daughter had a happy month together, almost more as affectionate pals than father and daughter. They went fishing, spun make-believe yarns, and read Uncle Remus stories, never mind that, at twelve, Margaret was a little old for them. In September, she went off to boarding school, while Porter continued to write and continued to have success. He found an especially receptive audience in *Ainslee's* and Gilman Hall, who, after a few acceptances, encouraged him to come to Gotham. As soon as he read those words, his mind was made up. A week later he wrote Margaret a letter saying he had to go away on another long business trip. At least this time it had the virtue of being true.

CHAPTER III

On his second night in New York, Porter dreamt that he was back in the OP, being led down a long corridor. There were no shackles on him, but somehow he had no use of his arms. As he walked by the cells, he could see inmates laughing at him. Their mouths were gaping open, but no sounds seemed to be coming from them. A feeling of dread grew in him and finally he woke up with a start. He lit the gas lamp and looked at his pocket watch. It was nearly four a.m. Further sleep was out of the question, so he sat up in bed, drew a blanket around him, and sat silently.

When light began to spill through his east-facing window, he dressed, walked downstairs and past a sleeping desk clerk in the lobby, and outside into the cool September air, vowing that as much of his next fee as required would go toward a new overcoat. It was still too early for breakfast so he went for a walk, inscribing an arbitrary rectangle in the city's capacious grid. He saw horse-drawn lorries making their deliveries, Waring's White Wings sweeping the streets, workers on their way to or from their shifts. (He could tell the difference by how much spring was in their step and how much starch was in their clothes.) At first slowly, then more and more rapidly, lights switched on in the windows of the skyscrapers and tenements and brownstone houses, until finally Porter had the sense that the city was properly awake.

He found his way back to Madison Square Park, where he saw a police officer in the process of rousing a vagrant sitting on a bench. The tramp got up, removed his derby hat, and flung it at the cop's chest. "What are you doing that for, Soapy?" said the officer. "You know I'll have to bring you in." And at that, he marched "Soapy" out of the square, presumably on the way to the precinct and thence to a bunk in prison. The bum went willingly and seemed, to Porter, to have a slight smile on his face.

At the corner of 23rd Street and Sixth Avenue, next to the elevated railway entrance, he could see a small structure, covered all over in fluttering sheets of paper. When he reached it, he realized that it was a newsstand, adorned with more periodicals than he would have thought existed. He noted with satisfaction the presence of both *Ainslee's* and *Black Cat*, in each of which he had a story, and was struck stronger than before with the wisdom of Hall's advice. Virtually all of the magazines were produced within two miles of where he stood, and he could almost feel a certain aura that emanated from them. Or perhaps a better metaphor—a gravitational force that inexorably pulled him in.

The stand had its own gravity, and as Porter walked toward it, he saw a horizontal shelf groaning with displays of the daily newspapers: the *Times*, the *Post*, the *Press*, the *Herald*, the *Tribune*, the *Telegram*, the *Mail and Express*, the *Evening News*, the *Commercial Advertiser*, the *World*, the *Sun*, the *Journal*. He had no loyalty to any of them and was momentarily paralyzed. Scanning them, he saw that the *Times* cost one cent, the *Sun* two, and the *Tribune* three. He picked up a copy of the *Times* and laid his penny down.

He wandered along 34th Street for a few blocks, until his eye was caught by a chef behind a large plate window cooking cakes on a griddle; "Childs," said the letters etched in the glass. He walked in, and a man in a white uniform showed him to a table near the front. The theme of Childs, apparently, was the color white. The floors and walls were white tile, the counter top white marble, and the waitresses wore white hats and starched white embroidered collars and cuffs, with the only contrasting note being their black bow ties.

One of the waitresses, a small-statured blonde with a wit as quick as her feet, was exchanging repartee with the occupants—all male—of three tables at once. One gent hailed her and demanded, "Is my order coming?" The response was quick: "Yeah, and so's Christmas"—which drew smiles all around. Meanwhile, she was performing astounding feats with orders of bacon and eggs, sausage and wheats, and any quantity of things on the iron and in the pan and straight up and on the side.

After delivering an order to a table next to Porter, she glided over to him and demanded, "What's yours?" He had never heard of butter cakes, but there was nothing questionable about the two words that constituted their name, and the price was right, so he ordered them along with a cup of coffee, black. "Three off," the waitress called to the griddle man in the window. And to a man in a white coat next to a coffee urn behind the counter: "Draw one—have it in the dark."

The coffee quickly arrived, and Porter perused the paper as he sipped it. A headline on the top of the front page caught his eye:

WOMEN CAUGHT IN RAID STRICKEN WITH PANIC

Handsomely Dressed Bevy Found in Alleged Poolroom

The day before, police officers had forced their way into an apartment on West 62nd Street and found "a room elegantly furnished and with a large racing chart, a telephone, racing cards, and other poolroom paraphernalia about." When the officers entered

> all but three of the women wept and broke out into wailings, pleadings, and prayers. The three silent ones had fainted. They were revived by two of the policemen. The other women meanwhile were in a pitiable state. Several were so hysterical they did not know what they were saying and mingled laughter with their tears. "What will my husband say to this?" was the cry from nearly all of them.

The article went on to describe how the telephone rang in the flat. An officer answered and listened as a potential customer attempted to place a bet on a horse race.

It was capital stuff.

By the time he finished the article, Porter's butter cakes had arrived. They turned out to be as tall as biscuits, but browned on both sides; the "butter" was applied by the diner, along with maple syrup, a good quantity of each was set before him by the sharp-tongued waitress.

Another front-page article had to do with a terrific crush of people at the City Hall Station of the Third Avenue elevated line during the previous day's afternoon rush, stemming from a delay in train service due to a bridge closure. When a train finally did arrive, the crowd on the platform surged toward the cars, while the passengers trying to get off couldn't do so. The *Times* reported that

> one man, with gray hair and beard, and wearing a frock coat and silk hat, was borne down in the crush, and his coat almost torn off him. His hat was knocked off and trampled upon until it was a shapeless mass. A woman with a child in her arms was caught in the moving human mass, and her skirt literally torn off her. Several women became semi-hysterical and cried out that they were being crushed and trampled down.

It was true that the train hadn't fallen from its track to the ground. But still Porter's resolution not to ride the elevated was redoubled.

He turned the paper over to the back page, page 16, with the intention of reading the latest dispatches from the world of sport. Once there, he saw that the Giants had been defeated by the Boston Beaneaters at the Polo Grounds before a crowd of 1,100. Mathewson had allowed only six hits and two runs, but his teammates had supported him with but a single tally.

Porter's eyes wandered to the bottom of the page, and what he saw there made him almost stand up in his seat. The headline was "FIT-THROWER'S" TRICKS. The unsigned article read:

> Imitations of epileptic fits and attacks of heart disease have yielded George Gray, twenty-six years old, and in other respects a plausible beggar, an income of from $15 to $20 a day, according to his own admission, now that he is in the hands of the police. The "professional fit thrower," as they call him, is also a curiosity of nature in that he possesses the power of accelerating or retarding his heart action at will, according to the physicians at the Presbyterian Hospital.
>
> Gray tumbled down in front of the residence of Isaac N. Heidelberg, at 42 East 17th Street yesterday, just as Jesse I. Straus of 49 East Seventy-fourth Street was coming out. "Heart failure; digitalis—quick, I am dying!" he gasped as Mr. Straus, Milton Einstein of 15 West Seventy-ninth Street, and others ran to him. Another minute and he would probably have been carried into one of the handsome residences of the block and treated with restoratives and cash, but Bicycle Policeman Walter Leazenbee came along just then and noticed an army hat and the cavity of a missing tooth, the salient points of his police description. Admitting his identity, Gray pleaded that he was sick, and so affected was Mr. Einstein that he protested that it was a shame to arrest a man in such a condition, and gave the prisoner 50 cents as he tottered away to the hospital.

It was, he realized, an account of the very scene he, Hall, and Duffy had witnessed the day before! And he kicked himself for not doping that it was a graft. Clearly, the New York City cons were of a higher order than he was used to.

Porter called for the bill, paid it, and left a one-cent tip. On the way out the door, he reflected on his good fortune, both in having such an excellent meal for eleven cents and in having landed in New York. Hall's comment was proving to be on the mark. Porter wouldn't necessarily weave George Gray, the professional fit-thrower, into a short story, but his presence on the back page of the *Times* augured well. Whereas previously he had had to seek out tales, or stitch them together from haphazard incidents, or worst of all, contrive them from his fancy, it seemed that in this city, they might very well fall into his lap. And how many of them involved vice, grift, or deception!

On his way back to the hotel, he thought about his walk with Duffy and Hall, and specifically the uncanny way the city operated on a grid. All its life moved on tracks, in grooves, according to system, within boundaries, by rote. The streetcars, autobuses, and elevated trains traveled on their perpendicular routes; the people streamed by in straight rows. And strategically placed within the grid were green squares, including the three he and the editors had successively encountered: Washington, Union, and Madison. A notable feature in all of them were the New Yorkers, from seemingly every stratum of society, sitting on the benches, looking straight ahead, as if in a waiting room. But what were they waiting for? By the time Porter had ascended to his barren room, an idea had hatched and was already trying to stumble forward on two thin legs. He gathered some paper, sat down in the room's one chair, and began to write in his neat Spencerian hand. The story, as it developed, was about two souls sitting in a New York park—a man and a woman—and the web of misunderstanding which turns out to connect them.

By supper time he had finished the story and given it a title: "His Courier." He put it in an envelope, bought some stamps from the clerk in the lobby, and posted the package to Dana at *The Smart Set.* He realized he had written straight through the midday meal and was right hungry. He decided he had earned one of the New York lobster dinners he had read so much about. And a good bottle of white wine.

CHAPTER IV

THE FOLLOWING DAY, Porter moved out of his hotel—chosen only because it was within view of the Hudson River ferry terminal—into the so-called Vallambrosa Apartment-House, near (but not on) Gramercy Park. "So-called" because it was not an apartment-house. Rather, it was composed of two old-fashioned, brownstone-front residences welded into one. Among the Vallambrosa's other roomers were stenographers, musicians, brokers, shopgirls, space-rate writers, art students, wire-tappers, and other people who leaned far over the banister-rail when the doorbell rang.

Porter secured rooms in the east side, on the third floor, but they were just two in number and modest in character. One contained a bed and a bureau, on top of which he placed his framed photographs of Athol and Margaret, and the third one. The notable inhabitants of the other room were a divan, an easy chair, and a table, on top of which were his sharpened pencils and a high stack of yellow paper.

He settled into a routine. Breakfast in his rooms and work on a story. Twice a week, a letter to Margaret. Lunch at a restaurant. And almost every afternoon, wandering: along the river fronts, through Hell's Kitchen, down the Bowery, dropping into all manner of places, and talking with anyone who was willing to pass the time with him. (He carried with him a small notebook in which he could take down notable instances of slang or striking turns of phrase.) He embarked on these peregrinations even though a part of him dreaded that some beggar or bum would take him in with a flash of recognition and say, "Well, look at yourself! I haven't seen you since the OP. How are the hell are you?" Or even worse, that one of the small number of Texans who *knew* would somehow have gotten himself to Gotham and—even less likely—found himself on the same sidewalk as Porter. Time and again, he told himself how improbable that was. And indeed, he felt a growing confidence—he didn't know where it came from—that he could establish and maintain his anonymity here. The metropolis sometimes felt like a terrific quicksand, shifting its particles constantly, with no foundation, its upper granules of today buried tomorrow in ooze and slime.

He often walked the streets and sidewalks at night, especially if he couldn't sleep. If he was in the vicinity, he would always find his way to the Bread Line at 10th and Broadway. Years before, Fleischmann, the baker, had undertaken to provide a half a loaf of bread to every man who presented himself, promptly at midnight. Each night, the homeless and the hobos and the hapless would line up well before that hour and silently wait their turn. In hard times or in the winter, there could be as many as four or five hundred. Porter would watch from a respectful distance as the Bread Line moved forward slowly, its leather feet sliding on the stones with the sound of a hissing serpent. Occasionally, he'd strike up conversations with one or two of the men, and if they were willing, ask them by what route they had arrived there. Sometimes, it was enough to look at them and imagine.

In December, the thought occurred to him that someone assessing his situation would expect him to visit his daughter in Pittsburgh, where she would soon be arriving from school for the holidays. It was but a train ride away. But that outside observer couldn't have understood that, already, New York had taken possession of him, as if it were a warden and he (again!) a prisoner. The city was more benevolent than the Ohio Penitentiary, to be sure, and its meals more sumptuous, but he was no more able to escape than he had been there. He wrote Margaret a letter saying that a business trip out west would prevent him from being there. He didn't spend any time pondering whether she would believe him.

One unseasonably warm day, he struck into Broadway, and abandoned himself to the spectacle of the laborers digging the foundations for a skyscraper at one of the corners. They had scooped forty or fifty feet into the earth, below the cellars of the old houses they had torn down, and were drilling into the everlasting rock with steam drills. A whole hive of men were let loose all over the excavation, pitching the earth and broken stones into carts, lifting the carts by derricks to the level of the street, and hitching the horses to them, and working the big steam shovels hanging from the derricks. The engines were snorting and chuckling and the wheels grinding, and the big horses straining, and the men shouting at them—the whole thing muted by the streaming feet of the multitude, and the whine of the trolleys, and the clatter of the wagons, and the crash and roar of the terrible elevated trains. It struck Porter that the scene would have been impossible to capture in print, or at least not with the skills he had at his disposal. Even a motion picture would be insufficient. It couldn't convey the sounds, the smells, the pulsations the city seemed to throw off.

Pretty soon, a mud-covered Italian ran out of the depths with a red flag, and the rest ran to cover, and puff! went a blast that tore up tons of rock, and made no more of a dint in the great mass of noise than if it had been the jet of white vapor that it looked like. Life in the city was on such a prodigious scale, Porter thought, and going on in so many ways at once, that the human atom lost the sense of its own little aches and pains, and merged its weakness in the larger human mass.

Another day, a week or so later, wanting to wander a bit in the teeming East Side, he took the Second Avenue streetcar downtown. The evening rush hour had just commenced, the car was crowded, and Porter stood surrounded by a variegated collection of what he had just begun thinking of as his fellow New Yorkers.

As the car approached Fifth Street, his thoughts about a stubborn plot point were interrupted by a woman in an elaborate hat who was speaking loudly—he realized—to him.

"Well, I have had enough with mashers like you!" she said. "At your age, you'd think you'd have learned to keep your paws to yourself!"

New Yorkers are notoriously circumspect when an altercation occurs on a public conveyance, but on this occasion, every head in the car turned to look at Porter.

He looked around him and said, "Madam, I assure you, I have done no such thing. Just look at me! One hand is in my pocket and the other is holding on to this strap. And I've been this way for several minutes.

She would have none of it. "Masher!" she kept repeating, with increasing volume. Most of the car gazed silently (and, it must be said, with a measure of vicarious enjoyment) at the exhibition, but one man near the door said, "If I didn't have to get off at this stop, I would knock your block off."

Despite himself, Porter felt his face reddening. After what seemed an eternity, the car arrived at Houston Street, and the would-be pugilist indeed exited. So did his female accuser, hurling one more accusation as the door closed. As the car began to pull away from the station, the other passengers gradually pulled their gazes away from Porter, and towards their newspapers, out the window, or merely into space. In order to escape the scrutiny of the one tight-lipped biddy who still stared at him, he made a ninety-degree turn and shifted the position of his hands, taking the strap with his left and putting the right in his pocket. When that hand arrived at that destination, it found nothing else there. His wallet was gone.

At that point he saw two street urchins, one of whom was wearing a red cap, making their way to the far end of the car. The metaphorical penny dropped, and Porter took off after them. Or tried to: because of his bulk and the crowdedness of the conveyance, the distance between him and his boys only increased, and soon he lost sight of them. But when the train stopped at Rivington, he took a gamble and got off. Sure enough, the ragamuffins were on the other end of the platform, and they didn't appear to see him. One of them took off down the street, and disappeared from view as he turned south on Ludlow. But the other—red cap—stayed on the street for half a block and then ducked into a storefront.

Porter took his time getting there. If the kid had slipped out a back door, there wouldn't be any hope of finding him; therefore, he kept his eye trained on the front, which saw no further traffic. As he got into view, Porter perceived that the boy's haven was a cigar store—a "cheap Charlie," as the locals called it. He took the chance of walking around the block to confirm a hunch; then he entered the premises. The shelves were suspiciously bereft of cigars. A half-dozen males—one of whom was diminutive and had a red cap on—were sitting around a table, so attentive to their card game that they paid no attention to the new arrival. The thirteen spades from a deck of cards were fastened to the table and arrayed around it, in numerical order. Small piles of bills and coins had been placed on top of the eight, the five, and the queen. A man in a straw hat—evidently the dealer—laid the jack of hearts on the table, then the six of hearts. He paused a beat, put down the eight of clubs. At that, one of the players pounded the table and stood up. The dealer produced another card, evidently of no importance, and then gathered up the money resting on the eight.

The game, Porter realized, was a variant of faro, a favorite around cowboy campfires and Austin saloons, one difference being that the cards were dealt from a bare deck and not a box. That made it easier, he noticed, for the dealer to deftly pluck a card from the bottom.

The loser swore and started to walk away from the table. That caused the players to look up, and take notice of Porter. When the kid saw him, he sprang up and made a dash for the door. Porter blocked his way and said, "Oh no you don't."

"What's the idea?" said the dealer, in a tone suggesting something roughly halfway between boredom and outrage.

"The idea is that this gutter rat either stole my wallet or was a party to that action."

At that point the kid emptied his pockets and stuck his tongue out at Porter.

"As I said, you were a party. You or your friend either guyed me, or helped create a commotion while one of your confederates did. You could even have handed the spondulicks to someone at this table." The card players immediately and unanimously looked at their shoes.

"There is a police station just around the corner. Not ten minutes ago, I met with an officer there who gave me a whistle, which is in my pocket. If I walk out that door and blow three short notes, he will immediately follow the sound, and I'll hand you over for arrest."

"Nuts," the kid said. "I don't have no money, of yours or nobody else's. And without it, the cops can't make me."

"That may be," Porter said. "But I'll testify that you picked my pocket, so even if you get cleared eventually, you'll be booked and detained. How would your mother feel about that?"

He had evidently struck a nerve. The boy was clearly past the point when a maternal allusion would elicit tears, but his face softened and he got a faraway look in his eyes. "So whaddya want?" he finally said.

Porter led the boy to Seward Park, where they sat down on a bench. He explained that because of the obvious circumstances of being shorn of his wallet, he had no funds at the moment, but if their arrangement were to continue, there would be some money in it for him. He mentioned the figure of two dollars. And he did have a couple of pennies in his pocket to buy the kid an ice cream from a Hokey-Pokey man, lured out to the streets by the unseasonable temperatures. Porter didn't know if it was the sweet, the promise of funds down the road, the threat of blowing the whistle, or merely a desire to get some things off his chest, but the kid proved talkative. He said his name was Bernie Scheuer and his age was eleven. The first question Porter asked was about the card game in the cigar store.

"Shimmy on the other side! You never seen stuss?" Bernie was incredulous.

Porter let that pass. "Tell me," he said, "—how long have you been picking pockets?"

"Since I was nine, I guess. Some of the boys I run with started showing up in fancy shirts and new shoes. I asked them about it and they brought me over to the cheder." In Bernie's mouth, the words came out "dem" and "dey."

"Cheder?" Porter had trouble reproducing the guttural sound of the first consonant.

"A school, I guess you'd call it. Only it was fun, at least at first. The first day I show up, the fagin, this guy with lamps so heavy he looks like he's asleep, he says he got a game for me. He drops two bits into his pocket and says they're mine if I can take the quarter out of his pocket without him noticing. He closes his eyes and I reach in and pull it out. I tell him I done it and he acts like he never heard of such a thing. I do it again, and then two more times. He says I'm an 'excellent pupil' and I should come back tomorrow. I walk home with a buck in my pocket."

Bernie finished his daub of ice cream, licked the brown paper on which it had been presented, crumpled the paper up, and tossed it over his shoulder.

"The next day, there's someone else there. This gazabo has tiny bells sewn all over his clothes. He's got something in every pocket: watch, purse, card-case, handkerchief, gloves. I had to show that I could empty every pocket without making a sound before the fagin let me go into the world and cop out boobs."

Porter had worried that he wouldn't be able to get the kid to talk. It struck him that the real challenge might be getting him to shut up. On the plus side, his notebook was filling up—"to beat the band," as the kid might say—with premium slang.

Bernie told Porter about the various ploys he had learned about and put into practice on "the boobs." One kid would bicycle through crowded Orchard Street, or Essex, and deliberately fall. While he clutched himself here and there and tried to get back up, his confederates picked pockets right and left. They surreptitiously handed the plunder to the bike rider, who was back on his wheels and off in a jiffy. Sometimes, Bernie said, he'd pose as a newsboy outside a theater's doors just as a performance was getting out. He'd thrust a newspaper into a gent's face, and in the ensuing commotion take his other hand and extract the contents of the mark's pockets. Then he'd hand the plunder to a swiftly departing confederate. If accused, he would employ "the baby game," simply bawling his eyes out till the accuser relented. On the handful of occasions this hadn't worked, and a cop who was not on the take could be found, Bernie's case would be handled by one of the shysters his fagin had on retainer. Without the booty there was no jail, but, as the kid had elucidated, the incidents caused no end of shame in the Schueur family, as well as promises on the part of Bernie to stick to the straight and narrow.

"And what was the caper you pulled on me?" Porter said.

"Simple," the kid responded, warming to his theme. "The lady with the hat and the guy who said he'd knock your block off were the 'stalls.' When the lady started yelling at you, you didn't think about nothing else except you didn't do it. That's when me and my sidekicker went for your pockets. He was the one who got the mazumas off of you. He handed your wallet to the stall, then he got off the car and hit the bricks before you got wise that it was swiped."

"All very interesting. But if your enterprise is so successful, why are you willing to spill the beans to me? It seems like you're not lacking any dough."

Bernie got quiet all of a sudden. In a voice smaller than previously, he said, "The fagin don't let us keep more than ten cents out of every dollar we steal."

"And what's the fagin's name?"

"Benny Fein. They call him Dopey Benny, on account of his eyes."

It was time to go home and, while it was still fresh in his mind, write down what Bernie had told him. Porter thanked the lad and set up a time to meet him the following week at a local candy store, where, he said, he'd not only bring the two bucks but stand him to a Charlotte russe and an egg cream. They went their separate ways. As he walked uptown, Porter patted himself on the back for the whistle bluff. He really should invest in one, he thought. He could think of no end of ways it could come in handy.

CHAPTER V

As the new year of 1904 arrived and took its first baby steps, Porter's productivity was impressive. He had no domestic duties, no duties of any kind for that matter, and, other than the occasional meal with Hall or another editor, no social obligations. At the Vallambrosa, he avoided the other tenants' chattering social whirl. This level of solitude might have been trying for someone else, but Porter hadn't come to the city to make friends. The presence of four million people in close proximity was enough to stave off loneliness; he didn't need to converse or share intimacies with them.

He had physical needs, to be sure. But the city offered abundant ways of meeting them. Hall had given him the lay of the land, so to speak, steering him away from the parlor houses in the Haymarket and the fifty-cent houses in Chinatown and East Side tenements, not to mention the streetwalkers in their plumage who came out in multitudes when the sun came down and whose pimps watched them with a cold eye, from under a street lamp or just around the corner of a building. ("A bad business," the editor had said.) There were two or three five-dollar-houses on Madison and Park that suited his purposes and among which he alternated.

As in his Ohio confinement, the expanse of hours seemed to unlock his fancy. *Smart Set* had bought "By Courier," and nearly everything else he submitted was accepted as well. By Easter he had sold thirteen stories—a half dozen of them to *Ainslee's*, which was taking so much of his work that, at Duffy and Hall's request, he supplied yet another pseudonym—James L. Bliss—so it would not appear that most of the book was written by O. Henry. ("Olivier" had been dropped by mutual agreement.)

Oddly—considering how far it was, in so many ways, from where he had come from—New York City had truly begun to feel like home. It seemed propitious that he had arrived when the city was creating a new version of itself, much as he was doing. In 1898, five years before his arrival, New York had more than doubled its population to four million with the consolidation of Brooklyn, western Queens, and Staten Island into the existing metropolis of Manhattan and the Bronx. That made it the second most populous metropolis in the world, propelling it ahead of Paris, Berlin, Chicago, Vienna, and Tokyo. Only London was bigger. And it wasn't merely a matter of numbers. The city was in a moment of astonishing flux, with new buildings, institutions, and demographics forming before its residents' eyes, and new populations still streaming in from Europe and other corners of the earth. All of it was raw material for his fancy.

And, improbably, he had landed in the center of American publishing at a moment when the American magazine had just reached its pinnacle as an enterprise, and the short story was the most popular medium not just in literature, but in entertainment broadly defined. Frank Munsey had arguably set things in motion, just a decade before. With the weekly paper he owned and edited and named after himself rapidly losing circulation, he realized that weeklies were being crushed by Sunday newspapers. He decided to create a monthly magazine—also named after himself, naturally—and sell it for the unprecedentedly low price of ten cents a copy; the "respected" journals like *Century* and *The Atlantic Monthly* cost three times that much, or more. It was a resounding success: circulation rose to more than 500,000 by the middle of the 1890s, and advertising had followed, eventually bankrolling Munsey's lofty perch in the Flatiron Building. Munsey was benefiting not only from his own commercial and editorial insight, but from a robust and growing market. The American population was increasing, as was the literate portion of the population, and even trends in interior illumination were favorable. (Nearly every dwelling had gaslights or, increasingly, electric ones.)

And so it wasn't surprising that other titles followed: by 1900, nearly 2,500 monthly magazines were being published in the United States. The monthlies that followed the *Munsey's* model—*McClure's*, *Everybody's*, *Ainslee's* and so forth—offered "muckraking" journalism, illustrations, humor, occasional essays, book reviews, and verse, but their lifeblood was the short story. As Munsey had written a few years earlier: "We want stories. That is what we mean—stories, not dialect sketches, not washed out studies of effete human nature, not weak tales of sickly sentimentality, not 'pretty' writing. . . . We want fiction in which there is a story, a force, a tale that means something—in short, a story."

Theater and vaudeville, even for city dwellers, were for special occasions. (Those in the hinterlands had to wait months for a road show to arrive in their town.) Motion pictures were a novelty. Novels required so much time. Thus, the triumph of the robust short story: with toothsome plot, noteworthy setting, distinctive point of view, and page count sufficient to provide amusement and engagement for an hour or two.

What Munsey and other editors wanted, Porter turned out to be eminently qualified to supply. In short order, the name "O. Henry" was on the lips of the denizens of the literary world—with the conversations equally divided between praise for his work and speculation as to precisely who the pseudonymous author really was. On that point, Hall had related to him an amusing story. It so happened that a Harvard undergraduate, who was an orphan and provided for by his wealthy uncle and aunt, was upbraided by that uncle one evening for doing poorly in his studies. The suggestion was that the lad might do better to find himself a job. His eye happened to land on a magazine lying on a table; the cover featured a story by O. Henry. The boy, in a flash of inspiration, declared that he indeed had been laboring mightily, writing and publishing short stories as "O. Henry." The uncle and aunt read the story, estimated it highly, cut it out, and sent it to a Harvard professor with the information that it was the work of their nephew. The professor read it, and a few days later in open class announced that there was a young man present who had written a story that showed a marvelous grasp of Western life and a knowledge of human nature that was almost incomprehensible in one so young. The rumor spread, and in due time a Minneapolis newspaper printed it as fact. The attention emboldened the student to enter, as "O. Henry," into negotiations for a first-reading agreement with *The Saturday Evening Post.* An editor at the *Post* thereupon called at the office of *Ainslee's* and asked to see Gilman Hall. He explained that his company naturally wished to proceed with every care and courtesy. Hall told the representative that the real O. Henry had never been farther east than New York, that his name was William Sydney Porter, that he was well into his forties, and that just an hour before he had been in those very offices.

Because of all the interest, Hall thought it would make sense for one of the cultural magazines to write an article about this new figure on the scene. He asked Porter to compile some background information, to supply to said magazine. The reply gave Hall a chuckle, and the resolution never to ask such a question again. Porter wrote:

> You say you will try to have an article about me printed in one of the literary magazines. Please have it stated that I am of a sedentary but slightly corpulent disposition. I compose with the greater ease on unruled paper and Fridays. My favorite authors are Carolyn and Artesian Wells. Generally feverish, with thirst of mornings. Admire writings of Billy Burgundy and the prophet Jeremiah. Presbyterian. Bilious. Slightly ignorant.

Unsurprisingly, the article was never written.

For the moment, it seemed Porter could pluck ideas from anywhere, even, to some extent, from the regions of his past that he never, ever talked about with anyone. One day, a fancy struck him and he picked up his pen and started in on a letter to his fellow Recluse Club member Al Jennings.

Jennings was a little man with face so wrinkled and tanned it resembled a baked apple. On the outside, he wore a big hat, which he needed to keep his long and unruly red hair in check. He came by the hat rightfully. Born in Virginia, he ran away from home at the age of eleven and wound up as a junior hand on the 101 Ranch in Indian Territory. At sixteen, he went back east to study law, and returned to the future Oklahoma to join his father and his brothers Ed and John—lawyers all—in the town of Woodward. Then tragedy struck. A rival attorney shot Ed and John, killing the latter, and Al declared that henceforth he would neither practice nor follow the law. He proceeded to form a gang consisting of his third brother—Frank—and a handful of other desperadoes.

In the universe of outlaws, their exploits were not the most prolific. In 1897, they did manage to rob three passenger trains in Oklahoma Territory, but the results were mixed. The first time out, their dynamite failed to blow up a Wells Fargo safe on the train, and they made a narrow escape. They couldn't break the safe the second time, either, and their haul consisted of a couple of hundred dollars from the passengers, plus a bottle of whiskey and a bunch of bananas. The gang's most successful robbery was of a train in Berwyn, a few miles north of the Texas border, which netted about $30,000. But in time the law caught up to Jennings, and he was sentenced to life in prison, his sentence to be served at the Ohio Penitentiary.

Not long after his arrival, he met Bill Porter. Rules and conventions in a penitentiary are as formal and strictly adhered to as in civil society, if not more so. Chief among them is the prohibition from asking a fellow inmate about his past life. And so Jennings was ignorant of Porter's biography, other than his sentence, his pharmaceutical training, and his southern heritage—betrayed by his accent. (Jennings' own exploits, the subject of illustrated newspaper feature articles, were familiar to all.)

There was one more thing Jennings knew about Porter. The Oklahoman discovered it after he had embarked on a memoir of his bandit days. The ambition was not unusual. Every man in prison considers his life an adventure of the most absorbing interest. What set Jennings apart from the mass of convicts was that he actually set pen to paper. Indeed, his book—which he called *The Long Riders*—was galloping ahead at a furious pace. That was, to some extent, a problem. There were chapters with 40,000 words and not one climax. There were other chapters with but seven sentences and as many killings as there were words.

He showed the manuscript to his friend Billy Reidler, who was in for train-robbing as well. Reidler insisted that a man be shot in every paragraph. It would make the book "go," he said.

"If I have any more men killed," Jennings said, "there'll be nobody left on earth."

"I'll tell you what you do," Reidler said. "You ask Bill Porter about it. He's writing a story, too."

When Jennings and Reidler dropped in on Porter that evening, their awareness of his literary pursuits appeared to embarrass him. But after a few moments, he acknowledged that yes, in the nighttime quiet, he occupied himself with a pen. He asked Jennings to read aloud a few choice passages from *The Long Riders.* The passage he picked was an account of a particularly gruesome gunfight. When Jennings finished, Porter smiled and closed his eyes for a minute.

"Colonel," he finally said, "you have a good story to tell. Perhaps too good. I suggest that as dramatic as the events might be, so should the writing be *un*dramatic. That is, write in as simple, plain, and unembellished a style as you know how. Make your sentences short. Put in as much realism and as many facts as possible. That advice may not be as easy to follow as it seems, but I believe it will hold you in good stead."

Jennings tried to follow the advice, but he still hadn't finished the book by the time he was set free. His liberty was the product of three qualities that *had* stood him in good stead: cunning, some influential friends, and luck. During the long days and nights at the OP, his cunning fixated on the fact that he had been convicted for robbing the mail, which had a minimum sentence of life, when in fact he had merely robbed several passengers and one safe. Thanks to the two other qualities, his case was brought to the ear of Mark Hanna, the Republican Senator from Ohio and adviser to President McKinley, who saw to it that his sentence was commuted to five years. On his release in December 1902, Jennings returned to Oklahoma Territory and resumed the practice of law.

In his office one day about a year later, he went through the mail and found a letter from none other than his old friend Bill Porter. After some initial pleasantries, Porter got down to tacks.

> I have been doing quite a deal of business with the editors since I got down to work and have made more than I could at any other business. Behold me, the lazy man old Jean at the Recluse Club used to guy, averaging $250 a month.
>
> I have struck up quite a correspondence with the editor of *Everybody's Magazine*. I have sold him two stories for the current issue, which I enclose. You will not see "William Porter" among the contributors, which is explained by the fact that on this island, William Porter does not exist. Hence, "O. Henry." I am determined that no man here learn of my identity or my past. So far, I have found that a city of four million is a good place to keep a secret.
>
> In any case, in writing to the *Everybody's* man some time ago, I suggested an article with a title something like "The Art of Holding Up a Train," telling him that I thought I could get it written by an expert in the business. As you might know, the best-seller of the moment

> is a cowboy novel written by a Philadelphian, and the President's tales of wrestling bears and such in Wyoming are eaten up like candy. Just imagine how western stories written by Westerners would go over. I propose we collaborate.
>
> Now, I will give you a sort of general synopsis of my idea—of course, everything is subject to your own revision and change. The article, we will say, is written by a typical train hoister—one without your education and powers of expression but intelligent enough to convey his ideas from his standpoint.
>
> Comment on the moral side of the proposition as little as possible. Do not claim that holding up trains is the only business a gentleman would engage in, and, on the contrary, do not depreciate a profession that is really only financiering with spurs on. Describe the facts and details—all that part of the proceedings that the passenger sitting with his hands up in a Pullman looking into the end of a tunnel in the hands of one of the performers does not see.

Here Porter gave what he called "a rough draft of my idea"—the sequence of the proposed article. What was the "manner of the hold-up" including the details of topping the train, and "How is the boodle gotten at?" And: "What could two or three brave and determined passengers do if they were to try?"

"I apologize if this seems excessive," he wrote.

> I merely send along the ideas that occur to me casually. You will, of course, have many far better. I suggest that you make the article anywhere from 4,000 to 6,000 words. Get as much meat in it as you can, and, by the way—stuff it full of western genuine slang—(not the Eastern story paper kind). Get all the quaint cowboy expressions and terms of speech you can think of.

> Try her a whack and send it along as soon as you can, and let's see what we can do.

He asked after Billy Reidler and some other mutual acquaintances, then concluded: "Write me as soon as you feel like it and I assure you I will be glad to hear from you. I am surrounded by wolves and fried onions, and a word from one of the salt of the earth will come like a clap of manna from a clear roof garden."

Jennings stayed up till three that morning transcribing everything he could think of about train-robbing. He mailed the pages to Porter, who sent back some questions and suggested revisions. They had two more exchanges, after which Porter presented the happy news that *Everybody's* had accepted the piece. When he later sent on Jennings's half of the fee, the $75 cheque was more thrilling than any loot from a train heist.

And he felt kind of proud when he read the "Author's Note" at the beginning, signed "O.H.":

> The man who told me these things was for several years an outlaw in the Southwest and a follower of the pursuit he so frankly describes. His description of the modus operandi should prove interesting, his counsel of value to the potential passenger in some future "hold-up," while his estimate of the pleasures of train robbing will hardly induce any one to adopt it as a profession. I give the story in almost exactly his own words.

The "almost exactly" was gracious on Porter's part; Jennings took it as his due.

As the weather began to warm, however, Porter's output slowed. He found himself spending more time and money in the saloons than he knew he should, to the detriment of his productivity. The equation was unmistakable and troubling. Now that he was patronizing those saloons and New York's finer restaurants, and was meeting and paying young Bernie Scheuer and a couple of other informants on a regular basis, his expenses were rising. Savings: depleted. Income: declining. And his obligations remained steady: the $25 he sent each week to his in-laws towards Margaret's tuition, clothing, food, and so on, and the $50 each month that was transferred by Western Union, under his name, to a party in Texas. What's more, against his own better judgment, Porter couldn't resist picking up—or at least putting up a good and sincere fight for—the tab when he dined with others.

The evening of May Day, a Sunday, found him without funds, or food, except for a lone onion. He eyed it warily and remembered how cowboys would eat them, like apples, for a mobile meal on the trail. But he told himself he was in the East now, where a raw onion was not an acceptable repast. He left it on the counter; it seemed to cast a cold eye on him as he tried to write.

The story, such as it was, was based on an incident Gilman Hall had related to him. Hall had recently decamped to the suburb of New Rochelle, and had found some surprising conflicts and competition among the newly landed gentry there. Over lunch earlier that week, Hall had told him about two men who'd actually engaged in fisticuffs for an unlikely prize.

The idea was promising, but, wanting nutrition as he did, he couldn't summon the means with which to propel it from anecdote to story. Finally, he gave up, got up, walked out the door, and began pacing up and down the landing.

Another resident of the Vallambrosa was Hetty Pepper, a sharp-featured woman of thirty-three, who worked as a feather curler. Rather, had worked. That very day, while she was laboring on a lobster plume, Mr. Blumenstock himself, while wandering through the shop, pinched her arm kindly, three inches above the elbow. She was not in the mood to be pinched and slapped him three feet away with one good blow of her muscular and not especially lily-white right. Thirty minutes after that, Hetty walked out of H. Blumenstock, Ostrich Feathers, for good, with one dime and a nickel in her purse.

The entire sum went to the butcher, for two pounds of rib beef, priced that day at seven and one-half cents per pound. Hetty mounted with her rib beef to her $3.50 third-floor flat. One hot, savory beef-stew for supper, a night's good sleep, and she would be fit in the morning to search for a new position. In her room she got a graniteware stew-pan out of the 2×4-foot earthenware closet, and began to dig down in a rat's-nest of paper bags for the ingredients she wanted. She came out with her nose and chin just a little sharper pointed. There was nothing there. She was sorely disappointed, for a one-ingredient stew was a mean repast. But, in an emergency, with salt and pepper and a tablespoonful of flour (first well stirred in a little cold water), beef alone will serve.

Hetty took her stew-pan to the rear of the third-floor hall. According to the advertisements of the Vallambrosa, running water was to be to be found there. In truth, it only ambled or walked through the faucets, but that is a mere technicality. There was also a sink where the female roomers often met to dump their coffee grounds and glare at one another's kimonos.

At this sink Hetty found a girl with plaintive eyes and masses of heavy, deep-brown hair, washing two large potatoes. From house gossip, she had learned that the girl was a miniature-painter living in a kind of attic—or "studio," as landlords preferred to call it—on the top floor. The girl was quite slim, and handled her potatoes as an old bachelor uncle handles a baby who is cutting teeth. She had a dull shoemaker's knife in her right hand, and she had begun to peel one of the potatoes with it.

"Beg pardon for being a buttinski," Hetty said to her, "but if you peel them potatoes you lose out. They're new Bermudas. You want to scrape 'em. Lemme show you." She took a potato and the knife and began to demonstrate. The decisiveness and swiftness of her strokes were testament to her years with Blumenstock.

"Oh, thank you," said the artist. "I didn't know. And I did hate to see the thick peeling go; it seemed such a waste. But I thought they always had to be peeled. When you've got only potatoes to eat, the peelings count, you know."

"Say, kid," said Hetty, staying her knife, "you ain't up against it, too, are you?" The artist smiled wanly.

"I suppose I am," she replied. "Art—or, at least, the way I interpret it—doesn't seem to be much in demand. I only have these potatoes for my dinner. But they aren't so bad boiled and hot, with a little butter and salt."

"Child," said Hetty, letting a brief smile soften her rigid features, "fate has sent me and you together. I've had it handed to me in the neck, too; but I've got a chunk of meat in my room as big as a lap-dog. And I've done everything to get potatoes except pray for 'em.

"Of course, potatoes ain't the only ingredient we need," she went on. "I'd ask the landlady, but I don't want her hep to the fact that I'm pounding the asphalt for another job just yet." She paused. "Say, kid, you haven't got a couple of pennies that've slipped down into the lining of your last winter's sealskin, have you? I could step down to the corner to old Antonio's stand."

"You can call me Anna," said the girl. "No; I spent my last penny three days ago."

"Then we'll make do," Hetty said. "Let's me and you bunch our commissary departments and make a stew of 'em."

The two began to prepare their supper in the former feather-curler's room. Hetty put the rib beef in cold salted water in the stewpan and set it on the one-burner gas-stove. Presently, the beef and potatoes were bubbling merrily. Sensing more water was needed, Hetty headed out into the hall towards the sink—and nearly hit Porter in the nose with the door.

The two tenants stared at each other for a full second. "I beg your pardon, ma'am," Porter finally said, "but I couldn't help noticing the delectable odors emanating from your room." He told her his name.

"I know who you are," said Hetty. "You write books and things in your rooms for the paper-and-rags man. I can hear the postman guy you when he brings them thick envelopes back."

Porter realized that he wasn't only hungry for a good meal. He could use some company, too. "You have me pegged," he said with a chuckle. "I'm afraid I don't know you nearly as well. We must keep different hours. To whom do I have the pleasure of speaking?"

Porter had found it amenable in New York to adopt a certain formality in his speech as well as his dress, including the transposition of prepositions to the beginning of sentences.

"Hetty Pepper, New York's finest feather curler." In making the acquaintance of someone new, especially a gentleman, Hetty preferred to be armed with a job.

"Miss Pepper, as I say, the odors coming from your apartment are. . ." He let the sentence hang.

She heard—or maybe she just imagined it—the growl of his stomach. "Well, Mr. Porter, you are cordially invited to share some beef stew with a miniature painter and myself. There's only one problem. A stew can be edible and even tasty with two ingredients, and we have beef and potato. But to be a proper stew, it requires a third."

"A stew without an onion," she said, "is worse than a matinée without candy."

The three tenants crowded around Hetty's table. "Crowded" because it was a table designed for two and Porter, even putting it kindly, took up the space of one and a quarter. His positioning was even more awkward than this might suggest, because of the mild contortion he was attempting to perform: keeping his attention on Hetty, who in the course of monopolizing the conversation (a common state of affairs, he surmised) was offering up some potentially usable material, while stealing as many glances at Anna as propriety would arguably allow.

Hetty was describing, at Porter's encouragement, the fine points of feather-curling—catching and correcting herself, more than once, after employing the past tense. "The method," she was saying, with a precision and formality that suggested she might have memorized a manual, "consists of holding the feather in the hand, then placing the fiber of the feather between the thumb and the edge of the knife and drawing it along swiftly, being careful not to curl the fiber too tight. Only the end of the fiber should be curled. And then the feather, or tip, is laid down on the edge of the table on its underside, and it's combed into a regular roll along the edge."

She leapt up to the counter, where she grabbed Anna's knife, recently used for potato peeling. Then she plucked a couple of long leaves from the rubber plant in the corner and demonstrated some of the different styles she'd mastered—Prince of Wales tip, lobster plumes, snake plumes, drooping willow plumes, and Prince de Galles. The plant was more or less behind Anna's chair, which allowed Porter, he reckoned, to surreptitiously divide his attention between the feather-curling exhibition and her admirable profile.

"You mentioned the thick envelopes the postman brings back to me," he said to Hetty. "In the interest of having them stay put at the magazines I send them to, I have been trying to emulate the quality associated with M. Zola and his fellow Frenchmen. I speak of naturalism. As I understand it, that includes cold facts, figures and details, the more and the truer to life the better. And so I hope you'll not think me rude if I inquire as to your salary."

"I made . . . *make* . . . ten dollars a week," she said. Porter noted the correction. He also heard the pride in her voice and deemed it well-placed. He had never heard of a woman—in a respectable position—bringing home that much. Hetty, thinking of the job search she would embark on tomorrow, added, hopefully, "A good curler has always been in demand—and will be, until milliners start decorating their hats with something other than feathers." From her slight giggle as she made the last comment, Porter inferred that the likelihood of such a development was nil.

"I'm surprised you're so interested in my craft, Mr. Porter," Hetty said. "I find the attention of most gentleman goes '23 skidoo' at about the fourth word."

Porter chuckled. "Naturalism again. And the fact that the

more I know—about *anything*, it appears—the quicker stories seem to flow. Right now I am pursuing a fascination with shop-girls. . ." Hetty and Anna both looked up from their stew. "Not in that sense, I assure you," Porter quickly said. "But at the current moment, department stores seem to me to occupy the heart of the metropolitan scene, and it's the shopgirls who make them run. I declare, if Henry James had gone to work in one of those places, he would have turned out the great American novel."

The stew was tasty, Porter's only regret being the absence of something more potent to wash it down with. When they were finished, Hetty picked up the dishes and went down the hall to clean them. Porter took the opportunity to express his admiration for miniatures, and indicate how delighted he would be to view a selection of Anna's. She agreed—but not, she said, until she'd finished a series she was working on.

The following morning, his stomach reasonably full and his spirits buoyed by the prospect of seeing his upstairs neighbor, he directed his attention once again to his refractory short story. On Hall's suggestion, he had read de Maupassant's "The Necklace" and had been much affected by the surprise ending—the revelation that Madame Loisel, having sacrificed and gone into debt and more or less ruined her life to replace a borrowed necklace she'd lost ten years earlier, was the victim of a misunderstanding, for the necklace was a fake. The scope and tragic irony of such a story, he understood, was a bit beyond him at this point in his career. But he still could glean something from it. Could the suburban husbands coming to blows be a twist ending? No. But, he realized with a jolt of excitement, it could be part of a twist *beginning*. He crumpled up the paper that contained the forlorn 150 words he'd managed the day before, pulled up a new sheet, and started to write.

> Again, to-day, at a certain street, on the ragged boundaries of the city, Lawrence Holcombe stopped the trolley car and got off. Holcombe was a handsome,

> prosperous business man of forty; a man of high social standing and connections. His comfortable suburban residence was some five miles farther out on the car line from the street where so often of late he had dropped off the outgoing car.
>
> The conductor winked at a regular passenger, and nodded his head archly in the direction of Holcombe's hurrying figure.
>
> "Getting to be a regular thing," commented the conductor.

That was the start of the deception, and, with something like delight, Porter drew it out. When Holcombe, a bond broker, calls on "Katie," every phrase and adjective implies that his is a pursuit of the heart.

Holcombe makes his plea to her, and concludes, "Say 'Yes,' Katie, and I'll be the luckiest man in this town to-day."

Then his rival, Danny Conlan, appears on the scene and Holcombe improbably bests him in an abbreviated prize fight.

Porter put Holcombe on another train, heading out to his own suburb, where he meets an acquaintance, Bob Weatherly, who asks why he's looking so pleased with himself. The revelation and conclusion was swift, a mere seven short sentences.

> "Say, Bob, do you remember that Irish girl, Katie Flynn, that was with the Spaffords so long a time?"
>
> "I've heard of her," said Weatherly. "They say she stayed a year with them without a single day off. But I don't believe any fairy story like that."
>
> "'Twas a fact. Well, I engaged her to-day for a cook. She's going out to the house tomorrow."
>
> "Confound you for a lucky dog," shouted Weatherly, with envy in his tones and his heart, "and you live four blocks further out than we do!"

Porter went back through the six pages quickly and altered precisely three words. He gave the story a title—"The Struggle of the Outliers"—put the manuscript in an envelope, and addressed it to *Everybody's.* (Despite his dry spell, he still had stories under consideration at *Ainslee's* and *Smart Set.*) He was just in time to hand it to the postman.

Three days hence, the same individual brought for Porter, not the manuscript, but an acceptance and a check for thirty-seven dollars. Since this was his second story in the magazine, Cosgrave had raised his rate from one cent a word to two. He burst out of his room and knocked on Hetty's door, hoping to thank her for her hospitality by taking her out to Moquin's for dinner. There was no answer.

He proceeded to the rooms of the landlady, Mrs. Purdy, and asked about Hetty. She told him she had moved out two days before—giving not a word of notice and no forwarding address. Another one claimed by the quicksand, Porter thought.

Mrs. Purdy was speaking, he realized. "Would you know of anyone who might be interested in a cozy third-floor back? Four dollars a week, and a bargain at that."

CHAPTER VI

A COUPLE OF mornings later, Porter was working on a story about Con's Tavern, a joint on Irving Place he had begun to frequent, when the mail arrived, containing a single letter. The envelope was thin, which happily meant it didn't contain a rejected manuscript, but the writer's relief on that score quickly evaporated. The content of the single sheet of paper inside bore a letterhead and a brief typed message:

CHARLES W. GARDNER
PRIVATE DETECTIVE
The Mohawk Building
160 Fifth Avenue
New York City

Dear Mr. Porter:

I have become aware that certain parties have obtained sensitive information about your past—dating from the period before "O. Henry" existed. This information pertains to an institution near Columbus, Ohio.

I would be pleased to meet with you to discuss this intelligence. Neither a reply to this letter nor an appointment is necessary. Merely come to my office during business hours.

Yours sincerely,

Charles W. Gardner

Porter flung the paper into the air with such force that for a second he thought he might have dislocated his shoulder. He watched the page slowly float to the ground. A moment later he picked it up, stuffed it in his pocket, put on his hat, and walked out the door.

The Mohawk Building stood on the southwestern corner of Fifth Avenue and 21st Street, a ten-minute walk from the Vallambrosa. The directory in the lobby said Gardner's office was on the fifth floor, low enough for Porter to indulge his fear of aboveground conveyances and take the stairs. When he opened the door on which Gardner's name was etched in glass, he was breathing heavily. Inside he saw the authoritative hedge of an iron railing, behind which sat a furrowed man, clearly a secretary, who looked a bit like an animated cork-screw. Porter approached and gave his name; the man looked up with interest but little surprise and said, "Give me a couple of minutes. I'll tell Mr. Gardner you're here." Porter took a seat and looked around the room. Two other men who looked as vexed as he felt also sat there. One was intently studying some cryptic notes he had made; the other was staring at the ceiling. Only darkness could be seen through the doors to the secretary's right and left; the left one occasionally opened just far enough to permit a very diminutive call-boy to be squeezed through. In a prominent place on the wall was a large blackboard whereon were marked the figures from 1 to 20, over some of which the word "Out" was written. Every few moments a bell rang, some words emerged through a speaking tube next to the secretary's desk, and he scrawled "Out" over another number.

Presently he stood up and walked into the room to his right. He emerged half a minute later and announced, "Mr. Gardner will see you now." Porter followed him into the dim seclusion of the room and regarded a man of roughly his own age, wearing shirtsleeves and an owlish expression.

"Mr. Porter." Gardner stood up and extended his hand. He shook Porter's, then motioned to an oak-framed library chair, upholstered in light green velvet. "As a devotee of literature, I am right pleased to meet the man who is breathing new life into the short story. Though given the Western theme of so many of them, I'm a bit surprised that you are not wearing a Stetson hat and spurs." Porter looked at him without expression. Then he took the letter out from his pocket, smoothed it on his leg, and held it before him. "Sir," he said in an even tone, "what is the meaning of this?"

"Yes, you will be wanting an explanation, and I will give you one," Gardner said. "You will excuse me if it takes a few minutes to unfold. I think you will sympathize; certainly, one of your characteristic plots does not reveal itself on the first page.

"Let me start by telling you a little about my business. I don't presume to know what *you* know about private detectives, but in the public mind they are associated with the labor agitation of the Pinkertons, on the one hand, and the squalid details of front-page divorces, on the other. I do not pretend that those things don't exist and aren't a part of the trade. But the enterprise, at least as I practice it, is much more than that. Broadly speaking, it concerns the gathering of intelligence.

"Now, as to why I asked you to see me. Two days ago, I received a letter—an anonymous one, it almost goes without saying. The correspondent identified himself as a newspaperman and said he was sitting on a 'scoop.' You won't be surprised to hear that the scoop concerned you."

Porter noticed that his hands were squeezing the arms of his chair rather tightly.

"His exclusive is the following: He has learned that the identity of the mysterious 'O. Henry,' whose short stories have been appearing in the leading periodicals over the last year, is in fact William Sydney Porter. And he has learned that before arriving in this city, William Sydney Porter spent the better part of four years in the Ohio Penitentiary, serving a sentence for embezzlement."

Porter looked away for a moment, digesting what he had just heard. Now, apparently, three people in New York City knew his secret, or at least one part of it: himself, Gardner, and apparently this reporter. He thought about the expression "bated breath." For the first time in his life, he really understood what it meant.

As if aware of the tension and desirous of prolonging it, Gardner prepared a pipe, lit it, and took a puff. "For ease of discussion," he said, "let's call this reporter McManus. Like most men, McManus has a price, and his is in fact lower than the average."

So he didn't know the rest. Porter allowed himself to let out a slight sigh. He looked the detective in the face: "You are talking about blackmail."

"Well, it is McManus who was talking about it. Nothing to be surprised at there: newspapermen are paid so poorly, have so few principles, and come into such variegated nuggets of information that they are notorious for this proclivity. In this case, McManus's proposition would hold back the information for a fee of fifty dollars a week, wired to a Western Union account with no name, only a number. He sought me out and proposed that I act as a conduit, for a fee of ten dollars a week, which I refused."

"Bully for you!" Porter said. "You would still be nothing but a middleman to blackmail, which strikes me as no better than the crime itself."

"Not at all. Please permit me to reach the end of my explanation, which at this point is near. I am not in the business of blackmail. Some years ago, before your arrival in this city, I was accused of that crime, and it took me two full years to clear my name. Some time when you and I meet in more pleasant circumstances, I will tell you all about it. For now, here is what I propose. For a certain amount of time—a brief one, I am confident—you will pay Mr. McManus his fifty dollars a week, through our offices. We will take no commission."

Gardner paused. "You noted the large board in the outer chamber?"

Porter gave a barely perceptible nod.

"Those numbers represent the 'shadows' in my employ. These are men—and women, I should note—whom I deploy, as needed, from this office to all corners of the city. It is well that they not be widely known, and, so as not to be seen by my clients, they have a separate entrance. My shadows are very good at not being noticed and they are very good at accruing information."

"I dispatch my shadows first and find out Mr. McManus's true identity. That shouldn't be excessively difficult. To start, I will call in my 'connections' at Western Union. The company boasts that it offers complete anonymity, but I've found that when pressure is strategically applied, that wall can start to break down. Once we have a name, we will look into his actions and his past. My experience—and his own eagerness to enter into this very scheme—makes me almost certain that we will find something useful, and rather quickly. At the very least, I wouldn't think he would be happy at the prospect of his current employer or any future ones knowing he is a blackmailer.

"At that point, we will broker an agreement with McManus. As long as he doesn't publish his story about you, we will not reveal what we have found about him. My experience tells me he will readily agree.

"If this arrangement is to your liking, we shall proceed. We can come to an agreement regarding a fee when our mouse has been trapped."

Porter had been silent for a long time. He was thinking how foolish his vow to Jennings had been: "No one shall hold the club of ex-convict over me." How had he expected that his past would not catch up with him? And he found himself wondering about this "McManus" character. He had known his share of unsavory newspapermen back in Texas, but none who were blackmailers. A thought occurred to him.

"Can you show me McManus's letter?"

Gardner reached into his desk and produced a piece of paper. The text was typewritten and much as the detective had described it. But something struck Porter's notice. McManus—or whatever his name really was—had written that he was involving Gardner because he knew the detective "specialised" in sensitive matters. Porter put the paper on the desk and jabbed his finger at the word.

"That's British spelling—an American would have written I-Z-E-D. You tell your shadows to look out for an Englishman."

Gardner lightly coughed and stared at the paper. "Yes, I'd noticed that. But full credit to you for the observation. Rest assured—I've already told my men about it."

Porter reached into his coat pocket and pulled out a cheque book. He asked Gardner for the use of his pen, and with it filled out a draft for fifty dollars, payable to William C. Gardner. He wordlessly walked out of the offices, and then down the stairs. By the time he reached the bottom, he had allowed himself a tight smile.

Porter needed a drink, and decided he would seek it uptown at the Metropole Bar. Gilman Hall had taken him out for drinks at the bar's round table, a hangout for journalists, and Porter would occasionally go there and enjoy the shop talk and barbs from the habitués, like Will Irwin, a reporter on *The Sun*, and Jimmy Swinnerton, a cartoonist on Hearst's *Evening Journal.*

By the time he had walked up Broadway to the hotel's entrance between 41st and 42nd Streets, his head had cleared a little bit. The anonymous newspaperman, it was clear, had divined part of his secret but not the entirety. For the time being, he would pay Gardner the money his blackmailer had demanded. It might mean increasing his productivity or his rates, or both. But it could be done.

He had an inkling that it might be worth his while to find out something more about this newspaperman, independent of Gardner. Of the Broadway flotsam and jetsam who frequented the Metropole, reporters and editors and their colleagues were the most numerous, and he felt it was at least possible that he might unearth some useful information from them.

When he entered the room, and his eyes adjusted to the dim light, he saw that the big round table in the middle of the room was already well-occupied. Irwin wasn't there, but Swinnerton was. A decade younger than Porter, he was a native Californian whose comic strip, "Mr. Jack," about an anthropomorphic philandering tiger, was the first thing everyone read when they picked up the *Journal.* Porter made his way over to the table, and Swinnerton made the other introductions, as the men stood.

"Gentlemen," he announced, "you have probably read at least some of the works of O. Henry in all the best magazines. Here he is in the flesh, and the surprise ending is that his name isn't O. at all, but Bill—Bill Porter. Perhaps he will be prevailed upon someday to explain why he made the change. Probably not. He is a reticent sort."

Swinnerton gestured to a man on his right with a broad-brimmed hat, a hawk's beak, and ropy, pendulous mustaches that resembled those of a catfish. "This here is Appetite Bill. Nobody has ever discerned his last name. You would not know it to look at him, but he is a gastric phenomenon, capable of out-eating Diamond Jim Brady. Popcorn is his specialty—he could eat two pounds of it before dinner, as long as somebody else paid for it."

Indicating the man next to Appetite Bill, Swinnerton said, "This is Jim Thornton, the singer, monologist, and composer. If you ever hummed 'My Sweetheart's the Man in the Moon' or 'When You Were Sweet Sixteen,' you hummed one of his tunes.

"Here we have two new members of the cartooning community, both lately arrived from the West Coast to labor for my employer, Mr. Hearst—George Herriman and Tad Dorgan." Herriman was a rather diminutive man who didn't appear to be much older than twenty; under his derby hat, his hair was close-cut, dark and curly. Dorgan was taller and had sandy hair parted in the middle, a prominent nose, and a high collar. He kept his right hand in his pocket and stuck out his left to shake; Porter followed suit.

The other member of the table was a good ten years older than Porter. He was sawed-off and stumpy-legged, with a stub nose, and wore a flat-topped derby similar to the one associated with John D. Rockefeller. The only two things that kept him from resembling a steamfitter's helper on holiday were his eyes. They were like smooth ovals of gray schist. Shaking hands, Porter looked into them for a moment and they glinted back at him like flecks of mica.

Swinnerton said, "Bill Porter, meet Bat Masterson."

Porter was nonplussed. He associated the legendary name with shootouts in the West, not with a table full of Broadway sports, and he would have expected a more dashing figure than the unprepossessing gentleman in front of him.

Masterson had clearly faced this kind of reaction many times before, as he was ready with an abbreviated *curriculum vitae.* "Pleased to make your acquaintance," he said, holding out his hand. After they shook, Masterson motioned for Porter to sit beside him. "I came here from Denver," he went on, "following what's been my main interest in life these past decades—what Pierce Egan called 'the sweet science of bruising.' Boxing has led me to your field, the literary one: I've been chronicling the ring and related topics for *The Morning Telegraph.*"

Porter nodded. "I will make sure to pick up the paper. I take it your days as a lawman are over?"

"They ended twenty years ago, when the citizens of Trinidad, Colorado, voted me out as city marshal. But, say, I have read some of your stories of the West, and they strike me as the real article—unlike most of the tales concocted by Harvard and Princeton men for the monthly magazines. You've spent time on the prairies?"

"I have," Porter said. "I spent. . ." He paused. "I lived a number of years in Texas, and came in contact with a fairly wide swath of humanity. That's served me in good stead in my literary efforts."

The topic being discussed at the table before Porter's arrival was the topic on the front page of all the New York newspapers and on all New Yorkers' lips: the killing of Caesar Young, the gambler, the day before. (The victim's real name was Francis Thomas Young, but he was called "Caesar" because his haircut resembled the Roman emperor's.) What made the story especially juicy was that his paramour, Nan Patterson, wasn't just any showgirl, but a onetime member of the celebrated Florodora Sextet. These were chorus girls for a musical show called *Florodora*, which had opened on Broadway in 1900 and proved an immediate sensation, primarily because of the Florodora Girls. They were all exactly five feet four inches tall and weighed just 130 pounds and, in the most famous scene, sashayed about onstage demurely while male choristers sang, "Tell me, pretty maiden, are there any more at home like you?" Famously, each member of the original sextet married a millionaire, and the many subsequent replacements, like Nan, were known for being pursued by stage-door Johnnies.

The consensus at the Metropole was that Nan would be arrested and stand trial for murder.

"In the cosmology of humanity, the chorus girl occupies a low rung," said Thornton, taking up the theme again. "I never encountered this Patterson, but the sisterhood is devoted to digging for gold. I understand Young's wife had given him an ultimatum—'leave the girl or give up my fortune.' Presumably what he had to tell her in the cab was more than she was prepared to accept."

"Well, I knew Caesar Young and I liked him," Masterson said. "And I know that his friends repeatedly tried to induce him to break off the alliance with the girl, but he stubbornly refused to do so. He practiced all manner of deception of his lawful wife in order to be with the Patterson woman."

All eyes were on Bat, whose authority on such matters would seem to be rock-solid. All, that is, except Tad Dorgan's, which appeared to be directed at his lap.

"It may seem cold-hearted," Masterson went on, "but I can see no good reason for wasting sympathy on Caesar Young. He was a good fellow, and it is too bad he met such an untimely death; but there seems to be no one to blame but himself."

"So what do you think the outcome will be?" Swinnerton asked.

"I predict Nan Patterson will be brought to trial, more or less as a matter of public necessity. And the result of the trial will be an acquittal, as there are no witnesses. Nan is the only person who knows what really happened, and her claim of suicide or accident will be impossible to categorically refute.

"But the case will drag on for months. If I were still a betting man, I'd wager that the D.A.'s next move will be bringing in Nan's brother-in-law, Morgan Smith, for questioning. I understand that he knows a good deal about the case."

That seemed to sum things up; conversation turned to other matters. It occurred to Porter that this might be the moment to have a private word with Masterson, and he shifted his chair so as to face the famed lawman. "As a man of wide experience, in law enforcement and now in journalism, you, I think, might be able to counsel me in a sensitive matter." Masterson turned, attentively, to face him. "Not to beat around the bush," Porter said. "The matter is blackmail."

For an instant, the mica in Masterson's eyes glittered. "And you are the blackmailer's prey?" he asked. Porter nodded.

"Come to my office at the *Telegraph* at Eighth Avenue and Fiftieth Street," Masterson said. "You can find me there at four or so in the afternoon, Monday, Wednesday, and Friday, struggling to find *le mot juste*. Perhaps you can even help me with that. I reckon I can help you."

Unaccountably, Porter felt himself overcome with gratitude. But he just said, "I thank you," and the two men shook hands for the second time. This time they held the grasp two beats longer.

Porter had long since finished his beer. If he was going to boost his productivity, this would be the time to start. He had on his desk three stories in various stages of completion. He'd already gotten advances on all of them, but he might be able to extract the rest of the fee from Hall, at least. He rose and began to make his exit. Before he could complete it, Dorgan stood and handed him a sheet of paper. It was a drawing of him and Masterson, deep in conversation. As a grace note, Tad had placed prairie tumbleweeds on the Metropole floor, and provided a heading.

Porter laughed and pumped Dorgan's left hand. He walked out with the drawing under his own left arm.

Two Sons of the West
"Bat" Masterson
"O. Henry"

CHAPTER VII

Anna Lockhart had come to the wicked city from Hull, Ontario, in the spring of 1903. Her border-crossing wasn't a happy one. Her parents had perished in the great Hull-Ottawa fire of 1900, a catastrophe that severed the already fraying ties between her and her brother, Thomas, two years younger. The terrible event destroyed the family home and gave Thomas a rough push in the direction of dissolution—namely, the race track and the bottle. In her vulnerable state, Anna agreed to an offer of marriage proffered by the owner of the local dry-goods store, whose name was Owen Magnuson and who for years had sent heart-felt glances in her direction from his nearby pew in church. Their wedding followed quickly, and even more quickly after that came her realization that Magnuson was a dullard, a boor, and an alcoholic, and that the union was a dreadful mistake. Unfortunately, Ontario didn't sanction divorces, and Anna didn't have the funds to pursue the only domestic possibility, a petition to Parliament for a statutory settlement. A local solicitor told her that the only other option—short of Magnuson's death—was to go to the United States and obtain a divorce there. She chose New York as her destination because it aligned with her long-held dream of seeking her fortune as an artist.

In the local library, she found the name and address of the secretary of New York's Young Women's Christian Association, and wrote to her requesting information about respectable and cheap boarding-houses. That person responded with a number of names and addresses, among them that of Miss Elmira Jamison, "a lady of very high Christian ideals." And so Anna gathered the $1567 she had inherited from her parents (the sum represented what was left after legal fees), packed a small bag, and snuck out of the house early one morning under cover of darkness. Her day of travel began very early but seemed to stretch endlessly—the ferry to Niagara Falls, the railroad hop to Buffalo, the longer journeys to Albany and then Grand Central Terminal, and finally a hansom cab to the boarding house, hard by the Hudson River in Hell's Kitchen. She didn't arrive till close to midnight, and was greeted by Miss Jamison herself, wrapped in a faded French flannel kimono, her face smeared with cold cream, her hair done up in curling kids. They arranged terms on the landing in front of Miss Jamison's bedroom door, and the housemaid conducted Anna aloft to a tiny chamber under a skylight that fortunately was warmed by a small Jenny Lind stove.

When Anna saw her at breakfast the next morning, the proprietor—a short, plump, blonde lady in the middle forties—had been transformed by a snug corset, an undulated pompadour, and a powdered face. The breakfast, which was meager and less than toothsome, convinced her that sooner rather than later, she would require new lodgings. The little bedroom under the skylight and three meals per day of none too plentiful or attractive food required the deposit of five dollars a week in advance. Wandering around Manhattan later that day, she came upon the Vallambrosa, with a sign in the window advertising an available room. The price was two dollars. She would have to provide her own meals, but she calculated that ingredients could be obtained and prepared for less than three dollars. She secured the room, and six days later, she moved in.

Once ensconced, Anna took heart and two painting lessons a week from Professor Angelini, a retired barber who had studied his profession in a Harlem dancing academy. The professor's specialty was miniatures, the medium Anna had chosen a couple of years before after being inspired by the work, seen in magazines, of Theodora Thayer, Virginia Richmond Reynolds, and other exemplars of the new school. The old school of miniatures had been done in by advent of photography, which could create faster, cheaper, and better likenesses of dear ones than was possible by hand. Its successors didn't strive for photographic perfection but rather to capture the subject's soul.

In New York, Anna leapt to accept the commissions that infrequently came her way, but most of her pictures were of the characters she remembered from her home town: her family, a couple of her schoolteachers, an innkeeper, the haughty banker, and the tramp who survived on charity. She tried to distill one or two of the characteristics of the subject into each picture, and together, she felt, they constituted a portrait of Hull. The work was satisfying; less so was what she found when she made inquiries as to the possibility of obtaining a divorce. The Hull solicitor had neglected to mention that the only permissible grounds in New York were adultery. For all Magnuson's failings, philandering wasn't one of them, at least as far as Anna knew. So she resolved to bide her time and continue to try to build a life in the city.

But as the weeks passed, the economics of her decision came into starker and starker relief. They were not unlike those that Porter, her future fellow tenant, a practitioner of a different art, would confront. The expense side was fixed: rent, food, her materials (ivory, water colors, and brushes), and the lessons. The income side, by contrast, went back and forth like an elastic band. But mostly back, alas.

One day, she wandered down to Mulberry Street and was astounded by the sights and sounds of the street market. She bought some apples from a friendly vendor named Giuseppe with whom she had fallen into a conversation. His friendliness extended to allowing her to display her pictures on a corner of his cart (a small corner—they were miniatures, after all), in return for a commission of ten percent—or one dollar—per sale. However, week after week, Giuseppe's apples and plums proved more popular than her small portraits. Some weeks she would sell two, but then six weeks would go by when she would go home with the same collection she had carefully arranged on the pushcart. Eventually, she dispensed with the lessons from Prof. Angelini, but her balance sheet remained less than robust.

Other than Giuseppe, most of Anna's intercourse was limited to the fellow residents of the Vallambrosa. On warm evenings she would sit on the steps of the high stoop of the building, accompanied by silent rejoicing on the part of the gentlemen roomers. But Miss Longnecker, the tall blonde who taught in a public school and said, "Well, really!" to everything you said, sat on the top step and sniffed. And Miss Dorn, who shot at the moving ducks at Coney every Sunday and worked in a department store, sat on the bottom step and sniffed. Anna sat on the middle step and the men would quickly group around her.

Especially Mr. Skidder, who had preceded Porter as Vallambrosa litterateur, who wanted to write for the theatre, and who had cast her in his mind for the star part in a real-life romantic drama. (Once she let Mr. Skidder read to her the three acts of his great, as yet unpublished, comedy, *It's No Kid; or, The Heir of the Subway.*) And especially Mr. Hoover, who was forty-five, fat, flush, and foolish. And especially very young Mr. O'Reilly, who set up a hollow cough to induce her to ask him to leave off cigarettes.

The success of the ruse sufficiently emboldened Mr. O'Reilly to ask her to accompany him to a dance on an October evening. That gentleman, whose first name was Edward, had been born and raised in an East Side tenement. He was a bright young man who applied himself to his studies, and after graduation from high school secured a position as a clerk at a firm that imported rugs from the Near East. As his income and social standing ascended, his place of residence correspondingly moved north. Yet he retained ties to the old neighborhood, including membership in the Clover Leaf Social Club. Every Saturday night, that club gave a hop in the hall of the Give and Take Athletic Association on the East Side, and Anna agreed to attend, in part because "Clover Leaf" and "Give and Take" sounded exotic enough to have come from a fairy story.

On the appointed night, they met on the stoop in front of the alternately watchful and forlorn eyes of Miss Dorn and Mr. Skidder and took the Sixth Avenue streetcar to Broadway and Grand. They walked east and, once they passed Center Street, were assailed, from a series of doorways, by the glare of lights and the blare of music—a waltz or a two-step pounded on the piano and emphasized by an automatic drum. The competing managers stood outside, each announcing the special features of his dance hall. Anna and O'Reilly might have been on an esplanade at Dreamland instead of a street in Manhattan.

The Give and Take Athletic Association was in Orchard Street and lived up to its name, as the hall of the association was fitted out with dumb-bells of assorted shapes and sizes and intricate muscle-making contraptions. With the fibers thus built up, the members were ready to engage the police and rival social and athletic organizations in joyous combat. But one night a week, such endeavors were put aside for a dance. (It didn't escape outsiders' notice, however, that on dance nights most Give and Takers shed their jackets and wore form-fitting shirts, the better to display their musculature.)

Mr. O'Reilly paid ten cents to check his and Anna's hats and they went inside. About thirty couples were doing the two-step to Sousa's "Washington Post" march, their forms indistinctly seen through clouds of dust which followed them in broken swirls through air so thick that the electric lights were dimmed. Somewhere in the obscurity, a dark, diminutive, and very young man whose name apparently was "Izzy" was doing his noisiest best on the piano. A striking number of the women wore black gowns. When Anna remarked on this, Mr. Reilly said, "That's the mark of the dance-mad girl." He explained that when you spend every evening going from one dance hall to another, a light evening gown would soil rapidly. Replacing or even laundering it would be costly. Hence, black. The other thing Anna noticed was that every single one of the girls seemed to be chewing gum.

Izzy segued into with a waltz whose refrain—discernible from the way the majority of the dancers full-throatedly sang it—and, presumably, title was "After the Honeymoon." Mr. Reilly took Anna's hand and led her to the floor. He was a good dancer, and Anna, to her surprise, remembered the steps and fundamentals she had been taught at the Sunday School dance academy back in Hull. She skimmed over the floor as lightly as a swallow. On the turns, her partner insisted on the "gliding reverse" without a step, and the couple threaded their way in and out of the closely-packed dancers as swiftly and surely as a needle in the hands of an expert seamstress.

For the last chorus, all the dancers stopped and sang along in unison:

> I'll wager my life there are millions of men
> Who wish that their wives were their sweethearts again
> After it's Mister and Missus
> There's often a year between kisses
> A sweet wedding cake only gives you an ache
> After the honeymoon

The waltz wasn't the only step on display. Some of the couples did what Mr. Reilly informed her was known as "spieling." They moved with a steady, rotary motion on one spot; their extended arms marking time more or less accurately with the music. Anna could tell that spieling's advantage, compared to the traditional style of dancing with extended steps, was that it enabled a great many couples to dance at one time on a small floor. She also noticed that the male spielers had a tendency to hunch forward when dancing, thus bringing their face closer to their partner's than if they stood up straight.

At the end of the song, Anna was besieged by a crowd of young Give and Takers who proffered their cards and begged dances for the remainder of the evening. And Mr. Reilly was besieged by friends to "put them next." The next hour was a whirlwind. On the floor, many of the couples bobbed backward and forward in "The Rocking Horse Gallop"; some of the men executed the "backward rock" with such force as to lift their companion several feet off the floor. "Pretty raw," commented Anna's partner, whose name she had not caught. Izzy was playing a rag of doubtful character and practically the entire floor was a picture of flying skirts and lumbering couples, swaying with the peculiar step of a pacing horse.

When the song was over, Izzy stood up abruptly and walked out the door. "I'm surprised Berlin played for that long—must have gotten carried away," her partner said. Anna looked puzzled and he went on: "Usually it's five minutes on, twenty minutes off. The whole point of these hops is to sell the hooch. Why do you think they keep the windows locked shut, when it's so hot? Speaking of which, I've got a powerful thirst. Come on." He took Anna's hand and led her down a staircase in the corner of the hall.

Anna did not like being led about like a cow, and she took a brief glance in search of Mr. Reilly. But he was nowhere to be seen, and, as she realized she was thirsty herself, she followed down the stairs, to a smoky room with a bar and a couple of dozen tables. Before Anna sat down, she picked up a small pile of colorfully printed cards that were on the chair. She glanced at them and found she could barely understand the language in which they were written:

> Don't miss the ball given by Joe the Greaser, and Sam Rosenstock, at Odd Fellows' Hall, October 20th.

> See the Devil Dance at the Reception and Ball given by Max Pascal and Little Whitey, at Tutonia Hall, Tuesday evening, Nov. 3.

> Reception and Ball given by two well known friends, Max Turk and Sam Lande, better known as Mechuch, at Appollo Hall. Floor manager, Young Louis. Ticket admit one 25 cents.

"There's a racket every night," Anna's companion said as he took the cards from her hand and strewed them on the floor. "And they're big money. Dopey Benny walks down Grand Street, hands out these throwaways, and somehow persuades every storekeeper to buy a couple of tickets. A lot of them throw in quite a bit more. Pretty persuasive guy, wouldn't you say?"

He stuck out his hand and grinned so broadly she could see the gold fillings in his teeth. "I don't think we've been properly introduced," he said. "I'm Mike Gaffigan." Anna told him her name and shook his hand.

Mike pulled out a pack of Sweet Caporal cigarettes, and as he lit up, Anna stole a couple of glances at him. He had an angular face, piercing, relentless eyes, and dark hair and dark mustaches. He couldn't have been much older than she was, but his every gesture or movement gave off an air of experience. He wore patent leather boots, pinstriped pants, a vest, a shirt with a wing collar, and a flashy tie with diagonal navy stripes on a field so red it made Anna think of spilled wine. Or blood.

A waiter approached. Mike ordered a beer and Anna hesitated, somewhat at a loss. "Have what I'm having," Mike said. "It'll soothe your thirst." Anna demurred. Her parents had been teetotalers; she had inherited the proclivity, and had never liked the taste of alcohol. "Then maybe a creme de mint," he said. "You know, peppermint juice." That sounded all right, and the waiter left to fill the orders. He returned within moments and set before her a small, stemmed glass with a conical bowl. In the bottom were inviting particles of cracked ice. Surmounting it was a liquid, clear, dark green in tint. From the glass protruded two short straws, suggestive of the soda fountain in the drug store back home. The fresh odor of mint cooled Anna's nostrils. She put the straws to her lips and took a tentative sip. It was refreshing, with a subtle taste she couldn't quite place. She took more sips, and slowly there stole over her a kind of warmth.

Mr. Reilly was just upstairs and Misters Hoover and Skinner just a mile uptown but suddenly the three of them and their dull remarks, sitting on the stoop, seemed very far away. So did the hours she spent working away in her studio, and the endless blocks she'd covered trying to sell her work. This new world, of Giving and Taking and rackets and spieling, wasn't like anything she'd experienced before. It felt a little bit dangerous, but at the same time alluring and slightly thrilling. It had never occurred to her before that those qualities could arrive together.

Mike was asking her a lot of questions, and she found herself answering with a fullness and ease that surprised her in spite of herself. He had never heard of miniatures, but when she found herself confessing her financial straits, his ears pricked up. Indeed, his entire body seemed to stiffen with a kind of animal alertness.

"Say, I'm sorry to hear that, little kiddo," he said. "But it doesn't have to be that way." He reached into his pocket, extracted a ten-dollar bill, and placed it on the table. "Take it, it's yours. If you stick with me, you can make one of those every night. With your looks, you can probably double it."

The sight of the bill was like a slap to the face; the warm glow her drink had delivered immediately dissipated. She looked around the basement room and saw, for the first time, the heavy makeup on the women, the way some of them were sitting on men's knees, their dresses drawn up. Without a word, she stood and climbed the stairs to the main hall. In the middle of the floor, she saw Mr. Reilly waltzing with a red-haired girl. She walked up to him and said, simply, "I would like to go home now."

He offered his apologies to the redhead, and they left the hall. As they walked along Orchard Street, he made a couple of attempts to initiate a conversation. But Anna answered softly and distractedly and he gave up. The evening was cool, and they walked the rest of the way back to the Vallambrosa in silence.

On the afternoon of New Year's Eve, 1903, Anna strolled to Brentano's bookstore at Union Square and 16th Street, where she splurged and purchased for one dollar *The Calendar of Famous Artists*. As the clock ticked to the end of a cold December 31, it was pleasant to look at the cover, a watercolor by Henry McCarter depicting an idyllic fountain surrounded by lush greenery, billowy clouds, and the ruins of what looked like a Greek temple. At the edge of the fountain were two maidens wearing flowing white gowns; in it was a tot wearing nothing.

Business picked up a little in spring after a hard winter, but not enough. In April (a rather eerie depiction by Howard Pyle of a woman carrying a jug through a snowscape, ravens picking at the bottom of her white gown), Mr. Schrum, an art dealer, told her of a rich man in New Jersey who wanted a miniature of his daughter painted. Anna took the ferry to Jersey City, and then a trolley to the man's home in Newark, to show him her work. When she told him the price would be twenty dollars he laughed like a hyena and, when he recovered, said, "An enlarged crayon twenty times the size would cost me only eight!" Anna held her tongue, gathered up her pictures, and retreated to Manhattan.

Rent and food were her only necessary expenses. The rent was immutable, so her outlay for food by necessity was reduced. Bread and butter and black coffee for breakfast, bread and butter for lunch, and potato soup and bread and butter for supper. The beef stew she shared with Hetty and Mr. Porter on the first of May, needless to say, was a rare treat.

CHAPTER VIII

FLUSHED WITH the success of the train-robbing story, Al Jennings picked *The Long Riders* up from the high shelf on which it had been gathering dust. Naturally, he sought his old friend's counsel on the matter of publication. And naturally, Porter gave it, along with a geographical imperative. Come to New York, he implored. As he put it in one letter, "The publishers are all grouped here, in a zone of perhaps forty square blocks. You can call on them successively, like touring the animal cages at the zoo."

The idea appealed to Jennings' fancy. After all, he had no wife or family to keep him in the West. The law had lost its luster. And he was amused by the notion of sharing the streets of Gotham with his OP pal and observing Bill's way through the world. Within a week, he had packed his bag and set off for the big city. Somewhere along the way, he lost the letter that contained Porter's address. But he didn't fret about it; surely his old friend's fame would make that immaterial. He knew that New York was a big place, but he had an idea that Porter would tower over the Manhattoes like Gulliver among the Lilliputians.

His train terminated in Jersey City. The ferry ride across the Hudson River to the 47th Street Pier was a grand one, as the skyscrapers of Manhattan came closer and closer into view. On landing, Jennings commenced to wander up one street and down another, a queer-looking vision with his red whiskers and wide fedora, a Pullman bag in his right hand. Every now and then Jennings made bold and plucked the sleeve of some man, woman or child. "Hey, pard, can you tell me where Bill Porter lives?" They stared at him coldly and moved on. Jennings heard one young fellow titter, "The poor babe from the woods."

Suddenly, the name "Gramercy Park" materialized in his head—it was the neighborhood his friend lived in, he recalled. People seemed to be willing to give him the directions to that location, and in short order he arrived at the northwest corner of the picturesque fenced square. Proceeding counter-clockwise, with a rather painful dignity, he went up the steps of every house and rang the bell, inquiring for Bill Porter. Of those who answered, not a soul had heard of him. Shortly after making his first left turn, he found himself outside a large brownstone building with three stone pillars. He looked up at its second- and third-floor balconies, each with cast-iron balustrades, and then to a brass plaque in front that said, simply, "The Players."

Jennings walked in to a large hall and presented the question to a flunky: "Where is Mr. William Sydney Porter, the writer?"

"Don't know, never heard of him," was the response. "But there's someone here you can ask." He led Jennings down a couple of steps and through glass doors into a room dominated by a pool table, next to which a somewhat familiar-looking white-haired man in a white suit was holding a cue. The clerk indicated a diminutive fellow sitting at a table with two others; he had keen gray eyes and an ample, humorous face. "That's Gilman Hall, the editor of *Ainslee's*. If your man indeed makes his living by the pen, Hall will know him."

Jennings walked over and presented his question. Hall's face lit up like an arc lamp. He jumped up and his hand swooped down on Jennings'. "Do I? I should say so! Do you?"

"Hell, yes, he's an old pal of mine."

"He is, is he? What part of the West does he come from."

Jennings paused. Clearly, his friend had them guessing already. He sensed with some satisfaction that in this metropolitan world, Bill Porter's secret was multifaceted and profound. For a moment he didn't answer. Finally, he said simply, "He's from the South—and he calls his friends 'Colonel.'"

Hall's gaze softened and he clapped Jennings on the back like a long-lost friend. He said, "Head over to the Vallambrosa, on Twenty-fourth Street between Park Avenue and Lexington. You'll find your man."

Jennings duly made his way to that establishment. Finding no landlady or porter, no markings to indicate who lived where, he ascended to the top floor, the fifth, and proceeded to knock on doors. None of the tenants appeared in. On the fourth floor, he awoke a young man who, he angrily informed Jennings, had recently gone to bed after his overnight shift on the subway. But on the third floor, he knocked on the door closest to the stairs and received a cheerful invitation to enter. It was a small room opening on the usual air shaft. It was bare of furniture and destitute of the appurtenances of physical comfort. A bed, a chair, and a trunk—that was all.

As he came in, he saw in the shadows a man sitting at a desk, putting something in a drawer and closing it. The figure stood up. "Colonel!" Bill Porter said. "That red hair is a sight for sore eyes, to be sure."

Porter wore a handsome gray suit, with a rich blue tie, a glove and cane in his right hand.

Jennings looked him up and down. "Say, Bill," he said, "why don't you carry a forty-five instead of that trinket?"

"Well, there are folks in Manhattan who object to the custom, notably the Legislature."

It felt as if it had been two days since the men had been together, not two years. Porter put down his cane and glove and they stood there shaking each other's hand and nodding to each other like a pair of mutes. Finally, Porter gestured to the chair and balanced himself on the edge of the trunk.

Like a pair of farmer boys who had grown up together and ducked in the same creek, they sat back, swapping reminiscences of the place they had both endured.

"It's good you've been there," Porter said. "It's the proper vestibule to this City of Damned Souls. The crooks there are straight compared to the business thieves here. If you've got two dollars on you, invest it now or they'll take it away from you before morning."

He looked at his pocket watch. "Dinner time is nigh. You will be my guest at Moquin's."

The two men walked over to Sixth Avenue and turned uptown; within five minutes and three and a half blocks, they were at their destination, an imposing three-story structure of brick and wood. "This used to be called the Knickerbocker Cottage, and it's been around since the only white men in these parts were the Van Dykes and the Van Loons," Porter said. "It's hard to believe"—he gestured to the elevated train, the tall buildings, and the pedestrian throng—"but in those days, all this was farmland."

They ascended up an awning-covered stairway, walked through a pair of glass doors, and immediately were absorbed in a din of muffled conversation and clinking glassware, regularly punctuated in a sort of clockwork sequence by peals of laughter and shouts of remonstrance. Before them was a large red dining room and to the right a series of smaller private rooms. Porter directed Jennings to an interior stairway to the left. "At Mook's one goes up to go down," he said.

At the bottom of the stairs was an even louder large room, finished in white enamel and gold, with mirrors along the walls. Marble-topped tables were set close together, and leather-cushioned seats lined the walls. A waiter glided up to them and said warmly, "Bon soir, Monsieur Porter. Suivez-moi."

"Thanks, Max," Porter said

After they were seated at what seemed to be the only remaining empty table, a banquette against the wall, Porter said, "A funny thing—every waiter here is Emile, Max, or Pierre. Sometimes a Jacques shows up, but before too long he's Emile, Max, or Pierre."

The men glanced at the menus they'd been handed, and Jennings turned his face down on the table. "Bill, I don't know if you polly view, but I sure don't," he said. "This thing might as well be in Cherokee. They know you here and you must know the grub, so go ahead and order for the both of us."

His companion grunted in agreement. The next time their Max approached the table, Porter ordered what he always did: the Salade Méli-Mélo (lettuce, tomatoes and green peppers with a French dressing), at thirty cents, and Chicken Fricassée with rice a la Henry IV, at sixty cents. Since the occasion was indisputably a special one, he selected a quart of Listrac Médoc, '93, a dollar extra.

"I trust the food is as rich as the prices," Jennings said after the waiter walked away.

"Algernon," Porter said, "I can happily stand you. As I wrote to you, this literary business has been treating me well. There is something about the New York air that seems to have unlocked my fancy. In any case, as long as I can complete stories, I find no end of buyers."

"I am well aware of that, Mr. 'Henry,'" said Jennings. "And while we're on the subject, where did you come up with that handle?"

"You'll appreciate this more than most," Porter said. "You'll remember there was a captain of the night watch at the OP named Orrin Henry. In the prison records, he used to sign his name with this first initial. For some reason, I liked the look of it, and it's served me well.

At that moment Max arrived with the wine. The two friends raised their glasses and drank a toast to freedom.

"Porter!" The shouted name came from a mustachioed man of about forty at a table at the south side of the café. "Come join us!" Porter gave a half-smile and a wave of his hand whose clear meaning was, "Another time."

Turning to Jennings, he said, "A noisy little corner of Bohemia. That's Robert Henri, the painter. George Bellows, another painter. Flanagan and Bartlett, both sculptors. And Fredric Gregg, a writer on *The Sun.* You would find their conversation tedious; they try to outdo each other in their contempt for the bourgeoisie you and I are happy to have become members of. And besides, we have a lot of lies to tell each other."

By the time they drained the second bottle of Médoc, they had reminisced about the Recluse Club and their mutual acquaintances, and filled each other in on all that had happened since their last meeting. At one point, they fell silent, and Jennings felt the time was right to ask the question he'd never posed on the inside but that felt rather pressing at the moment.

"Bill, what did you fall for?"

Porter regarded his friend with a look of quizzical humor, and waited a moment before he answered. "Colonel," he said, "I have been expecting that question, lo, these many years.

"I was a bank teller in Texas. The charge was embezzlement, but it was simpler than that. I borrowed four from the bank on a tip that cotton would go up. It went down, and I got five."

Jennings knew the answer to the next question, but he thought Porter might be expecting him to ask it, so he did: "Bill, do any folks in New York know of your history?"

Porter's eyes flashed with such vehemence that they almost seemed to turn red. "Not a word!" he shouted. He made a visible effort to calm himself. "Not a word," he repeated, more softly. "My past is a locked book and I vow it will remain so." He was tempted, for a minute, to tell Jennings about Charles Gardner and the blackmailer. But he was about to spill the details to Bat Masterson, and he figured that, for now, that was probably enough.

After a pause he went on. "Every time I step into a public café I have the horrible fear that some ex-con will come up and say to me, 'Hello, Bill; when did you get out of the OP?' It has not happened yet, and I honestly don't know what I will do if it ever does.

"The prison label is worse than the brand of Cain. If the world once sees it, you are doomed. It shall not see it on me. I will not become an outcast. I will not and I could not endure the slanting, doubtful scrutiny of ignorant human dogs. No one shall hold the club of ex-convict over me."

"Lots of other men have said the same," Jennings replied. "And there is always someone to hunt them down. You can't get away with it. And think about this. You and I spent many an hour talking about the degrading conditions behind bars. With your gift, you can bring them to the attention of the public. Maybe even get something done about them."

"I will do nothing of the sort," Porter said, again, nearly shouting. He was as riled up as Jennings had ever seen him. "I shall never mention the name of prison. I shall never speak of crime and punishments. It is not my responsibility to cure the diseased soul of society. I will forget that I ever breathed behind those walls."

A quarter-hour earlier, Max had put the bill on the table, nearer to Porter than to Jennings. But now Jennings grabbed the tab, took a quick look at it, and, before Porter had a chance to protest, laid it down with a ten-dollar bill. "Consider this a partial payback for setting me up with that train article."

Porter, who had regained his calm, acceded with a bow of his head, and the two men retraced their steps out of the now nearly empty restaurant. They had barely gotten half a block away when they heard, from behind them, the French-accented cry "Monsieur Porter!" and heard the clomping of swift footsteps. By the time they turned around, Max had nearly reached them. He was holding a ten-dollar note.

"Thees eese counterfeit. Look!" The three men gathered around the note, with its portraits of Meriwether Lewis on the left, William Clark on the right, and an American bison in the middle. "See how blurry," Max said, pointing to a couple of spots in the engraving. "And look, here it says 'Dollar,' not 'Dollars.'" Clearly, Max had experience in these matters.

Porter looked at Jennings. Jennings looked at the bill. "Ah yes, to be sure, you're right, Max. My abject apologies." He took the note, extracted from his pocket a legitimate tenner, and handed it over. The waiter, without a word, turned on his heels and hightailed it back to the restaurant.

"Sorry about that, Bill," Jennings said sheepishly—though not *exceedingly* sheepishly. "That was actually a souvenir from a counterfeiter I made the mistake of defending back in Oklahoma. It's meant to remind me never to go up against the feds. I plum pulled it out by mistake."

Porter didn't say anything, but on the inside he was giving himself a good talking-to. Here he thought he was capable of smelling a grift a mile away. But he didn't pick up the smell of funny money right under his nose.

CHAPTER IX

IN HIS MIND, Porter constructed a picture of his blackmailer. He was dark and thin, almost to a degree suggesting consumption had claimed his flesh. For some reason he was wearing a plaid suit. And, of course, he had a British accent.

He was looking forward to calling on Bat Masterson at *The Morning Telegraph* and getting the lawman on the case, but in the meantime, there was someone else he thought might be useful. The egg cream and Charlotte russe—not to mention the two-dollar retainer—had proved satisfactory compensation for young Bernie Scheuer, and he and Porter had a standing appointment for the first and third Tuesday of each month on the Seward Park bench on which they'd first talked and about which they came to develop proprietary feelings. Porter set the time at 4 p.m., so as not to give the youngster a reason to play hooky. Indeed, Bernie claimed his attendance at P.S. 17 was perfect, that the funds from Porter went straight to his mother's purse, and that he had abjured pick-pocketing for Dopey Benny Fein. Porter had no way of knowing whether he was telling the truth.

Porter arrived first for their next tête-a-tête. Presently he saw Bernie approaching from the east, wearing a cotton undershirt and pants supported by one suspender and a safety pin. More surprising, was the sight, as he got nearer, of a scalp bereft of hair. Porter looked at him quizzically and mimed running his fingers through his hair; the boy said, "My ma shaved it off on account of the lice."

That reminded Porter of something else he thought the boy might help him with. He was working on a story about an East Side pharmacist in love with a factory girl, but realized it wanted local color. So he offered Bernie an extra greenback (immediately accepted) to provide a walking rubberneck tour of some of the neighborhood sights, capped off with a visit to the Scheuer home. They walked west through streets so packed with people and dwellings that, Porter thought, Calcutta could not have been their match. His attention was caught—as how could it not be?—by a veritable brigade of whores sprawling indolently on tenement stoops and chairs, brought outside for the nice weather. They gossiped and chirped in the warm sunshine like parrots. Some knitted shawls and stockings. Others chewed Russian sunflower seeds and spat out the shells. Porter stole a glance at his young friend; Bernie met it.

"Are the . . . ladies always out in such force?"

"Yeah. And before you ask, I know what they sell. I known it since I'm five years old."

In Orchard Street, pale, bearded peddlers shouted to passersby. Their wares seemed of infinite variety: calico, clocks, sweet potatoes, oranges, herrings, potted geraniums, galoshes. A melancholy old man limped by with six derby hats stacked one over the other on his head and a burlap sack on his shoulder. "I cash clothes!" he wailed. On the corner stood a swarthy man with a fierce, pointed moustache. He wore a Turkish fez, white balloon pants, and a red sash; on his back hung a brass kettle with a long spout.

Bernie looked at Porter plaintively. "It's only a penny a glass. Please?" Porter got the Turk's attention and handed him two cents. The vendor thereupon bowed to the pavement as if in prayer; from the spout over his shoulder, lemonade poured first into one glass, then another. The man and the boy both finished theirs in one draft.

The Scheuers lived in Forsyth Street. As Porter and Bernie turned onto the block they encountered another feminine scene, this one more benign than the first. A group of little girls were happily dancing to sounds supplied by an Italian organ grinder. The girls' faces were flushed with joy, as they jogged to and fro, twirling about like tops.

"See the one with the pigtails? That's my sister."

The girl in question was the most energetic of the dancers, and she was so absorbed in her whirling movements that she took no notice of the boy. Art is to be found in unexpected places, Porter thought to himself. The dancers provided the rare gift of happiness, albeit temporary. A cop leaning against a lamppost. A grim old graybeard with a live chicken under his arm. Mothers watching from the tenement windows. All of them, smiling.

After a moment they left the scene and entered the dark hallways of a tenement. They climbed to the third floor, and on each landing they were greeted with the smells of cabbage, of onions, of frying fish, and the sound of whirring sewing machines, each sensory burst all the more pronounced because the door to every apartment was open. Bernie explained that in a contest between privacy and a small measure of air and illumination, the latter usually won out.

Like the others, the Scheuers' door was open, and they stepped into a living room that was stale and dingy, despite the light from the hallway and from a single gas lamp within. Porter could see two smaller rooms leading off from it, gray and spidery dens. There were two sewing machines thrumming in the living room, and more in the other rooms, from the sound of it; indeed, Porter's main sensory impression was the noise of the machines, their treadles clacking against the linoleum floor. Every inch of the flat seemed to be crowded: the machines, the chairs beside them, and a small amount of necessary furniture, including an improvised bed made from a mattress resting on four chairs.

"How many live here?" Porter asked, whispering to Bernie.

"There's me, my brother and my sister, my mother and my father. And the boarder. So, six." While the fact that the boy produced this number without using or even looking at his fingers didn't prove with certainty that he'd been attending school, it was worthy of note.

Toys, newspapers, pieces of cloth, and tailor's trimmings littered the floors. The walls were drab green. On one of them hung a calendar displaying a chromo of Teddy Roosevelt charging up San Juan Hill. There was also a large crayon enlargement in a fly-speckled gold frame. It showed Bernie's mother and father on their wedding day; she standing in her white bridal veil, holding a bouquet, he sitting in solemn bridegroom's black at a table.

Bernie's father sat hunched and cross-legged on a table under the gas jet. He was sewing knickerbockers—"knee-pants," in the local parlance. A dirty rag was tied around his throat, and a towel around his forehead. Mrs. Scheuer sat across from him, working on her own machine. The hair that emerged from her kerchief was gray, her brow wrinkled, and Porter had to make an effort to connect her with the untroubled young woman in the photograph.

After a minute or so, Mr. Scheuer stopped the machine and looked up, apparently having reached a target in his work. "Hallo, mister," he said. Turning his attention to Bernie: "This is the fellow you meet in the park?" The boy nodded. His father stood up and picked the mattress up off the chairs, leaning it against the wall. "Sit, sit."

Porter did so, and at that moment, a shadowy figure emerged from a room in the rear. Moving into the dim light, he was revealed to be a youth of fifteen or so, with milky white skin and abundant curly black hair. This was Bernie's brother, name of Danny, a strikingly handsome lad, who immediately put Porter in mind of an ancient Greek bronze sculpture of a boy he had recently seen at the Metropolitan Museum on Fifth Avenue.

A visitor in the house was apparently an occasion for a respite from work. Mrs. Scheuer busied herself with making tea, the boys joining her in the kitchen, while Porter and Scheuer sat facing each other in the chairs, whose ancient scratchings looked like hieroglyphics.

The father looked the writer up and down. "I have to say, I was suspicious when the boy started bringing home a dollar from you," he said. Porter heard something like a muffled cough from the kitchen. "But then his grades started to get better, so it seemed all right. But I still don't get what you want from him. Are you some kind of welfare worker from the Settlement House?"

Porter made an attempt to explain his trade and the demand it made for "local color"—leaving out the circumstances of his and the boy's meeting. Scheuer's face did not betray any understanding; rather than get deeper into the intricacies of the short-story market, Porter promised to return on Sunday and hand-deliver a copy of *Munsey's*, with one of his stories in it. Scheuer said it would be gibberish to him—Yiddish was the only language he could read—but Bernie would recite.

Mrs. Scheuer brought out three saucers, on each of which was a glass of hot tea, a slice of honey cake, and two sugar cubes. The boys repaired to the rear of the apartment, and Porter watched as the couple each soaked a cube in the hot tea, then placed it between their teeth, and then sipped from the cup. He tried to replicate the process, spilling only a couple of drops on his tie. It was a splendid detail, which he would be sure to work into a story. The thought reminded him to ask his hosts about the particulars of their own work.

Porter suspected that Scheuer's willingness to divulge them had at least partly to do with extending this unplanned break. He said that, working twelve hours a day, he, his wife, and his two older children could turn out fifty dozen knee-pants per week, for which the "sweater" paid them forty cents a dozen.

The output struck Porter as remarkable, the payment remarkably skimpy. "How do you live on that?" he asked.

Mrs. Scheuer laughed, and then spoke for the first time. She recited the expenses as if she knew them by heart, as she surely did. Rent, fifteen dollars a month. Bread, fifteen cents a day; two quarts of milk a day at four cents a quart; one pound of meat for dinner at twelve cents; butter, one pound a week at "eight cents a quarter of a pound." Coffee, potatoes, and pickles completed the list. Porter couldn't do all the calculations in his head, but he didn't need a pencil and paper to know that the margins were razor-thin, and that the dollar every two weeks from Bernie was a help. He didn't blame the kid for pocketing the other simoleon.

The accounting reminded him that it was time to get back to work. The couple quickly finished their tea and cake, and Porter did the same, this time abjuring the sugar cube.

"It was a pleasure to make your acquaintance, mister," said Mr. Scheuer, extending his hand. As Porter shook it, Scheuer called for Bernie to show their visitor to the street. Man and boy walked down to the street. When they got outside, before he turned and walked to the west, Porter told Bernie that now that the school term was about to end, he had some extra work for him. He outlined what he had in mind, and what he was willing to pay. Then he said that if Bernie brought his brother to their next meeting, there would be an extra two dollars in it.

Porter took the streetcar home, had a light dinner at Con's, and decided to clear his mind with work. He had four stories to choose from, each in a different stage of development, and each having sprung from one of the fields that, in his brief tenure as a full-time writer, had proved fertile. Initially, he had specialized in stories from the West—cowboys and ranches and sheriffs and outlaws, still fresh in his mind a half dozen years away from Texas.

But soon he had begun to draw tales from his new home of New York. Gotham situations and characters stealthily and steadily emerged from his imagination and observations, like green shoots growing out of the cracks in the sidewalk.

The last two "fields" were surprising, given how zealously he kept aspects of his life secret. Several of his tales were set in "Anchuria," a Central American banana republic, and based on his experiences with the ragtag collection of lost souls he had encountered in Honduras while he was on the lam.

Even more remarkably, he was beginning to mine his prison

experiences. His first foray was the train-robbing story on which he'd collaborated with Al Jennings. He had not (nor would he ever) actually set a story behind bars, but he'd written several tales about the exploits of second-story men, grifters, and the same paper-hangers who'd apparently schooled Jennings in their trade.

One story was based on Dick Price, the safecracker who'd taught him the cackle-bladder grift. Price had been sent away for a long sentence, but then there was a financial scandal involving a company in Ohio's capital, Columbus. Suspicion fell upon the treasurer of the company, who promptly placed a trove of documents in the company safe, locked it, and fled. (No one seemed to understand why he didn't just burn the papers.) The authorities appealed to the penitentiary for an inmate who could open the safe. The warden offered Dick Price, and meanwhile offered to Price the possibility of a pardon. The prisoner consented to the job, and—by a brutal method in which he filed down his fingernails to the quick, until his fingers were so sensitive, they could feel the every vibration and hitch in the tumbler—opened the safe. When they were both out, Porter and Price had joined forces in Harrisburg for some grifting.

Porter decided to call his character "Jimmy Valentine," as a sort of homage to the moniker Price had used in their cons together. He changed just about every other detail as well, including Price's method. As he told Al Jennings, "Colonel, it chills my teeth to think of that gritting operation. I don't like to make my victims suffer." Another change: At the opening, Jimmy is being released from prison, and Porter skated on thin ice with some of the knowing details, betraying a rather suspiciously intimate familiarity and resentful attitude, if anyone had cared to think about it: "He had on a suit of the villainously fitting, ready-made clothes and a pair of the stiff, squeaky shoes that the state furnishes to its discharged compulsory guests." Jimmy goes back to his safecracking ways—until he travels to a small town, falls in love, and decides to go straight. But then one of his beloved's nieces is trapped in a bank safe. Jimmy steps forward and uses his tools to open it. The twist is that a lawman, Ben Price (Porter chose the surname as another nod to Dick), has tracked him down to the town, prepared to arrest him. But he's also seen the life Jimmy has started to make for himself. In the last scene, Jimmy walks up to Ben, ready to be taken into custody. Ben pretends he doesn't know him and walks away. The calculated gamble Porter made in baring his familiarity paid off. *Cosmopolitan* immediately accepted the story, which he called "A Retrieved Reformation." His editor there, Dreiser, told him the story had drawn more reader mail than anything they'd published in the past five years.

(When he next had dinner with Al Jennings at Moquin's after the story came out, the Oklahoman was flabbergasted at how much he'd revealed.

"Bill, I thought you wanted nothing more than to keep your past a secret," he said.

"That's a fair estimate of the situation," Porter said, tucking into his *poulet*.

"Then why publish a story like that?"

Porter laid down his fork. "Colonel, over the past year and change, I've given a good deal of thought to the economics of the literary game. I've got two things in my favor: the capital of my experiences and a certain skill at spinning yarns. If I'm going to make good, I've got to use both to the fullest

"Now, you mention the details of my past. It turns out that the reading public actually gives an author credit for imagination. I made Dick Price into Jimmy Valentine, and no one said a word, after they had finished praising my inventive imagination. Now let's talk of happier things.")

That success emboldened him to embark on a story he called "A Call Loan," and which he picked up after coming home from the Scheuers'. This one was about a Texas cattleman, Bill Longley, who had opened a bank in a small town. On the very first page, Porter had introduced a dyspeptic national bank examiner—the very type of person who had led to his own catastrophe. The official examines the books, looks at the president through his double magnifying-glasses, and declares:

> "You are carrying one very bad bit of paper—one that is so bad that I have been thinking that you surely do not realize the serious position it places you in. I refer to a call loan of $10,000 made to Thomas Merwin. Not only is the amount in excess of the maximum sum the bank can loan any individual legally, but it is absolutely without endorsement or security. Thus you have doubly violated the national banking laws, and have laid yourself open to criminal prosecution by the Government. A report of the matter to the Comptroller of the Currency—which I am bound to make—would, I am sure, result in the matter being turned over to the Department of Justice for action."

Longley had made the loan in good faith to a friend from his cowpoke days, on the expectation of a big cattle payoff—a payoff that has not as yet come to fruition. The examiner gives him a day to call it in, or otherwise get his hands on the amount of the loan. That was as far as Porter had gotten in the story. Now, sitting at his desk, he picked up his pencil and began to write. Longley does not flee, but—to protect his friend rather than himself—endeavors to take a most drastic action. He is prevented from doing so . . . Well, the thing could be wrapped up in the morning in another two paragraphs, Porter reckoned. He walked over to his bed, took off his shoes and his tea-stained tie, turned out the light, and descended into a dreamless sleep.

CHAPTER X

THE FOLLOWING evening, Porter met Bat Masterson at the *Morning Telegraph.* The newspaper's office was in Fiftieth Street, near Eighth Avenue, in what had been the stable for a street-car railway, put out of use by electrification. On entering, Porter thought he detected a faint lingering odor of horse. He saw Masterson across the room, and the legendary lawman waved him over. Porter's path was not direct, as he had to step over the (long) legs of what appeared to be a couple of chorus girls, waiting for their escorts for the evening to finish their columns.

Masterson was looking over the copy for his own column. Without any ado, he said to Porter, "How's this?"—and proceeded to read:

> There are those who argue that everything breaks even in this old dump of a world of ours. I suppose these ginks who argue that way hold that because the rich man gets ice in the summer and the poor fellow gets it in the winter, things are breaking even for both.

He looked up, clearly expecting a compliment. Porter, complying, said, "Nicely turned. And as a student of slang, I now resolve to use 'gink' in a story."

"I got that one from Tad Dorgan," Masterson said. "Hang around that boy, and your vocabulary will be enriched beyond your dreams."

"I will make one suggestion," Porter added. "You've got 'rich man' and 'poor fellow.' That's needless variation. Make it 'rich man' and 'poor man' and your euphony is improved."

Masterson took a pencil and immediately made the change. He held up his three sheets of foolscap and yelled out, "Copy!" Nobody stirred. Masterson chuckled and motioned to a desk on the other side of the room where a gent in shirtsleeves was dealing out cards. "Until deadline is nigh, the copy readers occupy themselves with poker," he said. The two men walked out of the room, and on the way, Masterson dropped his column on a pair of kings that was apparently the winning hand.

They went downtown a couple of blocks to the Metropole and, in contrast to their previous meeting, took a quiet table in the corner. "You've improved my copy, so the first round is on me," said Masterson. After their order had been taken, he said, "I've been looking into Charles Gardner. Do you know anything of his history?"

"Not a thing. Except, I recall he said something about once being a blackmail victim himself."

Masterson snorted. "I've taken the liberty of looking into Mr. Gardner's past. I think you'll be interested in what I've found."

He took some notes out of his jacket pocket, and a book out of a satchel, and laid them on the table. He opened the book, out of the top of which stuck little torn bits of paper, presumably marking passages of interest, to show the title page:

The DOCTOR and the DEVIL,
OR Midnight Adventures OF
Dr. PARKHURST.

BY CHAS W. GARDNER,
EX-DETECTIVE PARKHURST SOCIETY.

GARDNER & CO.,
NEW YORK.
1894

"A lending library is a wonderful thing," Masterson said. "You're familiar with Dr. Charles Parkhurst?"

Porter shook his head.

"He's a man of the cloth," said Masterson, "who preaches in your neighborhood, Madison Square. I suppose you worship elsewhere." Masterson raised his eyebrow; Porter acknowledged the irony by bowing his head. "For years he crusaded against the vice in his environs, but his harangues fell on Tammany's deaf ears. So one night, about a decade ago, he enlisted the same Gardner to dress him in mufti and take him and another witness on a tour of the worst spots. A bit like Virgil leading Dante through the circles of Hell. Famously, after each stop on the tour, the Reverend had the same refrain: 'Show me something worse!'"

Masterson opened the book to the page with the first bookmark. "Gardner spares no details," he said. "This is where he tells of introducing Parkhurst to 'the worst vice that New York holds' at a place on Third Street called The Golden Rule Pleasure Club." Masterson read in melodramatic tones:

> The basement was fitted up into little rooms, by means of cheap partitions, which ran to the top of the ceiling from the floor. Each room contained a table and a couple of chairs, for the use of customers of the vile den. In each room sat a youth, whose face was painted, eye-brows blackened, and whose airs were those of a young girl. Each person talked in a high falsetto voice, and called the others by women's names.
>
> I explained. The Doctor instantly turned on his heel and fled from the house at top speed. "Why, I wouldn't stay in that house," he gasped, "for all the money in the world."

He went on to describe how, at a bordello a few blocks from the Madison Square church, run by a madam named Hattie Adams, Gardner paid five girls three dollars each to take off their Mother Hubbard dresses and perform a nude "dance of nature."

"This next bit is choice," Masterson said. He read:

> Then the five women, to a lively jig, danced the "can-can." "Hold up your hat!" shouted one of the girls, a tall blonde. I grasped the Doctor's black derby hat, and held it up. The girl measured the distance with her eyes—I held the hat about six feet from the floor—then gave a single high kick, and amid applause sent the hat spinning away.

"After that," Masterson said, "if you'll believe it, the naked girls played a game of leapfrog, jumping over Gardner one by one.

"And then there was the infamous 'French circus' they witnessed in another house, a performance by the nude prostitutes so 'vile' and 'unspeakable' that Gardner says he cannot describe it."

"That is all quite remarkable," Porter said. "But what does it all have to do with the threat Gardner passed on to me?"

"Just this—our detective is not the figure of moral rectitude he makes himself out to be. The first problem is his profession itself. When hired by suspicious husbands or business enterprises, men of his trade are always anxious to produce exactly what is desired, and as a result their reports are often lies, manufactured to suit the occasion. Worse, there are multiple instances of detectives engaged in extortion, blackmail, outright partnership with criminals."

Porter said nothing, but was aware of a queasy sensation in his stomach.

"Secondly, I find it curious that Gardner appears to have been so familiar with the places he took Parkhurst to."

Masterson jabbed his finger at a slightly yellowing cutting from the morgue of the *Morning Telegraph* and continued. "Now, as to Mr. Gardner himself, here is the interesting point. Not long after he and Parkhurst testified about what they saw, one of the women he named, Lillian Clifton, came forward and said Gardner had demanded fifty dollars a month for the protection of her house, which she gave him, and that in the course of her dealings with him she had been on a number of drinking bouts with him in various places in the city. The time came when he demanded a hundred and fifty dollars on threat of imminent prosecution. That prompted Mrs. Clifton to go to the police, who supplied her with three marked fifty-dollar bills. The next day, she paid him the money, and they took a cab to a saloon. When he got out, the police were there waiting for him. He pulled a roll of bills out of his pocket and threw it on the sidewalk. It was the marked money. The police arrested him and found fifteen hundred dollars on his person. Now, how would a humble private detective get hold of that kind of green?"

The question did not require an answer and Porter didn't give one.

"During the trial," Masterson went on, "a parade of witnesses painted Gardner as a charlatan with a history of blackmailing prostitutes and dime museum operators, going back decades. He was found guilty of attempted extortion and sentenced to two years hard labor at Sing Sing."

Porter nearly spat out his beer. "You sure this is the same man I am dealing with?"

"As sure as I'm standing here," Masterson said. "Now, to finish the story, Gardner didn't serve the full sentence. After about a year, the state Supreme Court—dominated by Tammany men—ruled that he should be released because he hadn't used any force or fear in his dealings with Clifton, and therefore it wasn't technically extortion. That is why he is permitted to ply his trade, such as it is."

Masterson drained his glass. "And that," he concluded, "is why I am highly skeptical of the tale he peddled to you."

"Then what's the truth of the matter, Bat?"

"Don't know yet," Masterson said. "But if I'm going to find out, you're going to have to trust me. I know it ain't going to be easy. But you're going to have to tell me the dark secret hanging over your head. Anyone with functioning eyes can see it there, right above you."

Not easy. Masterson wasn't aware of how far those words understated the matter. Porter swallowed some beer, less from thirst than to avoid immediately responding. He thought back and realized that he had never told the whole truth to anyone. And now this figure out of frontier storybooks was asking him to reveal it all. But what, really, did he have to lose? Maybe some of the weight of that secret Masterson had observed pressing down on his head. What was it that the English said? "In for a penny, in for a pound."

"All right, Bat," he said, "here it is. I'm a jail-bird. Served three and a half years in the Ohio Penitentiary."

"That's all? Hell, I'd think in your line of work, that would be a badge of distinction. Mark you as a man of the world who 'knows whereof he speaks,' unlike the palefaces who've been chained to their desks since the age of eighteen and have to dream up their yarns." He looked across the table and Porter felt the steel of the man's gray eyes.

"But moving on," Masterson continued, "what did they get you for?"

Having begun the process of revelation, Porter felt somehow energized, and a full twenty pounds lighter. Propelled by the unaccustomed momentum, he answered the question without hesitation: "Embezzlement."

"Did you do it?"

Porter paused. Lightening his load was one thing, and, indeed, he had told Masterson all that the blackmailer who had contacted Gardner seemed to know. He could end the matter by saying "Yes," and was tempted to do so. No one—not his in-laws and his other Texas friends and supporters, not his fellow inmates in Ohio—no one except four other people, half a continent away, knew the full truth. And he was sure they would never tell. He found, however, that having started on this road, he could not help himself from continuing. "Well, Bat," he said, "that is a long story, and it calls for another round." He lifted his arm to summon a waiter.

When the liquid fortifications arrived, Porter began to speak.

"The simple answer to your question is yes. This all happened a dozen years ago. By day I was a teller in an Austin bank. The rest of my hours were devoted to a humor magazine I was attempting to instigate. Unfortunately, it never made money, and soon I was in debt. On a couple of occasions I took deposits at the bank and used them to pay the magazine's expenses. Of course, I intended to pay it back. I knew that it would be a while before the magazine turned the corner, so I invested half the money in cotton futures. It seemed a sure thing. But cotton prices fell and the money was gone."

He paused, then said, "Here is where it gets complicated. Or more complicated. I will back up a little bit, to when I had just started working at the bank. The president was a fellow named Bob Brackenridge. He was a doctor, a veteran of the War Between the States, a Bible-thumper of the Calvinist persuasion. But his pious appearance was deceiving. Texas banks in those days were famous for their laxity in operation and record-keeping, but the First National took the cake. For years, Brackenridge had been skimming money from the coffers to pay off gambling debts. His position got to a point where he was forced to sell the bank, to a fellow named Frank Hamilton. Brackenridge continued to run the operation, however.

"That was around the time when I went into debt myself and bought *The Instigator*, soon to become *The Rolling Stone*. When I pocketed those deposits, Hamilton, who was a sharp customer, spotted the discrepancy in short order. The total amount was around $900. I explained the situation to him, and he seemed to understand. We set up a repayment schedule. With interest.

"I tried my damnedest to get the paper off the ground. But as time went by, I found it was getting difficult to be funny. The spontaneity seemed to depart from my humor. Quips and droll sayings no longer emanated carelessly from me. I found myself constantly crooking my ear to catch available ideas from my friends. Let a bright saying, a witty comparison, a piquant phrase fall from their lips and I was after it like a hound springing upon a bone. My friends, consequently, started to shun me. Nor was I a delight to be around at home, on the increasingly rare occasions when I was there.

"Then there came a night when I felt that the well was completely dry. I closed up early at the magazine and went to a place called Spicer's Tavern. I wouldn't be missed at home, as my wife, weary of my grouch, had taken our daughter to stay with my in-laws for a few days. I thought perhaps at Spicer's some of the merriment might rub off on me.

"There was a woman there. A beautiful, dark-haired young girl. As fate would have it, I found myself talking to her. I learned she worked for Brackenridge and her name was Maria. Maria Montez. She was there to buy a cordial for Mrs. Brackenridge. Purely medicinal, you understand. I got to talking to her, told her of my connection to her employers, insisted on buying her a drink, then two. I was charmed by her. She was unused to alcohol and when she left to leave, she stumbled a bit. I played the gentleman and offered to walk her home. On the way, we jostled against each other. I took her in my arms and kissed her.

"I ain't proud of what happened next. I took Maria home and had my way with her."

Masterson said nothing.

"I walked her to the Brackenridges' in silence. By the time we arrived, I had concocted a story to explain her absence, and the missing cordial. She had taken a wrong turn, and wound up in an unfamiliar part of Austin, where some bad men had taken her drink and attempted to take her. But she had managed to run from them, then knocked on the door of what turned out to be a friendly residence. She stayed there an hour and managed to find her way home.

"She seemed to understand but she didn't say anything. I could not find words to speak either, so I made a pitiful bow to her and walked back to my house. When I got there, it was past dawn, so I made some coffee, splashed some water on my face, and made my way to the bank."

Masterson spoke after a long pause. "I can understand your regret over the incident. But I can't imagine that this blackmailer, or anyone, would know—"

Porter cut him off. "There's more. Maria."

Masterson opened his mouth but no words came out. He seemed to know where Porter was going. "That's right," the writer said. "She was . . . well, she was expectant. Apparently one day she broke down crying. Mrs. Brackenridge got the story out of her. Maria didn't know my name, but the Brackenridges figured it out. First thing the next morning, Bob Brackenridge storms into the bank to confront me. But Frank Hamilton catches him first. He's had a tip from the other bank in town that an inspector will be in town in a few days. By this time Hamilton—who's sharp, as I said—has figured out what Brackenridge did and is in a state, convinced that the examiner will see it too."

Porter took a long drink of his beer. The Metropole was almost empty. The pre-theater crowd had long since departed; in a few minutes, the post-theater crowd would start streaming in.

"I'm piecing this together from what I learned later," he finally said. "Brackenridge thinks for a minute and says maybe a deal can be made. He tells Hamilton about Maria. They call me in and tell me about her condition. They promise to keep the story quiet, and they will help me pay for her expense in raising the child. In return, they will fix the books so that all the missing funds look like they're my doing. They reasoned that if the inspectors found this sort of activity among the officers, they would shut down the bank. I was the perfect fall guy. I had already taken what wasn't mine, they said. It hardly mattered what the amount was.

"What did I say? What could I say? I agreed.

"For a while, it looked as though I might escape the law. In due time charges against me were presented to a grand jury, but Hamilton and the Brackenridges pulled strings to get an inside man as foreman. And Frank testified that I had intended no wrong but 'had merely made a series of mistakes.' The grand jury failed to indict.

"It seemed I was in the clear. I got a job with the *Houston Post* and gave up *The Rolling Stone.* While I was in Houston, I got word that Maria had given birth to a boy. Soon after that, she married one of her own people, who took the child as his own. Naturally, this fellow wouldn't allow me to have any rights of fatherhood, or even the opportunity to visit. But on a couple of occasions, when I was in Austin, I drove a buggy by their place, and got a glimpse of him playing outside. I had a Kodak camera, and once I even snapped a picture of him kicking a ball across the yard.

"Every month I mailed the Brackenridges twenty-five dollars towards the boy's rearing—they added it to Maria's pay, so her husband would have no way of knowing about the source. When I was in prison, I didn't have access to funds, but since I've gotten out I've doubled the amount I send. The boy's ten now, and I'm going to keep it up till he's eighteen. Nobody knows it, but that's why I'm always short of funds. Needless to say, paying this blackmailer has made me even shorter.

"At that time, back in Texas, finances weren't a problem. The *Post* paid me well, and it looked like the difficulties at the bank were done. The thing I didn't count on was the bank examiner, a terrier of a fellow named Gray. He was flabbergasted that the first grand jury didn't indict, and none of the witnesses he requested were called. He kept the pressure on the case and a few months later, they called a second grand jury. This time I was indicted."

Porter paused. "I am like Lord Jim, because we both made one fateful mistake at the supreme crisis of our lives. My mistake was that instead of returning to Austin to stand trial, like a man, I fled. I took a train to New Orleans and spent a few weeks wandering the French Quarter and writing for the local papers. Then an Austin friend put me in touch with a Frenchman in the import-export business. This fellow said there would be an opportunity for me in Honduras. So I shipped out to Trujillo."

"And what of your family?" asked Masterson.

"I missed them, of course," said Porter, rather hollowly, "but I felt they would be safe and secure with Athol's parents. My plan, such as it was, was that I would send for them once I made the export business a going concern. Then, in seven years, once the statute of limitations had taken effect, we would go back to Texas. As for Brackenridge and Hamilton, they would have no reason to spill the truth."

"But the plan didn't have enough time to hatch. After a few months, I got word that Athol's consumption had gotten worse, and I came back. The reports were true. She died on July 25. The trial was a formality. I asked everyone I knew to stay away, and I didn't speak in my defense. My agreement was still in effect. The penalty for embezzling ten thousand dollars wouldn't be any worse than for one thousand, or anyway, not so much as to risk the disgrace. And with my wife gone, the disgrace would have been a hundred times worse."

Porter found he was exhausted. For a moment, the two men sat silently, drinking their beer. Then Masterson said, "Bill, I thank you for your truthfulness. I agree—this blackmailer, whoever he is, doesn't seem to know the full story. But knowing it myself will help my efforts. And the first thing I'll do, I think, is find a little more about where our Mr. Gardner's interests and inclinations lie. Tailing him for part of the day would no doubt yield some interesting results, but unfortunately I don't have any deputies at my disposal up here in the concrete canyons."

"I might be able to help in that regard," said Porter.

"Do tell."

"Some months back I made the acquaintance of an East Side guttersnipe. He feeds me material for my stories, and I keep him supplied with egg creams. Anyway, he has friends, all of whom have a lot of time on their hands. And they're good at slipping in and out of crowds."

"Well done, Mr. Porter. I will make some more inquiries about Gardner, and if your guttersnipe and his mates can uncover some intelligence, so much the better."

They clinked glasses and downed what remained of their beers.

"Just one more question," Masterson said. "I can understand, now more than ever, that you would have wanted a nom de plume. But why 'O. Henry'?"

"I would never deign to compare myself to Mark Twain," Porter replied, "but we both took names from our former professions. His came from riverboat terminology. When I was a pharmacist, the main work of reference was called *The United States Dispensatory*, in which several mentions are made of a European chemist named Etienne-Ossian Henry. In the text, he is referred to by the initial 'O' and then his last name. I liked the sound of that."

"Fascinating," Masterson said. "And for certain, 'O' works better than 'Etienne-Ossian' would have."

"Indeed. Just one more thing before I take my leave and head for home. Could I borrow that book? If there are any fines from the lending library, I am good for them."

CHAPTER XI

Soon after the arrangement with Gardner began, Porter's financial situation significantly improved, easing (to a point) the sting of paying blackmail money. The reason for this was a chain of events that began when F.L.H. Noble, the managing editor of *The Sunday World*, summoned an assistant, Robert Davis, and, very much in the same manner that Henry M. Stanley was shipped to Africa to locate Dr. Livingston, sent him uptown to find the elusive O. Henry. It was a distinctly difficult task. All anyone seemed to know about the author was the rather indefinite rumor that he lived "somewhere next to a restaurant" in the neighborhood of Gramercy Park.

Noble's idea, and Davis's brief, was to make arrangements for O. Henry to write a weekly short story for *Sunday World*'s feature supplement. "Offer him eighty dollars a week," the editor said. "If he balks jump to ninety. The third and last call is a hundred dollars."

And so Davis, on an unseasonably warm day, in a manner quite similar to Al Jennings's earlier quest, began a survey of every structure in the neighborhood that that adjoined an eatery and seemed open to a transient populace. Relying on the courtesy of landlords, he combed four buildings, without result. The fifth happened to be the Vallambrosa. Like Jennings he found himself knocking on a door on the third floor and being invited to enter. In the dim light, Davis could make out a rather corpulent figure in his shirt sleeves and with his suspenders down, seated beside a washstand upon which reposed a huge bowl containing perhaps five pounds of cracked ice in which nestled a half dozen fine Bartlett pears. The fat man put something in a desk drawer, arose with considerable dignity, and bowed.

"Come in, mister," he said.

Davis entered and closed the door. "I am looking for Sydney Porter," he said, "otherwise, O. Henry."

"I am both," came the reply. "Here's a chair. Have some fruit. It is nice and cool. I suffer like hell from the heat. What can I do for you."

"I have a proposition to make."

Porter fixed his blue eyes upon his visitor, wiped the perspiration from his brow, and cupped his left ear with his hand. There was something about his demeanor that suggested the utter absurdity of bargaining.

"In fact, I have three propositions," Davis said. "I will make the last one first.

He took two bites out of a Bartlett for purposes of concentration and then fired the shot:

"The New York *World* authorizes me to offer you one hundred dollars a week for a weekly short story."

Porter gazed out the air shaft for a few seconds. "If this last proposition is the best," he said, "you needn't make the other two; I accept your offer. Moreover, you can have the balance of the pears."

Davis thanked him and put one of the pears in his pocket. They shook hands on the agreement. Then Davis said, "There's just one more matter to discuss, and I confess it's more a matter of personal than professional curiosity. Your byline. Is 'O. Henry' your real name, and if so, what does the 'O' stand for?"

Porter chuckled. "No, my birth certificate reads 'William Sidney Porter.' Please call me Bill."

"Where did you come up with your nom de plume? It has quite a ring to it."

"Don't know much about plumes, but the moniker comes from

my Texas days. There was a colored ranchman who was quite a tale-spinner. People called him 'Old Henry,' then the 'Old' got shortened to 'O.' When I started sending out my little yarns, I thought I needed something a bit more, well, poetic than plain old William Porter. Then it seemed to bring me luck, so I kept using it."

Porter stopped abruptly, as if he had already said too much. In just the one short meeting, Davis already felt the writer's most notable quality to be reticence—not a reticence of social timidity but a reticence of deliberateness. It proceeded from the fact that civilly, yet masterfully, he was taking in every item of the person with whom he was conversing (in this case Davis), while at the same time revealing as little as possible of himself.

To commemorate the arrangement, Porter got his coat and the two men withdrew to the restaurant next door, where, in spite of the humidity, they had a full course French dinner including a quart of imported wine. The banquet lasted until four p.m.

Porter's deadline for his first piece for *The World* was Wednesday. On Thursday, Davis sent a messenger to Porter's rooms to pick up the copy. The writer told him to go back to *The World* and return with a cash advance; when he did so, Porter sent him back again, with the message that he would deliver the story in person on Friday, which he knew full well was the actual deadline for the Sunday paper. The story was called "The Elusive Tenderloin," and it was a confection about an out-of-towner from out West who comes to New York intent on sampling the famous sins of that district. However, the worst he can find is that "the dissipated bootblacks was sleepin' in their chairs, and the roast peanut whistles sounded gay and devilish among the mad throng that leaned ag'inst the awnin' posts." Porter still needed a kicker, however, and a little before noon he came up with one. He capped his pen, rose from his chair, walked out the door, and journeyed to Park Row.

When he ascended from the subway station, he strolled across a small park toward City Hall to get a better look at his destination, the New York World Building. He turned and regarded it with admiration and a small sense of pride at being selected to participate in such a grand endeavor. The building was no longer the tallest one on the planet (that honor had been seized several years before by a neighbor, the Park Row Building), but it was monumental nonetheless. Its façade was made of red sandstone, brick, and terra-cotta; the arched entryway had accents of red and gray granite. Nestled in the entry was a large box score showing that the Giants led the Brooklyns by 2-1 in the second inning. Above it were statues of four bronze female torchbearers, meant to symbolize the arts. Atop the building was a capacious gilded dome topped by a cupola; if Porter craned his neck and squinted, he could make out a couple of dozen rubberneckers who had ventured there for (literally) a bird's-eye view of the city.

He walked back to the building, entered the grand lobby, and announced himself to a guard who said he would summon Mr. Davis by telephone. While he was waiting, Porter strolled over to a large poster and read:

> In this building you will find Shorthand and Typewriting experts, a Restaurant, Barber Shop, Turkish Bath, Bootblack, Telephone Pay Station, Dentist, Tailor, two Telegraph and Cable Companies, Steamship Ticket Office, with Express, Money Order, Drafts and Baggage Checking; and stores for the sale of Drugs, Soda Water, Cigars, Flowers and Fruit, Candy, Stationery and Magazines, Shoes, and Children's Aeroplanes.

His marveling at this assortment of wonders was interrupted by Davis, in shirtsleeves, accompanied by a boy. The editor pumped Porter's right hand and took the two pages of copy he held in his left. He read them quickly, making some inscrutable marks in black pencil, and handed them to the boy, who hurried off. He turned to Porter, took a breath, and said, "Let me give you the Cook's Tour." He led the way to a circular elevator—

reserved for the use of *World* staffers—and they shot upward in a car crowded with telegraph messengers, each carrying one or more envelopes, some of them bearing in bold black type the words: "News!—Rush!"

They took the car to the last stop, at the top of the dome. From there they ascended by stairs—Porter clutching the railing continuously—all the way up to the cupola, where the writer consented to remain long enough to briefly take in the remarkable view. Regarding the full circumference of the vast city suddenly brought back to his mind his predicament. Among the four million souls beneath him was one who knew and intended to profit by his secret. Porter's reputation as master of the ending was already established, but none of the possible outcomes of his predicament—as his mind flitted back and forth between them—seemed acceptable. The most favorable would be Gardner exposing the rogue and somehow leveraging his silence, but that seemed less likely than an endless détente of payment and silence. Or (he almost shuddered to think of it) the reporter deciding that printing what he knew was worth more to him than the cash. Just being in this building made Porter comprehend that exclusives provided the energy on which it ran, and the scandalous news about "O. Henry" would no doubt be a scoop that would capture the distracted attention of New Yorkers for a day. Or maybe two.

"It's quite peaceful and still up here now." Davis's words interrupted Porter's reverie. "Not so last summer. You were in the city then?" Porter shook his head. "Well, we had a suffocating heat wave. As a publicity stunt, the *Evening World* brought in a self-styled 'rainmaker,' a fellow from Arizona called Bishop. He came up here and set off a couple of dozen 'rain bombs,' he called them. In fact, they were dynamite charges, and all of lower Manhattan came out on the streets to see what was causing the explosions." Davis gestured to the east. "The Brooklyn Bridge was lined with the curious."

"And did it rain?" asked Porter.

"Not a drop."

Davis pointed down to a rather squat contiguous building to the south. "That is the headquarters of one of our competitors. Rumor has it that Mr. Pulitzer chose this particular location so he could quite literally spit on *The Sun.* Charles Dana's retort was to compare the World Building to 'a large brass tackhead.'"

Davis, who was both a little younger and a little heavier than Porter, had something of the quality of an eager and demonstrative dog. What he liked to bestow, instead of wet kisses, was pieces of information. He had found, to his disappointment, that people normally weren't that interested in hearing them. But he discerned that Porter was just as eager to learn as he was to present. And so he didn't restrain himself.

They descended from the cupola and walked down three flights of stairs to the second floor of the dome. Davis led Porter through an open door to a disheveled office. Behind the desk was a bald-headed man in short sleeves; he looked up from a manuscript that had more cross-outs than typed words. "Mr. Noble, may I present O. Henry, who has brought with him his first short story. O. Henry is his name on the page; in life he goes by Bill Porter." Noble grunted, and Porter infinitesimally flinched. "Bill, Mr. Noble, editor of *The Sunday World.*"

Noble returned his attention to the manuscript, made a couple of more marks, summoned a copy boy to take it to the typesetter, and turned to face the two men.

"I am trying," he said, "to give the Sunday supplement features the reader won't find in the *Journal* or *Times.* I've got Dorgan and Herriman's comics, and lots of talented journalists who can provide colorful articles and profiles. But the short story is the emblem of our time. The modern American is too busy to delve into a lengthy novel, yet retains the human thirst for narrative. A short story can provide that in an hour or less. It befits our age of efficiency. And that's why stories fill these magazines." He gestured to the issues on his desk. "I want a good one in our paper every Sunday. And I think you are the man to provide it."

"Now, here is what I require. First, a commitment that you

will provide a story every week, deliverable on Wednesday." He paused, rather pointedly. "That will be a challenge even for someone with your fecundity. And second, that all the stories have a local subject and setting. I imagine that won't be as difficult to fulfill as if we were, say, the *Paducah World*. You'll retain future publication rights, and I can assure you pieces will be illustrated by the best men in the field. And you'll have readers—our circulation has recently passed 500,000. Unless I'm mistaken, this relationship will make your name as the American Maupassant."

"Colonel," Porter said, "I am honored by the faith you've shown in me. And I believe I am up to the task."

To the right of Noble's desk was a closed oak door. Davis gestured to it and said, "I wonder if it would be all right if I briefly showed him Mr. Pulitzer's office." Noble grunted twice, which apparently indicated consent. Davis opened the door to a room filled with light from three windows facing the south and east. Frescoes were on the ceiling and the walls were of embossed leather. After half a minute to take it all in, Davis led his guest out past Noble (who didn't even bother to grunt) and back to the stairs. "Unfortunately," he said, "the magnificent view is lost on our proprietor—he's been completely blind for more than a decade."

They walked down one flight. The lowest floor of the dome was the great news-room. At the various desks or in the aisles were perhaps fifty men, most of them young, none of them beyond middle age. They were in every kind of clothing imaginable, from the most fashionable summer attire to an old pair of cheap and stained duck trousers, collarless shirt open all the way down the front and suspenders hanging about the hips. Some were writing long-hand; others were pounding away at the typewriter; others were talking in undertones to typists taking dictation to the machine; others were reading copy and altering it with huge blue pencils which made cryptic smears wherever they touched the paper. In and out scurried a dozen office-boys, responding to calls from various desks, bringing bundles of proofs, thrusting copy into boxes which instantly and noisily shot up through the ceiling.

"It's always bedlam in here," Davis said, "but today is especially mad because of the rush to get leads on the Caesar Young murder." The case was still on every New Yorker's lips and therefore on the front page of every New York paper.

Porter said he was familiar with the case. "I understand Young's wife had given him an ultimatum—'leave the girl or give up my fortune.' I guess what he had to tell her in the cab was more than she was prepared to accept."

"From what I hear, the D.A.'s next move will be bringing in Nan's brother-in-law, Morgan Smith, for questioning. The talk is that he knows a good deal about the affair."

Davis glanced at him with what seemed to be a new measure of respect. "You seem to be up-to-the-minute on this case. If you ever give up the short-story game, there might be a place for you in the newsroom."

"My newspaper days are over. But speaking of that, tell me something. Do you know of any British reporters working on New York papers?"

"Why do you ask?"

"It's nothing important. Just a detail I might want for a story I'm working on."

Davis thought for a minute. "One name that comes to mind is Frederic Villiers, the correspondent and artist. Do you know the name? He's lately been covering the Russian-Japanese war for the *Daily Graphic*, and on his way back to London he's been based in the *Graphic* bureau in New Jersey for some months. He's done a few sketches for us—capital fellow."

"The only other person." Davis went on, "is a bit of a curiosity. A lady reporter by the name of Midy Morgan. She's a striking presence—over six feet tall, I'd hazard, always decked out in tweeds and a bonnet. You might call her the animal correspondent of the *Times*—always present at the dog shows, the horse shows and races, the cattle yards."

Neither one seemed a likely candidate for blackmail. The animal correspondent, well, for obvious reasons. And Villier's eminence, Porter thought, would probably preclude his involvement. But he'd check both out nonetheless.

Davis led the way to an adjoining large room. As he opened its heavy door, a sound, almost a roar, of clicking instruments and typewriters burst out. Here again were scores of desks with men seated at them, every man with a typewriter and a telegraph instrument before him. "These are our direct wires," Davis explained. "Our correspondents in all the big cities, east, west, north, and south, and in London, are at the other end of these wires.

From the newsroom they went up a flight to the composing room—a vast hall of confusion, filled with strange-looking machines and half-dressed men and boys. "It's getting late," said Davis. "The final rush for the first edition is on." Up through the floor of the room burst boxes filled with "copy." Boys snatched the scrawled, ragged-looking sheets and tossed them upon a desk. A man seated there cut them into little strips, hanging each strip upon a hook. A line of men filed rapidly past these hooks, each man snatching a single strip and darting away to one of the machines at which scores of men and a few women were seated. These devices responded to touches upon their keyboards by going through uncanny internal agitations. Then out from a mysterious somewhere would come a small thin strip of almost hot metal, the width of a newspaper column and marked along one edge with letters printed backwards. The strips would be assembled into blocks of type, which the copy boys hurried away with.

Following their trail, Porter and Davis came to another part of the great room with many tables, on each a metal frame about the size of a page of the newspaper. Men placed galleys of type into them under the direction of the city editor—his name was Charles Chapin, Davis said, and he was universally feared—and his staff. As soon as a frame was filled, two men began to even the ends of the columns and then to screw up an inside framework which held the type firmly in place. Then a man laid a great sheet of what looked like blotting-paper upon the page of type and pounded it down with a mallet and scraped it with a stiff brush. When he was done, he dropped it into what seemed like an elevator shaft. "It's now in the sub-basement," said Davis, "two hundred and fifty feet below us. They are already bending it into a casting-box in the shape of the cylinders on the presses; metal will be poured in and when it is cool, you will have the metal impression of the page. It will be fastened upon the press and printed from."

They rode the main elevator down to the ground floor and then went down a dark and winding staircase until they faced an iron door. Davis pushed it open and they entered a sort of gallery where they could view the press-room. Its temperature was blood-heat, its air heavy with the odors of ink, moist paper, and oil, its lights dim. Below them on all sides were the huge presses, silent, motionless, waiting. "Within an hour, those presses will swing into action," Davis said. "They eat six hundred thousand pounds of paper and four tons of ink a week. They can throw out two hundred thousand complete papers an hour—papers that are cut, folded, pasted, and ready to send away."

They ascended to the lobby, where the two men agreed to meet for dinner in the future, shook hands, and parted. At the park outside, Porter found a bench and took out *Pudd'nhead Wilson*, a Mark Twain novel he'd recently found in a Fourth Avenue bookshop. He read four chapters, then looked up when he heard a commotion. It was a group of newsies picking up their copies of *The Evening World*, hot off the presses. Porter walked over and plunked down a penny for a paper. His eye was drawn to the lead article:

FREEDOM DENIED NAN PATTERSON AFTER HEARING

Justice Clarke Reserves Decision on Habeas Corpus Writ, Refusing to Grant Her Freedom on Bond, for Which Lawyers Fought at Two Sessions of Court

He scanned the first paragraph, which added a few details to the headline, then read the second:

> Central Office men Cary and Flay took J. Morgan Smith, brother-in-law of the young woman who was in the cab when Young was shot, to the District-Attorney's Office on a "forthwith subpoena. Smith was at once taken into the office of Assistant District-Attorney Garvan and questioned in the presence of Police Captain Sweeney, of the Leonard street station, concerning "Nan" Patterson, the ownership of the revolver which figures in the case, and Smith's own whereabouts at the hour of the shooting.
>
> Smith, it is reported, refused to answer any of these questions.
>
> Smith's refusal to reply is said to have been on the ground that it might tend to incriminate or degrade him or to connect him with the case. As Mr. Garvan had no further recourse he had to let Smith go, having learned no more from him than before.

The Giants had won 7-2, behind the pitching of Christy Mathewson.

CHAPTER XII

On the first day of May, Anna flipped over a pencil sketch by Joseph DeCamp, of a woman whose steady gaze she had frankly found a little disconcerting, and was pleased to see that the McCarter water color would be her companion for the next thirty-one days. (There are two kinds of people in the world—those who look at every page of a calendar as soon as they can, and those who patiently wait for each month to arrive before turning the page. Anna was in the latter group.) Perhaps inspired by the sylvan scene on her bureau—or, more precisely, by the distance between it and her own circumstances—she had that morning come to a decision. She had put her brushes, color-box, ivories, easel, and miniatures (these wrapped in their own snug case) into a sack, and put that under her narrow bed, next to the wall, and resolved that the very next day she would look for a job. That night, she dined on potato, onion, and beef with her fellow tenants. The story she told to the stout man who spoke so oddly—Mr. Porter—about the series of paintings she needed to finish was an invention, concocted so that she could devote all her resources to the task at hand.

In the morning, she bought a newspaper and, over her coffee, bread, and butter, perused the want ads, which filled many columns. Work was plentiful enough; it nearly always is. The question was not how to get a job, but how to live by such jobs as one could get. The low wages offered to green hands—two and a half to three dollars a week—might do for the girl who lived at home;

but Anna had to pay rent and car-fare and buy food. Five dollars a week, she reckoned, was the minimum salary she would settle for.

The advertisements for cigar and cigarette workers were very numerous. As it sounded like humble work, she thought she might stand a better chance in that line than any other, and circled three positions. The first was at a factory in Avenue A, which wanted "bunch-makers." The foreman, a young German, heard her petition in a drafty hallway through which a small army of boys and girls were pouring, each one stopping to insert a key in a time-register. The foreman cut her off unceremoniously by asking to see her "working-card"; and when she looked at him blankly, not having a ghost of an idea what he meant, he strode away in disgust.

Undaunted—for she meant to be very energetic and brave that morning—she went to the next factory. Here they wanted "labelers," and as this sounded easy, she approached the foreman with something like confidence. He asked what experience she had, and was given a truthful answer. "Sorry, but we're not running any kindergarten here," he replied curtly and turned away.

The third foreman was an elderly German with a paternal manner. He listened to Anna kindly, said she looked "quick," and offered to put her on as an apprentice, explaining in a pompous manner that cigar-making was a very difficult trade, at which she must serve a three years' training period with no pay before she could become a member of the union and entitled to draw union wages. She left, finally disillusioned of her cigar-making ambitions.

"Girls wanted to learn binding and folding—paid while learning." The address given under those words took Anna to the Brooklyn Bridge and down a strange, dark thoroughfare running toward the East River. Above was the great bridge, unreal, fairylike in the morning mist. She was looking for Rose Street, which turned out to be a zigzag alley that wriggled through one of the bridge arches into a world of book-binderies. Rose Street was choked with moving carts loaded with yellow-back literature done up in bales. The superintendent proved to be a civil young man.

He did not need her before Wednesday, when he said she should come back at half-past seven and bring a bone paper-cutter with her. He paid only four dollars a week, but she accepted, with the hope that over the following two days she might find something better.

It was half-past three, and she had one more name on her list. "Rose-making" sounded appealing, and she walked up to Bond Street, a wide thoroughfare that had become the forcing-ground or nursery of artificial flowers. Its signs on both sides, even unto the top floor, proclaimed some specialization of fashionable millinery-flowers, feathers, or wire hat frames. On the third floor, rear, of a once grand mansion now fallen into decay, she stumbled into a room, radiantly scarlet with roses. The jangling bell attached to the door aroused no curiosity whatever in the white-faced girls bending over their work, but was signal for a thick-set, beetle-browed young fellow to bounce in from the next room and curtly demand her business. "We only pay a dollar and a half to learners," he said, smiling unpleasantly over large yellow teeth. She fled in dismay and spent a precious five cents to take the Broadway elevated train back to the Vallambrosa.

So the binding and folding job was her best prospect. It would pay a dollar less than the figure she had set. But, she told herself as she heated up her supper of potato soup, she could economize by walking to the factory. And cutting out molasses. As she ate, she opened up the *Evening World* she'd bought on the way home, with the thought of taking one more look at the ads. What she saw was that Siegel-Cooper was hiring and expected applicants to present themselves at the Big Store at eight a.m. the next day.

After her long day of job-hunting, it might have been expected that she would be unwilling to endure one interview more. But Anna had nothing if not resolve, and it wasn't drained yet. Assuming that in two days she could find out what a bone paper-cutter was, and acquire one, she was still assured of a job. She decided to make one more try.

The following morning she walked to the department store at

6th Avenue and 18th Street. She admired the elegant sundresses and summer coats on display behind large plate-glass windows, and walked through the middle one of three towering portals. Inside, a standing sign directed hopeful shopgirls to enter and proceed to the third floor.

She found the moving stairs and took them up one flight, pausing on the second floor long enough to admire the music department. The extensive display of the songs of the moment, each with a fanciful and colorful cover, made her wish, for a moment, she had kept up her piano lessons in Hull. Then she remembered she had no piano to play and swiftly rode the stairs up one more floor.

What confronted her when she alighted reminded her of the distorting mirrors at Coney Island: she saw dozens of versions of herself, all in white waists and black skirts, but some slim and some full-figured, some short and some tall, some fair-haired and some dark. She joined the mass of girls, arrayed in three lines, and presently realized that they were being assessed, indeed, inspected, by three men in dark suits. One of them approached her. He moved slowly, and his appearance was slow, phlegmatic, gentlemanly. He motioned to her and said, "You, stand to the side." He didn't ask about her experience, merely looked at her; up, down, and around. Apparently he was satisfied with what he saw, for he said, "You start tomorrow at nine a.m. in the toy department. Your pay is five dollars a week. Go to payroll on the first floor and they'll put you on the books." There she provided the details of her life, and in turn was given a number: "424," by which she was known during her time at the Big Store.

The next day was a blur. She got up at half-past five to make herself a cup of coffee on the oil stove. Then she ate a bit of bread and rushed out into the street thronged with a lunch-carrying humanity hastening to the downtown district, passed by cars packed with pale-faced, sleepy-eyed men and women. At the toy department, Anna found nine other girls who were to be her companions in toil. The place was a dazzling array of all kinds of toys, from a monkey beating a drum to a doll that said "mamma" and a brightly painted hobby-horse. The business of the ten of them, Anna found, was first to dust and condense the stock, and then to stand ready for customers. They served in the double capacity of floorwalkers and clerks, and their business was to see that no one escaped without making a purchase. As soon as the elevators emptied themselves on the floor, there was one mad rush of clerks with a quickly spoken, "What would you like, madam?" Customers reacted alternately with rudeness, amusement, and alarm. One young boy, on being assailed by half a dozen at once, threw up his hands in horror, and said: "For God's sake, let me get out of here!" and fled down the stairs, not even waiting for the elevator.

The phlegmatic supervisor hadn't told her, or if he had, she hadn't quite comprehended it, that she was expected to stand up all throughout her shift. After three hours behind the counter, she spotted an inviting stool next to the stockroom and took a delicious rest. Almost immediately the supervisor—not so phlegmatic now—spied her and said, loud enough for all the girls to hear, "Get up out of that, you lazy hussy. I don't pay you to sit around all day!"

Anna's first customer was an angular woman with a businesslike expression who in peremptory tones demanded that she be shown building blocks. They were dutifully produced and presented, but proved unsatisfactory. Then dolls' buggies, boys' sleds, laundry sets, and skates were examined in slow succession, and were catechized in a thoroughly pedagogical manner regarding the prices and merits of the same. When the last skate had been critically examined, the angular woman fixed a patronizing gaze upon Anna and said: "I do not intend to buy today; I merely wished to examine your goods."

"Was she a revenue officer?" was the first thought that came to Anna's mind. "Oh, no!" said the next clerk over, a friendly blonde girl named Maisie. "She's just a rubber-neck."

Thus reassured, she started out on a second exercise in the art of sales. This time it was a small boy who wanted to buy, and the bright-faced little fellow did her good. He had eighty cents, he said, and he wanted presents for the baby, and Tom, and Freda, and cousin Jack, and several others. Anna suggested one thing after another, till finally he had spent his money; so she made out her first check and looked at it with pride. It read thus:

SOLD BY				AM'T REC'D
424				.80
1	"Dewey" bank			05
2	Sets dishes	15		30
1	Laundry set			15
1	Mother Goose ladder . . .			12
1	Rubber ball			10
2	Bb'ls clothespins	04		08
				80
CASH NO.				AMOUNT
127				.80
				.80

Her first day ended at half-past six. She went wearily to the cloak-room and more wearily to the Vallambrosa. When she arrived there, she could only throw herself upon her narrow bed. Soon she was dreaming that blows from an iron mallet were falling fast upon her. In a little while it was morning, and another day was begun.

On her way out the door one morning a week later, she ran into Bill Porter, coming back from his constitutional. She greeted him, but he merely looked at her white waist and black skirt, then at his pocket watch, and then back at her. Anna felt her annoyance rising. She saw his silence as a sign of discomfort at catching her in a lie about her work. But she hadn't lied at all.

"Yes, you are permitted to wish me good morning without offending me, Mr. Porter," she said in a rush of words. The color in his face grew almost imperceptibly redder.

"Believe me, my dear girl, any offending implication could not be farther from my mind. Please accept my apology if I gave that impression. I merely was not expecting to see you."

"Well, see me you have. And I am about to disappear from sight because I have to be at the Siegel-Cooper toy department in fifteen minutes. You indicated when we dined that you hoped to write about New York shopgirls. I am now one of them. And if you will excuse me. . ."

She started down the stairs. "Please"—the one word stopped and swiveled her. "I hope you haven't forgotten your promise to show me your miniatures."

"Oh, those," Anna said. She had indeed forgotten. "I'm afraid they're hidden away," she said, after a pause. "Perhaps some time away from the world will impart them a value they haven't been able to achieve in it."

"I'm very sorry to hear that. When the time is right, I should be very happy to see them. But in the meantime," Porter smiled, "I have not yet written the shopgirl story, but I have studied the subject enough to know they aren't required to work on Sundays."

It was Anna's turn to smile.

"The weather looks to be fine for the next few days. Would you be willing to accompany me to North Beach on the Lord's Day? I am confident the Lord won't mind."

Anna was surprised to be struck by the feeling that this particular moment, standing on the stairs of the Vallambrosa, was a critical one in her life. She had no idea why. She looked up at Porter. In part because she had no plans for Sunday, in part because she had always wanted to see North Beach but never had the money to go there, in part because she was in a hurry, and in part because sharing beef, potato, and onion with someone seemed to create a sort of ineffable bond, she said, simply, "Yes."

PART II

CHAPTER XIII

THE TWO had arranged to meet at the foot of the steps at one o'clock Sunday. (While Porter was no churchgoer, he suspected Anna might be, but it seemed a bit too sensitive a question to broach—hence the proposed time.) It was a warm day, and they wore light clothing—she a summer dress, he shirtsleeves and a boater hat. They walked east. At Third Avenue, Porter glanced at the elevated train tracks and said, "Don't you think traveling close to the ground is more civilized?" He didn't seem to require an answer, and they continued two more blocks to First Avenue, where a horse-drawn trolley had just come to a stop, as if it had been summoned for them. Porter paid their fares and led them to seats on the east side of the car. As the streetcar moved north and more spaces began to appear between buildings, they caught glimpses of the East River, and eventually Blackwell's Island, notorious home to prisoners and incurables.

They alighted at 99th Street and walked a block to the pier, where a ferry was just pulling away. While Porter and Anna waited for the next one, they had a chance to observe their fellow summer merry-makers, who were arriving swiftly and excitedly. Notably, English was at best the third most commonly spoken language, Italian and German carrying the day. Family groups predominated, each one carrying enough food in baskets and cloth bags to survive on for a month. When the next boat pulled in, Porter paid their ten-cent fares and they walked aboard. It was an old-time ferry, with an upper deck running half the width and the entire length of the boat, and even though they would be traveling for a mere half-hour and would not leave New York City limits, the whole enterprise had the feel of a much more ambitious excursion.

The other passengers kept Porter and Anna entertained as the boat traveled up the East River, then eastward through Hell Gate. Most of the women were without hats, and wore large, plain gold earrings. The men, as soon as they found seats for the wives or companions, flocked to the lower deck and smoked cigarettes. To draw out the avian metaphor: they also had the more resplendent plumage. There were not only velvet coats in brown and black, but velvet trousers, with stripes, as carefully creased as if they were country club dandies. The fellows wore scarfpins stuck in the center of bow ties, and outing shirts, with a dizzying variety of color. "This is the most picturesque sight I've seen in New York," Anna said. "I only wish I had my paints and brushes."

Suddenly music was in the air, and the Vallambrosa pair turned to see a band consisting of a harp, two violins, and a piccolo. If they'd been riding a boat to Coney, the passengers would be singing "In the Good Old Summertime" or "What's the Matter with the Moon To-night?" or some other popular song of the moment. But this band immediately plunged into "La Donna è Mobile," to great fanfare from the spectators. A mustachioed man stepped out from the crowd and took the vocal part, with gusto. His performance grew still more rousing as he went on, and at the end he was hailed with "bravos" and offers of cigars and drinks.

After the song, the deck was cleared and the children had their chance. They competed in their own version of spieling—high-kicking and cake-walking dances, just as they would do to the accompaniment of street organs in front of their tenements. Porter glanced at Anna and noticed her mouth was open in what looked like wonder. The day was starting out splendidly.

On arrival, they poured off the boat with the rest of the passengers, to a long and wide boardwalk. They walked westward with the crowd, the water and some bathhouses on their right, a rollercoaster and then a carousel on their left. The carousel's crown was decorated with portraits of every president but the current one. "By next summer, Teddy will be up there, too," Porter said. Children squealed as they revolved on the camels, horses, and large dogs, to the sound of calliope and drums.

The view over the water was lovely; the odor was . . . not. Anna resisted saying anything, but she couldn't help wrinkling her nose. Porter noticed and gestured to a body of land not far off shore. "That's Riker's Island, where the city dumps its refuse," he said. "Unfortunately, the tide as well as the wind brings traces of it. And that is why, if we decide to go bathing today, I will recommend the swimming pool, on the other end of the promenade. It's the biggest one in New York, and a constant flow of salt water is pumped into it. I've come here early in the morning when the heat threatens to be oppressive and found scores of uptown residents going for their swims. Let's make that our destination, shall we?"

Anna said, "You seem to know a lot about this place. Do you come here regularly?"

"I don't have an occupation in the usual sense, and I don't have a boss. Therefore, I can come and go as I please. Being separated from my pen means being separated from income, of course, but I've found that coming to North Beach on a weekday, when there aren't crowds like we see today, does me good. It isn't the wide-open plains, but still it clears away the congestion of Manhattan."

Porter's reflections were interrupted by the buzzing and bustling of a dozen or so clumps of people, each apparently intent on observing something in the center. "Try your luck," they heard from the middle of one cluster, and then the same words from another. "You've heard of 'bunko'?" Porter asked. "This is its purest form. Let's move on—I'll give you a guided tour of the fakirs later."

Soon they arrived at North Beach's most famous attraction—the Shoot the Chutes. Small boats were mechanically pulled up a steep ramp the length of football field, then sent down a watery parallel ramp, reaching a speed almost that of the fastest locomotive. At the bottom they were shot through the air for an impressive three or four seconds, before landing with a splash in a man-made lake. Anna had never seen anything like it and was inspired to work up her courage to give it a go. But customer trade was suspended for the moment, for a performance by (a sign announced) "Young Ajax and Dare-Devil Hurley."

It was quite a show. First, Ajax, dangling from a rope, glided from the top of the chute tower to the lower end of the lake, dropping off into the water below. Then "the Dare-Devil," who didn't appear to be older than sixteen, rode down the chutes on a bicycle. On reaching the bottom of the slide, he separated from his bike in mid-air and made a flying dive of twenty-five feet, before splashing into the water. For their finale, Hurley mounted a bike with concave tires that fit over the slack wire cable and carried Young Ajax, who was suspended by his teeth from a pendant attached to the bicycle. From the top of the tower they rushed a mile a minute down the wire incline. At a given signal Ajax dropped into the lake. Hurley, on being released from the weight of the human pendulum, shot forth like ball from cannon, only to topple over into the water below.

Having seen their exploits, Anna lost any fears about doing a "regular" run, and she and Porter immediately climbed the stairs to the top of the tower. From there they had a splendid view of not only all of North Beach but four of the five boroughs of New York City, incorporated now for just four years. (Staten Island was just too distant to be perceived.) Porter pointed out the green rectangle of Central Park, the Flatiron Building, and the twin flagpoles on top of the Park Row Building in Lower Manhattan, the tallest structure in the world.

When it was their turn, they climbed into a boat with three others. Speeding down the chute and splashing into the water was so much fun that Anna insisted on doing it a second time. By that time, the two Manhattanites were both sufficiently sprinkled with water that they agreed they'd forgo the swimming pool and find some refreshments. The Fort Andersen Pavilion was in view and they walked inside, where the dim light and comparative coolness was refreshing. When her eyes adjusted to the light, Anna noticed that on every table, whether empty or occupied, was a square slice of white bread. After they'd been led to a table in the middle of the hall, Porter said, "I pray you. Do not eat that bread."

Anna looked mystified. "It's the Raines Law," Porter went on. "When President Roosevelt was police commissioner of New York, a decade or so ago, he pushed a bill through the legislature prohibiting Sunday drinking—with a few exceptions. One of them is that an establishment is permitted to serve alcohol if it also serves 'meals.' And so they set out food that's not meant to eat, merely to satisfy the letter of the law. This slice of bread is actually one of the more toothsome examples. Some saloons serve the notorious 'Raines Law sandwich'—two slices of bread surrounding a brick."

A waiter came and took their orders: a beer for Porter, a crème de menthe for Anna. She asked him to take away the bread but he declined with a smile. "You don't look like inspectors but you never know," he said. "House rules is the bread stays."

The drinks—after they finished one round, they ordered a second—propelled them, or Anna, at least, to a further level of frankness. She confessed the failure, as she saw it, of her career as a miniature artist, the indignities of the day she had spent looking for work, and her nervousness about working at Siegel-Cooper. As for her companion . . . from the moment she had met him over stew in the Vallambrosa, Anna had sensed that Porter was close-lipped about personal matters, and so she wasn't surprised that his "confession" amounted to revealing he was sometimes "lonesome" in the city. That led her to ask where he had been born and brought up. He merely smiled and said, "Points south and west"—then immediately changed the subject. His literary success—completely unexpected, he said—had been sufficient to warrant a move, the following week, from the Vallambrosa to more commodious lodgings in an Irving Place flat.

Something about the day, and the surroundings, prompted Anna to push. "Mr. Porter," she started but he promptly interrupted: "Please, call me Bill."

"Then Bill. I notice that any time I ask you about yourself, or you start to reveal something, you change the subject. Just what are you hiding?"

Her tone was light but Porter seemed to take it quite seriously. He was silent for a minute, the soft evening breeze brushing against his skin. The setting, the circumstances, the company, cracked open something in him that had been closed off for a long time.

"You've pegged me pretty good," he said. "A long time ago, I learned that saying too much can get you in trouble. I guess I learned that lesson too well.

"But look." He turned to face her, and words seemed to fail him again. "Here's the thing," he finally said. "I've been by myself since, well, since I can remember. And it's no good. Honest, I would like to try to make room for someone in my life. But I don't know. . ."

Anna didn't know either. She was silent for a minute. When she was a little girl, her best friend next door, Penny, had found a stray kitten with an injured leg and nursed it back to health. Anna had observed the process with interest but no particular desire to join in or replicate it on her own. Now, the man across from her seemed to be asking to be taken on as a comparable sort of rehabilitation project. She surprised herself by not dismissing the idea out of hand. Clearly, for all his failings and all his missing pieces, he was no Owen Magnuson. She chuckled internally at the low standards she had apparently established for herself. She finished her drink and suggested strolling about in the cool evening air.

They made their way to the booths along Old Bowery Bay Road, one of which had a sign that read "African Dodger." There was a counter with baseballs on it and, at a distance of twenty-five feet, a canvas curtain, sticking out of which was the head of a Black man. A living head of a living Black man, to be precise.

When Anna looked at Porter, uncomprehendingly, he said, "You have three chances to hit the target, for the prize of a cigar. It's harder than it looks—these fellows are quick. Probably bred into them from centuries of dodging tigers in the jungle."

Anna was horrified. "Maybe that counts as fun where you're from, but for a civilized person, it's . . . it's not."

Porter put down a baseball, realized he was grinning, and carefully rearranged his lips into a noncommittal horizontal line. He apologized, with a reference to the misbegotten land in which he'd been raised. He led Anna to a shooting gallery a couple of doors away and asked if she'd like to try her luck. When she declined, he paid two bits, picked up a rifle, and hit three bull's eyes in succession. For his prize, he picked out a piece of chalkware and handed it to Anna. She wasn't proud of it, but the trinket, modest as it was, mollified her a bit. She said, "Mr. Porter, you implied you were from the west, but you said nothing about being a sharpshooting bad man."

He said, "I'm going to keep asking you to call me Bill till you learn it."

"Bill it is. And speaking of names, there's something I've always wondered. Why are your stories signed 'O. Henry' rather than 'William Porter.' There doesn't seem to be anything objectionable about your given name."

"Unobjectionable, true," Porter said with a chuckle, "but rather dull, wouldn't you say? I wanted something that would stand out and be memorable. As for the moniker I chose, since you're obviously a sensitive soul, I'll let you in on a secret.

"Back in my Texas days, I had . . . well, let's call her a lady friend. She owned a cat called Henry. It never seemed to come when I called it, until one day when I positively bellowed 'Oh, Henry!' From then on, I signed my correspondence with my friend 'O. Henry.' She signed hers 'Polly-O.' When I began writing stories and needed a signature, I remembered the name and it seemed just the thing."

They decided it was time for supper, and they backtracked to

Daufkirch's Casino, famous for its goulash and big-name entertainers. The wooden pavilion was square and high, with a roof that looked rather too large for its body, like an overgrown suburban railway station. There were as many tables under the outer roof, screened by a vine-covered trellis and commanding a view of the Ferris wheel, as there were indoors. Porter suggested eating inside. "I think it will be more amusing," he said, gesturing to the stage at the far end of the room on which, at the moment, Gus Williams was doing his Dutch act. They sat down, and the goulash soon arrived, accompanied by steins of beer for both of them. As they ate, a series of performers came and went: a girl with a Southern accent who sang pathetic ballads of the lost cause; a tramp-magician who praised and blamed himself with "Oh, pretty good! oh, pretty rotten!"; a comedy sketch, all butlers and footmen, and criss-cross love-making between Jack and someone else's wife so as to cure Jack's wife of going about with the other lady's husband and convince her that there is nobody like Jack; German acrobats and acrobatesses; and a man in a high hat and long overcoat, unbuttoned to show his evening dress, who balanced feathers on the point of his nose and kept a paper wad, an open umbrella and a small dinner bell tossing in the air.

Afterwards, the orchestra began playing waltzes and couples began twirling on a generous square in front of the stage. Anna was fairly certain Porter wouldn't ask her to dance. He didn't.

When they went outside, darkness had fallen, and they began making their way home. The electric lights every hundred feet, erected by William Steinway (the piano scion had developed what became North Beach as a resort for his workers at the factory nearby), reflected on the waves and shined through the trees in the busy picnic groves, making a picturesque tableau. The boardwalk was crowded, as before, but this time they made their way to the inside of one of the clumps of people. At the center was a very fat man with a benevolent, fatherly face, operating a device on which were written the words "The Swinger." It consisted of a suspended pendant, in the form of a heavy wooden ball, and a wooden cone placed at the precise spot the ball would rest if it dangled freely. The way the game worked, the fat man was explaining in rapid tones, was that the player put up fifty cents. He took the ball, and raised it to an angle and height of his choosing, then let it go. If it swung passed the cone and then knocked it down on the return movement, he won $2.50. If the cone remained upright (this was said almost *sotto vocce*), he would lose. But he could always "represent"—go again for double or nothing.

A man in knickerbockers stepped forward from the crowd, put four bits down, and said, "I'll give it a try." Porter leaned in to Anna's ear and said, "He's going to lose, then win."

The man pulled back the ball and released it. On the downward swing, it grazed the cone, which toppled. The fat man said, "Hard luck. Would you care to represent?"

Knickerbockers said, "Sure," and exchanged his fifty cents for a dollar. He let the ball go again. This time it hit its target on the return swing. The fat man presented him with a five-dollar bill, and he strode happily away.

Porter whispered to Anna, "We'll watch three losers, then leave." And sure enough, on the next three attempts, the descending ball struck the cone. Porter and Anna extricated themselves from the crowd. When they were a sufficient distance away, he said, "I almost feel sorry for the suckers, but they really should know better. The Swinger's one of the oldest bits of bunko in the book. The laws of physics and gravity are such that, unimpeded, the ball will almost always hit the cone on the way back. But not after the operator does some 'fine work.' The uprights holding the ball and string are always made a little loose, so that a very slight pressure from the shoulder on the part of the manipulator makes the ball miss. Everybody's so intent on the ball that they don't see what he's done. And of course the fellow in knickerbockers was what they call a 'capper'—a prearranged winner who primes the pump."

Porter led Anna down the boardwalk a ways, to another cluster of people—at least fifty of them, all men. As they made their way to the front, he appeared to be making an examination of the crowd. Once they reached the center, he led her a quarter of the way clockwise around the table positioned there, excusing himself as they went and explaining they wanted to get a better look. "Have you ever seen anything like it?" he asked Anna loudly. "Can't wait to tell the home folks." She was sure his Southern accent had just gotten at least fifty percent stronger.

On the table was a large glass cone with an opening at the top. The operator, a short, balding man in suspenders, lifted it, revealing another cone nested inside. This smaller cone was studded with protruding nails, and around its base was a ring of open-topped, numbered compartments. Also on the table was a grid marked out in black paint. Each square was marked with a number corresponding to one of the chambers encircling the bottom of the inner cone, and contained either a dollar amount from $1 to $25, a small prize, or the word "Blank."

"Who'll try his luck at the 'Hap-Hazard?" cried the barker. "Drop the marble in and around it goes—hap-hazardly, hence the name. The box it drops in determines your prize!"

The man standing next to Porter and Anna was as tall as the barker was short. He was wearing a boater hat, striped pants with suspenders, and shiny yellow shoes. Next to him was a blonde woman and next to her was a tow-haired little boy. The man leaned in to Porter and said, "Say, friend, I can see that the game is perfectly fair and I'd like to take a chance, but I'm restrained by the presence of my family here. What do you say you take my dollar and play it for me. If I win, I'll meet you over there"—he gestured to a carousel—"and you can hand me the winnings. If you lose, no harm. Either way, you'll have all the excitement of gaming without any of the risk."

"Why, sure," Porter said, and accepted the dollar. The exaggerated accent was still there, Anna observed—it sounded as if he were saying, "Wah sho." Porter stepped to the front, and handed the dollar to the barker in exchange for the marble. He dropped it through the hole in the top cone, and five seconds later it landed in compartment number 23. On the grid, the 23-box said $10. The barker promptly handed Porter a bill and shouted, "This gentleman's luck will rub off on the next person—I guarantee it. Who's next!"

Porter took Anna's arm and led her out of the crowd, not toward the carousel but in the opposite direction, toward the Grand Pier, where a ferry to Manhattan was waiting. Seconds later, the tall man in suspenders overtook them and said, "Say, reuben, what's the game? Hand over those simoleons."

Porter said, "I think not my friend, and I don't think you'll make a fuss." Anna noticed that his Southern accent had subsided. "If you do, I'll tell that crowd all about the hidden levers at the bottom of the cone. Don't think they'll be too happy about it."

He took Anna's arm, turned, and swiftly walked to the boat. "Not likely that he'll come after us, but we'll be safer when we're on the water in any case," he said.

As they neared the boat, she started to pose a question: "How . . . ?

Porter jumped in. "I made him for a capper by the yellow shoes. The yellow-haired moll was a clue as well."

They got on board, and the boat pulled out less than a minute later. Porter took a five-dollar bill from his wallet and handed it to Anna. "Your share of our winnings," he said.

They stood on the deck and looked over the water, not saying a word, each seemingly comfortable in their own thoughts. Porter was thinking about the "bumpkin," in his fashionable yellow shoes, and how he might work his way into a short story. And Anna contemplated how New York, which had always seemed somehow constricted to her, despite its grandeur, now felt a more capacious place. Having doubled her weekly salary from Siegel-Cooper didn't hurt.

There were no fireworks at North Beach on Sundays. But as they leaned on the rail, they were witness to a more modest display. As the boat headed to Manhattan, they gazed back at Riker's Island. From the massive mounds of coal that had been dumped came smoke, which, as it rose to the sky, created an eerie light show against the stars.

CHAPTER XIV

Bill Porter had two brothers. David was born when Bill was three and died at six months, just after their mother's passing. His older sibling, Shirley Worth Porter, known as "Shell," was Bill's opposite number in every conceivable manner: rough and tumble, he never opened a book, scorned those who did, and left home when he was barely in his teens to begin his life's work as a laborer in Carolina lumber camps. Bill hadn't seen him since a brief visit to Greensboro more than ten years earlier. (He still carried a measure of affection for Shell, however. When he was on the lam in New Orleans, he had signed his articles in the local papers "Shirley Worth.")

With that absence in mind, it perhaps wasn't surprising that soon after their professional relationship began, he began to develop a rather filial friendship with Bob Davis. Porter responded to the younger man's earnestness, decency, and humor. Davis also had some rather impressive hidden talents, which intrigued Porter. Some years earlier, he had recruited to the *World*'s pages a muckraker named Jacob Riis, whose book, *How the Other Half Lives*, was illustrated with his own photographs of tenement sweatshops and the like. Riis had sold Bob a used box camera at a minimal cost, showed him how to operate it, and even how to create sufficient light for indoor photographs with flash powder.

Porter appreciated, as well, Davis's respect for privacy. Perhaps surprisingly for someone in the newspaper trade, he had a moralistic strain, sometimes coming off as a bit of a prude. That was one reason among several that Porter told him nothing about the roles played in his life by Bat Masterson, Charles Gardner, Anna Lockhart, or even Al Jennings; when an inadvertent reference to one of them passed Porter's lips, Davis never pressed the point.

The two men enjoyed sending each other letters back and forth, filled with word play and high-flown language. (The telephone was reserved for emergencies which, happily, never seemed to come.) One day Porter received, by messenger, a missive from the editor.

> My dear Bill:—
>
> If you are not otherwise occupied, and feel in the mood, I will be pleased to take sufficient time off tomorrow to go with you down to Port Washington, and mingle with the Yeomanry. It will be a pleasant trip for both of us, particularly for you, as I am light and gay in the country.
>
> Let me know by this boy whether or not you are next, and I'll get busy looking at the time tables, etc. If the idea appeals to you, why not 'phone me?
>
> Ever and anon,
>
> RHD

The idea did have a certain appeal; at that moment, landing a fish seemed a more likely prospect than catching his blackmailer or finishing the short story that had lain inert on his desk for three days. Bright and early the next day, a mild one, he and Davis filled a lunch basket with provisions, took a ferry to Long Island City and then the train to Port Washington. There they found a boatman, who took them out on an oily tide through a web of seaweed strewn with flotsam and jetsam. They followed the ebb until it flattened, at which point a pitiless sun took up the work of parboiling both men. Porter, who was of a florid complexion, cooked first and became as pink as a boiled lobster. The fishing was atrocious and the small fry swiped bait as fast as the men could put it on hooks. Three weary hours resulted in two flounders and four sea robins.

Finally they gave up. Porter directed the boatman to land near a broad expanse of lawn, with three boathouses. When they stepped out, Davis recognized it as Jay Gould's estate.

"Well," Porter said, "he can't do any more than ask us in to lunch. Do you reckon he'd like to have both flounders, or do you want to keep yours?"

They lay on the beach in the shade of the boathouses, and made overtures to their lunch basket. A gentle breeze blowing seaward from the Gould garden brought the perfume of flowers and wet grass. The environment stirred Porter to philosophy—or, at least, as close to that realm as he ever ventured.

He took an object from his coat pocket and said, "Here is a notebook. It contains a dozen pages of blank paper. With a lead pencil I wrote on these several sheets a tale three or four thousand words in length. An editor such as yourself buys the tale and prints it in a magazine. If it is a good tale it gets into a book and perhaps it is dramatized and put on the stage. It goes on and on reaping profit yet it is never anything but the figment of my imagination converted into words."

He paused and ran a stream of sand through his hands, one above the other, like an hourglass. "It emanates from my mind, but it exists; it survives the years."

"Now, I have a daughter," he continued, after a long pause. "A child of my own flesh and blood, bone of my bone. She looks and acts like me. In three score and ten, according to the Biblical injunction, she will return to the earth, and that will be the absolute last of Margaret Porter, daughter of William. But my written words set down methodically, laboriously, on these sheets of white paper, fugitive recollections at best, move on. Queer, isn't it. Flesh: mortal. Thought: immortal."

A comment on Davis's part didn't seem called for, and he didn't make one. Porter fussed about in the yellow sand and uncovered a small tortoise shell hair comb from which the luster had faded.

"Here's another story," he said. "Who owns it? Lady in waiting or lady in wading? Maid or mistress? White or Black?"

Porter put the comb in his pocket. Out of his, Davis took an elegant pocket watch, looked at it, and said, "We had better leave now, unless we want to miss our train and spend the night on Long Island." The two men rose and walked down to the boat. When Davis boarded, the boatman had a quiet word in his ear. "Your friend," he said, "appears to be kind of a nut."

Three weeks after his first meeting with Charles Gardner, Porter posted his cheque for fifty dollars and received a brief note in return: "We are circling the prey. Patience.—CG." The following week, Porter decided to deliver the funds in person so as to find out exactly how tight the circle had drawn. Once again, he traveled to the Mohawk Building, ascended to the fifth floor, sat in the ante-chamber watched over by the furrow-browed secretary, and entered Gardner's office. He asked the detective how his investigation was proceeding.

Gardner cleared his throat. "There are twenty-six Western Union Offices in the city. I don't have operatives in all of them, but I'm fairly well covered. On Thursday, my spy in the Forty-second Street branch, name of Retzlaff, came in for his shift and saw in the log that the payment had been picked up just a few hours earlier. All our man needed to get it was a signature, but needless to say it wasn't his real name, or even the 'McManus' he supplied to me."

Porter asked what the name on the signature was.

"Why would you possibly want to know that?"

Porter smiled. "I reckon I might put it in a story. If our blackmailer sees it, maybe it would put a little of the fear of God into him."

Gardner nodded his understanding. "I'll ascertain it, but I think we have a quicker means to identification. When the man on the earlier shift came in the next day, Retzlaff asked him for a description of the fellow. Of course, a day had passed, and his colleague hadn't been paying great attention, and most of what he said was useless: medium height, medium build, brown hair, mustache. But he did notice that the man walked with a limp."

"So where does that get us?" Porter asked. "Seek far and wide in New York for a mustachioed gimp? Seems a fool's mission."

"Patience, patience. I count it highly likely that our prey will keep on picking up his money at the same Western Union office. Why wouldn't he? I'm on my way to recruiting all four clerks who work in the branch. They'll be under instructions to telephone the office the minute they spot McManus on his way in. Or if they don't have time for that, as soon as he leaves, along with the dope on the direction he's heading. I'll immediately dispatch some operatives uptown and I'll warrant one of them will spot him and nab him. Or if not this week, then soon, for certain."

Porter didn't feel certain at all, but he held his tongue.

"All that is the good news," the detective continued. "Here's the bad. McManus has sent us another letter." Gardner handed it to Porter, who scanned it and found it replete with predictable bluster. He noticed there were no Briticisms. Indeed, the brief letter concluded with the statement, "If you had any doubts about the information I possess and any suspicion that my demands are based on a pretense, please see the enclosed." The American "pretense" rather than the British "pretence."

Porter looked to Gardner, who handed him a page cut out of the brand-new issue of *The Critic*. It contained a short unsigned article which read:

> Less than a year ago the readers of popular magazines began to be startled and delighted by certain fantastic and ingenious tales, mainly dealing with Western life and bearing the strange device "O. Henry" as a signature. In a short time people began to talk to each other about the stories, and very soon they began to ask who the author was.
>
> It was then that a new problem fell upon this over-

> puzzled age,—who is "O. Henry"? No one seemed to know the author's real name, and immediately vague and weird rumors began to be afloat and the nom-de-guerre was soon invested with as much curiosity as surrounds an author after his decease.
>
> But, like most mysteries, when it was probed there was no mystery about it. "O. Henry's" real name is Mr. Sydney Porter, a gentleman from Texas, who, having seen a great deal of the world and having had many savoury and unsavoury experiences, happened to find himself in New York, and there discovered a market where people would buy stories of his experiences.
>
> Being of a lazy disposition he very naturally quitted active life and took to his desk. He signed the name "O. Henry" merely because he did not take his real self seriously as a maker of fiction. He really does shun notoriety—a most unusual characteristic among present-day writers—and he disclaims any intention of having purposely created a mystery about his identity. But he is still not too old to become a professional.

Above the paragraph was a photo of Porter from his Austin days, complete with a curled-up mustache.

Porter grunted; there didn't seem to be anything to say. But "lazy disposition" rankled.

"I take this as our man's proverbial shot across the bow," Gardner said. "In revealing your Texas background and hinting about some unnamed trouble, he is warning us he is prepared to reveal the rest.

"Whether you continue to pay him is of course up to you. But I hope I've convinced you that we have a good plan to catch him, which may come to fruition very soon."

Wordlessly, Porter took the cheque from his coat pocket and handed it to Gardner. He left the office and descended the stairs to the street. This time, there wasn't a smile on his face.

CHAPTER XV

As THE DAYS, then weeks, went by, Anna started to feel comfortable at the Big Store, and to get some pleasure from observing, and in due time getting to know, her fellow employees. She got along well with Maisie, and they always took their lunch together. The store had a paternalistic attitude toward the shopgirls and (perhaps as a preemptive rebuff to any criticisms of the low wages it paid) regularly offered instruction in such pursuits as calisthenics (on the roof) and ballroom dance. The latter took place in a space carved out in the basement and proceeded in time to the piano-playing instructor's barking "*One*-two-three, *one*-two-three." The steps and the airy way the girls held each other (taking turns on who would lead) were a far cry from the goings-on at the Give and Take Athletic Club.

One striking thing Anna witnessed, in herself and others, was the development of the famous "shopgirl refinement." It was, she came to realize, a thing unto itself, and for the most part a manufactured article—indefinable, but immediately identifiable to anyone who witnessed it. Girls who came from rough surroundings changed rapidly, as if by osmosis. A red-head named Pearl, with a peculiar chuckle, entered the store as coarse as a bog-trotter. She got in because she was pretty, but how awkward! She used to shut her eyes, stick out her lips, and say "For land's sake!" or "Oh, my!" Anna took some interest in observing her. Initially, she had the high-ratted pompadour and the exaggerated straight-front associated with the shopgirl type. Her skirt was threadbare but had the correct flare, and she wore her short broadcloth jacket as jauntily as though it were Persian lamb.

Over the course of four weeks, the transformation of Pearl from the raw material to the finished article was effected with remarkable speed and efficiency. She worked in Ladies' Gloves, and she was an apt pupil, learning from the way her customers comported themselves. From one she would copy and practice a gesture, from another an eloquent lifting of an eyebrow, from others, a manner of walking, of carrying a purse, of smiling, of greeting a friend, of addressing those inferior in station. From her best beloved model, Mrs. Van Alstyne Fisher, she acquired that excellent thing, a soft, low voice as clear as silver and as perfect in articulation as the notes of a thrush.

One day, Anna was in the dressing-room on the second floor. This space, with its rocking chairs, framed prints, stacks of newspapers and magazines, and large sign reading, "Look Pleasant When You Speak to a Customer," was a popular refuge for the girls. They would walk in as if coming off the stage, peek at their hair in the mirror, and give it a swift touch; if they had a spare minute, they would gather to gossip. On this particular day, a girl named Dulcie was holding forth about her exploits on the way home the previous evening: "This feller sashayed up, so he did, and gave me the matinee eyes, and his song and dance. I turned him down cold and made a sneak; but he followed me down to Eighteenth and tried his hot air again. I says to him, 'Ain't you the fresh thing! Who do you suppose I am, to be addressing such a remark to me?' And what do you think he says back to me?" Several heads—brown, black, red, and yellow—bobbed together; the answer was given; and an irrefutable parry to the thrust was decided upon, to be used by anyone who needed it, whenever the occasion arose. At that moment, someone swept in and asked the time. Pearl replied, "It lacks twenty minutes of two."

After a probationary period, Anna's salary was raised from five dollars a week to six. It might appear to be impossible to live even on the larger sum, yet she did. She had her lunches in the Big

Store restaurant at a cost of sixty cents for the week; dinners were $1.05. On weekdays her breakfast cost ten cents; she cooked her eggs over the stove while she was dressing. On Sunday mornings she feasted royally on veal chops and pineapple fritters at Billy's Restaurant, at a cost of twenty-five cents—and tipped the waitress another ten. She found a factory where she could buy broken crackers for three cents a pound, and another place where she got a pound of broken candy for a dime. The evening papers—and she had quickly learned that taking the daily papers was something every New Yorker did—came to six cents; and two Sunday papers were a nickel each.

Two dollars went for her room, the attic studio. Couch-bed, dresser, table, washstand, chair—of that much the landlady was guilty. The rest was Anna's. On the dresser were her treasures—a formal photograph of her parents and her brother, a gilt china vase presented to her by Hettie, *The Calendar of Famous Artists*, some rice powder in a glass dish, and a cluster of artificial cherries tied with a pink ribbon.

The immutable total weekly expenditure was $4.75, give or take a penny. She tried (with varying success) to save ten cents a week, and with what remained, she had to cover all additional expenses. That usually left nothing for entertainment, or even for venturing by streetcar beyond her immediate neighborhood. Unless she was treated, of course.

One Saturday night, she hurried out at six o'clock—Saturday being the one weeknight when the doors had the good grace to shut and stay shut—and entered streets filled with the rush-hour floods of people. An ineffable magnetic force drew her in to a shop where goods were cheap; her eye caught, and she bought, an imitation lace collar for fifty cents—more than she could afford, but it had been so long since she'd splurged, she couldn't resist. She made the rest of the journey home without incident or further expenditure. At ten minutes to seven she was ready. She looked at herself in the wrinkly mirror. The reflection was satisfactory. The dark blue dress, fitting without a wrinkle, the new lace collar, the hat with its jaunty black feather, the but-slightly-soiled gloves, all were becoming; a neutral observer wouldn't even guess at the self-denial they represented. And her absolute best feature, her hair, flowed and shone as it always did. For a moment she forgot everything else except that she was beautiful.

There would be no self-denial tonight. She had been invited to the roof garden atop Hammerstein's Victoria Theater. There would be a grand dinner, and music, and splendidly dressed ladies to look at, and wonderful things to eat.

Somebody knocked at the door. Anna opened it. The landlady stood there with a spurious smile, sniffing for cooking by stolen gas. "A gentleman's downstairs to see you," she said. "It's the fellow who used to live here. Mr. Porter."

Mr. Porter indeed. What was there to be done about him? The thing that made him most infuriating, Anna reckoned, was that he had no idea there was any problem. On their day at North Beach, and the first few times he called after that (he had moved to new rooms, in Irving Place), she allowed herself briefly to entertain the thought of a future together. One evening, spurred by romantic reverie, she painted a miniature of herself and gave it to him. He was so touched he was speechless. But the fancy didn't last long.

First of all, the Magnuson situation had not changed, there was no prospect of it doing so, and unless or until it did, marriage was simply not a possibility. And second, there was Bill Porter himself. She found it fitting that the world knew him by another name, because when they were together, she felt she was with only part of a man.

His shell, you might say, was functional. Certainly, he was never less than pleasant. She enjoyed—to a point—his old-fashioned manners and apparently never-ending supply of New York lore; and she was flattered by the extensive interest he took in the particulars of her life (while knowing he was spelunking for material for his stories). But there was a hollowness at his core. It was eminently clear that there was also a great deal that was not—and could not be—discussed. For one thing, anything related to his life before the day he set foot in New York. For another, anything related to what the two of them meant, or might one day mean, to each other. It didn't help that he would periodically make awkward passes at her. The first couple of times, she was lonely enough that she played along up to a point. But once she came to realize they had no future together, his attempted embraces grew to seem curious and unsavory, and she nipped them in the bud.

All that being the case, when Bill would turn up and ask to take her out, she always contemplated saying no. But she never did. She felt herself protesting "And why shouldn't I permit myself to be treated by him?" to some disembodied and disapproving internal voice. Without their days and nights on the town, she would be left to a life of penury, cooped up and counting her pennies in her mean flat. And so she allowed him to take her to dinners at restaurants like Rangeneschi's, where she ate spaghetti for the first time, and the Hofbrau Haus, where she had sauerbraten and lager and heard the famous call, "Jannsen wants to see you!" They went to nickelodeons and vaudeville houses. One Sunday they took a rubber-neck bus around the city, and one Friday night they went on a slumming tour of Chinatown led by the so-called "mayor of Chinatown," Chuck Connors, dressed in the pearly button-covered attire of the Cockney costermonger, with his derby hat which he never took off and the eternal cigar in the corner of his mouth. They'd eaten chop suey (Connors himself had instructed Anna in the proper use of chopsticks), attended a kind of opera, gone to the Mott Street "joss house," and as a grand finale, been escorted to an opium den, where wide-eyed Chinese people lolled around, seemingly dazed within an inch of unconsciousness. Walking out, Porter informed Anna that they were all actors.

(Bill got a short story out of the rubberneck tour, which he called "Sisters of the Golden Circle." "The car glided up the Golden Way," he wrote, by way of description of the rubberers' journey.

> On the bridge of the great cruiser the captain stood, trumpeting the sights of the big city to his passengers. Wide-mouthed and open-eared, they heard the sights of the metropolis thunder forth to their ears. In the solemn spires of spreading cathedrals they saw the home of the Vanderbilts; in the busy bulk of the Grand Central depot they viewed, wonderingly, the frugal cot of Russell Sage. Bidden to observe the highlands of the Hudson, they gaped, unsuspecting, at the upturned mountains of a new-laid sewer.)

On this Saturday, Anna walked down the stairs to greet him, and they emerged into a warm summer evening. They were both happy to set out on foot, walking east, with the setting sun at their backs. At Sixth Avenue, as they turned to the north, there was a station for the elevated train, but Anna didn't even bother to mention it.

They walked past the notorious Haymarket, the grand new home of R.H. Macy's department store, and (after bearing left on to Broadway), the Herald Building, with its statues of the goddess Minerva and twenty-six owls; giant printing presses, clanging and banging audibly through the glass, were already producing the next day's early edition. At 39th Street they came to the ornate, Italianate Metropolitan Opera House, which occupied a full city block. Chauffeured motor cars and horse-drawn carriages were dropping off patrons in monochromatic evening dress.

"Behold, the swells," Porter said. "They pay top dollar to hear Italian operas, but they wouldn't allow an Italian at their clubs."

At 42nd Street, Broadway met Seventh Avenue and they were at their destination. The grand building, crisscrossed with fire escapes, dominated the intersection.

They walked into the lobby, where a portly gentleman with a Van Dyke beard, wearing a reversible plug hat and carrying a gold-headed cane, was pacing to and fro among the crowd and puffing on a cigar. "That's Hammerstein, the owner," Porter whispered to Anna. "His son Willie runs this place. Willie is the master of stunts, including the thermometer one." He walked her over to a corner where a large instrument showed the temperature to be sixty-seven degrees, at least fifteen degrees cooler than it actually seemed to be. Porter lifted a corner of the tablecloth on which the thermometer was sitting. Underneath was a large block of ice.

They made their way to an elevator and ascended with a half-dozen other patrons. They emerged onto a roof that seemed another world. A big world, as it combined the roofs of Hammerstein's Victoria and the adjoining theatre, The Belasco. To one side of them was a large performance space enclosed by glass walls on two sides and open on the rear, on whose stage was a man, announced by a sign to the side as The Great Spedoni, juggling heavy iron weights. To the other side was . . . well, it appeared, improbably, to be an actual farm. Porter and Anna began to stroll through it and saw: a windmill whose sails revolved in a Catherine wheel effect of colored lights, a miller's cottage with a stork's nest in the chimney, a small pond with ducks swimming in it, a vegetable garden containing sprouting cabbages and potatoes, a waterwheel turning with realistic plash and gurgle, and a live and actual cow, at that very moment being milked by a pair of maidens dressed in Swiss costumes. Waiters carrying glasses and bottles and victuals crossed a rustic bridge that led to higher terraces. But for the faint sound of buses braking and automobile horns sounding, Anna and Porter might have thought they were in the countryside of their separate childhoods, and they stood a moment in silence, taking it all in.

They found a table at the open end of the theatre, put in their customary order (beer for him, the Manhattan cocktail Anna had come to favor for her), and proceeded to be entertained. This put them in the same position as a plain and rather somber-looking woman seated on the side of the stage. A sign announced that she was known as "Sober Sue," and that the management would present $100 to any comedian who could succeed in making Sue laugh.

Sue, Anna, and Porter saw:

- Don the Talking Dog, whose vocabulary seemed to be limited to two words, "Hunger" and "Kuchen."
- Rajah, a snake charmer.
- Machnow, "The World's Tallest Man," whose performance consisted of walking through the audience and shaking hands. (Machnow was indeed tall, but the impression of height was enhanced by his Cossack fur hat and thick boots, and by the fact that the "assistant" who accompanied him was distinctly short.)
- The singer Maggie Cline.
- Mademoiselle Alexis, billed as a "Whirlwind Dancer," in whose set piece, "The She Devil and the Demon," she was confronted by a masked fiend and tried to elude him in a dance of Spanish wriggles and twists, twirls and swirls, graceful contortions and picturesque postures. As a climax she tied herself into a double-bow knot, then lay down and, apparently, died. Great applause.
- Unthan the Armless Wonder, who played cards, fired a rifle, and played the violin, all with his feet.
- Hoey and Lee, Hebrew comedians.
- The Three Keatons, being a man, a woman and their six-year-old boy, "Buster." The woman played the saxophone to one side, while the males, gotten up as stage Irishmen, did their rather alarming act. Buster would goad his father by disobeying him, to which the latter would respond by throwing him against the scenery, into the orchestra pit, and once even into the audience. If you looked closely, you could see that a suitcase handle was sewn into Buster's clothing to aid with the constant tossing.

The next act was a young man billed as "Will Rogers, Lasso Expert." Rogers came on stage in cowboy garb accompanied by a horse with felt-button boots buckled on its feet like galoshes. An assistant mounted the horse and proceeded to ride it back and forth across the stage at high speed, while Rogers deftly roped horse, then rider. Porter commented, "I've seen vaudeville rope spinners who clearly haven't been west of New Jersey. This man is the genuine article." Rogers then tried to rope both horse and rider simultaneously, but missed the rider, and said in a Western twang, "I'm handicapped here, as the management won't allow me to curse when I miss." The whole audience laughed, including Porter and Anna. But Sober Sue remained stone-faced, as she had through each of the preceding acts.

After Rogers took his bows and left with horse and assistant, a stagehand put up a sign reading "Ernest Hogan (The Unbleached American) and his 25 Memphis Students in 'Songs of the Black Folks.'" The troupe were not from Memphis, nor were they students. Rather, they were a rousing ragtime band fronted by Hogan—the noted composer, singer, and comedian—and conducted by a gentleman who led the players not by waving his arms but by actually dancing out the rhythm. At the right moments, the players put down their instruments and sang and danced themselves. The music swelled to fill the whole great roof garden, and the audience appeared to be swept away.

The finale was billed as "The Zancigs: Two Minds With But a Single Thought." The Zancigs were a man and his wife, dressed in ordinary street clothes, both of whom spoke in Nordic accents. The husband roamed through the audience while the wife—on the stage, blindfolded and behind a solid screen, so as to allay any doubts about the opacity of the blindfold—described aloud what he encountered. She did so accurately, consistently, and (anyone would have to conclude after the fifth successful "shared thought") without the use of "plants."

It was quite remarkable. At one point, Zancig approached a man seated in the center of the theatre and asked if he would whisper his birthday. Upon hearing it, the mentalist closed his eyes, tapped his forehead, and said, "Go on—I want you to please give me the number." Immediately his wife shouted out, "February 15!" The audience member, bewildered, pumped Zancig's hand for a good ten seconds before sitting down again.

Anna noticed that Porter was staring at Zancig more intently than he had at any of the other acts, even Mlle. Alexia. The performer walked towards the rear of the theatre and asked a woman to produce an object from her handbag. She did so and handed it to Zancig, who tapped his temple as before and said, "Quick, the article!" Mrs. Zancig said, "It's a snuff box"—whereupon Zancig held above his head, for everyone to see, that very thing. As she was clapping (along with the rest of the audience), Anna turned to remark her amazement to Porter, only to see that he was standing up. When the applause died down, he called out, "Mr. Zancig! Come here if you please. I have an object for you to communicate."

Zancig approached the table. When he arrived, Porter reached into his pocket and removed from a handkerchief Anna's miniature. In the process of doing so, he said (and Anna noticed that his Southern accent was again in the ascendant), "I have only one request—that you transmit your thoughts to your wife completely silently. That is, not to say anything, or even snap your fingers or clear your throat." At that, Zancig looked to the side of the theatre and gave a slight, almost imperceptible nod. Immediately two burly men came swiftly walking towards him. Each took one of Porter's arms, and they lifted him up and carried him all the way to the elevator.

Zancig said loudly to the crowd, "My apologies, ladies and gentleman. That man whispered a threat to me. Do not fear for your safety. A couple of Mr. Hammerstein's employees will see him to the street. . . Now, would anyone care to divulge to me the country they have most recently visited?"

Anna looked down on the table and saw that the miniature was sitting on it. She picked it up and rushed to the elevator. Under the big sign and the fire escapes out on the Seventh Avenue side of the theatre, she found Porter, brushing himself off.

"No permanent damage," he said. "And by the way, that Sober Sue—my guess is she has facial paralysis. But the important thing—do you have the miniature?"

She silently held it up, and he took it, with a slight bow. Something in her eyes gave Porter cause for concern. "I'm sorry to have ended the evening so abruptly, but I—"

She didn't let him finish the thought. "I cannot figure you out, Bill Porter. You seem to have appointed yourself the ultimate exposer of graft and trickery. But there is nothing about yourself you're willing to reveal. You have the mysterious skill of marksmanship with a rifle. Your Southern drawl comes and goes. Any question I ask, you deflect it. I don't even know where you were born! What are you hiding, and why don't you think you can trust me with it?"

"I'm sorry," was all he seemed to be able to bring himself to say, again.

"I finally understand," she said. "Your stories about the poor, beleaguered shopgirls, and all your talk of sympathizing with us, are bunk. And you are as much a fakir as that mind-reader."

Porter reached for her hand. He seemed to be about to say something, but no words came. Eventually she pulled free and turned up the Avenue, first walking swiftly, then running. Porter watched her until she was two blocks away and the crowd had swallowed her up. He realized that his right hand was in his pocket, and it was holding Anna's miniature.

As the days passed, Anna stopped thinking very much about Bill Porter, but she did start thinking about her life in a new, colder way, as a sort of business proposition. She spent her days selling expensive toys. In a way she was an expensive toy herself, on display along with all the others. But she and her fellow pretty objects didn't share in the proceeds. They were sent home with a pittance and the admonition that they should be grateful for that.

She had begun skipping a meal every other day. She had nowhere to go for help. Her parents were dead, her brother vanished with the winter wind, her friends—the ones who didn't live with their parents—were in the same straits as she was.

Since she'd started working at Cooper-Siegel, she had noticed a few sharply-dressed men who hung out at the employees' entrance at the end of the day, leaning against the building or pretending to read a newspaper, smoking cigarettes, and now and again talking to some of the girls. She'd noticed one or two of them answered the men's fresh remarks, as she herself walked swiftly by, showing them her heels. In due course, those girls disappeared from their posts at the store. One of them was Dulcie. She had shown up on the customer side of Pearl's counter just this week. Anna had seen her from across the floor. She was wearing a fine dress and hat, and rather ostentatiously made a purchase of a pair of kid gloves.

The girls talked about her in the dressing room. "She's working in a parlor house in Hell's Kitchen," Maisie said. Anna nodded knowingly, though she didn't know precisely what a parlor house was. By the end of the conversation, though, it was clear.

That evening, when she walked out the door, she purposely walked more slowly down the street than usual. There was the usual group of men there, but today, she saw to her surprise, one of them was the man she had danced with months before at the Give and Take Athletic Club, Mike Gaffigan. He was slouching against a lamppost and wearing a bowler hat. When he recognized her, a grin swept over his face. "Well, if it isn't the kiddo," he said.

Anna didn't say anything, but she walked a little more slowly.

"You left me in the lurch downtown but that don't put a grouch on me," he said. "I don't imagine that you could use a bite to eat? Why don't you come on with me to Rector's. We'll order a couple of lobsters and put some meat on them bones."

Anna stopped and turned to face him.

CHAPTER XVI

Al Jennings had initially planned to stay in New York for several weeks, then go back to Oklahoma. But something about the city struck his fancy—above all, a fairly self-evident equation: the greater the population, the more numerous the marks. And so he decided to stick around for a while. He filled out his days walking the concrete canyons, sometimes in Bill Porter's company, more often alone. He learned fairly quickly to play up his Western talk and garb. They earned him no small number of free drinks. One night, he thought they'd won him the companionship of a big blonde named Flossie. But when things reached their conclusion, it turned out she expected to be paid. That inspired Jennings to embark on a study of New York women, still to be completed.

He was by himself one day, on West 23rd Street, when he came upon an odd sight. A wooden tripod was planted on the sidewalk. Atop it was a rectangular black box, about the size of a small suitcase, and behind the box stood a man. His head was covered by some black fabric, and he was turning a crank on the side of the box. Jennings sidled over so he was next to this spectacle, a dozen feet away, where he could hear a whirring sound emanating from the box. He looked in the direction toward which it was pointing and saw . . . nothing. Or, rather, he saw the typical scene on a typical New York street: streetcars and carriages passing by, people crossing 23rd, the normal run of pedestrians going to and fro. Of the last, all ignored the man and his contraption, except for a boy of eleven or so, who planted himself in the middle distance and stared at it with rapt fascination.

Presently a woman in a white dress and a man in a dark jacket and a straw boater hat began to approach. They walked straight toward the man under the black cloth and his machine. When they were just a few feet away, they stepped atop what must have been a wind grate, for the man's necktie started fluttering and the woman's skirts flew above her knees. They would have gone higher, but she quickly gathered them; then she laughed raucously and they stepped aside.

Immediately, the man under the cloth emerged; he had a generous nose, a black mustache, and hair parted in the middle. He enthusiastically clapped the man and the woman on the back.

"Well done," he said. "Alfred, you kept a straight face, and Florence, you didn't, but it's all to the good. That giggling will make the piece."

Jennings, never one to let politeness get in the way of curiosity, edged closer and asked the mustachioed man what it was all about.

"'What it's all about' is Thomas Edison's latest production," was the reply. "I came upon this wind grate the other day, and figured it would make for a wow of a short subject."

"Ah, so this is a camera and you were making a moving picture. Marvelous. The name's Al Jennings." He stuck out his hand.

The photographer took it. "Mr. Edison paid enough to secure the patent, so we call it the Kinetograph. But camera will do. I'm Edwin Porter. And my players, Mr. Abadie and Miss Georgie." Handshakes all around. "Al Jennings, I take it from your accent and your hat that you do not hail from the Isle of the Manhattoes."

Jennings assented, and told him an expurgated account of his history, claiming, not completely inaccurately, that he was in New York on "an extended vacation." Among the things he left out was the other Porter who had brought him to the city.

"Can you ride a horse?" asked Edwin Porter, rather abruptly. Jennings affirmed that he could.

"That's possibly quite fortuitous," Porter said. "I am a native of Pennsylvania but, as is the fashion in my field and others, I've developed an interest in western things. Over the past couple of years, we've made some films of Buffalo Bill and his Wild West show. You may have seen them at Huber's or the Eden Musée, down the street."

Jennings had not but pledged he would seek them out.

"You are in luck, for our most recent short, which opened at Huber's last week, is our best. We based it on Buffalo Bill's showstopper at Madison Square Garden, 'The Hold-up of the Deadwood Stage.' We got some of Bill's riders to be the cast. There's some remarkable action. The desperadoes ambush a stagecoach. They point their Winchester rifles at the driver and order him to halt and the occupants to step out. The outlaws get all the booty they can, and are just departing when an armed Sheriff's posse arrives. They pursue the bandits, ending in a desperate chase, and the bad men vanquished. And all this was filmed in the wilds of New Jersey, near Mr. Edison's old studio, not fifteen miles from where we're standing now.

"The reason I am telling you all this, Mr. Jennings, is that we're about to embark on a sort of sequel, of an unprecedented length—ten minutes or more. It's inspired by the exploits of Butch Cassidy and his Hole in the Wall Gang in Wyoming. You may have read about them in *The Police Gazette.* Alas, Buffalo Bill's engagement has ended, his company has left the city, and I am in desperate need of players who do not look like they just stepped out of a Manhattan office.

"What do you say about being in my train-robbing gang? The work will not be arduous, the pay is reasonable, and you will have some good stories to tell the home folks back in Oklahoma."

Jennings looked at him like a man not sure if his leg was being pulled. "Train robbing, you say?"

Interior filming was to start in three days' time, at the Edison studio in Twenty-first street. Jennings reported there at eight a.m., as requested, and—also as requested—in the same suit and hat he'd been wearing when he met Ed Porter. He also brought with him a copy of a recent issue of *Everybody's*, open to page 611.

He ascended to the top floor, and met Ed Porter in a small room that, Porter explained, did triple duty as dressing room, dark room, and business office. Jennings handed him the magazine and asked him to read the first paragraph aloud. When he was done, Jennings said, "I am the man O. Henry refers to." Porter took a step back. "Don't be alarmed, my friend. My outlaw days are behind me. But, like Butch Cassidy, I have robbed a train or two in my time. That's why I had a start the other day when you mentioned the subject of your picture.

"A couple of months back, I happened to meet Mr. . . . ah, Mr. Henry at a watering hole in Irving Place. I guess the drink loosened my tongue. He proposed I write this article, which he would submit under his name. I did, he did, and you are holding the result in your hand. Every word is true."

Porter finally found his own tongue. "A remarkable set of circumstances," he said. "I am doubly glad to have you as a player in this film, and I hope you'll agree to be technical adviser as well. If you consent, I'll raise your pay from twenty dollars to thirty."

Jennings said he'd be delighted (and that is exactly why he had brought *Everybody's* along). "But keep my name out of it, if you don't mind," he said after a pause. Porter agreed, and immediately set off to procure a copy of the scenario for him to read.

It was two pages long and a typical tenderfoot fantasy.

Jennings put it down on a table and took a deep breath. "The scenario specifies two robbers. Like I say right there on page one in *Everybody's*, the ideal number is five. I understand you want to save on salaries, but I'd suggest adding at least a couple of more men. That'll make the chase and the gunfight more exciting as well." Porter made a note in his copy. "The other thing that occurs to me is, if you want to add a note of veri. . . veri. . . of accuracy, have the robbers unhitch the locomotive from the rest of the train. Makes for an easier getaway."

Porter scribbled a note to that effect as well and exclaimed "Capital! I can use a couple of fellows from the barroom scene in the gang. Mr. Jennings, you've already earned your salary and we haven't begun shooting. And speaking of which, let's head upstairs."

Porter explained that there were two studios on the roof, one large and glass-enclosed and one small, with a skylight. The "interiors" were to be shot there. Porter led Jennings into the small room, which was curiously bifurcated. Two of the four walls were white and unadorned, and a Kinetograph (it looked like the same machine he'd seen on 23rd Street) was set up in the corner where the walls met. The other half of the room was made up to look like a simple office, with a door, a desk, and a large window, outside of which could be seen employees' comings and goings on the roof. "I tip my hat to the set boys," Porter said. "Wouldn't you take this for a Western Union office out west?" Jennings answered in the expected affirmative though it was a good deal more spacious than the cramped warrens of his experience.

As he finished talking, three men entered the studio and presented themselves to Porter: one in a white shirt and a vest, each of the others in dark clothes, a broad hat, and a belt holding a revolver. "My cast has arrived, Al. Excuse me while I prepare them."

Within minutes, the scene was ready to go. Jennings stood next to Porter and watched the action unfold. The man in the vest was at the desk, writing. Suddenly the other two entered the room, brandishing their six-shooters and ordering the clerk about. He scribbled something on a piece of paper and handed it through the ticket window. At that point, Porter said, "Now!" and one of the bad men conked the clerk on the back of the head with his revolver; he slumped to the floor. Jennings found the swift tidiness of the operation not a little unlikely; in his experience, unconsciousness was a good deal harder won. But once again he kept his counsel. As he did (as well as stifling a laugh) when the "victim," as his hands were being tied, clearly appeared to move his right arm, as if to help out in the procedure. Even with the assist, the tying-up was belabored: Jennings counted out an even thirty seconds before it was finished. Then the bad men gathered their guns and walked out the door, and Porter stepped away from the camera and said, "Thank you, gentlemen."

In short order, a small girl stepped up, wearing a sort of Red Riding Hood cloak. Porter wrapped her in his arms, and, upon releasing her, introduced her to Jennings as his daughter, Mary. He whispered something in her ear, and she walked by the telegraph operator—still prostrate on the floor—and out the door. A moment later, Edwin Porter positioned himself by the camera and yelled "Action!" The operator roused himself, made his way to the desk, but then collapsed again. Moments later, Mary walked through the door, looked at the man, and raised her face and hands to the heavens, apparently in an attempt to convey deep emotion. She busied herself with the ropes tying his hands and feet, then took a cup of water from the desk and splashed it on his face. He rose to his feet. End of scene.

Porter stepped out from under the cloak and asked Jennings what he thought.

"Very impressive. But I have a question. All the time you've been filming, people have been walking back and forth out that window." Jennings gestured at the opening, behind which the three actors he'd just seen were strolling by. "Won't that look odd?"

"Ah, the magic of motion pictures. There's a technique I've picked up from the Lumière brothers that I'm eager to try out here. The key to this scene is that a train arrives. And when viewers watch this in a theater, they'll see through that very window a train pulling in. The effect is derived through the use of mattes. Look at the lens of the Kinetograph." Jennings did so and saw that a tiny rectangular piece of cardboard was affixed to it.

Porter went on, "Because of the matte, I didn't actually take pictures of the window, and that portion of the film remains unexposed. When we're on location at a train station in New Jersey, I'll take the same film and shoot a train coming to a stop. Only this time, I'll cover up the *rest* of the lens. And voilà! I will have a scene of the telegraph office, with the train viewed through the window."

Jennings nodded, though he didn't really understand.

"That was child's play compared to our next scene," Porter said as he walked to the larger studio (followed by the Kinetograph, which an assistant was wheeling along on a dolly). They walked in, and Jennings saw it had been gotten up as a Western saloon with a dozen people in it, four of them women. A man with an accordion and one with a sort of stand-up fiddle were on a small raised stage. The director gave Jennings his direction for the scene. Jennings had an idea in turn, and Porter nodded enthusiastically. He called for the prop man, who in short order returned with a revolver and handed it to Jennings.

And then Porter yelled "Action!" and the scene commenced. The musical duo pounded out a two-step and four couples executed a pretty fair country quadrille. After twenty seconds or so, the door opened and in walked a man in a suit and a derby hat, evidently a dude. One of the cowboys led him to the center of the circle, and the stranger started dancing the buck-and-wing. At that point, Jennings took out his gun and fired it in the general direction of the dude's feet—though not too close (as the director hadn't needed to caution him). The poor fellow continued for a few seconds, then bolted out the door. General laughter, and more dancing. And then the door opened again and the telegraph operator from the first scene entered, waving his arms excitedly. Everybody followed him out the door, including the musicians. Jennings was the last. He was so engrossed in the proceedings that he almost forgot his cue.

Nor, in the heat of the moment, had he noticed that in the course of the action, a man in a black suit had sidled up to Porter. He was about fifty years old and had white hair, black eyebrows, and a friendly demeanor. When he walked back in through the door, Porter motioned him to come over. "Al Jennings," he said, "I have the pleasure of introducing you to Thomas Edison. It's not often that the Wizard of Menlo Park ventures in from New Jersey, but the commencement of production on *The Great Train Robbery* is a momentous occasion."

The two men shook hands. "I take it shooting at the tenderfoot was your idea," Edison said.

"That's right. I once saw a cowboy pull that stunt in a saloon in Muskogee, and it stuck with me."

"Glad it did. I'm from Ohio, Porter's a Pennsylvanian—if we want to have the real flavor of the West in our picture, we're lucky to have an authentic cowpoke like yourself."

The next day, Jennings awoke at an ungodly hour, dressed, picked up a satchel from where he had left it on the floor the night before, walked to the ferry station, rode the ferry to Hoboken, and from there took the Erie-Lackawanna train to Orange. From Orange he walked ten minutes or so to a nearby livery stable, following the directions he'd been given yesterday. There he found Ed Porter, the bad men and saloon carousers from the day before, and some new faces. Gesturing to the two bandits, Porter said, "This is Frank Hanaway—he served the U.S. cavalry. I cast him because he can fall off a galloping horse without killing himself. And this here is George Barnes—I found him on the stage of Huber's Museum, and I thought he looked ornery enough to be a robber. He's from Scotland but don't hold that against him. And our next two bandits, added at your suggestion." The director called over a handsome young man. "Meet Max Aronson. He was the star of one of our comedy shorts, 'The Messenger's Mistake,' and he's ready for bigger things."

"I didn't tell you, Ed," said the youth. "I'm changing my name for the stage—it's Anderson now."

Porter let that pass without comment. "And finally, Alfred Abedie, whom you've met." With Abedie in Western garb, Jennings almost didn't recognize the gent from the wind-grate gag on 23rd Street.

Porter and the four men got on horses, and the director led them to a stretch of train tracks not far from the station, where there was a substantial water tower. Jennings followed on foot and saw Porter put them in position crouched behind the tower. Then he gave a signal, and a train approached. When it stopped to pick up water, the four scurried over and surreptitiously climbed between the first two cars. Then the train pulled away.

That was probably the simplest scene in the whole production. For the rest of that day and the entirety of the next one, Jennings and the other players went from one situation to the next, with little time in between to catch their breaths or make sense of what just happened. And indeed, the plot initially seemed an exercise in absurdity. The company went from the water tower to a hilly, wooded part of Essex County Park a couple of miles away, with the bandits being pursued by the posse from the dance hall, including Jennings; Hanaway indeed pantomimed being shot from his horse, and survived the fall without a scratch. That was followed by a scene in which Jennings (having switched from a broad-brimmed hat to a derby and dispensed with his bandanna) and a few dozen other people who had been recruited from a nearby factory were forced from the passenger cars at gunpoint and robbed by the bad men. Jennings was bewildered until Barnes explained to him that moving pictures characteristically were shot out of sequence; all the elements were sorted into the right order in the editing room.

Jennings wasn't in the most exciting scene. The others told him about it over beers at a West Orange tavern after shooting was finished. Following Jennings' suggestion, the locomotive and the coal car, or tender, had indeed been separated from the rest of the train, and Porter set up his camera in back of the tender. As it ran, Hanaway and Barnes climbed up on the car and Hanaway held the engineer (a real engineer on the Lackawanna line) up at gunpoint. Meanwhile, the fireman (likewise the genuine article) emerged with a shovel and attempted to engage Barnes in combat. In a furious fight, the bad man got him on the ground. At that point, Porter stopped shooting and directed the engineer to stop the train.

"The fireman got off and was replaced by a dummy in the same outfit," Barnes said. "The train and the camera started up again, and I pummeled him with a lump of coal and threw him off the train. We happened to be on a bridge about a hundred feet above a road, and the fake fell directly in front of a trolley car packed with passengers. Well, it shrieked to a stop, and the motorman and all the passengers came running toward the 'victim' in high panic. When they realized what it was, all they could do was stare up at us, completely perplexed."

Jennings caught the last ferry back to Manhattan. In his pocket were thirty dollars and Edwin Porter's business card. His satchel was empty, as he had presented to Porter its contents—the manuscript of *The Long Riders*—and the director had promised to read it and consider it as the basis of his next "Western." It was just the latest sign that the trip to New York, taken as a sort of lark, was proving to be unexpectedly profitable.

CHAPTER XVII

One evening Porter wandered over to the Vallambrosa. He had been avoiding calling on Anna because he was embarrassed by what had happened at Hammerstein's. A good part of the embarrassment, he rather dimly realized, stemmed from the fact that he cared for her. As such, he wanted to know how she was doing. But when he knocked on the door there was no answer, and the landlady informed him she had left the week before, no forwarding address.

He proceeded to walk down to Chinatown. He was drawn by curiosity. A week or so before, on Pell Street, a Chinese man with the rather peculiar name of Mock Dock had been shot, apparently by members of a tong, or gang, that was challenging his own organization, Woo Ling, for supremacy. That interpretation was supported when, two nights later, there was a gunfight between members of the two tongs. A member of Woo Ling was arrested, and the newspapers reported that he was wearing a coat of mail weighing at least seventy-five pounds and consisting of little rings of steel woven together. The protective garment was so heavy that he couldn't run away, hence his capture.

Porter figured things had died down enough that it was safe to take a look around. From Chatham Square he ventured into narrow, brief Doyers Street; it had a sharp turn roughly at its midpoint, dubbed the "bloody angle" because of the way marauding tongs escaped behind it for cover.

He found himself in front of a striking scene. A diminutive

woman was gathering crates and boxes and assembling them under the fire escape of a tenement building. She climbed the flimsy structure and attempted to propel herself onto the fire escape, but it was too high. She descended back to the street and peered up into a second-story window. Behind it, the face of a Chinese man regarded her with (it appeared to Porter) a combination of impassivity and disdain. There was no question but that Porter would cross the street to talk to her.

As he approached, she raised her eyes to look at him. She was wearing a dark suit and a dark hat, she was about his age, and—he was surprised to note—she was Black. It was too late to change the sentence he had composed in his mind, but he was able to round off some of the flat vowels of his native accent. "Might I be of assistance, ma'am?"

The woman took a moment to assess him. "Well, sir," she finally said, "that depends on how far you are willing to insinuate yourself into a difficult situation." Porter said nothing and she went on. "I know this to be a disorderly house, and managed to gain entry earlier this evening. Behind a closed door, I heard the cries of a girl, pleading to be let go. When I tried to get in, the men threw me out. As you saw, I had no luck gaining entry through the fire escape."

Though habitually reserved, Porter was only on rare occasions speechless. This was one of them. Finally, he managed to get out a question. "Is this the first time you have attempted such a rescue?"

"Hardly," she answered, without changing her expression. "Releasing girls from this form of bondage has been my occupation for ten years or more. But Mr. . . ." Porter gave his name, and a slight bow. "Mr. Porter, I would be happy to recount my history on some other occasion. But time is pressing. I don't know if that girl is in physical danger, or possibly about to be spirited out through a rear entrance. You asked if you could be of assistance. Does the question still hold?"

The writer nodded.

"Good," the woman said. "Now, I happen to know a patrolman

in this precinct who, unusually for his breed, is not in the pocket of the pimps and cadets. The 6th precinct station is around the corner. I will go fetch the officer if you stand watch. If you see anyone leave this building, call for me, as loudly as you can." He nodded again, and she turned and walked away quickly, almost running. She looked back over her shoulder and said, "My name is Hattie."

Porter had watched the door for less than five minutes when Hattie swept back, a young police officer in her wake. She had apparently informed him of the circumstances, for he climbed the stoop of the building and began banging on the front door. There was no response. He turned to Hattie, looking rather sheepish, and said, "This is a strong door. I don't think I'll be able get it down without a battering ram, and we don't have one at the precinct."

"I don't think that'll be necessary," Hattie said. "Mr. Porter, come with me. Officer Maloney, wait here."

Oddly, it didn't seem odd that Hattie was giving the orders. Porter followed her around the corner to Pell Street, where she knocked on a door and was given a friendly greeting by an older woman, also Black. The three of them went to the rear of the house, against which was leaning a ladder. Hattie hoisted the front, Porter the rear, and they transported it back to Doyers Street, creating a spectacle which heartily amused the passersby.

At their destination, they placed the ladder against the building and Hattie and Maloney climbed to the fire escape, then ascended to the roof. Porter lost sight of them, but seconds later he heard a crash of glass. Presently, they emerged from the front door. Maloney had his arm around a Chinese man, and Hattie had hers around a girl of no more than sixteen, wearing a simple frock that a charitable observer would call a dress, and a less charitable one, rags.

The four paused when they got to Porter. Hattie said, "I had a feeling we could get through the skylight. Mr. Porter, assistance you offered and assistance you gave, for which I thank you. And now I am taking this unfortunate child to the Gerry Society."

Porter said, "Can I see you again?" Hattie seemed nonplussed, and he quickly added, "I would like to offer whatever help I can." She said, "I am on the streets every night. I usually embark from Chatham Square around six." And then she turned on her heel and strode away.

The following day, Porter needed to finish a story for *Everybody's*. It was based on a yarn he'd heard at the penitentiary from a Recluse Club member from Knoxville, Tennessee. This fellow claimed to have enlisted a Native American graduate of Carlisle College to masquerade as a chief and monosyllabically endorse a snake-oil remedy at county fairs across the Plains. The tricky part was getting down the voice of the narrator, whom Porter called Jeff Peters. By lunchtime, he had a sentence in which the cadence revealed itself. The grafters' product, he wrote, was called "Sum-wah-tah, the great Indian Remedy made from a prairie herb revealed by the Great Spirit in a dream to his favorite medicine men, the great chiefs McGarrity and Siberstein, bottlers, Chicago."

After that, the story, which he called "The Atavism of John Tom Little Bear," came easily. He telephoned Cosgrove, the editor, and instructed him to send a messenger by five o'clock, with the remainder of his fee. (Porter had already spent the first seventy-five percent.) He only made the boy wait fifteen minutes. The last thing he wrote was a line at the end of the first paragraph, referring to Jeff Peters: "He is a man of the Hadji breed, of a hundred occupations, with a story to tell (when he will) of each one." Some of those stories, he felt sure, would pour out in the months and years ahead.

All day, every time he put down his pen, he found himself thinking about the previous night's adventure, and his closing question to Hattie. "Can I see you again?" Where had *that* come from? He smiled at the thought of how the home folks back in Greensboro would react to his speaking that way to the likes of her. But his next thought was that he had left Greensboro behind, long ago. He walked out the door and made his way to the Third Avenue trolley.

Stepping out at Chatham Square a minute before six, almost at once he saw Hattie entering the square from the east, accompanied by a brown-haired girl of about twenty. Porter greeted them, and gestured to a bench where all three could sit. Hattie took the seat between Porter and the girl, smoothed her skirts, and said, "Mr. Porter, I had a feeling I would encounter you again, but frankly, not so soon."

Porter made a slight bow. "To be frank myself—I have never witnessed anything as extraordinary as the events of last night. And it left me with a lot of questions."

"I will try to answer them," Hattie said. "But first I have one for you. Your speech tells me you are a not a native of these parts. So where do you come from?"

His accent was one thing Porter couldn't fully disguise. (No doubt there were others as well.) So he told her the truth.

"I thought you sounded familiar," said Hattie. "I am from Randolph County. Grew up on a farm there. Perhaps our people had some connection in times past."

The suggestion hung in the air for a minute, like a child's balloon. Porter had no comment, nor could he concoct one, and Hattie went on.

"I'll tell you a little about myself, and if you have any remaining questions, I can try to answer them. My last name is Rose. I came to this city more than twenty-five years ago, and for a few years, I . . . I plied the trade. Then I realized the advantage lay with the people who had control of the operation. I acquired a house downtown—in Wooster Street—then took on several more, in the Tenderloin, on San Juan Hill. White houses, and colored houses, and some black and tans. I paid the police the protection they asked for, and I wasn't bothered. My downfall was playing policy. I relied on *The Policy Player's Dream Book*, and it led me down the garden path. I kept putting too much on the wrong number, and before I realized that my dreams were unreliable, I was down $10,000 or more. I couldn't afford the protection, and I got sent to the Island."

She was referring, Porter knew, to Blackwell's Island, a sliver of land between Manhattan and Queens that housed New York City's jail, as well as various workhouses and asylums. It was where Soapy, the bum Porter had seen hauled off on his first morning in town, had presumably spent the winter. That thought led Porter to an amusing notion.

Hattie interrupted his reverie. "I was raised in the church," she went on. "During my time in the business I told myself that if I weren't doing this, someone else would. And that I treated my girls well. But lying on a cot in a cell, such statements felt more and more empty and vain. When I was released, I turned over the proverbial new leaf. And since 1893, I have devoted my time to investigating the social evil and helping girls escape from it."

"Emma Hartig is one of those I've helped," she said, gesturing to her companion. "Emma, please meet Mr. Porter, who aided me in rescuing an unfortunate last night and who is interested in my battle because. . . well, why is it, sir?"

"I write stories," he said, and immediately realized how blunt that sounded. "Yes," he went on, "I write short stories for the magazines. You may have seen one or two. I sign them 'O.Henry.'" The women showed no sign of recognition.

"I hasten to add," he continued, "that my tales are not like the Arabian Knights or Red Riding Hood. What I try to do is illuminate the lives of not the Four Hundred but . . . but the four million, of people in this city of all the walks of life.

"Therefore, I seek my fellow citizens out and listen to what they have to say. It is a little surprising how ready, sometimes eager, they are to talk. But I am not—or I do not like to think of myself as—a dressmaker, merely in search of material as a commodity. Each of the four million is a person, with his own sadness, aspirations, occasional joy or triumph. I want to do right by them."

It struck Porter that he had just given his longest speech since his time seeing the town with Anna, when, for some reason, he had so often found himself in an expository mode.

Hattie chuckled. "A writer," she said. "Well, that is a new one. But we will take help where we can get it."

"I applaud your efforts," Porter said. "But isn't yours a dangerous pursuit for a lady, even one as accomplished as you?"

Hattie smiled. "I have been threatened, and on a few occasions struck, but never suffered serious injury. I know my way out of a dangerous situation. And if the moment calls for it, I have this." She opened her purse and took out a Double Derringer pistol.

After putting the weapon away, Hattie explained that she had long had her eye on a house around the corner at 116 Pell Street, but had not been able to gain entry. "Are you willing to be an under-cover investigator?" she asked Porter. Before he had a chance to answer, she said, "I must say that this will not merely be a matter of observing and taking down notes for a short story. I am employed by the Committee of Fourteen, and in order to take action against an immoral resort, the Committee needs evidence. What I mean to say is, you will have to pretend to be interested in obtaining the services offered. Then you will have to follow through, playing the part, until just before you would have . . . committed the act. If that's not acceptable to you, we can part on friendly terms right now."

Porter's immediate impulse was to demur. He was a writer, an observer, not a crusader. But he held his tongue. It occurred to him that New York, in its vastness, gave one cover to try on a different identity. He certainly had some experience in acting, not only in the cons he used to pull, but in the various masks he donned—a different one, it sometimes seemed, for every person he was with. At the very least, this enterprise would provide some prime material for future stories. He told Hattie he would undertake the assignment.

She didn't seem surprised. She gave him more complete instructions—mostly that he should make a mental note of as many details as he could, and that, to the extent possible, he should refrain from making an actual request for services, instead letting them be offered to him—and told him to meet them, when he was done, at Chay Heong Hen, a basement restaurant around the corner in Doyers Street.

The two women walked Porter up Bowery to the corner of Pell, then took their leave, so it would appear that he was alone. He approached the door of 116, opened it, and found himself in a barroom. There were twelve or fifteen men in the place, and he felt twenty-four or thirty eyes were fixed on him. He understood that to carry out his assignment, he had to be "one of the bunch." So he had a glass of beer at the bar and joined the men in telling stories and singing songs. After a while, he was approached by a man in suspenders and a derby hat.

"Do you want to go upstairs?" he asked, with no preamble. "We have twelve girls and you may find three or four to your disposal."

Porter nodded and, passing through what struck him as a dirty small hole of a room, came to the hotel entrance hallway. He ascended the stairs and, as he reached the fourth floor, he saw, in fact, nine or ten girls, all in fancy costume, seated and standing around the room. A dark-haired, heavyset woman not much older than the girls—Porter would have estimated her weight as 160 pounds and her age as twenty-two or twenty-three—was sitting in a rocking chair, and at that moment receiving half a dollar from one of the girls. Porter took a seat, and in a matter of a quarter hour observed at least ten men enter the room. He noticed the pattern. They would not speak to a girl, but nod their head or beckon. With that, the girl would go to the sink, take a tin pail and fill it with water, get a towel from the bureau, and silently lead her customer down the hall to a chamber.

The setting made him think about the uptown houses he'd frequented from time to time. They had a patina of decorum and even glamour. While you were there, you could forget the transaction that lay behind them. But at the root of it, he thought, were they any different from this tawdry hallway?

Eventually the madam glared at Porter and said, "Hey mister, hurry up and get fucked. There is others waiting." So he gestured to the girl closest to him, who had red hair and a downcast expression. It occurred to him that she was only a couple of years older than Margaret. She took the towel and the bucket of water and led him into a room without windows, about eight by ten feet in diameter, containing nothing but an old bed, a washstand with a piece of soap on it, and one chair. Cheap chromos hung on the wall, dingy with age. To counter his nervousness, Porter concentrated on Hattie's instruction to take note of everything that happened.

He sat down on the chair and asked the girl her name. She said, "We don't give our names here." She asked for fifty cents, which Porter handed to her. Next, without a word, the girl opened his pants, took out his penis and washed it with the towel, the soap and the water from the bucket. It all happened so suddenly that Porter didn't have a chance to protest or even react. Then she lay down on the bed and pulled her clothes up above her shirtwaist. She was wearing nothing, Porter saw, but the skirt and the waist. It all happened so quickly that he had no words. His only (rather ridiculous) thought was to try not to blush.

The girl said, "Come on, hurry up."

Hearing the words seemed to restore Porter's equilibrium and power of speech. He figured that by this point, he had followed through to Hattie's specifications. "Oh hell, I am too drunk," he said. "I can't do it. Get up and get dressed."

The color rushed to her face. "I'm sorry that happened—but it's not my fault is it?" Porter assured her it wasn't. The girl rose from the bed and put on her clothes. The two of them walked silently into the parlor, where she gave the madam the fifty cents and produced a white card, in which the madam appeared to punch a hole.

Porter retreated down the stairs. When he reached the saloon, the man in suspenders said to him, "Well, how do you feel since you have satisfied your animal passions?" Porter didn't answer, just walked out the door into the night air.

He made his way to the pre-arranged spot, to find Hattie Rose and Emma Hartig outside, waiting for him expectantly. They walked down a few steps into the restaurant, which was bright, clean and spare. The polished-wood tables had no condiments on them, just simple flatware; the walls were bare except for a sign warning customers to look after their own coats and umbrellas. Hattie explained to Porter that there were choices: chop suey with a cup of tea and a bowl of rice for twenty-five cents, or the same with mushrooms added to the chop suey, for thirty-five. Porter opted for the fungi-less version, as did his companions. Hattie relayed the order to a pigtailed waiter, with whom she seemed to be on familiar terms.

In a couple of minutes, the waiter set one cup, containing dry tea leaves, and two saucers in front of each of them. He poured boiling water in the cups, then covered them with saucers. Hattie explained that they needed to wait for the tea to steep.

Porter nodded and said, "Well, Hattie, your suspicions were confirmed. One hundred and sixteen Pell Street is indeed an immoral house."

"Mr. Porter," Hattie said, "I am not a doctor of literature, but I know enough to say that your sentence would not be acceptable in a short story. It is completely lacking in detail, and general enough to be useless. Please tell us the particulars of your experience. Whatever it is, I'm sure both Emma and I have heard and seen worse. And have some tea before you start. It will fortify you for the task."

All three of them took a sip of the hot brew. Porter related what had happened, sparing little (except the full measure of his own embarrassment). When he had finished, Hattie said, "Well done, sir. All the Committee will need is an affidavit spelling out what you just told me, signed by you and notarized."

"Narratives are my line of work," he said. "Deadlines are usually my downfall, but rarely am I in the position where my writing can achieve some good. I will be sure to have it posted by the end of the day tomorrow."

"But let me ask you some questions," he went on. "Is this the typical set-up for an operation of this sort? What is the punch-card system? And what about the girls? How are they recruited? How are they compelled to stay? And—"

Before Hattie had a chance to answer, the waiter arrived with three heaping dishes of chop suey, three bowls of rice, and three small dishes of black sauce. Hattie and Emma bowed their heads in grace. Porter had no difficulty going through the motions. He had had a lot of practice.

Hattie raised her head. "Those are good questions, but I would need a lot longer than one evening to answer them fully. I can make a start, however. The establishment you visited is known as a parlor house. They are spread all over Manhattan, and the other boroughs as well. One sixteen Pell Street is a fifty-cent house, the lowest.

"As you saw, the madams or housekeepers have a punch similar to those used by railroad conductors. When a customer is secured, the girl hands the madame a square piece of cardboard, in which she punches a hole. At the end of the night, for each hole punched, she is paid half the proceeds. I have seen one such card from a notorious one-dollar house in West 28th Street, representing a single day's work by one inmate. It had thirty holes in it.

"Now, understand that this woman did not keep fifteen dollars. She has to pay back the fee or commission her procurer had received for her. She has to pay exorbitant prices for the jewelry and gowns she was given as part of her costume. She has to pay for regular medical examinations, and she has to pay for room and board, charged at twice the rate of a boarding house. As a result, not only has she no money but she is in constant debt to the madame and whoever *her* boss is. One hears of 'white slaves' being drugged and kept in chains, and other such fairy stories, but lack of money, in my opinion, is the real reason why they stay."

Hattie hadn't touched the meal in front of her. She took a bite and seemed to find it satisfactory. "As to how the girls join the enterprise in the first place, my own experience took place some twenty years ago," she said. "If Emma is willing to tell you her story, you will get a better sense of what happens nowadays."

The younger woman nodded. "It was about four years ago," she said. She had the remnants of a German accent. "I was fifteen years old. I could no longer live at home. I wanted to go and take a position somewhere. I took a German newspaper, the *Herald and Journal*, and there was an advertisement for a waitress at Number 32 First Street. I meant to go there and do a respectable business as a waitress, but when I got there I found myself in an improper place."

"Why did you stay?" Porter asked.

Emma replied immediately. "Because I would not return home."

"Were things so bad with your parents?"

"I did not like to go back to my father. I didn't like to go back home because my father never treated me right. So this woman who kept 32 First Street said she would be a mother to me, and I thought I would stay. I didn't know she wanted me to do anything wrong until I was there for about two or three hours. From that place, 32 First Street, I went to 212 Forsyth Street. That was a bad house, too. From Forsyth Street I went uptown to Fourth Avenue, No. 89.

"There were a good many girls in those places, and a great many young girls circulating through all those places on the East Side. A few as young as I was. But a great many, sixteen and seventeen years of age. I could not count them, there is so many.

"There are a great many men living in that district who take money away from the girls when they earn it. These men do nothing to support themselves, they just live idle lives and go around and don't do any work—just take the money of the girls. Some of those men stand on the sidewalk in front of the houses on the East Side and invite other men to go in, like a puller-inner at a store.

"Those men, first they make out that they like the girls, and then after they say: 'Well, now, if you don't stick to me, I'll tell the police,' and all that kind of stories, and the girls get kind of frightened, and then they commence to give their money to him, and sometimes if they don't give the money to him they get licked. I know such a man as that. He throwed a chair at me to make me give up my money. He hurted me."

"Did you think of going to the police?" asked Porter. Emma and Hattie exchanged a glance, and the girl uttered a sort of muffled laugh.

"I don't think the police are much good," she said. "Sometimes the police go in these houses and get treated to drinks and whiskey and they don't care much about it if a girl goes on the street. A police officer in uniform came into the house regularly. He never paid. The proprietor of the house was glad to have policemen come, because if they come in it is easier for them to treat the policemen so they keep their mouth shut. I remember when I was at No. 32 First Street, a police officer coming in. We used to call him Charlie; he used to come there once or twice a week, and sometimes oftener, and the madam would call me because I was the youngest girl in the house."

"The madam once told me, 'There's no danger of being pulled as long as I come up with the long green.' After a while," she went on, "I got going to McGurk's."

Porter recognized the name. McGurk's had been closed now for a couple of years, but in its time, as he had read in the endless accounts in the yellow press, it was known as "Suicide Hall" because so many women who plied their wares there tried to commit suicide in the saloon or the hotel above it—reportedly six deaths and seven failed attempts in 1899 alone. The most notorious, Blonde Madge Davenport and Big Mame, made a pact to end their suffering and bought carbolic acid at a nearby pharmacy. Davenport took her dose and died in agony. But Big Mame inadvertently splashed most of the acid on her face and was left with a life sentence of disfigurement and misery. Porter asked Emma if she had known any of the girls who had taken their lives.

Emma nodded. "I was one of them. I was one of the girls that got tired and took poison, not enough to kill me, thank God. I was arrested in a raid, and I got better, and that resulted in my changing my life. I am living now outside of the city, with decent people, and enjoying a comfortable, good life. I only come down to the city sometimes to help Hattie or Rose Livingston."

Hattie explained that Rose, dubbed "the Angel of Chinatown," was in the same line of work as she was. Her particular advantage was that she was slim, had a masculine looking face, and cut her hair short; when she wore men's clothes on undercover missions, no one suspected she was a woman. And, of course, she was white.

Emma had come to the end of her story. "All of this I experienced in five months," she said. "Pretty rapid life for a little girl. I am glad I am out of it."

It was past ten o'clock, and they had all had a long night. Porter picked up the check, which amounted to seventy-five cents, and paid the cashier next to the door. They agreed to meet the next day, same time, same place. They parted outside the restaurant and Porter walked home under a starless sky. The entire way, and into his rooms, until he finally succumbed to sleep, he had in his mind's eye the image of the young girl without a name, approaching him with downcast eyes.

CHAPTER XVIII

A WEEK LATER, Porter sought Hattie Rose out in Chatham Square as she was beginning her nightly rounds. He told her, with as much delicacy as he could muster, that he wanted to continue aiding her cause, but was not prepared to continue the role he had played in Pell Street. She said she understood and would call on him, as needed, for other services. Just two nights later, as he was laboring on another Jeff Peters story, the telephone rang. It was Hattie. She said she could use him that evening: she wanted to visit a suspicious saloon called Barron Wilkins' Little Savoy, in the Tenderloin, and unaccompanied ladies were not admitted. Would he act as her escort? He said he would be there.

"Dress for a night out on the town," she said, before hanging up.

When he reached the entrance—in Thirty-Fifth Street, west of Sixth Avenue, Hattie was already there. Porter greeted her with a bow, then hesitated. Something had been on his mind and he was reluctant to divulge it. She sensed his discomfort. "What's the trouble, Mr. Porter?" she said. "I promised I wouldn't force you into anything like the other night, and I don't go back on my word."

"It isn't that. But I wonder. Will we be accepted as . . . as a pair?"

"Oh, I see. You can put your mind at ease. Wilkins is a colored man, and the Little Savoy is a 'black and tan.' The rare sort of establishment where people like you and people like me are equally welcome." Porter felt his face redden. "And it would be good, anyway," she went on, "for us to keep our distance. I need to see how, or if, you are solicited. Let them wonder about the exact nature of our relationship."

A few steps into the entrance they were enveloped in tobacco smoke and loud music, coming from a three-piece band, that to Porter sounded like a cacophony. "Ragtime," Hattie whispered to him. When his eyes focused, he saw couples—Blacks and whites, women and men, paired in every possible combination—dancing in a way that left nothing to the imagination. It was certainly nothing like the ice cream socials where he and Athol had waltzed and courted, back in Austin. The dancers wrapped their arms around each other, cheeks and bodies touching, as if burrowing into each other. One girl had a black cigar in her teeth, which seemed to greatly amuse the others. The women dressed in a bizarre array of outfits: knee dresses, or tights to the hips; Buster Browns with bare arms; a boy's swimming costume; baseball uniforms; jockey suits; and even an ordinary boy's knickerbocker suit, with very short and skimpy knickers. All had low-cut tops showing plentiful decolletage.

The place was rather opulently done up. Tables and Vienna chairs were arranged around the bandstand and dance floor; there was a long bar at one end, and the wall in the rear was covered with a large mural of a nude woman. Porter and Hattie found a table to the side, sat opposite each other, and took in the surroundings. After a couple of minutes, a woman with curly brown hair sat down at their table, without invitation. She ignored Hattie, introduced herself as Ruby, and asked Porter if he would "treat" her to a Champagne cocktail. After he flagged down a waiter and made the order, she asked what kind of work he did. He relied on his powers of invention for a living, but at this moment his mind was a blank. "I'm a writer," he said, rather dully.

"Oooh, a writer," said Ruby. "I know a poem:

Here is the girl with the big brown navel,
The cheeks of her ass as round as a table,

The color of her pussy is red as a rose,
And how many she fucked, Christ only knows."

For the second time in ten minutes, Porter blushed. That seemed to embolden Ruby, who said, "Why do women wear black stockings?" Porter gathered that was a riddle, and he didn't really want to know the answer, but Ruby presented it anyway: "Their legs are in mourning for all the stiffs that have been buried alive inside of them."

"Who's this?" she asked, gesturing at Hattie.

Porter gave the first answer that came to mind: "A business colleague."

The girl grunted. "Well, what do you say?" she demanded. "The rooms are right upstairs."

Porter glanced at Hattie with an imploring look. She seemed to understand it, and gave a slight nod. "Look here, Ruby," he said. "It is delightful to make your acquaintance. But I will be frank. I am not going to be a customer for you tonight and I don't want to waste your time. If you find yourself thirsty, please come back and I'll buy you another drink. But otherwise, I promise that you will find greener pastures elsewhere."

Ruby stood up and, with an aggrieved expression on her face, said, "I am sure I do not understand what you mean. Good evening to *you*, Mr. Writer." She drained her cocktail and disappeared to a room behind the bar. Porter had noticed women coming in and out of it since he and Hattie had entered.

"Well done, Mr. Porter," Hattie said. "And you do not have to worry about our Ruby. She earned half the price of that drink, and I have no doubt she'll do very well for herself before the night is over."

Presently a Black woman walked to the bandstand and started to sing low songs. She slurred the words to the point and Porter couldn't make most of them out, but he heard her sing, "There'll come a time when a whore won't need no man, lordy, lordy." Then she sang a song that began "O, that night of mystery," and after that, a rendition of "Row, Row, Row," with lyrics Porter had never heard before, which left nothing to the imagination, and which the audience greeted with peals of laughter. When the band went into instrumental sequences, she affected a look of boredom and picked up a novel by Victoria Cross.

After one number ended, Porter glanced toward the door and saw two uniformed police officers walk in. His first thought was that the saloon was going to be raided. His first thought was wrong. In short order, one of the cops had taken off his hat and coat and was dancing with a woman. They fit right in with the tough dancing done by the other patrons, with one addition: the cop gave his club to his partner, and she put it on the floor and used it to imitate a Scottish Highlands sword dance.

After about an hour, Hattie told Porter she had seen all she needed to in order to present her report. They began preparing to leave, but then Porter saw something that stopped him in his tracks. The door behind the bar opened, and out of it stepped . . . Anna Lockhart. She looked as he had never seen her before, lips painted, cheeks rouged, hair pinned up high above her head, wearing a tight-fitting red dress with a decolletage that left little to the imagination. But it was her. For a moment he didn't know whether to flee the place or stay. But the decision was made for him when her gaze landed on his, and a look close to horror came over her face. She slowly walked to the table. By the time she got there, her visage was composed and Porter was standing. "Miss Lockhart," he said with a bow, "please make the acquaintance of Miss Rose."

For a moment the three of them sat in awkward silence. Hattie Rose broke it. "You can call me Hattie," she said. "And may I call you . . ."

"Anna. And yes, of course."

"I have only known Mr. Porter . . . how long has it been?" Hattie asked, seeming to consult her own memory rather than his. "Well, I suppose two weeks, though it seems longer. But each time I meet him I find out something new. Anna, you appear to have a somewhat longer acquaintance with the gentleman."

"Yes, we have a history. You'll excuse me if I don't care to go into all the particulars at the moment. But as I recall, the last time we saw each other was outside Hammerstein's roof garden theater."

"Ah," said Hattie. "That is a bit farther uptown than I generally go. But I understand that the entertainment and the atmosphere are wonderful."

"Yes, wonderful," said Anna.

Porter had the sense that he should say something, too. "Wonderful," he repeated.

Another uncomfortable silence ensued. This time it was Porter who spoke first. "Miss Lockhart, it would be a great honor if you would join me for luncheon tomorrow."

Anna opened her mouth but nothing seemed to come out.

"I insist," Porter said. "We have a lot to discuss. Among other things, I have never properly thanked you for this."

He reached into his pocket and pulled out the miniature she had given him. When he opened it, he was struck by how young she looked. "Miss Lockhart is a woman of many gifts," he told Hattie. To Anna, he said, "One p.m. at the New Amsterdam Hotel, Park Avenue near Twenty-first Street. Do I have your word?"

Anna found herself nodding, despite herself.

"And now," Porter said, "we really must go."

Over the next fifteen hours—or all but two or three of them, when he fell into a troubled sleep—Porter thought about little other than Anna. He wasn't really surprised by her fate. It was what happened to working girls who disappeared, was it not? But why hadn't he fully recognized that she *had* disappeared, and made more of an effort to find her? In the period just before dawn, lying in his bed fully alert, his own defenses and justifications had broken down enough for him to construct a clearly connected sequence of events: their "courtship" and the false promises he had never laid out in words but had nonetheless implied; their confrontation outside Hammerstein's; her disappearance from the

Vallambrosa. Why hadn't he bothered to seek her out at Siegel-Cooper? He had no answer. What Porter had to do, he realized, as dawn finally arrived and he permitted himself to rise, was learn what had happened in the gaps. And set things right, as best as he could.

"Setting things right" would surely involve yet another financial obligation, and thus an even more pressing need for income. So in the morning he tried to apply himself to a story. But nothing came to him, and finally he gave up and decided to take a long walk to clear his head. At luncheon the day before, Bob Davis had mentioned "the most picturesque bit of rear tenement that exists in New York," and given the location. And so Porter made his way to Sixth Avenue and walked south, past the Jefferson Market Police Court, into Greenwich Village, past Sheridan Park, and down Grove Street to the very end. Between the front houses, Nos. 10 and 12, was the spot Davis had referred to—an opening leading onto a bare, dreary yard. At the back of it were three three-story houses, the windows of which looked out diagonally on the blank side of the brick house twenty yards away. An old, old ivy vine, gnarled and decayed at the roots, climbed halfway up the wall. Some malady had stricken its leaves from the vine until its skeleton branches clung, almost bare, to the crumbling bricks.

For some reason, the scene put him in mind of an episode in Murger's *Vie de Bohéme*; he had recently been reading the novel and was amused by the implicit comparison between the original Bohemians and their New York descendants, Sloan and Bellows and their circle, whom he had encountered at places like Moquin's and who were starting to populate these very Greenwich Village streets. He had just read the chapter about the love affair between the painter Marcel and the "honest and pretty girl" Musette. When they meet, he buys her a pot of flowers, and she promises to stay in his garret as long as the flowers remain unfaded. Day after day, they keep their life. Then one morning, Marcel wakes up early and finds Musette watering the flowers, as she has done each night while he sleeps.

Something of the sort could be done, he thought, with the old vine on the brick wall.

He made his way uptown and arrived at the restaurant with five minutes to spare. Presently, he spied Anna approaching from the north on Fourth Avenue. She walked with a sort of regal bearing and, in an uncanny way, the other pedestrians seemed to shrink before her. As she came into view, Porter saw that she was dressed very differently from the night before. She wore a dark gray wool suit. The bodice was double-breasted and sharply tailored, with a double row of buttons and leg-of-mutton sleeves. Her skirt was simple, fitting closely at the waist and spreading at the bottom to form a short train. She wore a cream-colored shirtwaist topped with a stiff collar and black necktie. To top it off, she had on a large, broad-brimmed hat adorned with a rainbow of ostrich feathers, which made Porter think of their old feather-curler friend Hetty.

He had chosen the New Amsterdam less for its cuisine than for the privacy it afforded. It actually contained four different dining rooms—each with its own entrance on the avenue. Porter selected the door farthest south, which opened on just a mite of a room, decorated in warm reds and quiet greens. A waiter led them to the table Porter had reserved. Before they even picked up their menus, Anna said, "If you could have seen the look on your face last night."

Porter, nonplussed, said nothing.

"Actually," Anna went on, with a light laugh, "it looks a little bit like your face right now."

"I hadn't seen you for so long, and, admittedly, I was not expecting you to appear at the Little Savoy."

"It's where I ply my trade, just as you produce your sentences in your rooms in Irving Place."

"Look here, Anna," Porter said, "I cannot continue to talk calmly about what I witnessed. Looking at you today, you appear to be in good health. I see no bruises or signs of distress. But how did you end up in such a locale? Were you drugged? Abducted? I have had some personal experience with the white slave trade"—he found himself blushing, yet again—"and cannot bear the thought of what you must have endured."

Anna took a long look at him. "Let's order our luncheon," she said, "and then I can tell you the whole sordid tale."

They perused the menu and called for the waiter. Anna said, "I'll have a celery salad and a Vichy water." Porter looked at her quizzically and said, "And nothing else?"

"No," she replied, "That will be sufficient." He shrugged and asked for a tenderloin steak with mushrooms and Lyonnaise potatoes, and a bottle of Ballantine Ale to drink. He had planned to order a dozen oysters as well, but that seemed excessive in the light of Anna's Spartan repast.

When the waiter had departed, Anna began to speak, dispassionately. "There was no abduction or knock-out drops. If you ask your friend Hattie Rose about it, she will tell you such cases are quite rare."

"Then why?..."

"Why," Anna repeated. "I'm reminded of a clever remark you once made after you had sold a couple of stories to *Munsey's Magazine*—'*Munsey's* is the root of all eatables.' It would appear that, more often than not, money is the 'why.' To put it simply, I didn't have enough."

"There is a special place in hell," Porter said, "for the men who hire working-girls, and pay 'em five or six dollars a week to live on." Once he had expressed that fine sentiment, he realized he was a bit too late for it—and he also realized that Anna was probably thinking the same thing. Pushing the thought aside, he said, "Why didn't you come to me for assistance?"

Anna smiled. "You might have a hard time believing it," she said, "but I have my pride."

She said that she had made the acquaintance of a man named Mike, who bought her nice dresses and jewelry and treated her to fine dinners. She had no illusions about what his intentions were (she said this rather pointedly), and so she wasn't surprised when, after just two weeks, he brought her to visit an establishment he funneled girls to, one of Rosie Herz's parlor houses, and asked if she would be willing to "sit in company."

Porter showed no recognition of the term, and Anna said, "On Friday and Saturday nights, there's a heavy demand, and madams bring in extra girls to handle the overflow. When I arrived at the house on the first night, I was greeted by two girls I knew from Siegel-Cooper. And I found out that most of those who sit in demand work as shopgirls or in factories and are trying to eke out a living."

"And you agreed?" Porter tried, not completely successfully, to keep the incredulity he felt out of the question.

"I did. I will never ceased to be amazed by the capacity of men to be shocked and amazed. The decision we make is to trade our bodies. Not our souls."

Porter had no response to that, and Anna went on. "Our souls wouldn't fetch nearly so high a price, in any case. What I earned in two nights nearly doubled my Siegel-Cooper salary for a week. The exchange seemed fair, and I returned the following weekend, and two more after that. Then I realized that if I worked on a full-time basis, the money would be even better.

"I could quickly see that continuing on with Rosie Herz would be a losing proposition. In quiet moments, I gathered information from the other girls, and came to the conclusion that the best course would be working out of a concert saloon and making an arrangement with a Raines Law hotel." She smiled. "As I recalled, it was you who first told me about such establishments, on our day out at North Beach."

Porter nodded. It seemed a long time ago.

"Mike introduced me to Barron Wilkins and a couple of other proprietors. The arrangement is the same at all the saloons. They supply a steady stream of potential customers. I keep all of the money I make from my customers, plus get half of what they pay for the room. I'm expected to convince my customers to buy a steady stream of drinks, and I take a cut of the bar tab.

"I have to take out expenses, of course—for clothes, rent, protection from the police, a few dollars to Mike. But I'm still left with a tidy sum. I am eating more than potatoes for my supper, and have far better accommodations than in the Vallambrosa days. And if I were still at Siegel-Cooper, do you think I would be able to afford this ensemble?" She struck a pose in the manner of a Charles Dana Gibson drawing. "I don't know how much you fetch for your stories, but I daresay that on a good week I make as much as you. Or more."

It was a lot to take in. In the moment, Porter found he was able to respond as if her life were a ledger. "Your prospects appear favorable," he said. "The only expenditure I would question is to this fellow Mike. Do you really need him."

"Oh, he's all right," Anna said. "And besides the police, he provides an added layer of protection."

They had finished their meals, and the waiter came to carry the plates away. Anna said to him, "Come to think if it, I will have a pork chop, and another Vichy. Bill? A sweet? This is on me."

In the event, Porter was able to wrestle the bill from Anna's hand, and even to refuse her offer to "go Dutch." He did not doubt that she could afford to pay for their meals, but—though everything she said had a surface logic to it—he left the restaurant less than fully convinced that she was as content as she made herself out to be. When he arrived back at his flat, he wrote a short letter and sealed and stamped it in time for the afternoon post.

Later that day, Charles Gardner left his office in the Mohawk Building at the usual time of five o'clock. He turned south on Fifth Avenue; by the time he crossed 20th Street, he had two young men in his wake, at a distance of roughly half a block. One of them wore a red cap. They stayed with him for a mile or so, as he made his way to the Bowery and finally went inside an establishment with a discrete sign that said "Little Buck's."

CHAPTER XIX

THREE NIGHTS later, just before the clocks struck nine, a stub-nosed man in a derby hat walked into Barron Wilkins' Little Savoy. He took a table for two in the corner farthest from the bandstand, and ordered a ginger ale. Each time a girl approached him, he waved her away, until they got the idea and left him alone. His steely glare seemed to convince the toughs that frequented the place to steer clear as well. Only the bald-headed waiter came to the small table, every twenty minutes, a fresh glass of ginger ale in hand.

The man in the hat surveyed the room every few minutes. Everything he saw was to be expected, with the exception of a tall young man sitting alone at a table in the opposite corner. He was wearing an odd sort of Tyrolean hat, and he had in his lap what looked to be a large sketch pad. He would look up for a moment, apply himself to the pad, then repeat the process. Across the room, the derby hat dropped a little bit lower on its wearer's brow.

The scene unfolded much as it had the previous Friday, when Porter and Hattie Rose had visited. The band struck up its syncopated tunes, the singer vocalized in her sultry way, and the diverse couples performed their primal dances. The girls descended on their quarry; more often than not, after a drink or two, the couple walked through the door behind the bar arm in arm. Then the girl would return, alone, twenty minutes later.

And, as before, a painted woman with luxurious brown hair, slightly older than the rest, walked through the door and looked around the premises. But this time she was intercepted by a mustachioed man who had been sitting at a table not far from the man with the derby hat, and who strode across the room until he stood just inches from her. He grabbed her by the arm and said, "Kiddo, you shortchanged me ten bucks yesterday."

"Mike, you know that's not true," she said.

He let go of her arm and slapped her across the face.

The man with the derby hat got up from his table and sprang across the room with a speed that belied his stolid physique and gray hair. In what seemed like an instant, he had planted himself between the woman and Mike, grabbed Mike's belt with his left hand and struck two blows with his right—the first to the midsection, the second square in the face. Mike dropped to the floor, and blood started to trickle from his nose. Looking up, he reached inside the leg of his pants and withdrew a stiletto. The man in the hat kicked Mike's arm with such force that the knife flew across the room. Then he grabbed Mike's belt again, lifted him to his feet, and struck a mighty blow to his jaw. Mike fell to the floor, face down. He didn't stir.

The man in the hat turned to the woman, who still had her hand to the cheek where she had been slapped. "Anna, is it?" he asked.

She nodded.

"You are coming with me," he said. The statement seemed to brook no dispute. "I've been instructed by a mutual friend to bring you to his flat."

He placed his jacket around her shoulders and walked her out the door. "You can call me Bat," he said.

Outside, Bat Masterson hailed a hansom cab, and within ten minutes it alighted in front of a house on the west side of Irving Place, between Seventeenth and Eighteenth Street. Number 55 was a narrow four-story brownstone. On the parlor floor was a window as large as a storefront. Standing behind the window were two men, one heavy-set and one even heavier-set. The latter was

Robert Hobart Davis; the former was William Sydney Porter, whose place of residence it was. When Porter saw Masterson and Anna step out of the cab, he rushed to greet them in the street and ushered them in through the big oak front door.

They all gathered in the parlor, illuminated by a glass-beaded chandelier. The light made Anna conscious of the thick layer of make-up she was wearing, and she asked Porter where she could wash; he directed her to the bathroom in the rear. Once she had washed, she rather regretted having done so, as the red marks left by Gaffigan's slap were in full evidence. What's done is done, she thought, and walked back in with her head high. Porter introduced Davis to her and Masterson, as the three men made an obvious and concerted effort to avert their eyes. An uncomfortable silence was broken by Davis's offer to leave what was obviously a delicate moment. Porter said, "No, Colonel, we will need the benefit of a disinterested party. Please stay."

"Yes, by all means stay, Mr. Davis," said Anna. "The more the merrier."

She directed her attention to Porter. "You should know the circumstances by which your agent, Mr. Masterson, had occasion to bring me here. They are these: he intervened in a private affair of mine, wreaked mayhem in my place of business, and essentially abducted me. I went along with him because I didn't want to create even more of a disturbance. Now, if you'll excuse me, I will bid you good night." As she rose, Masterson and Porter also leapt up, each grasping one of her forearms.

"Anna, my dear, I am not in the business of abduction," Porter said. "Of course you are free to go if you wish. But will you be willing to hear me out for just five minutes?"

She nodded—somehow managing to execute the nod in a begrudging manner.

"You don't seem to be familiar with the name Bartholomew 'Bat' Masterson," Porter said. Anna shook her head. "Then I will tell you that he is no mere ruffian. If you had grown up a little boy rather than a girl, you would have read pulp magazines and known he made his reputation as a buffalo hunter, civilian scout, and Indian fighter on the Great Plains. And as a sheriff in Dodge City, Kansas, he prevailed in some of the most notorious gunfights of the past century. He is now a resident of Bagdad on Hudson, and has turned in his six-shooter for a typewriter."

Porter pulled out a pocket watch and looked at it. "I see I have almost four minutes remaining," he said. "Bat, can you tell Mr. Davis and me what you witnessed at the Little Savoy?"

Masterson briefly recounted the altercation between Anna and Mike. "I did what was necessary," he said.

"But he didn't hurt me!" Anna remonstrated. "Really, that slap was just for show. Believe me, I know how to handle Mike Gaffigan."

The words seemed to ring hollow in the bright room. For a moment no one spoke.

"I will be brief, and blunt," Porter finally said. "In fact, I don't believe you. I know enough from what Hattie Rose has told me, and from my own eyes, to know that these pimps—and let us call a spade a spade—are no good. What they call protection is really possession. Masterson saw him slap you once, but I would wager that wasn't the first time. Nor would it be the last. You have enough experience with that sort of man to know this is so."

Anna's said nothing, merely lowered her eyes to the floor.

"How much of your earnings do you give him?" Porter went on. "And with how many other girls does he have such an arrangement?"

Again, she was silent.

"You were handed a raw deal by . . . I don't know, by the world," Porter said. "I understand that in doing what you did, you were following a sort of economic imperative. I know that at the moment, the ledger seems to be favorable. And as I say, I have no wish to hold you against your wishes. But hear me out. I cannot see your arrangement with Gaffigan as having a happy ending. I have felt that way since I saw you last week. I sent Masterson to investigate, and he confirmed my fears.

"Since then, I have been working on a plan for you. I have sung your praises to Miss Rose, and she has agreed to take you on as an undercover investigator for the Committee of Fourteen. She tells me that, often, a woman's eye is called for—one who can fit in and not attract attention, as she tends to do. You would merely enter these places with an escort and report on what you find. The pay would be ten dollars a week.

"Now I know that is less—far less—than what you currently earn. But I have another idea up my sleeve. There are a number of academies in this city that train young women to be type-writers. I will pay for you to take the course, and, once you've completed it, further commit to hire you at a good rate to convert my scrawl into neat rows of letters and words. Davis, once she has mastered the skill, will you be willing to recommend Miss Lockhart to the other writers you deal with?"

Without hesitation, Davis nodded his head.

"And I will spread the word to my other editors," Porter said. "With so many scribblers, and so many magazines, you're certain to find work."

A surge of emotion appeared to come over Anna. She had not been in New York very long, but so much had happened in that time. It was as if the city were a vast wave, buffeting her to and fro with a force that, had she not known better, she would have deemed malicious. She had had no choice but to ride it out. But now she felt the tempest beginning to calm. She closed her eyes and was able to control the urge to cry. When she opened them again, she said, "All right." But then a thought occurred to her. "What about my things? They are at my apartment and Mike is likely there. I can't face him."

Porter wrapped her in an embrace. "And you won't have to," he said when he released her. "If you give us a sense of where everything is, Masterson and I will go there and retrieve your belongings. On the way, we'll secure a room for you at the New

Amsterdam. Davis, will you stay with Miss Lockhart and bring her to the hotel in two hours' time?"

Bob Davis briefly consulted his pocket watch before turning to face Anna. "I certainly will," he said.

CHAPTER XX

NINETY MINUTES later, Porter, Masterson, and a large trunk entered the New Amsterdam Hotel. In the lobby, Davis and Anna had their chairs pulled together over a small table and were so deep in conversation that they didn't notice the two men had arrived until Masterson loudly cleared his throat. They carried Anna's trunk to the room that had been secured for her on the second floor, not without some strain.

The men bade her goodnight, then made their way to Con's, the tavern across the street from Porter's place. It had a forty-foot rosewood bar, a tin ceiling, black-and-white tiled floor, and an ornate chandelier hanging over the cashier case. Porter greeted the bartender, Con, and nodded to several members of "The Club," as he called the coterie that hung out at the bar: Bill Williams, the young *World* reporter (who recognized Davis as a colleague and raised a glass); a cabbie from the livery stable across the street; a Sicilian shoemaker; and "the Professor," a diminutive German who taught his language to a few private pupils.

Porter ordered three Mamie Taylors from Con and ushered his guests to his favorite booth, the second one in from the door. When the drinks were mixed, he collected them at the bar, and the three men toasted Anna's health and fortune. Davis asked how things had gone at her flat.

Porter chuckled. "We slipped her key in the door and opened it to find that oleaginous pimp, Gaffigan, lounging on the bed.

After his initial surprise, he made a lunge at us, but then he recognized Masterson from their altercation earlier. That memory, and the presence of a second man, albeit a middle-aged and corpulent one, gave him second thoughts about confronting us physically. But he challenged us as to what we were doing there. Masterson told him in no uncertain terms that his arrangement with Anna was over. I'm not sure he was convinced of that proposition, but he had no choice in the moment but to leave.

"I don't doubt that we'll encounter him again. He is of a cowardly type, but I'll warrant that he's not willing to give up his meal ticket without a struggle."

He looked square at Davis. "And how did you get on with Miss Lockhart?"

The editor took a sip of his drink—Scotch whiskey, with ginger beer, lime juice, and ice—before answering. "Rather eye-opening. I learned a bit about how someone might find herself in . . . that position." He blushed, seemed to perceive that the others noted his embarrassment, then quickly continued. "I was interested to learn of her background in the arts. And we have in common that we're both from small towns—though in different countries and separated by most of a continent."

"Where do you hail from?" Masterson asked.

"Born in Nebraska, grew up in Carson City, Nevada. I worked on newspapers in San Francisco, then followed Mr. Greeley's advice in the reverse and joined *The World*."

Masterson raised his glass. "Another toast. To every Westerner who comes to New Amsterdam to seek his fortune." The men drained their glasses. Davis insisted that he would stand the next round, and he set off to convey the order to Con.

A few seconds after he had gotten up, Masterson leaned into Porter and quietly said, "I have some news about Mr. Gardner. Can I speak frankly in front of Davis?"

"I have some as well," Porter said. "No reflection on the gentleman, Davis is a fine fellow—but here in New York, my past is a closed book. After this round, let's call it a night. Davis lives in the 'Village.' When we part, he'll go downtown, I'll walk you uptown towards your flat, and we can pass on our intelligence."

When Davis returned with the drinks, the men proceeded to chat—about their home towns, newspapers, and the fair sex. At the appropriate point, Porter said, "It's been a long night, and I thank both of you for your considerable help. But I have two—no, three—deadlines tomorrow, so let us make our way home."

When they walked out Con's door, Davis turned to the left on Irving Place and the other two turned right. Masterson said, "The full account will take some time—are you game for a substantial walk?" Porter nodded, and Masterson began to speak.

"There's a New York cop, name of Gargan, who's always had it in for me. In fact, the day after I set foot in the city, the bounder arrested me. The claim was that I had fleeced a Mormon elder in a crooked faro game. Nothing could be further from the truth. But I had to have my mug shot taken and stew for hours in a jail cell before some fellows who knew me by reputation came with my bond. The Mormon skipped town and the charges got dropped, but that doesn't mean I don't want revenge on that bent cop."

"I remember the incident well," Porter said. "I read all about your arrest in the papers, never dreaming I'd make your acquaintance barely two years later."

"That publicity is important," Masterson said, "as it supplies my entrée to Gardner. I figured the best way to trap him might be with honey—in this case, a combination of flattery and financial considerations. I sent him a letter saying I want to extract some revenge from Gargan, along with a lot of fancy language to the effect that he's the only man for the job. I got a note by return mail suggesting we meet, and the following day I was in that strange office in Fifth Avenue."

Porter was impressed by the speed of the proceedings, and said so.

"Gardner's fast response bespeaks his interest in this sort of enterprise, which is a good thing," Masterson said. They crossed Twentieth Street and reached Gramercy Park. They looked beyond the locked gates to the patch of green, empty and quiet in the darkness. As they turned to the west, Masterson continued, "I never used the word blackmail. But I made clear what I was interested in. I said I wanted to besmirch Gargan's reputation, as he had done mine, and I was sure there was no shortage of opportunity to do so—that I just needed someone to dig up the dirt. And that I wouldn't turn my back on profiting from the operation.

"Gardner hung on my every word, and when I was done, he said he was sure we could do business together. He said he had a man who specialized in sensitive matters such as this—but discretion required that this fellow not come in to the office. A bit of further conversation revealed that Gardner is an enthusiast of the sweet science. There happens to be a fight card at Sharkey's this Friday, and we arranged that the three of us would meet there. I should emerge from the evening with a good deal more information on Mr. Gardner's modus operandi. And afterwards, I'll put the tail on the other fellow, and see what it yields."

They were approaching Broadway, and when they reached that avenue, Masterson said, "You mentioned you had something for me."

Porter nodded. "It's from Bernie Scheuer and his brother Danny, and it's intriguing. You remember how you read to me some choice passages from Gardner's book? There was one about a place called 'the Golden Rule Pleasure Club,' where men dressed as women and did unspeakable things. It seems it was no mere happenstance that Gardner brought William Parkhurst there. The Golden Rule is long gone, but there is a place on the Bowery called Little Buck's that operates much the same way. The Scheuers report they witnessed none other than Charles Gardner head into Buck's."

"Capital work by those lads! I take it you told them to stay on the case?"

Porter nodded.

"Tell you what," Masterson said. "Let's meet again in Con's, Saturday at eight, and we'll compare the progress on both fronts.

"And in the meantime, keep an eye on that Davis. He may come off like a bit of a stick-in-the-mud, but I'd wager a week's salary that he has his sights set on our Miss Lockhart. It won't be long before he makes his move."

The Sharkey Athletic Club's upstanding name belied the reality of its circumstances. Since 1900—shortly after Corbett knocked out Jeffries in Coney Island—boxing had been banned in New York State. Or, more precisely, it was banned except when taking place in "chartered athletic clubs"; both the fighters and the attendees were required to be members of said organizations. Not surprisingly, the law led to a proliferation of such clubs, on barges, in storefronts, and in the backrooms of saloons like Sharkey's, which was in Sixty-fifth Street, near Broadway.

Also unsurprisingly, the clubs' membership procedures were less than stringent, as Masterson found when he arrived and inquired at the bar. There was no application to fill out, interviews to submit to, or references to supply; lifetime dues were one dollar, which he handed over to the man behind the bar. The man looked at Masterson with a glimmer of recognition.

Masterson returned the look. "Sailor Tom Sharkey," he said. "Mighty pleased to see you. The last time we met, if I recall correctly, was in San Francisco in '96, when Jeffries took you down."

"And within a year he was heavyweight champion of the world," Sharkey said in his Irish brogue. "Hello, Bat." He extended his mammoth hand.

Besides his size, Sharkey's most notable feature was his swollen and twisted left ear, which jutted out from the side of his head like a gas lantern on the flank of a coach, a casualty of a career of fights. A couple of years earlier, Sharkey had famously placed an advertisement in a New York City newspaper which read: "I will pay the sum of $5,000 to the person who can provide me with a new ear, or do a suitable job on the one I have." More than three dozen doctors came to his rooms at a Broadway hotel to have a look. He selected a noted eye, ear, and nose specialist, Dr. Joseph Bell, who told a reporter: "I have treated several persons to correct what is commonly called 'Cauliflower' ear. The surest method is by lancing. I shall be delighted to treat Mr. Tom Sharkey's ear, and I believe I can guarantee success." But Sharkey had changed his mind, and on the morning scheduled for the surgery was sleeping soundly on a train to Chicago.

Now retired from the ring, he at least had confidence that the ear wouldn't get any bigger. And Masterson observed that he had apparently developed a strategy to obscure the protuberance: he wore a large Stetson hat pulled down low, and also tilted his head to the left, leaning his right side across the bar.

"How's tonight's bill?" Masterson asked.

"You should get a good write-up for the *Telegraph*. As a result of this damned law, the fighters can only go three rounds. But there'll be plenty of action. The main event is a bout between two sailors—an American and a John Bull."

There was a door behind the bar. Periodically, Sharkey would open it for a "member of the club" to enter, and the sounds of shouts and cheers would emerge. He did the honors for Masterson, who walked in to a virtual Bedlam. What appeared to be roughly a thousand people—all men—were packed into the chamber, surrounding a makeshift ring. Up close to the ropes, a section had been cleared for the big spenders; their faces, illuminated by the half-dozen gas lamps hanging from the ceiling, shone with sweat, glowing around the four sides of the ring like a secondary source of lighting. Diamonds flashed from expansive shirt-bosoms, and big, fat, black cigars sent clouds of smoke to the dingy ceiling. In the spectators' midst was a young man in a Tyrolean hat, tall and slim, who was clearly not of their number. Masterson recognized him from the Little Savoy a few nights earlier. He sat on a stool and was furiously drawing on the sketchpad in his lap.

The room was so compact that it seemed to breed an instant

intimacy and partisanship over the beer mugs and the smell of resin and cigars. Masterson spotted a relatively unpopulated section in the far corner, and made his way over there, managing not to spill anyone's beer as he went.

In the ring, two lightweights were facing off; a white one and a Black one, both so young that they appeared to be barely out of short pants. Each clout and grunt rallied boos and cheers demanding a dramatic finish. No one seemed to want a decision, only a comatose body on the canvas and a bloodstained, hysterical victor standing above him, held back by the referee to prevent sheer murder. But it wasn't to be. After the third round, both were still standing, and the referee declared the bout a draw.

A few minutes later, fresh buckets, sponges and towels were brought to the corners. First the British sailor, Cockayne, entered the ring, to jeers and catcalls from the American contingent, and cheers from a few of his countrymen. When his opponent—Reine—made his appearance, American sailors, who were plentifully sprinkled about the crowd, set up a hoot over his rather diminutive appearance. "Who is that guy?" shouted a tar standing near Masterson. "I could lick him wid me one hand." A group of sailors tried to crowd their way to the ringside, shouting "Take him down!" Sharkey, who was to referee the featured bout, managed to prevent them from going over the ropes, and finally quiet was restored. Cockayne stood with his hands in the pockets of his long dressing-gown, nonchalantly scraping his feet in the powdered rosin. Reine jumped up on the platform, stepped between the ropes, and sat down on the chair in his corner.

In the center of the ring, four gloves lay on a piece of wrapping-paper. Cockayne selected two of them, and one of Reine's handlers did likewise. The announcer, Jim Buckley, shouted the conditions of the match in an ear-splitting tenor voice, and then Sharkey called both men from their corners to give them final instructions. "You'll box straight Marquis of Queensberry rules. Break when I tell you, and protect yourselves in the break-away."

When the two men stood together, the contrast in their physiognomy was unmistakable, and the jeers intensified. The American had a high, thin, Roman nose, a weak chin, dull, sandy hair, and uncertain brown eyes. Cockayne was notably taller and heavier—a round-necked, deep-chested fellow with long, well-muscled arms, and a sturdy-looking pair of legs. There was a delay while the boxers were posed in the middle of the ring; a battery of cameras stood at attention while a nervous photographer spilled flashlight powder all over his hat and nearly set it on fire.

Sharkey gave a sign and the gong rang for Round 1. Cockayne immediately showed himself a boxer in the old-style manner, squatting low, setting himself squarely before administering a punch, and apparently making little effort to dodge his opponent's blows. He wagged his left fist from side to side and smiled a defiant smile. Reine, meanwhile, stood far off and made whirligig movements of the forearms such as six-year-old boys display when they are challenging.

Cockayne looked surprised and stood up at full height. He advanced slowly and cautiously and darted out his left fist in a straight jab. He followed the blow with a right hook on the American's jaw. Reine began to swing both fists wildly in short, hooking blows. Cockayne mixed it with him. The blows were flying fast, but not heavy. For perhaps twelve seconds each drummed on the other's head and then Reine backed away. The Englishman followed, and swung a hard right hook on the back of his opponent's neck.

Reine smothered up, but Cockayne jabbed his left on the nose and followed with a right hook to the jaw. Reine somehow managed to throw in a right hook of his own, but it was feeble and only made Cockayne grin. He jabbed the American again and again, as he pleased. At the clang of the bell, Reine hurried to his corner on shaky legs. He seemed to be looking for a hammock to crawl into.

Masterson could hear his cornerman shouting: "For Heaven's sake, stick out your left! Stick out your fist and let him run into it. You can lick him."

He was so absorbed in the spectacle that he was startled by a tap on his shoulder. He turned and saw two men had squeezed into seats behind him. The first was Charles Gardner; the other, sitting directly behind him, was a fellow in a fedora, with a ginger mustache. The three men pantomimed gestures of greeting. It was too loud for conversation.

The fight, meanwhile, was turning into a rout. Most, if not all, of the spectators were aware of the fact that just two weeks before, a boxer who went by "Kid Groog"—his real name was Nathan Rosenberg, and he was eighteen years old—had died from a blow he took during a fight at the Mount Morris Hotel, uptown. In what was obviously an effort to avoid such a result, Sharkey announced that each of the final two rounds would be limited to one minute.

The second round began with the American looking a little tired of things. Cockayne, by contrast, was just beginning to warm up to his work. After barely half a minute of fighting, the Englishman's right landed in the American's solar plexus. It was not a heavy blow, but Reine went down. He was saved by the gong.

In the third round, Cockayne jabbed Reine in the mouth with his left and floored him with a right-hooker sledgehammer swing on the left jaw. The American collapsed rather limply and next moment was in a sitting posture. He took the count, and presently Tom Sharkey declared, "All over. Shake hands, fellows." Then something happened that changed the hisses and hoots to a big, good-natured roar of laughter. The boys grasped hands and the big Englishman, putting his arm around the American's neck, reached over, and gave him a resounding, smacking kiss.

When the racket died down, Gardner leaned forward and commented, "Not the finest example of the pugilistic art, wouldn't you say, Bat?"

"Hardly. But it would have been worse if it had gone on longer—Sharkey was wise to put an end to things."

"This is the operative I told you about, Frank Hanaway," Gardner said. "I assure you, if there are goods to be gotten on the fellow we discussed, Hanaway can get them. Now, what can you tell him by way of background?"

Masterson was at an age when turning completely around was a physical difficulty, if not an impossibility. So he rotated his head as far in Hanaway's direction as he could and told him all he knew about Gargan, which was a not inconsiderable amount. Like many members of the force, he was a bounder; Masterson gave the names of several businesses he strongly suspected of paying Gargan protection money, and the name of a man who, he had heard from a reliable source, had been brutalized by Gargan. It was only as he spoke that a realization set in: the scheme he'd cooked up with Porter might actually kill two birds with one stone; ambushing Gardner and at the same time bringing Gargan down. The indignity of what he had done still rankled.

When he'd concluded, Gardner turned to his associate and said, "That should be enough to get you started, eh?" Hanaway nodded and grunted in affirmation. "All right then," said the detective, "we'll take our leave. You and I are both well-known in our individual ways, so it's best to go out separately and not get any tongues to wagging." With that, Gardner and Hanaway made their way out of the arena and through the door of the bar.

Masterson waited about twenty seconds and followed suit. Once he got to the bar, he walked briskly out the door. But not briskly enough. When he reached the sidewalk, he saw that the two men had boarded the stairs to the elevated train stop on Columbus Avenue, just to the east. By the time he arrived at the station and climbed the stairs, they were already on a southbound car.

PART III

CHAPTER XXI

At the age of thirty-three, Bob Davis was a confirmed bachelor. At least, he thought he was, until he met Anna Lockhart. He lived on the east side of Washington Square, in a bachelor apartment house whose official name had long been forgotten; a wag had once dubbed it "The Benedick," after the vociferous bachelor in *Much Ado About Nothing*, and the name stuck. A routine developed: Davis would stop at the Benedick after work to drop off his briefcase full of manuscripts, then call on Anna to go on a long walk around the Village. They would end up dining together at small restaurants that had a foreign tinge and where the prices weren't out of Bob's range: Maria's, the Black Cat, the Café Liberty, the Hotel Griffou, the old Brevoort before the French regime. On weekends they would often explore Central Park, sometimes taking a picnic lunch. They talked about the weather, about the news of the day, about her work.

Sometimes Bill Porter joined them. The avuncular pleasure he took in their burgeoning relationship was palpable. Privately, Bob and Anna thought of him as their own superannuated and corpulent Cupid.

Even privately, two topics were never brought up. The first, of which only Anna was aware, was her marriage back in Canada, still in good standing under the eyes of the law. The second was her former profession. Once, on a stroll, they had passed a salon where she used to have her hair done in those days. She lightly made mention of this, but Bob's stonily silent reaction gave her to understand that the subject pained him, and she resolved not to mention it again.

As to her current work: she had indeed gone on several undercover missions with Hattie Rose, but soon confessed that she didn't have the heart for it; she found the emotions it stirred up were too strong. Fortunately, she fared better in her new profession. Porter had acquired for her a Remington typewriter, and Davis had procured a copy of Mrs. Barnes's *How to Become Expert in Typewriting,* a manual of the modern system of eight-fingered writing by touch. Through applying herself assiduously to book and machine, Anna had within two weeks learned to type at a rate of sixty words per minute, with fewer and fewer mistakes. Davis had indeed secured her commissions from some of the writers he worked with; the more practice she had, the faster she became, and the more money she made.

On the rare occasions when he had the time (that is, when he wasn't handing a just-finished manuscript to a waiting messenger), Porter hired her to type his stories. She could tell he was pleased with her work.

"Good typewriting is the main thing in a story, isn't it," she commented one day, not averse to casting her line for a compliment.

Porter bowed his head. "No one whom I have ever known knows as well as you do how to space properly belt buckles, semicolons, hotel guests, and hairpins.

After a month, she overruled her two friends' protests and paid Porter back for the typewriter and Davis for the book.

She was so pleased with her progress that, on a lark, after seeing a newspaper advertisement for a contest at the Lexington Armory, she entered. On the night, she hauled her Remington to the Armory and found herself up against some thirty other women and precisely six men, all seated at a double column of desks on an improvised stage. Some of the contestants wore dark green celluloid eyeshades; a few of the women, disconcertingly, were in evening gowns, while the rest, like Anna, wore office dress.

At the appointed time, the starter said, "Get on your keys.

Set. Go!" A tin horn sounded and they were off, their eyes on the printed copy next to them (the first chapter of Henry James's new novel, *The Golden Bowl*), their fingers flying over the keyboards. Some of the contestants bent low over their machines like drivers of racing automobiles, while others, including Anna, sat up straight, never looked at the keys, and emanated a sense of calm. When a page was finished, it was jerked out, thrown on the floor, and a fresh sheet inserted with no appreciable pause.

The rapidity with which her rivals went through their pages made Anna realize, early on, that she had no chance of winning. Yet she persisted, in part because it simply wouldn't do to give up, in part because she found herself interested in James's convoluted characters and endless sentences. When the horn sounded again to signal the end of an hour, Anna had gotten about two-thirds of the way through the first chapter. She waited while the judges huddled over the contestants' pages. Finally, they announced a winner: Miss Florence Wilson, of New York, had made it all the way to Chapter Two, writing 7,020 words—a rate of 117 per minute—to take the $1,000 prize. Anna had achieved 73 words a minute, not enough for a cash prize, but higher than she realized she was capable of, and enough for her to leave the premises with her typewriting honor intact. As she exited the Armory, she overheard Miss Wilson responding to a newspaper reporter's query about her training regimen: "I find I eat pickles and pie rather more frequently before a contest."

Anna made one satisfactory professional connection on her own. Next door to the New Amsterdam (which she deemed a suitable lodging place, for the time being) was an establishment called Schulenberg's Home Restaurant. One evening, after dining at Schulenberg's forty-cent, five-course table d'hôte, she took away with her the bill of fare. It was written in an almost unreadable script, neither English nor German, and so arranged that if you were not careful you began with a toothpick and rice pudding and ended with soup and the day of the week.

The next day Anna showed Schulenberg—a diminutive, hyperactive fellow whose English was almost as hard to understand as his menu—a neat card, on which the offerings of the day were beautifully typewritten with the viands temptingly marshalled under their right and proper heads, from "hors d'oeuvre" to "not responsible for overcoats and umbrellas." She then presented him with an agreement to which he willingly committed. She was to furnish typewritten menus for the twenty-one tables in the restaurant—a new one for each day's dinner, and new ones for breakfast and lunch as often as changes occurred in the food or as neatness required. In return for this, Schulenberg was to send three meals per diem to Anna's hall room by a waiter and furnish her each afternoon with a pencil draft of what Fate had in store for his customers on the morrow.

Mutual satisfaction resulted from the agreement. Each afternoon, the waiter delivered the following day's bill, Anna would sit down to her typewriter, slip a card between the rollers, and, in an hour and a half, have the twenty-one menu cards written and ready. As a result, she had nourishment on the days she didn't dine with Davis, and Schulenberg's patrons now knew what the food they ate was called, even if its nature sometimes puzzled them.

A third person benefited as well: When Anna told Porter about the arrangement, he turned on his heels and immediately headed home. By this time, she knew him well enough to recognize the look in his eyes when he had a story in his sights.

One sunny Saturday, Anna and Davis were talking in his flat, preparatory to going for a walk, when the mail arrived. Davis glanced at the contents: two bills, a letter from his mother in Nevada, the latest issue of *Harper's Weekly.* He mindlessly flipped through the last, until he was stopped in his tracks by page seventeen. He stiffened so visibly that Anna asked him what the matter was. He wordlessly handed her the magazine. On the page was an article titled "A Blow Against the Social Evil," with text and illustrations credited to George Bellows. The first page was dominated by a drawing that showed, with striking verisimilitude and a minimum of melodramatic exaggeration, the contretemps at the Little Savoy. Bat Masterson (identified in the caption as "The Legendary Western Lawman") was hauling off and about to land a blow on Mike Gaffigan's face. Standing just to the side, a horrified look on her face, was—unmistakably—Anna.

The real Anna began to read aloud: "It is well known that the social evil is alive and well in Gotham. Rare is the street on which a male passerby is not accosted by rouged and painted ladies of the night, peddling their wares. And liberally strewn across the island of Manhattan are parlor houses and saloons where willing customers can find and procure any sort of female companionship they desire, no matter how perverse.

"One such establishment is Barron Wilkins' Little Savoy, a 'black and tan' in the heart of the notorious Tenderloin. Your correspondent was there one evening, capturing the scene on charcoal and paper, when a series of dramatic events ensued. Sitting at a corner table was Bartholomew 'Bat' Masterson, the famed Dodge City sheriff who has been living in New York, writing about prize fighting for a local newspaper. Evidently his thirst for justice has not been quenched, for when Masterson saw a mustachioed procurer mistreating his . . ."

Anna flung away the paper and began to weep. Davis took her in his arms. It was the first time they had embraced. He could feel her heart thumping, and he counted the rapid beats. Eventually Anna pulled away and looked at him.

"Bob, can he do this? I mean, use my image and send it to parlors all across the country?"

"I'm afraid he can. There is, sadly, no law against recording and publishing what happens in a public place." He paused. "I understand that this is a shock, but it may not be so bad. You're not identified by name, and the emphasis is on Masterson striking that scoundrel. And you look quite different now from the girl in the picture. I predict that no one will make the connection."

Anna had stopped crying, but she hadn't stopped looking at Davis. He picked up the magazine, put it on an end table, and took her by the arm. "And now," he said, "let us proceed on our walk. It's a fine day and the ground should be dry. I propose Belvedere Castle as our destination."

The same day, Masterson and Porter met at the Metropole. Their mood was relatively somber. Masterson was forced to confess his lack of success at tracking down Gardner's mysterious operative, Hanaway, or at getting the goods—any sort of goods—on the detective himself. Porter was about to impart a piece of good news, but after reflection, he thought better of it.

"No reflection on you, Bat," Porter said, after draining his beer, "but I'm getting mightily tired of providing that scoundrel with my hard-earned dough."

"Then call his bluff. I know you're not inclined to listen to me, but as I keep telling you, your terrible 'secret' is not so terrible. Cut off the money to the blackmailer, whoever he is, and his power over you will vanish."

Porter was silent for a minute. "Let's give it one more week. If you can unearth some intelligence, we'll act on it. If not, well, I might just do as you advise. And say, I finished my story for *The World* last night and I'm at liberty today. Let's take a stroll downtown."

The two men emerged into the sunlight and headed down Broadway (just as Anna and Davis were walking up Sixth Avenue). Porter made a deliberate decision to banish thoughts of blackmail and deadlines from his mind, and the two had a pleasant perambulation, discussing the relative prospects of the McGraw's Giants in the coming season, the Russians in their war against the Japanese, Jim Jeffries's heavyweight challengers, and William Randolph Hearst in his quest for the Democratic nomination for president. They agreed that with the exception of the Giants—buoyed by the prospect of Mathewson building on his thirty-win campaign in 1903—all were slim at best.

At 23rd Street, where Broadway meets Fifth Avenue, they beheld the looming French Revival edifice of the Eden Musée and decided, on a whim, to visit. But first, for reasons he said Masterson would understand later, Porter led them to an Irish saloon on Fifth, where he purchased a pint of Irish whiskey.

At the Musée, they paid fifty cents each for entry, and two bits for a catalogue, and began taking in some of the dozens of waxwork tableaux. Those on the first floor were patriotic or otherwise high-minded: Washington crossing the Delaware, Abraham Lincoln striking the shackles from the slaves, Napoleon III lying in state, and a composite scene of Custer's last stand. The most populous was a tableau of more than twenty world leaders, including Queen Victoria, Pope Pius X, and Prime Minister Léon Gambetta of France, standing or seated expressionless, as if they didn't want to give away the nature of a forthcoming momentous announcement. Porter and Masterson decided to skip the more grisly displays in the basement, showing the horrors of the Spanish Inquisition, an execution in India in which an elephant was stepping on the victim's head, and Charlotte Corday killing Marat.

Porter led Masterson to a room on a first-floor corner, where they were greeted with the sight of a ten-foot-high, black-bearded seated figure gazing downward, seemingly constructed of papier mâché and wax. He wore a turban and a billowing red cape. Porter opened up the catalogue and read aloud:

"Visitors while on the gallery should not fail to see AJEEB, the mysterious chess and checker playing automaton. It represents a Moorish figure seated on a cushion, beneath which is a perfectly open table; in front is a small cabinet with doors, which are all open, as well as the back and chest of the figure. Any stranger is at liberty to play a game with the automaton; the movements of the figure are free and easy, and it shifts the pieces with as much accuracy as its living opponents and with much greater success, generally coming off the conqueror. In giving check to the king the automaton makes a sign by raising his head twice, and for checkmate three times."

Ajeeb was much as advertised. The chess board rested on his lap, and his outsized legs lay stretched beneath it. He grasped a hookah in his left hand and hosted a cockatoo on his right shoulder. As the catalogue said, doors at the front of his chest and the box beneath him stood open, so that the half-dozen spectators, who stood behind a rail, could peer inside and satisfy themselves that no human agency was at work. A sign in front advised that a game of checkers against Ajeeb would cost ten cents, and one of chess twenty-five, the fee to be collected by a uniformed attendant who stood next to him.

At the moment, a young fellow was playing chess against the automaton, evidently in an attempt to impress his sweetheart, who looked on with a curious admixture of adoration and skepticism. Ajeeb's manner was imperious and deliberate, though he rarely hesitated more than a second or two before moving. When he did, his right arm would swing over the board in a slow, graceful arc, pausing while his papier-mache thumb and forefinger closed on the piece to be played, and then moving it.

In short order, Ajeeb's bishops were exercising their power on open diagonals, the knights paused in the center of the board ready to leap into action against the young man's king, which stood in the center of the board, its fate nearly sealed. In a move of desperation, the challenger attempted to castle his king to move it to safety. Unfortunately, he'd already moved his king in the game. Ajeeb responded by throwing back his head in a gesture of mixed horror and scorn. He froze in that position while the attendant explained the error and moved the piece back to its original position.

With the challenger's king trapped in the center of the board, and all lines of escape blocked by bishops and rooks and even his own pawns that now stood thickly on their squares, Ajeeb's queen was able to sidle right up to the opposing king to deliver the "kiss of death." The king could not take her, because doing so would put himself into check. There was no other move to make. Ajeeb nodded three times, to indicate checkmate. The vanquished opponent slunk away with his paramour, who tried mightily to comfort him.

Porter stepped up and presented a dime to the attendant, who swept the remaining chess pieces off the board into a basket and replaced them with checkers disks. Porter was given red, Ajeeb white. Porter then did something odd. He withdrew the pint of Irish whiskey from his coat and slipped it under the automaton's robe. The attendant glared at him but said nothing. For his first move, Porter took the second-from-the-left piece in the forward row and moved it forward diagonally to the right. Ajeeb countered quickly at first, but then more and more slowly and—it must be said—erratically. It took little more than twenty moves for Porter to win, at which point the attendant glared at Porter even more belligerently, gestured towards the door with his chin, and fairly hissed, "Who will be the next to challenge the great Ajeeb?"

Porter and Masterson repaired to the house of wax, and the writer said, "You'll forgive me, Bat, but I cannot pass up the opportunity to get the better of a fakir. Ajeeb is admittedly a clever graft. The reason he's so big is that there is a small man named Harry Pillsbury lodged in his leg. There's a peep-hole in his torso, and Pillsbury is able to peep out of it, through that fake machinery, and see the board. He controls Ajeeb with two levers—the right controlling the motion of the arm and the thumb and forefinger that move the pieces, the left controlling the figure's head.

"Pillsbury, I don't need to say, is an expert chess player. But he is also a rummy, and being confined inside of Ajeeb for five and a half hours a day has only intensified his need for drink. He always accepts my offering, even though he knows it will be to his detriment."

By this time, they had made their way through the waxworks and down to the ground floor and the Winter Garden theater, where for years the Eden Musée had shown Cinematographs, its term for moving pictures. There was a line to get in, as its current offering had created something of a sensation in just two days of exhibition. When the two men reached the front, they paid an additional fifty cents and found seats in the darkened theater, where an organist was playing a medley of popular waltzes.

The projector began to whir and a title card announced the title of the presentation: *The Great Train Robbery.* Porter, Masterson, and the rest of the audience sat in rapt attention as the scene opened on what appeared to be a railroad telegraph office, with a clerk sitting at a desk. Two men wearing big hats and carrying revolvers burst into the office. Through a large window, a train could be seen pulling in. The intruders forced the clerk to send a message, then knocked him out and tied him up. The scene shifted to a railroad water tower, where the two bad men and two confederates were lying in wait. The train pulled up, the four men emerged and began to board it, and there was a ferocious fight on top of the tender, ending when one of the bandits hurled the fireman's body to the ground.

As if by magic, the spectators then saw what looked like a Western saloon. A square dance was going on, and the organist in the theater tried to keep time to the dancing with a lively two-step. In the film, a stranger in a bowler hat walked into the saloon and started to dance in the middle of a circle. Then a man pointed a gun at his feet and shot; the shot was silent, of course, but a few screams rang out in the theater. The camera lingered on the shooter's face for half a beat.

In the darkened theater, Porter and Masterson immediately turned towards each other and simultaneously began to speak.

"That's Gardner's blackmail operative," said Masterson.

"That's Al Jennings," said Porter.

One week later, in the town of Hull, Ontario, a uniformed mailman brought the daily post to a tidy clapboard house on the edge of town. Presently, the door opened and a man emerged, collected the post, and returned inside. He was neither young nor especially old, slim nor especially stout; indeed, he was not remarkable in any way save his ruddy complexion. He flipped through some letters and placed them on a roll-top desk, to be dealt with later. He took the remaining item that had been delivered, a copy of *Harper's Weekly*, and brought it with him to an overstuffed club chair.

He sat down and began to page through the magazine. He was making his way through it at a fairly rapid pace when something stopped him in his tracks. As he stared at the page, his face got even redder, till it began to resemble the color of a ripe tomato.

After about a minute, he stood up, went to the desk, picked up a pen and a piece of paper, and began to write.

CHAPTER XXII

PORTER BURST out of his seat at the Eden Musée, followed by Masterson. (And so they missed the pursuit of the bandits in the wilds of New Jersey, the climactic shoot-out by the robbers' camp, and the notorious final scene of *The Great Train Robbery* in which Arthur Barnes, in dramatic close-up, looks straight into the camera, lifts his revolver, and fires six shots in the direction of the audience. In the Eden Musée that day, not only were there screams, but two women fainted.)

Outside the museum, a hansom happened to be passing by at that moment and Porter hailed it. The two men stepped into the cab; the doors shut with a bang; Porter shouted his address up through the aperture; the driver's whip cracked in the air; and the hansom dashed away crosstown. In the brief ride, Porter laid out for Masterson his own history with Jennings, and then loudly reprimanded himself for not putting two and two together: after all, the Oklahoman was the only individual in New York to know of his history, and Jennings' own history showed a consistent willingness—if not eagerness—to break or bend the law if it could further his own ends.

"Don't feel too bad about it, Bill," Masterson replied. "Human noses are probably as large as they are so as to obscure the explanations that are usually right under them."

When the cab arrived, Porter instructed both the driver and Masterson to wait. He bounded up the steps faster than Masterson would have thought possible, returning with a large manila envelope under his arm. He got in the cab and gave the driver the address of Al Jennings' rooming house in West 38th Street. "And if you get there in ten minutes, there'll be an extra two bucks for you," he shouted in the direction of the cloudless sky. The whip cracked again.

They arrived at the address with a half a minute to spare. Porter paid the driver the fare plus the promised bonus, leapt out (again followed by Masterson), and bounded up the stairs at the same impressive velocity he had shown at the Eden Musée. A pounding on the door. The sound of footsteps within. The opening of the door—and Porter grabbed Al Jennings by his open-collared shirt. For a moment, all movement was frozen. And then Jennings broke into a grin and said, "I've been expecting this visit, Bill—though I have to say I never would have thought I'd see Bat Masterson again in these circumstances. It was all I could do at Sharkey's to keep from gushing like a schoolgirl." Porter loosened his grip. "What do you say," Jennings went on, "let's all take a seat and have some whiskey."

Each man took a chair at a corner of the room and swallowed some of the strong spirit. Jennings held up his right hand and said, "Let me hold off your questions at the pass. I'll tell you all you want to know, but first I have a question of my own: how did you finger me?"

Porter said, "Your thespian exploits betrayed you."

Jennings chuckled. "On the one hand, maybe I should have laid low. But on the other. . . well, we'll get to that. But first, I know it'll sound kinda hollow, but I apologize for what I did." Porter snorted; Masterson said nothing.

"I'll unravel the whole yarn, and when I'm done, you can decide what you want to do with me. It started innocent enough. One day out in Oklahoma Territory I got a letter from this fellow Gardner. He needed some bounty hunter work done, and I was happy to oblige. In the course of our correspondence, I happened to ask if he knew of 'O. Henry.' I mentioned that I was a pal of yours from Ohio Penitentiary days, and he got mighty interested—he'd read your stories and always wondered about the man behind the byline. I guess I might have played up the way you were determined to keep your past a closed book.

"Gardner never used the word 'blackmail.' He just started going on, in a casual sort of way, about how there might be a money-making opportunity for the both of us. He said you were striking it rich in the short-story game, and would barely miss a few bucks a week. And if it seemed like you were in danger of backing out, we could let out just a little bit of the story to prime the pump—which is what I did when I wrote the letter to that magazine about your Texas days. As time went on, I found my heart wasn't in it—as a matter of fact, I was half-hoping you'd call Gardner's bluff. You might recall that when we had dinner that first night at Moquin's, I urged you to come clean. If you had followed my advice then, you might have ducked a heap of trouble. But that's not for me to say."

"It certainly is not," Masterson interjected. "And mighty convenient that you came to Jesus at the very moment you're cornered."

"No argument on that score, Mr. Masterson. But I'm prepared to put my money where my mouth is." He got up, walked to a bureau, opened a drawer, extracted a stack of bills, and handed it to Porter. "That's my share of the graft. And maybe it will count slightly in my defense that I had the dough counted out and ready to hand it over."

Porter counted out $550 and put it in his pocket. "It's all there, Al. Pray tell, how did you come into this kind of green? I can't believe you didn't spend your ill-gotten gains as they came in—now that I think of it, you've been awfully free in picking up the check in recent weeks—and not with counterfeit notes, either. Edison can't have paid you that much for shooting at a tenderfoot."

"All true, Bill. Here's the goods. While we were making that picture out in New Jersey, I got to talking to a member of the company—he played one of the square-dancers in the barroom. We continued our acquaintance in the city. This fellow has ambitions as a director. He's also a smooth talker. He got hired by a competitor of Edison's called Biograph, and he persuaded them that to make a true and convincing Western story, the wilds of New Jersey just won't cut the mustard. To make a long story short: He got Biograph to bankroll a production of *The Long Riders* way out west in California. For the rights to the book and my services as 'technical adviser,' I got two hundred simoleons and a ticket to Los Angeles."

Porter estimated that fifty percent of what Jennings had just told him was bunkum. And what else would you expect from an Ohio Penitentiary alumnus? One of the few things prison taught a person was prevarication. Look at his own tales. They were equally meretricious; it's just that they were gussied up in linotype and printed in monthly magazines. To be sure, Jennings had transgressed by exploiting an old friend. But Porter had swallowed Gardner's tale whole, when he probably should have sniffed out that it was a grift. He thought of that oft-repeated line from the OP: "If they weren't greedy, they wouldn't have gotten into a mess in the first place." In his case, he understood, it wasn't greed but an equally powerful impulse to cast off the shame that persistently clung to him.

Porter didn't have the heart to berate his erstwhile friend anymore, much less roughhouse him. But before he left, he demanded that Jennings produce a sheet of paper and something with which to write on it. Such items did not exist in the flat, as Jennings' literary exercises were over and done with, but he went out into the hallway and borrowed them from the playwright who exercised his imagination next door. On his return, Porter dictated a statement for the Oklahoman to take down and sign.

Porter picked it up, folded it in thirds, and made his way to the door. When he was three-quarters of the way out of it, he turned around and said, "What's the name of this artiste you're following out west? I'll watch out for it in the papers, see if he makes a name for himself."

"Griffith," Jennings replied. "David W. Griffith."

The interview with Charles Gardner wasn't as amiable as the one with Jennings. It began with Porter and Masterson storming past the secretary and into Gardner's chamber. From the sight of the two men together, Gardner had reason to believe that he had been found out; from the looks on their faces, he could be sure of it. Porter unfolded the document Al Jennings had written and signed, then read it aloud. It was a brief but complete account of the blackmail scheme. From Gardner's silence at the conclusion, Porter gathered that Jennings, for possibly the first time in his life, had told close to the complete truth about an important matter.

Porter broke the silence. "Gardner, you're a scoundrel, and if I have anything to do about it, I will never—once you have paid back in full the money I've given you—see you again. And if one word about . . . my past appears in print—*anywhere* in print—I am going to the newspapers with this document. Since the scandal with Parkhurst ten years ago, your reputation has climbed back to the edge of respectability. This will send it right back into the muck."

"That's mighty big talk, jailbird." Gardner had finally found his voice. "But this Al Jennings is a convicted train robber, at least from what I read. Who's going to take his word over mine?"

Porter gave a mirthless chuckle. "Your depravity is matched only by your audacity. I imagined you might take this tack, and I took appropriate measures. You're familiar with an establishment known as Little Buck's?" Gardner tried to maintain a poker face, and failed. "And do you recall being there several days when there was a sort of flash explosion? Perhaps you thought it came from the excitement you felt from embracing a boy who looked like a Greek god. You probably wondered why he left soon after and didn't show up at the appointed meeting place. Twenty-eighth and Third, I believe it was."

Porter opened the manila envelope that was under his arm and took out a photo. It wasn't of the utmost clarity, but the two people it depicted were eminently identifiable: Charles Gardner locked in an embrace with Danny Scheuer. And Gardner appeared to be wearing blindingly white pancake makeup.

Gardner walked over to a safe in the corner of his office and applied himself to the combination. When the door opened, he counted out a stack of money, then handed it over to Porter. The writer counted it and gave a nod to Masterson, and then the two men walked out.

Standing outside on Fifth Avenue, Masterson said, "The hunter gets captured by the game. Well done, Bill. I demand a full accounting—and please, use all your storytelling skills."

Porter suggested they walk to the Metropole, where they would round out their day. As they embarked, the writer said, "Well, Bat, your initial suspicions of Gardner hit home. When you lent me his book, I scrutinized it as closely as a map of buried treasure. Two things struck me. One was a brief description of his childhood, where he mentioned being schooled by an English nanny. That more or less confirmed my suspicions about the British spelling in that first letter from the 'McManus.' You'll recall that I pointed it out to Gardner. From that point on, every letter from the supposed blackmailer was pure American.

"The other thing about the book was that his predilections came through, sort of between the lines. He took more space describing that Little Pleasure Social Club than all the other places he took Parkhurst to combined."

By this time they had reached Broadway and turned uptown. Porter continued: "I mentioned to you that the Scheuer boys had spied Gardner going into Little Buck's. At that point, I thought it made sense to keep your investigation and mine separate. You'll forgive me—it seemed that if we did it that way, we'd sort of double the size of our net."

"A tried and true method among lawmen," Masterson said.

"I appreciate that. Anyway, the boys and their associates kept on tailing the private dick, and I have to say it cost me a fair penny. One day, they see him heading into Buck's and our plan springs into action. The young one, Bernie, sprints to Bob Davis's place—fortunately, he was in, and Bob stuffed all his equipment into a big valise and headed to Buck's.

"So it was Davis who snapped the photo?"

"Exactly. That's one of his hidden talents."

"I'm surprised you were willing to take him into your confidence."

Porter chuckled. "Necessity is the mother of confession."

The writer continued: "So Gardner pays an exorbitant 'membership fee' and walks into Little Buck's. By his description, it's quite a place: men dressed as women, their faces painted, sashaying about and calling each other by ladies' names. The plan was for Danny, truly a beautiful boy, to sit down at Gardner's table and initiate a conversation. Davis would sit near them, but out of Gardner's line of vision, and intervene if things got out of hand. Fortunately, everything went like clockwork. When Gardner put his hands on the kid, Bob pulled out the gear, and at the moment of truth, he was ready to take the photo and high-tail it out of there."

"After a suitable lapse of time, so as not to appear suspicious, Danny extracted himself as well, after setting up a fake meeting plan. I paid the boy my weekly fee from *The World*, and I have to say it was worth every cent."

They had arrived at the Metropole. When they walked in, Masterson said, "No question about that. But with what you're carrying, you're still pretty flush." He raised his voice and addressed the whole barroom. "Order up, boys. The next round's on Bill Porter!"

CHAPTER XXIII

THE WEEKS passed in their usual ungainly succession. The contract with *The World* and the termination of blackmail payments did good things for Porter's finances—though his outlays to support his progeny in Texas and Pittsburgh and his habit for whiskey in New York went on the other side of the ledger. And it was always touch and go with the weekly deadline. Letters between him and Davis flowed fast and free: (almost) always with an affectionately humorous tone, and (almost) always with an edge of pleading, on the one hand for a short story, on the other for money. Forthwith, a sampling of missives from the editor to the writer:

> Sydney Porter, Esq.
>
> 55 Irving Place, N.Y.C.
>
> Dear Bill:
>
> It is important, desirable, and necessary that you begin sending a wad of copy into this office.
>
> Having left off secondary heads, all bars are down and there is no reason why you should not produce a tale fit to read ere the week is gone.
>
> You will get this letter probably at 9 o'clock Friday morning—that will give you until 4 o'clock to write 2000 words. How can they stop you.
>
> Very sincerely yours,

*

Sydney Porter Esq.
55 Irving Place, N.Y.C.

Dear Mr. Porter:

COPY?

Yours respectfully,

*

Mr. Sydney Porter
55 Irving Place, N.Y.C.
Dear Bill:

We are still desirous.

Yours willingly,

*

Sydney Porter Esq.
55 Irving Place, N.Y.C.

My dear Porter:

If I don't receive the goods from you purty soon, I'll come down and drink up everything in your house, including the ink and the mucilage.

Are you sick?

Do you need help?

Are you in love?

Respectfully,

*

The letters from Porter to Davis weren't as abundant but when deadline or creditors loomed especially threateningly, or when the editor appeared to absolutely require assuaging, he would set pen to paper. One day when financial matters seemed desperate, he posted this (it amused him to address Davis by his own name, "Bill"):

> Dear Old Bill:
>
> I have been under the weather the past few days but am better and can now continue to turn out the old blown-in-the-bottle brand of fiction.
>
> I am a man of few words. I want $125 (don't read that a dollar and a quarter). The sum will be more than covered by the moral and entertaining tale that I hereby agree to have finished and delivered to you by 10:30 AM Friday or perhaps earlier.
>
> Pursue the liberal policy, & get the best stuff.
>
> Personally and officially I greet you and make obeisance.
>
> Consistently,
>
> Bill, the Bedouin
>
> P.S. I want the dough not a check by the bearer (but a check will do).
>
> P.P.S. My best regards to the charming Miss Lockhart.

As for Miss Lockhart. . . As Masterson had predicted—and as anyone with functioning sensory organs would have seconded—Bob Davis had indeed "fallen" for her (in the language of the Broadway rounders). Their courtship proceeded at a pretty pace, and on an October Saturday, the couple repaired to one of their favorite destinations, the Lake in Central Park. They hired a rowboat at Vaux's picturesque boathouse and lazily paddled, enjoying the changing colors of the leaves on the surrounding trees.

When they were roughly in the center point of the Lake—making the possibility that Anna would attempt to escape fairly remote—Davis cleared his throat. "Will you tell me what I most wish to know?" he said in an oddly stilted manner.

"And what, pray tell, might that be?" Anna replied, a smile just beginning to dance on her lips.

"The happy day when we shall be married."

Despite herself, she broke out laughing. As Davis reddened, she said, "Oh Bob, I apologize. But that language isn't yours, or at least not what I'm used to. Did you get it from a gentleman's guide?"

His silence indicated she was on the mark. Davis finally said, "I fear I have misread our circumstances. And it's I who must apologize to you, for presuming too much." He lowered an oar into the water and began the journey back to the boathouse.

The levity had disappeared from Anna's countenance. Firmly, she put her hand on top of Davis's. "Stop. You misunderstand. Can we stay here for a while, and let the current take us where it will, while I explain something to you?" He nodded.

She took a deep breath. "Because you know of my time in the Little Savoy and the history that brought me there, you might think you know all my dark secrets. But there's one I've kept from you, and I feel awful about it. To put it bluntly, I am a married woman."

Davis had been observing the eddies in the water; now he looked up at Anna in shock. "He is called Magnuson, Owen Magnuson," she said. "My God, it feels strange to say that name. It seems that I haven't done so for years."

She described their brief, unhappy courtship and marriage, and her unsuccessful efforts to obtain a divorce in Canada and then in New York. "Long ago, I resigned myself to not being free, or at least not until his death, whenever that might come. But then a strange thing happened. Two weeks ago, I got a letter from Magnuson. He tracked me down through the only person in Hull I'm still in contact with, my cousin Jane. The letter . . . the letter said he had seen that picture in *Harper's Weekly* and recognized me immediately. 'Shameful,' he called it. 'Disgraceful.' He has long known of my desire to end the marriage. He could have afforded a statutory divorce in Ottawa but withheld it out of spite. The thought that *he* might find happiness with another has apparently not entered his mind." She laughed bitterly.

"Now he says that the shame is too much to bear and he will sue for divorce in New York on the grounds of adultery. There is one condition. I must pay his attorney's fee of two hundred dollars and whatever the court costs are."

Davis took her hands in his and looked into her eyes. "That is a small price to pay for the only thing in the world I can think of that will bring me happiness. And if we pay the money and achieve the desired result, will you marry me?"

Anna required a moment to take in the situation. In the pause —barely a second—she assessed, as if from a perch high above, all the transformations her circumstances had undergone since leaving home. And then she came back down to where she was sitting, in a boat, across from the man she now knew she would spend the rest of her life with. "Yes," she said. Davis leaned forward to kiss her, but the boat began tilting perilously, and he retreated to his seat, a capacious smile on his face, and started to row them back to the bank.

The petition for divorce was set to be heard in Magistrate's Court one week later, and (contingent on its success), the wedding was to take place the Sunday after that. That was not long in the future, and thus a great deal of bustling commenced. There was a minister to be engaged, a dress to be procured and altered, and a site for the ceremony to be arranged. As good fortune had it, Bob Davis was a parishioner in good standing at the Little Church Around the Corner, on the corner of Fifth Avenue and Twenty-ninth Street; no sooner had Anna given her consent than he asked the rector, George C. Houghton, for use of the Church's lovely interior courtyard. Houghton agreed, as would any legitimate man of the cloth, on seeing Davis's ardent high hopes. The reception would follow on the roof of the Benedick, which was open to residents when the weather was fine. And Anna and Bob dearly hoped that the mid-October weather would be as fine as weather can be.

As the days passed, Anna occasionally found herself in a panic because, since his initial contact, she had heard nothing from Magnuson. In fact, she sometimes wondered whether she had imagined the communication from him; on such occasions, she rushed to the lockbox on her bureau to assure herself that the letter was there, and it was real. She found herself making more and more mistakes in her typewriting. Once, while composing her daily menu, she wrote "wedding" instead of "venison" and delivered the bills of fare to Schulenberg without catching the error. He informed her of it next day and pretended to be stern until he got the mortified reaction he wanted. Then he broke into a belly laugh.

Their court date finally arrived. It was a gloomy Monday, and when Anna, Davis, and Porter (the future bridegroom and the writer had separately insisted on being there to provide moral support) entered the Magistrate Court, they found it to be a rather depressing place. They waited as various petitions, torts, and appeals to the court were heard and, in what seemed to them a random fashion, granted or denied. When it was Anna's turn, she and Davis stood before the judge, who was bald and wore wire spectacles. He looked the document that was in front of him up and down, then looked Anna and Davis up and down.

"You are Mr. Magnuson?" he said to him.

"No, your honor."

The judge turned to Anna. "And you are not Mrs. Magnuson?"

"No, your honor," she said. "I mean—yes, I am Anna Magnuson." Noting the judge's look of confusion, she explained the circumstances, identifying Davis as "a friend."

The judge cleared his throat. "As I understand it, Mr. Magnuson, who did not see fit to be here, is petitioning for divorce on the grounds of adultery. Do you acknowledge the truth of this charge?"

Anna's impulse was to say nothing—indeed, to flee from the grim courtroom. But she knew that in order to achieve what she so dearly wanted, she needed to speak. "Yes," she said, in a soft but firm voice. The judge asked her to repeat her answer, and she did.

"Very well. Everything appears to be in order. There is the matter of court fees, in the amount of five hundred dollars." Davis reached into his jacket pocket, withdrew a blank bank cheque, and made it out for that amount. He handed it to the judge, who, in keeping with his custom, looked it up and down. With a flourish, he applied his signature to the document before him and looked up again at Anna. And, wonder of wonders, a smile broke out on his face. "You are a free woman," he said.

The weather changed by Sunday, with a sky as bright as the guests' spirits. They were perforce small in number. Bob's father had been dead for six years, and the journey from Nevada was too far for his aged mother to make; a firm promise was made to visit her on the couple's wedding trip, by necessity delayed for at least a year. Anna's aunt and uncle and her cousin Jane sent their regrets and a cunning leather key basket. And lo and behold: Jane also reported that Anna's brother Tom had been located in Toronto, where he had forsaken the bottle and embraced Jesus.

Friends stood in for family: Masterson, Gilman Hall of *Ainslee's*, Giuseppe the apple seller, Hattie Rose, and Anna's old workfellow Maisie from Siegel-Cooper. The couple had asked Porter to be best man, and the emotion that ran through him at the request was so surprising and strong that it took a moment for him to find the words to accept. The matron of honor, so chosen because she was instrumental in the chain of connections that led the bride and groom to each other, was sharp-featured Hetty Pepper, late of the Vallambrosa. Anna had run into her on Fourth Avenue one day and was delighted to discover that she was now the proprietor of a thriving feather-curling shop of her own.

The ceremony was designed to follow the regular Sunday service at the Little Church. That was handy for Pastor Houghton; for the bride and groom, it was pleasant to have a relative multitude of sympathetic witnesses. Some congregants filled in as ushers, and the organist stayed on, offering a sprightly medley of Bach and Vivaldi. Presently she paused, and Davis (in a morning suit) and Hetty (in a floor-length black dress, face softened into a smile), appeared at the rear and began to make their way down the aisle. As the first notes of Wagner's Bridal Chorus commenced, Porter and Anna walked in, arm in arm. She had on a white veil and a long white dress and carried a bouquet of calla lilies.

The ceremony was rapid and joyful, and in a blink of an eye the celebrants were walking out the door onto Fifth Avenue, showered with rice and the organist's rendition of Mendelssohn's Wedding March. A crowd was outside, including members of the congregation and some passersby; at the couple's appearance on the church steps, they broke into applause. It didn't stop till the whole party had made their way into two waiting hansom cabs and begun the short ride downtown.

The cabs slowed to a stop outside the red-brick Benedick. Alighting, the guests took in the glorious Sunday scene on Washington Square—picnickers, strollers, lovers, dozers—then went inside and started climbing the stairs. As they reached the second floor, a dark-haired girl emerged from a doorway and rushed down the hall. "Even on Sunday," Davis said with a sigh. He hurried the others on and explained to Porter, *sotto voce*, that behind the door the girl had emerged from lay a warren of rooms to which the architect of the building, Stanford White, Augustus St. Gaudens, and some of their cronies repaired, to, as Davis put it, "satisfy their appetites." "If you can believe it," he added, "they call it The Sewer Club."

After climbing five flights of stairs, they emerged in the bright sunlight of the roof to find two tables laid with white linen and set with attractive China, stemware, and flatware. A diminutive man was unpacking the contents of two picnic baskets. Anna gasped and Davis chuckled. "Lovely, Mr. Schulenberg," he said. "And well done by you, in keeping the arrangements from the bride."

Anna looked at her employer, and then at her husband. "But can we . . ." she started to say.

Davis interrupted her. "You must be the best type-writer in all of New York, and Schulenberg must desperately want to have you back, for he agreed to provide the victuals at a very modest cost."

By unanimous consent, Schulenberg was asked to join the party, and he agreed. He had also brought up a half-dozen bottles of champagne, paid for by the best man. First one cork, then another, was popped and everyone toasted the bride and groom.

The tar and gravel floor of the roof was slightly sticky, but the sun shone and the views of Washington Square to the west and the river to the east were grand, and the large wooden-planked water tower took up fully a third of the roof and provided an air of modernity. Davis, who fancied himself a historian, said, "The location may seem plain—Schulenberg's settings excepted—but in fact that tower is a landmark in the history of art." When everyone looked at him blankly, he explained: "Winslow Homer, the painter, used to be a Benedick bachelor. You've seen his painting *Undertow* at the Metropolitan Museum?" More blank looks. "Well, he did the studies for it here. It shows two women bathers about to succumb to the surf, and two men rescuing them. Their clothes are all absolutely soaked, and Homer filled bucket after bucket from this very water tower and kept drenching his models till he got the proper look."

The party had dispensed with the canapes and were on to a course of cold roast chicken, when suddenly the door to the roof flew open. Standing in the doorway were Mike Gaffigan and someone Anna recognized as his underling, a lupine youth named Spencer. He was holding a revolver, and Gaffigan a length of thick twine.

For an instant there was only silence. Anna looked at Gaffigan in disbelief. How had he known? Then she caught sight of Maisie out of the corner of her eye. Her friend was mouthing a word. Or rather a name: "Dulcie."

Gaffigan broke the silence. "Sorry to crash the party, friends, but it's come to an end. Now I'll be asking you to stand up." The group complied, the only sound being the scratching of their chairs against the gravel floor. "Kiddo, you stay where you are. Everybody else, move against that table, nice and close, so Spencer can keep a good eye on you."

He directed his attention to Masterson. "The famous lawman," he said with a sneer. "The dime novels don't say how much you fancy a good sucker-punch." Gaffigan took the gun from Spencer. The kid searched Masterson for weapons. Finding nothing, he took the rope from Gaffigan and tied the lawman to the water tower's metal support. Gaffigan walked up to him, looked him in the eye, and pistol-whipped him in the face. "See how much you like it when the shoe is on the other foot."

Masterson looked at the cadet and spit blood at his feet. Gaffigan reared back and punched him in the stomach.

The rest of the party looked on in silence. Porter was pressed so close to Hattie, on his right, and Hall, on his left, that he could feel the rise and fall of their breaths.

Gaffigan walked up to Anna. "Kiddo, we had a good thing, and you ruined it. And you thought that was that. What you didn't understand is that there's no easy way to walk away from Mike Gaffigan. Maybe I can't have you anymore. But nobody else is going to, either. See how this fat boy of a husband likes kissing a face that belongs in a dime show."

He pulled out a small glass vial from his coat pocket. Porter immediately recognized it as vitriol—sulfuric acid. There was a sudden sharp pain in his right calf. Then another. Hattie, he realized, was kicking him. She hissed one word in his ear: "Gun!" Of course! Porter reached into her purse and pulled out Hattie's Double Derringer. He pulled the trigger once and shot Spencer's gun out of his hand. With the other bullet, he shot the glass vial, just as

Gaffigan was about to hurl it in Anna's face. The bottle shattered and the acid danced in the air. A few drops fell on Anna's right hand and she felt a terrible burning sensation. The rest landed on her calla lilies, which she had knocked from the table to the floor in the commotion. In seconds, the vitriol burned into them a pattern that an observer, if he didn't know better, might have said resembled a heart.

By that time, Hattie Rose had picked up Spencer's pistol and had it trained on the center of Gaffigan's forehead.

EPILOGUE

DECEMBER 24, 1904

Madame Sofronie, clearly no novice, had put Anna at her ease and done the deed swiftly. Only later did she realize that the Madame had immediately tucked away the mass of hair she'd removed into some drawer or chamber, thoughtfully sparing her from having to look at (or mourn) her missing locks. And, for no charge, she brought out a set of curling irons and gave the hair that remained on Anna's head a Marcel Wave, so as to send her out the door looking very *en vogue.*

She hurried through the snowy streets to the pawn shop on the Bowery; to her relief, the present she had been eyeing for Bob for weeks was still there. She handed ten dollars to the man behind the counter and was handed the merchandise in a plain leather pouch. She still had five left from the Madame, so she treated herself to a streetcar ride back uptown, and, at the liquor store on Third Avenue, bought a second bottle of Burgundy. One was never enough when Bill Porter was their guest.

She walked through the door to find Bob (smoking a pipe) and Bill standing and examining the gray cat in the backyard, who seemed not to have budged from his spot on the fence. She took off her hat, and both men stared at her for a full five seconds, mystification on their faces.

Finally, Bill Porter broke the silence. "I reckon it'll grow back," he said.

"Or perhaps it would be better if it didn't," Bob jumped in, still gazing at her. "With a simpler frame, your beauty is more striking than ever."

Despite herself, Anna blushed. She told them they would understand in due time, then set about heating up the supper—a supper she had stretched every dollar to assemble—and putting it on the table. First there was oyster soup, then the obligatory celery, roast chicken, mashed turnips, and baked squash. And the two bottles of red wine.

They ate heartily, and gossiped about the news of the day, the weather, Roosevelt's likely exploits in his second term. When they had all finished their second helpings, Davis leaned back and apologized to the writer for not being in touch over the past weeks, except professionally; starting a household, he explained, turned out to be more time-consuming than he had counted on. Their professional association (he didn't have to say) had been rewarding. The weekly O. Henry story in *The World*, kicked off with the "The Elusive Tenderloin," and followed by "The Social Triangle," "The Last Leaf," "The Cop and the Anthem," and others, had been such an immediate hit that it had been moved up to the front page of the Sunday supplement. He also left unmentioned the weekly deadline struggle.

But Davis did feel a compliment was in order. It was something he'd been thinking about since the first stories had come in. "Bill, many if not most of us in this city have migrated from parts near and far. The three of us around this table certainly have. But you, more than anyone else I've ever encountered, have . . . I don't know, been *absorbed* by Gotham. You have your finger on its pulse."

"I thank you, Colonel," Porter said. "It's a strange thing, but as soon as I stepped off the train from Harrisburg and onto these concrete corridors, I felt at home, as I never had before. And I sensed that New York would provide all the material I'd ever require, and more. Stories—there are four million of them, and I haven't scratched the surface."

"Say," Davis said with a chuckle, "do you think you'll ever put Bat Masterson into a tale?"

"The dime novelists have taken care of that," the writer replied. "And besides, after the recent fracas, Bat wants to lay low for a while. Keeping tab on the world of sport for the *Morning Telegraph* is keeping him plenty busy."

"And what about the man who . . . invaded our wedding?" Anna didn't want to say his name. The three friends had testified against Gaffigan and Spencer in their trials for aggravated assault and were gratified that they were sentenced to the maximum of ten years.

"I've banished him from my consciousness and I recommend you do the same," Porter said.

"I did get a letter from Al Jennings the other day," he went on. "Seems like his moving pictures scheme is proceeding apace out in California. Another fellow from *The Great Train Robbery* has joined the venture. The chap's name is Max Aronson, which he's changed to Anderson. But from here on in, he's to be known to one and all as 'Bronco Billy.'"

By this time, they had finished the nutmeg egg tart, the dishes had been cleared from the table, and it was time to exchange gifts. Porter claimed guest's privilege and retrieved a box from where he had placed it near the door. He handed it to Anna, who found, when she opened it, a simple but stylish cloche hat, adorned with a large white feather that seemed to shine next to the subdued grey of the hat.

"Snowy egret," Porter said. "Curled by our friend Hetty." Anna put it on and twirled in front of the pier glass. "This will come in handier than you even realized," she said. "Until my hair grows back, from the time I leave this apartment till the time I come back in, this hat will not leave my head. Thank you, Bill."

Bob's gift was a Waterman pen. As he was admiring it, Porter said, "I figured that if you have to strike through some of my flights of fancy, you may as well do it in style."

Bob and Anna had jointly conceived Porter's gift; Anna had executed it. During several visits to the writer's flat, she had surreptitiously but carefully studied the photograph of Margaret on his desk. And then, from memory, using the brushes and paints she had lately retrieved from storage, she had created a miniature of the girl. When Porter unwrapped the tissue paper and stared at his daughter's profile, he was overcome with emotion. He closed his eyes for a long time; on opening them, he managed to say, "I thank you from the bottom of my heart."

Finally it was time for the couple's presents to each other. Anna insisted that she give Bob his first. There had been no time to wrap it. She reached into her purse and withdrew the silver watch fob she had purchased on the Bowery just a couple of hours before. "I think it goes splendidly with the pocket watch you got from your grandfather, don't you? And a definite improvement over the tin chain you've been using."

Bob removed said chain and replaced it with the new one, which sparkled in the candlelight.

"It's perfect," he said. "And it explains the mystery of your missing locks."

"All in all," her husband went on, "it's a good bargain—a temporary loss in exchange for something permanent and exceptional. I'm afraid I don't have anything so grand to you, except for a promise." He walked over to his briefcase, which was standing against the wall, withdrew a small box, wrapped with gaudy paper, and handed it to his wife. She opened it and held up the contents. It was a small box of oil paints.

"In this gathering," Bob said. "Bill is the storyteller, and I am merely a literary midwife. You are the artist."

At that, he took out a bottle of port, filled everyone's glasses, and proposed a toast to the resumption of her career as a painter. Then Bill toasted everyone's health and happiness over Christmas and into the New Year. Judging by the number of similar toasts the party made before Porter took his leave, it would be a very good year indeed.

The walk to his rooms in Irving Place took less than ten minutes, but the cold air cleared Porter's head. He walked in, hung his coat on the rack, and found himself walking toward his desk. He sat in his familiar chair, looked out the big window on the familiar view (at this late hour, only a few stragglers walked by), and felt the urge to write.

That was odd, given his propensity for edging right up to a deadline and, more often than not, crashing right through it. But he figured he shouldn't fight whatever instinct was presenting itself. His holiday story for *The World* was already set in type—in fact, the early edition was already starting to be delivered to the doorsteps of New York, as Christmas fell on a Sunday that year. The tale was called "Christmas By Injunction," and it was the first Western story he'd published in the paper. It was about a prospector named Cherokee who strikes gold and resolves to play Santa. The problem is that there are no children to be found in any of the nearby frontier towns. Finally, a ten-year-old named Bobby is produced. For his description, Porter borrowed the features and stature of Bernie Scheuer. Bobby smokes cigarettes, uses slang like "Come off it!" and "Rats!" and says, "There ain't any Santa Claus. It's your folks that buys toys and sneaks 'em in when you're asleep. And they make marks in the soot in the chimney with the tongs to look like Santa's sleigh tracks." There was a surprise at the end, and a clear understanding that Bobby will come around.

But why not undertake next year's story now? The audaciousness of the idea amused him. He took out a fresh sheet of paper and his own Waterman and looked around his desk. His eye lighted on the tortoise-shell hair comb he had found on the edges of Long Island Sound while on his expedition with Davis over the summer. He thought about the exchange of gifts he'd just witnessed, and his fancy began to play with it. The beginnings of an idea began to present themselves . . . .

Bill Porter had a ritual before undertaking a story. He first touched the photograph of Margaret on his desk, and then the other one, of a young boy playing in a dirt yard—the one that, when visitors came, he always made sure to tuck away in a drawer.

He held it and ran his fingers over what he had written in ink on the bottom. "Oscar Enrique." O. Henry.

He started to write.

AUTHOR'S NOTE

The seeds of this book were planted more than half a decade ago, when the idea occurred to me to write a biography of O. Henry (1862-1910). I naturally looked at previous efforts, but when I got to Gerald Langford's *Alias O. Henry*, I stopped. Prof. Langford's book was published nearly *seven* decades ago, in 1957, but did such a good job of ferreting out the knowable facts of William Sidney Porter's life–including the precise moment when he changed the spelling of his middle name to "Sydney"—that I was pretty sure I wouldn't be able to substantially improve on it.

In the meantime, I had started to read O. Henry's short stories. I thought they were really good, and at the very least far better than their reputation as old-fashioned, sentimental, and manipulative. I proposed a new edition of the stories to the Library of America, which led me to read everything O. Henry published. (The edition was released in 2021 under the title *O. Henry: 101 Stories.*) What struck me about the stories was their humor; the consistent themes of secrets, deception, and disguise; and, maybe most of all, the portrait they painted of New York City in the first decade of the twentieth century. As I knew from the biographies, Porter had been born in North Carolina and, after a colorful (to put it mildly) four decades, moved to the city in 1902, and considered it home for the rest of his life. "The Gift of the Magi," "The Last Leaf," "The Cop and the Anthem"—featuring Soapy, the bum—and the rest of his roughly one hundred New York–set stories showed a remarkable understanding of and appreciation for the city in a tumultuous time. He wrote a bit about the upper crust, but the characters that really shine are those hanging on to the lower rungs–the shopgirl, the clerk, the starving artist, the cop, the waitress, the Lower East Side druggist, the tramp.

I started to read about New York in this period, notably in Mike Wallace's magisterial 2017 book, *Greater Gotham: A History of New York City from 1898 to 1919*. I learned that it was a time of amazing change. Most important, a massive wave of immigration was altering the complexion of the city, literally as well as figuratively. (My own grandparents were part of that wave, and my father was born in New York while O. Henry was still alive.) Beyond that, all sorts of institutions were coming into being, in interesting and sometimes wrenching ways: the department store, the Great White Way of Broadway, the subway system, the tenement sweatshop, a robust and sometimes cutthroat journalism culture (including dozens of thriving magazines, where short stories were the most treasured asset), restaurants from Childs lunch counters to lobster palaces like Moquin's, motion picture production, vaudeville, and even New York itself; it was not until 1898 that Brooklyn, Manhattan, the Bronx, Queens, and Richmond consolidated into one city. Fascinating, as well, was the widespread concern, sometimes bordering on obsession, about the so-called social evil of prostitution, which in certain circles spiraled into panic about a supposed scourge of "white slavery."

The thought occurred: why not pluck Mr. Porter/Henry out of the realm of verifiable fact and make him a character—as he himself had done to many in the parade of colorful figures he encountered while taking his habitual long walks on the streets of New York? Doing so would let me delve deeper into the city he chronicled, which, as I read more and more about it, seemed even more fascinating. I could also imagine possible origin stories for some of *his* stories, and have some fun by taking figures out of the history books and introducing them to Porter. (Of all the major and most of the minor characters in my book, only Mike Gaffigan the cadet and Bernie Scheuer and his family are pure inventions. Hetty Pepper the feather-curler steps out of O. Henry's "The Third Ingredient," and Anna Lockhart is an extrapolation of his most famous character.) When it seemed to fit, I could include near-verbatim descriptions from contemporary accounts. Finally, I could propose solutions to mysteries even Gerald Langford couldn't solve. What was the truth behind the case that brought Porter to trial in Texas in the 1890s? Why did he not say a word in his own defense? Why, once he arrived in New York, was he so obsessively secretive about his past? What closed him off to intimacy? What fueled his amazing productivity? (He published all of his short stories, close to three hundred of them, in the last dozen years of his life, and the majority between 1902 and 1906.) It was probably inevitable that he would write under a pen name, but why did he choose the one he did? (An amusing feature of Langford's biography is his recounting of at least half a dozen different explanations that Porter himself gave on various occasions.)

So I embarked on a novel about O. Henry in New York, the result of which you're holding in your hands. Some of the incidents in it really happened; almost everything else *could* have happened ("almost" because, for the sake of plot cohesion, I slightly changed the dates of some events). You will notice that I borrowed Gerald Langford's title. There was simply no way to improve on it.

ACKNOWLEDGMENTS

Thanks, first of all, to Heather Merrill, researcher extraordinaire. Digging in to New York in this remarkable period was truly a collaborative effort, and I hope she enjoyed it as much as I did. Beyond research, Heather was a valued and valuable sounding board and contributor on matters of plot and character. There was a lot that she found out that there wasn't space or a place for, but I'm very happy that both spieling and "the kangaroo walk" made their way into the story.

Thanks to the Guggenheim and MacDowell Foundations for grants that helped me complete the book.

Mike Wallace, the author of the definitive history of New York City, encouraged me to go the fictional route (while warning me, presciently, of its challenges), and his approval was quite a helpful thing to remember over the many months of researching and writing. Historians Charles Musser, Bruce Dorsey, Martha Hodes, and Jennifer Fronc provided valuable insights and suggestions. Actual novelists Jon McGoran, Jenny McPhee, Elizabeth Mosier, and Tom Piazza gave helpful counsel to a newbie. Lizy Yagoda dived into the Committee of Fourteen archives and emerged with some prime nuggets. Jonathon Green's monumental Green's Dictionary of Slang (www.greensdictofslang.com) was helpful on New York City argot, as was Jonathon himself. O. Henry fans John Jebb, Carrie Rickey, and Elijah Wald supported this endeavor, which buoyed me. Michael Tisserand was encouraging and supportive, in his typical way, especially regarding the sort of chess moves

Ajeeb would make, and the culture of turn-of-the-century cartoonists. And speaking of which, great thanks to Eric Hanson for producing the "Tad Dorgan" illustration.

Thanks to my agent of forty (could it be?) years, Stuart Krichevsky, for his helpful notes on early drafts. To Julia Sippel for her deft and insightful editing, which saved me from repetitions and infelicities and helped me improve the novel in many ways. And to Wes Davis, who introduced me to Paul Dry, who got it.

SOURCE NOTES

Full citations can be found in Works Consulted.

Prologue

"heaping the snow into huge mounds" Van Dyke, *The New New York.*
"engines belching smoke" Chotzinoff, *A Lost Paradise.*
"making lascivious gestures" Gold, *Jew Without Money.*

Chapter I

Description of match-game con ("the big smack") Maurer, *The Big Con*, 250-255; "Coin Matchers of Times Square Are Doing Rushing Business," *New York Times.*

"My home town is Greensboro" Some of Porter's quotes and stretchers in this scene are taken from "'O. Henry' on Himself, Life, and Other Things." *New York Times.*

"The streetcars, autobuses and elevated trains" O. Henry, "Squaring the Circle."

Chapter II

"surging odor of slumgullion" Jennings, *Through the Shadows with O. Henry*, 101.

Chapter III

"Draw one–have it in the dark" Younger, "Diary of an Amateur Waitress."

"Women Caught in Raid Stricken with Panic" *New York Times*, March 18, 1902.
"one man, with gray hair and beard" *New York Times*, March 18, 1902.
"'Fit Thrower's' Tricks" *New York Times,* March 18, 1902.

Chapter IV

"The metropolis sometimes felt like" O. Henry, "The Furnished Room."
"spectacles of the laborers" Howells, *Letters Home.*

Chapter V

"The original cause of the trouble" O. Henry, "A Chaparral Christmas Gift."
"I have been doing quite a deal of business" William S. Porter to Al Jennings, September 21 [1902], reprinted in *Rolling Stones*, Doubleday, Page & Co., 1918
"The man who told me these things" O. Henry, "Holding Up a Train."
Hetty Pepper O. Henry, "The Third Onion."
feather-curling "Ostrich Feathers," *Scientific American.*
"Again, to-day, at a certain street" O. Henry, "The Struggle of the Outliers."

Chapter VI

"the authoritative hedge of an iron railing" Crapsey, *The Nether Side of New York.*
"He was sawed-off and stumpy-legged" Cobb, *Exit Laughing.*

Chapter VII

"In the local library" Richardson, *The Long Day.*
"Harlem dancing academy" O. Henry. "Extradited from Bohemia."
"Bread and butter" Richardson, *The Long Day.*
"Clover Leaf Social Club" O. Henry, "The Coming Out of Maggie."
"the glare of lights" Israel, "The Way of the Girl."
"About thirty couples" Dorr, *What Eight Million Women Want.*

"maybe a creme de mint" Lytle and Dillon, *From Dance Hall to White Slavery.*

CHAPTER VIII

"Bill, what did you fall for?" Jennings, *Through the Shadows with O. Henry*

CHAPTER IX

"Porter decided to call his safecracker Jimmy Valentine" O. Henry, "A Retrieved Reformation."

"veritable brigade of whores" Gold, *Jews Without Money.*
"Bread, fifteen cents a day" Riis, *How the Other Half Lives.*

CHAPTER X

Morning Telegraph Broun, *The Collected Edition of Heywood Broun.*
"The spontaneity seemed to depart" O. Henry. "Confessions of a Humorist"

CHAPTER XI

"they shot upward" Graham, *The Great God Success*

CHAPTER XII

"work was plentiful enough" Richardson, *The Long Day.*
"Get up out of that" Fronc, *New York Undercover.*

CHAPTER XIII

"Most of the women were without hats" "North Beach Unique as an Amusement Resort," *New York Times.*
"a series of performers came and went" Howells, *Letters Home.*
"the Swinger" Quinn, *Fools of Fortune.*
"If you are not otherwise engaged" Davis and Maurice, *The Caliph of Bagdad.*

Chapter XIV

"My dear Bill" Robert H. Davis Papers.

Chapter XV

"she found a factory" Frowne, "The Story of a Sweatshop Girl."
"a cluster of artificial cherries" O. Henry, "An Unfinished Story."
"Catherine wheel effect" Montgomery, "The Roof Gardens of New York."
"The Zancigs" "Weird Mind-Reading Act Startles Orpheum Patrons," *San Francisco Call.*

Chapter XVII

"There were twelve or fifteen men in the place" Committee of Fourteen Records.
"As you saw, the madams" Kneeland, *Commercialized Prostitution in New York City.*
"It was about four years ago" New York, *Report of the Special Committee.* (Mazet Committee report.)

Chapter XVIII

"One girl had a black cigar" Committee of Fourteen Records.
"At the table next to his" Clement, *Love for Sale.*
"he heard her sing" Committee of Fourteen Records.
"two uniformed police officers" New York, *Report of the Special Committee.*
"Irving Place to Fourteenth" Maurice, "The New York of the Novelists"
"She wore a dark gray wool suit" Edwards, *How to Read a Dress.*
"There is a special place in hell" O. Henry, "An Unfinished Story."

Chapter XX

Tom Sharkey Lewis and Sharkey, *"I Fought Them All."*

Chapter XXI

"pleased with her work" O. Henry, "The Enchanted Profile.
"she hauled her Remington" "Typists in 'Race' for Speed Record," *New York Times.*
"Schulenberg's Home Restaurant" O. Henry, "Springtime a la Carte."
"Ajeeb's manner" Kobler, "The Pride of the Eden Musee"

Chapter XXII

"The two men stepped into the cab" O. Henry, "From the Cabby's Seat."

WORKS CONSULTED

O. HENRY/WILLIAM SYDNEY PORTER

Books

Clarkson, Paul S. *A Bibliography of William Sydney Porter (O. Henry).* Caxton Printers, 1938.

Davis, Robert H., and Arthur B. Maurice. *The Caliph of Baghdad: Being Arabian Nights Flashes of the Life, Letters, and Work of O. Henry.* Appleton, 1931.

Jennings, Al. *Through the Shadows with O. Henry.* A.L. Burt Company, 1921.

Langford, Gerald. *Alias O. Henry: A Biography of William Sidney Porter.* Macmillan, 1957.

O. Henry Papers: Containing Some Sketches of his Life Together with an Alphabetical Index to His Complete Works. Doubleday, 1925. Reprinted by Palala Press, 2015.

Smith, C. Alphonso. *O. Henry Biography*. Doubleday, Page & Company, 1921.

Articles

Carroll, Walter. "An Afternoon with O. Henry's Widow." *Prairie Schooner*, Summer 1952.

Courtney, Luther W. "O. Henry's Case Reconsidered." *American Literature*, January 1943.

Jennings, Al. "O. Henry's Story Revealed at Last." *The Washington Post Sunday Magazine*, August 3, 1919.

The Mentor, Special O. Henry Number. February 1923.

"O. Henry on Himself, Life, and Other Things." *New York Times*, April 9, 1909. The only interview Porter ever gave.

O'Quinn, Trueman. "O. Henry in Austin." *The Southwestern Historical Quarterly*, October 1939.

Sibley, Marilyn McAdams. "Austin's First National and the Errant Teller." *The Southwestern Historical Quarterly*, April 1971.

Online

The Portal to Texas History: O. Henry Collection. https://texashistory.unt.edu/explore/collections/OHENRY/. Contains facsimiles of original publications, in books and magazines, of almost all O. Henry's work, and a wealth of other documents and material

THE SETTING AND THE CHARACTERS

Contemporary sources

Manuscript collections

Committee of Fourteen Records, Investigator's Reports. New York Public Library, Archives & Manuscripts.

Robert H. Davis Papers. New York Public Library, Archives & Manuscripts.

Books and chapters

Ben Yusuf, Anna. *The Art of Millinery*. The Millinery Trade Publishing Company, 1909.

Bovie, Verne M. "The Public Dance Halls of the Lower East Side." In *Fifteenth Annual Report of the University Settlement Society of New York*. Eaton & Mains, 1901.

Broun, Heywood Hale, editor. *Collected Edition of Heywood Broun*. Harcourt, Brace, 1941.

Cahan, Abraham. *The Rise of David Levinsky: A Novel*. Harper & Brothers, 1917.

Chotzinoff, Samuel. *A Lost Paradise: Early Reminiscence*. Knopf, 1955.

Cobb, Irvin S. *Exit Laughing*. Bobbs-Merrill, 1941.

"Coin Matchers of Times Square Are Doing Rushing Business." *New York Times*, November 9, 1913.

Crapsey, Edward. *The Nether Side of New York; or, the Vice, Crime and Poverty of the Great Metropolis.* Sheldon & Co., 1872.

De Leeuw, Randolph M. *Both Sides of Broadway, from Bowling Green to Central Park, New York City.* De Leeuw Riehl, 1910.

Dorr, Rheta Louise Child. *What Eight Million Women Want.* Small, Maynard & Co., 1910.

Flynt, Josiah. *The World of Graft.* McClure, Phillips, 1901.

Frowne, Sadie. "The Story of a Sweatshop Girl." In *The Life Stories of Undistinguished Americans: As Told by Themselves*, edited by Hamilton Holt. J. Pott & Co., 1906. https://www.digitalhistory.uh.edu/voices.

Gold, Michael. *Jews Without Money.* Liveright, 1930.

Graham, John (David Graham Phillips). *The Great God Success.* Grosset & Dunlap, 1901.

Hapgood, Hutchins. *The Spirit of the Ghetto: Studies of the Jewish Quarter in New York.* Funk & Wagnalls, 1902.

———. *A Victorian in the Modern World.* Harcourt, Brace, 1939.

Herzfeld, Elsa G. *Family Monographs.* The James Kempster Printing Company, 1905.

Howells, William Dean. *Letters Home.* Harper & Row, 1903.

Hughes, Rupert. *The Real New York.* Smart Set, 1904.

Israel, Belle Lindner. "The Way of the Girl." In *A Coney Island Reader*, edited by Louis J. Parascandola and John Parascandola. Columbia University Press, 2015.

Kauffman, Reginald Wright. *The House of Bondage.* Moffat, Yard & Company, 1910.

———. *The Girl that Goes Wrong.* Moffat, Yard and Company, 1911.

Kneeland, George J. *Commercialized Prostitution in New York City.* The Century Co., 1917.

Lytle, H.W., and John Dillon. *From Dance Hall to White Slavery: The World's Greatest Tragedy.* Metropolitan, 1912.

New York Committee of Fifteen. *The Social Evil, with Special Reference to Conditions Existing in the City of New York.* G. P. Putnam's Sons, 1902.

New York (State). Legislature. Assembly. Special Committee to Investigate the Public Offices and Departments of the City of New York. *Report of the Special Committee of the Assembly appointed to investigate the public offices and departments of the city of New York and of the counties therein included.* J.B. Lyon, state printer, 1900. (Commonly referred to as the Mazet Committee report.)

Quinn, John Philip. *Fools of Fortune or Gambling and Gamblers, Comprehending A History of the Vice in Ancient and Modern Times, and in BothHemispheres; an Exposition of its Alarming Prevalence andDestructive Effects; with an Unreserved and Exhaustive Disclosure of Such Frauds, Tricks and Devices as are Practiced by "Professional" Gamblers, "Confidence Men" and "Bunko Steerers."* W.B. Conkey, 1890.

Riis, Jacob. *How the Other Half Lives: Studies Among the Tenements of New York.* Charles Scribner's Sons, 1904.

Richardson, Dorothy. *The Long Day: The Story of a New York Working Girl.* Century, 1905.

Street, Julian. *Welcome to Our City,* John Lane, 1913.

Van Dyke, John C. *The New New York: A Commentary on the Place and the People.* Macmillan, 1909.

Van Kleeck, Mary. *A Seasonal Industry: A Study of the Millinery Trade in New York.* Russell Sage Foundation, 1917.

Wharton, Edith. *The House of Mirth.* Scribner & Co., 1905.

Where and How to Dine in New York. Lewis, Scribner & Co., 1906.

Articles

"A Salesgirl's Story." *The Independent*, July 31, 1902.

"The Autobiography of a Shop Girl." *Frank Leslie's Popular Monthly*, May 1903.

Beet, Thomas. "Methods of American Private Detective Agencies." *Appleton's Magazine*, 1903-05.

Bowdoin, W. G. "Miniature Painting." *The Outlook*, 1901.

Bowen, Louise De Koven. "Dance Halls." The Survey, June 3, 1911.

"Crush and Panic at City Hall Station: Passengers Unable to Get On or Off Third Avenue Road Platform." *New York Times*, March 18, 1902

DeCottes, Mrs. J. M. "Women and Society." *The Montgomery Advertiser*, April 20, 1906.

"Experiences of a Street Car Conductor." *The Independent*, May 7, 1903.

"'Fit Thrower's' Tricks: Beggar Who Has Victimized Many Charitable People. Physicians Say He Is Able at Will to Accelerate or Retard His Heart's Action." *New York Times*, March 18, 1902.

"Five 'White Slave' Trade Investigations." *McClure's*, July 1910.

"Gray's Profitable Specialty." *The Brooklyn Daily Eagle*, March 17, 1902. (More on George Gray, the professional fit-thrower. See also "Eagle's Story Caused Arrest." *The Brooklyn Daily Eagle,* March 18, 1902.)

"In 'Lobster Palaces'." *New York Tribune*, May 3, 1903.

Israels, Belle Lindner. "Diverting a Pastime." *Frank Leslie's Weekly*, July 27, 1911.

Kent, Mariner J. "The Making of a Tramp." *The Independent*, January – December, 1903.

"Life Story of a Pushcart Peddler." *The Independent*, January 4, 1906.

"The Lure of the Dance Hall." *New York Observer and Chronicle*, August 10, 1911.

Maurice, Arthur Bartlett. "The New York of the Novelists." (Multi-part series.) *The Bookman,* 1915-1916.

McG, "Cute." "Experiences and Reflections of a Hackman." *The Independent*, January – December, 1903.

Montgomery, Robert H. "The Roof Gardens of New York." *Indoors and Out*, August 1906.

"North Beach Unique as an Amusement Resort." *New York Times*, July 2, 1905.

"Ostrich Feathers." *Scientific American*, July 31, 1852.

Phillips, Amy Lyman. "Famous American Restaurants." *Good Housekeeping*, January 1909.

"Queer Dance Hall Etiquette Prevails Among Half-Time Spielers in Brooklyn." *Brooklyn*

Standard Union, August 21, 1904.

"The Rockefeller Grand Jury Report." *McClure's*, August 1910.

Saint-Gaudens, Homer. "Modern American Miniature Painters." *The Critic*, 1905.

Springer, Louis A. "M. Henri Mouquin Tells of His 60 Years as a Restaurant Keeper." *The Sun*, April 20, 1919.

Talbot, Fannie Sprague. "The Hair and Its Care." *Good Health*, 1910. Nineteenth Century Collections Online.

Terhune, Katharine. "The Hair We Wear." *Good Housekeeping Magazine*, 1911.

Tindall, H. M. "The Modern Miniature Craze." *The Harmsworth Monthly Pictorial Magazine*, 1899.

Thompson, Vance. "The Roof Gardens of New York." *Cosmopolitan*, September 1899.

"Tons of Human Hair." *The Washington Post*, July 2, 1908.

Turner, George Kibbe. "The Daughters of the Poor: A Plain Story of the Development of New York City as a Leading Center of the White Slave Trade of the World, Under Tammany Hall." *McClure's*, November 1909.

"Typists in 'Race' for Speed Record." *New York Times*, November 13, 1912.

Waters, Theodore. "The Roof-Dwellers of New York." *Harper's Weekly*, August 8, 1903.

Watson, Elizabeth C. "Home Work in the Tenements." *Survey* 25 (4 February 1911).

"Weird Mind-Reading Act Startles Orpheum Patrons: Zany Team Gives an Exhibition That Sets the Audience To Wondering." *San Francisco Call*, July 18, 1904.

Younger, Maud. "Diary of an Amateur Waitress: An Industrial Problem from the Worker's Point of View," *McClure's Magazine* 28(1907): 543–552.

Online

"A Pictorial Description of Broadway." Mail and Express, 1899. https://digitalcollections.nypl.org/collections/a-pictorial-description-of-broadway#/?tab=about

Secondary Sources

Books and Chapters

Alexander, Ruth M. *The 'Girl Problem': Female Delinquency in New York, 1900-1930*. Cornell University Press, 1995.

Allen, Irving Louis. *The City in Slang: New York Life and Popular Speech*. Oxford, 1993.

Asbury, Herbert. *Gangs of New York: An Informal History of the Underworld.* Garden City, 1927.

Byron, Joseph. *New York Life at the Turn of the Century in Photographs.* Dover, 1983,

Chauncey, George. *Gay New York: Gender, Urban Culture, and the Making of the Gay Male World 1890-1940*. Basic, 1994.

Chinn, Sarah E. "Youth Demands Amusement." In *Inventing Modern Adolescence*. Rutgers University Press, 2008.

Clement, Elizabeth Alice. *Love for Sale: Courting, Treating, and Prostitution in New York City, 1900-1945.* University of North Carolina Press, 2006.

Connelly, Mark Thomas. *The Response to Prostitution in the Progressive Era.* University of North Carolina Press, 1980.

Davies, Marjery W. *Woman's Place Is at the Typewriter: Office Work and Office Workers, 1870-1930.* Temple University Press, 1982.

DeArment, Robert. *Gunfighter in Gotham: Bat Masterson's New York City Years.* University of Oklahoma, 2013.

DeVillo, Stephen Paul. *The Bowery: The Strange History of New York's Oldest Street.* Skyhorse, 2019.

Donovan, Brian. *White Slave Crusades.* University of Illinois Press, 2006.

Edwards, Lydia, *How to Read a Dress: A Guide to Changing Fashion from the 16th to the 20th Century.* Bloomsbury, 2019.

Erenberg, Lewis A. *Steppin' Out: New York Nightlife and the Transformation of American Culture, 1890-1930.* Greenwood Press, 1981.

Fried, Albert. *The Rise and Fall of the Jewish Gangster in America.* Holt, Rinehart, and Winston, 1980.

Fronc, Jennifer. *New York Undercover: Private Surveillance in the Progressive Era.* University of Chicago Press, 2009.

Goren, Arthur A. *New York Jews and the Quest for Community: The Kehillah Experiment, 1908-1922.* Columbia University Press, 1970.

Gorsline, Douglas. *What People Wore.* Dover Publications, 1994.

Grimes, William. *Appetite City: A Culinary History of New York.* North Point Press, 2009.

Guilfoyle, Timothy J. *City of Eros: New York City, Prostitution, and the Commercialization of Sex, 1790-1920.* Norton, 1994.

Heap, Chad C. *Slumming: Sexual and Racial Encounters in American Nightlife, 1885-1940.* University of Chicago Press, 2009.

Howe, Irving. *World of Our Fathers: The Journey of the East European Jews to America and the Life They Found and Made.* Harcourt Brace Jovanovich, 1976

Jackson, Kenneth T., editor, *The Encyclopedia of New York City.* Yale University Press, 1991.

Johnson, James Weldon. *Black Manhattan.* Knopf, 1930.

Joselit, Jenna Weissman. *Our Gang: Jewish Crime and the New York Jewish Community, 1900-1940.* Indiana University Press, 1983.

Keefe, Rose. *The Starker: Big Jack Zelig, the Becker-Rosenthal Case, and the Advent of the Jewish Gangster.* Cumberland House, 2008.

Keire, Mara L. *For Business & Pleasure Red-Light Districts and the Regulation of Vice in the United States, 1890–1933.* Johns Hopkins University Press, 2010.

Kroessler, Jeffrey. "North Beach: The Rise and Decline of a Working-Class Resort." In *Long Island Studies Evoking a Sense of Place*, edited by Joann P. Krieg. Heart of the Lakes Publishing, 1988.

Levy, Newman. *The Nan Patterson Case.* Simon and Schuster, 1959.

Lewis, Greg, and Moira Sharkey. *"I Fought Them All": The Life and Ring Battles of Prize-Fighting Legend Tom Sharkey.* Magic Rat, 2010.

Lui, Mary Ting Yi, *The Chinatown Trunk Mystery: Murder, Miscegenation, and Other Dangerous Encounters in Turn-of-the-Century New York City.* Princeton University Press, 2007.

Maurer, David. *The Big Con: The Story of the Confidence Man and the Confidence Game.* Bobbs-Merrill, 1940. Reprint, Anchor, 1999.

McBee, Randy D. *Dance Hall Days: Intimacy and Leisure among Working-Class Immigrants in the United States.* New York University Press, 2000.

Musser, Charles. *Before the Nickelodeon: Edwin S. Porter and the Edison Manufacturing Company.* University of California Press, 1991.

Nasaw, David. *Going Out: The Rise and Fall of Public Amusements.* Basic Books, 1993.

Nash, Jay Robert. *Hustlers and Con Men: An Anecdotal History of the Confidence Man and His Games.* M. Evans and Company, 1976.

Ohmann, Richard. *Selling Culture: Magazines, Markets, and Class at the Turn of the Century.* Verso, 1996,

Peiss, Kathy. *Cheap Amusements: Working Women and Leisure in Turn-of-the-Century New York.* Temple University Press, 1986.

Riess, Steven A. *City Games: The Evolution of American Society and the Rise of Sports.* University of Illinois Press, 1989.

Rosen, David. "Rev. Parkhurst Goes Slumming: The Birth of Modern Sexuality." https://davidrosenwrites.com/drwnew/wp-content/uploads/Sex-MatPankhurst.pdf

Rosen, Ruth. *The Lost Sisterhood: Prostitution in America, 1900-1918.* John Hopkins University Press, 1982.

Sante, Lucy. *Low Life: Lures and Snares of Old New York.* Farrar, Straus and Giroux, 1991.

Stein, Sarah Abrevaya. "The American Feather World." In *Plumes: Ostrich Feathers, Jews, and a Lost World of Global Commerce.* Yale University Press, 2008.

Traub, James. *The Devil's Playground: A Century of Pleasure and Profit in Times Square.* Random House, 2004.

Wallace, Mike. *Greater Gotham: A History of New York City from 1898 to 1919.* Oxford, 2017.

Articles

"Bowery Bay Beach or North Beach." Smithsonian Institution, William Steinway Diary project. https://americanhistory.si.edu/steinway diary/annotations/?id=955

Calvert, Robert A. "Nineteenth-Century Farmers, Cotton, and Prosperity." *The Southwestern Historical Quarterly*, April 1970.

Daltzell, Rebecca. "The Gilded Age Origins of New York City's Rooftop Gardens." Curbed New York (blog), July 16, 2014. https://ny.curbed .com/2014/7/16/10076106/the-gilded-age-origins-of-new-york-citys -rooftop-gardens

Eichler, Margrit. "Divorce in Canada." Published in *The Canadian Encyclopedia*. 2016. https://www.thecanadianencyclopedia.ca/en/article /divorce-in-canada

Holland, Evangeline. "Lobster Palace Society." Edwardian Promenade, December 6, 2008. https://www.edwardianpromenade.com /amusements/lobster-palace-society/

Jackson, Leon. "Digging for Dirt: Reading Blackmail in the Antebellum Archive." *Commonplace*, 2012. https://commonplace.online/article /reading/

Kobler, John. "The Pride of the Eden Musee." (About Ajeeb, the chess-playing automaton.) *The New Yorker*, November 12, 1943.

Koenig, Leah. "Lost Foods of New York City: Butter Cakes from Childs Restaurant." Politico, January 6, 2012. https://www.politico.com /states/new-york/albany/story/2012/01/lost-foods-of-new-york-city -butter-cakes-from-childs-restaurant-067223

Nelson, Walter. "The Forbidden Ragging Dances." Mass Historia. http://www.walternelson.com/dr/node/3896

Perry, Elisabeth. "Cleaning Up the Dance-Halls." *History Today*, October 1, 1989.

Pliley, Jessica R. "Trafficked White Slaves and Misleading Marriages in the Campaigns Against Sex Trafficking, 1885-1927." *Federal History*, 2019.

Schultz, Dana. "The History of Bowery Bay Beach, the 'Coney Island of

Queens.'" 6sqft. 2014. https://www.6sqft.com/the-history-of-bowery-bay-beach-the-coney-island-of-queens/

Stevens-Garmon, Morgen. "Up on the Roof, Entertainment en Plein Air." Museum of the City of New York Blog: New York Stories, June 10, 2014. https://blog.mcny.org/2014/06/10/up-on-the-roof-entertainment-en-plein-air/

Tasha. [Last name not given.] "LGBTQ History: Bleecker Street." Off the Grid Village Preservation Blog. 2014. https://www.villagepreservation.org/2014/11/18/lgbtq-history-bleecker-street/

Taylor, Stephen J. "The 'Bird Bills': A Tale of the Plume Boom." Hoosier State Chronicles, March 8, 2016. https://blog.newspapers.library.in.gov/the-bird-bills-a-tale-of-the-plume-boom/

Voight, Henry. "Rector's." The American Menu, August 22, 2015. https://www.theamericanmenu.com/2015/08/rectors.html

Werner, M. R. "That Was New York: Dr. Parkhurst's Crusade." *The New Yorker*, November 19, 1955.

Websites

The Bowery Boys. https://www.boweryboyshistory.com/

Crain, Esther. Ephemeral New York. https://ephemeralnewyork.wordpress.com/

Miller, Tom. A Daytonian in New York. http://daytoninmanhattan.blogspot.com/

Vaudeville America. http://vaudevilleamerica.org/

Ben Yagoda is the author, coauthor, or editor of fourteen books, most recently *Gobsmacked!: The British Invasion of American English* (Princeton University Press, 2024) and *O. Henry: 101 Stories* (Library of America, 2021). He has written about language, writing, and many other topics for the *New Yorker*, *New York Times Book Review* and *Magazine*, *Slate*, *The American Scholar*, *Rolling Stone*, *Esquire*, and publications that start with every letter of the alphabet except X and Z. Yagoda has been awarded Guggenheim and MacDowell Fellowships to support his writing about O. Henry. His podcast, "The Lives They're Living," focuses on people whose achievements deserve renewed attention; episodes have included Gene Seymour on Ishmael Reed, Michael Tisserand on Jules Feiffer, Carrie Courogen on Elaine May, and Dwight Garner on Calvin Trillin. Yagoda lives in Swarthmore, Pennsylvania. *Alias O. Henry* is his first novel.

www.ingramcontent.com/pod-product-compliance
Lightning Source LLC
Jackson TN
JSHW020038071225
95014JS00001B/3